The slap of feet faded deeper into the alley. Janna charged. There could be dozens of traps there, even monofilament. Hit that at neck height and she would slit her throat to the spine and be dead before she felt the wire.

But if Tony eluded her, and changed his appearance again, how long before they caught him?

The footsteps veered left. She heard them just in time to avoid running into a wall as the alley changed direction. Seconds later they came out on a street. Tony dashed into the street, dodging cars, toward an alley mouth on the far side. Janna plunged after him.

Tony could not be allowed to reach that alley. Once in the dark he'd stop running, pull into a hole, and cut off his trail.

He reached the far sidewalk. The alley lay just strides away.

But a truck bore down on Janna, too big, too heavy to stop in time. She dropped, rolling. Turbulence from the truck's fans kicked at her, battering her. Pain lanced up her leg, and down her back . . .

*   *   *

"Interesting people, knowledgeable extrapolation of police procedure, and a world with an admirable lived-in quality."

—*Chicago Sun-Times* on *Spider Play*

DRAGON'S TEETH

ALSO BY LEE KILLOUGH

SPIDER PLAY

Published by
POPULAR LIBRARY

LEE KILLOUGH

DRAGON'S TEETH

POPULAR LIBRARY

An Imprint of Warner Books, Inc.

A Warner Communications Company

POPULAR LIBRARY EDITION

Copyright © 1990 by Lee Killough
Popular Library®, the fanciful P design, and Questar®
are registered trademarks of Warner Books, Inc.

Cover design by Don Puckey
Cover illustration by Michael Herring

Popular Library books are published by
Warner Books, Inc.
666 Fifth Avenue
New York, N.Y. 10103

W A Warner Communications Company

Printed in the United States of America

First Printing: May, 1990

10 9 8 7 6 5 4 3 2 1

For Pat, who heard most of this book a chapter at a time at one in the morning, and for Officer Bob, Kansas City leo. Thank you for helping with technical information on the KCPD and Kansas City, and certainly for your critiques of the chapters set in Kansas City.

ONE

It had to be the most tensely awaited case assignment of the year
. . . and every investigator in the Crimes Against Persons squad
was praying for it to go to someone else.

Bad enough that the night before, during the cocktail hour
before the Democratic Party fund-raiser dinner, seven men, six
armed with needlers carrying explosive needles, had entered the
Rotunda Ballroom of the Capitol Sheraton and stripped the guests
of all their valuables . . . guests who included many of the city's
richest and most influential citizens.

Worse, though, was a fact newscanner stories overlooked but
which affected leos—law enforcement officers. Pass-the-Word
Morello, the squad clerk, knew, however, as always, and gleefully informed the day watch as they reported for roll call that
two of the victims had been the wife and ex-governor father-in-
law of Thomas Paget, director of the Shawnee County Police
Department.

Mentally counting her current cases, Sergeant Janna Brill
swore. The arrests for the Maguiers rape and the Cobb hit-and-
run left her with just two. Two. And Lieutenant Hari Vradel,
the squad commander, standing up there with a printout detailing
all current cases, would know that.

"Kazakevicious and Cardarella," Vradel said.

Janna sighed in relief.

"Take Brill and Maxwell's current cases so they can concentrate on this robbery."

Janna snapped her notebook shut and said, "I just cut you off my Christmas card list, Lieutenant."

One corner of his mustache twitched up. "Cruz and Singer work on it, too."

Groans came from the far end of the squad room.

He shook his head. "Such enthusiasm. Cruz, give your cases to Agosta and Yoo. Statements and stolen property lists are on the table in the first interview room. Feel free to start on them now."

Janna shoved her notebook in the stash pocket of a thigh boot and followed her colleagues to the interview room.

"I don't need this," Daniel Singer sighed as he closed the door behind them. His broad shoulders sagged. Even his rusty mustache and the yellow stripes in his jumpsuit sagged. "I've got a partner who spends our days off trying to kill me in choppers and airships, a sister so pregnant she looks like she's going to give my partner a whole litter of little Cruzes, and a cohab who's hinting she wants a marriage contract. I don't need the third floor looking over my shoulder."

His partner Emile Cruz—gray-eyed and dishwater blond despite his name—grinned. "Don't worry; these jons had to be off their ticks, riffing high muckies. Wickerticks make mistakes."

Janna hoped so. She did not need this aggravation, either, not on a day that had already begun with the April monsoons resuming in time for the weekend and her barely making roll call because her conscience would not let her leave the house until her partner was up. The man did not sleep; he went comatose. When was he going to find another place of his own? It had been almost three months since she offered him the temporary use of her other bedroom. The couple downstairs hadn't helped her humor, hurling insults and household objects at each other all night, and then having the balls to pound on the ceiling complaining about the noise *she* made knocking on the bedroom door that morning.

The cross in her life appeared undaunted by the assignment, however. He grinned even more broadly than Cruz, teeth bright in the dutch chocolate darkness of his face. "Look at it this way, Singer. It's our chance to mix company with castlerows instead of deeks and slimelife for a change."

Janna sighed. Yes, he would enjoy this case, Mahlon Sumner Maxwell being off his tick, too. Look at his nickname, Mama, and at *him* . . . standing even taller and bonier than her lanky hundred eighty centimeters, all arms and legs and angles. He always had to be different. Why else would he wear the clothes he did—today a bodysuit and tabard in a harlequin pattern of fluorescent green and orange—insist on correcting his myopia with cumbersome glasses instead of practical contact lenses, and pride himself on being egg bald when almost every other leo in the department wore a conservative long style, such as a braid down the neck or a mane of tight curls like her own smoky-blond hair.

"Jan and I are excited, right, bibi?" he said.

She rolled her eyes. "Let's just get to work and see what we're dealing with."

"Starting with visual aids." With a flourish Mama dug under his tabard and brought out a video chip case.

The rest of them stared. "What's that?"

"A copy of one of the video chips the media videographers at the fund-raiser turned over to Criminalistics for enhancement. While you were racing up the stairs to be on time for roll call, I went by the lab and talked them into a temporary loan of this."

That explained why he came in ten minutes later than she had when they had arrived at headquarters together.

"How'd you know there'd be chips in the lab?" Cruz asked. "And why did you want one?"

He shrugged. "Well, I glimpsed Paget's wife on the news-canner story last night and—"

Janna blinked. "You what!"

"—knowing how light our caseload is right now, I thought there might be a chance we—"

She stiffened. "You *what*!" The son of a bitch! "And you didn't *say* anything!"

Singer blocked her lunge for Mama's throat. "Take him apart in the gym after the shift."

"Meanwhile, that chip is hard to watch in your hand, Maxwell," Cruz said.

Mama grinned. "I borrowed the solution to that, too." A circle around Janna took him out the interview room door where a minute later he came back carrying a small video chip player.

She had wondered why he came into the squad room carrying his trench coat bundled under his arm instead of draped over it in careful folds. He wanted to hide the player until the dramatic moment for producing it. Mama may have switched from theater arts to criminal justice and law in college but he had never given up Theater.

"It's showtime." He flipped up the viewscreen of the player, shook the chip out of the case labeled: *Station KADN, Wichita*, and pushed the metal edge into the chip slot in the player's front.

After an initial flurry of static, the screen cleared to reveal the camera panning a room filled with people, people glittering with jewelry and wrapped in color. Beyond them, photomuraled walls replicated one level of the statehouse rotunda . . . pillars, corridor entrances, statuary, and historical murals. Janna started to count the number of entrances their perpetrators had, only to realize that the photomural completely hid them.

Presently, however, doors appeared. One of the red-white-and-blue jacketed waiters slid back a panel in the middle of the wall to the camera's left, revealing a glimpse of round tables set up for the banquet. Other waiters and a number of waitrons, robotic waiters, glided in and out through a second door obviously connected to a service corridor behind the ballroom. Like the waitrons delivering orders in bars and fast food restaurants, the cylindrical service robots had broad bases, though they stood twice as tall as their cousins, nearly two meters, their brass-colored shafts pierced by a scattering of sensor openings and girdled by three shelves in place of carrying a single tray on top.

"Anyone see the main doors?" she asked.

They appeared as the camera panned, two pairs of double doors standing open to reveal a piece of lobby/corridor outside.

"So unless there are other doors we haven't seen, our jons have three ways in," Singer said.

All of which should be guarded. No one held an event like this without security.

The camera continued panning, zooming in for close-ups of notables, occasionally catching other videographers circulating through the crowd, the little cvc camera headsets down over one eye giving them the appearance of cyborgs. Janna spotted Haley

Jubelt, the Director's father-in-law, and Senator Andrew Docking, home from Washington, easily identified even from the back by the prominent ears voters found so endearing.

"Quite a fashion show," Mama said.

Janna shook her head. Trust him to notice clothes . . . though he was right of course. For a formal occasion like this the men all wore tuxedos, of course . . . breeches tucked into ankle boots and the high-necked tunics divided diagonally across the front, the upper section silver, gold, or opalescent white, the lower section the same bright color as the breeches and rest of the tunic. Scarlet or turquoise blue appeared to be the popular colors this year. The women wore a whole spectrum of colors and fabrics in all styles and lengths.

Then Janna caught herself. Damn! He had her doing it, too. "Just fastscan to where the riff starts!"

Movement became a frantic scurry. She watched, frowning. Three doors, all guarded, or supposed to be. The perpetrators must have come in as legitimate guests. The number of castle-rows and public figures here could be expected to make the guards hesitant about giving anyone more than a polite patdown at the door, making it entirely possible to wear in a gun.

So did that bulge under a tunic represent a needler, or just a waistline spread by good living?

"Who's handling the security?" Mama asked.

Obviously the same thought had occurred to Cruz, who was scanning the reports even before Mama's question. "Beria Security has the contract to supply the hotel with security equipment and—"

"Maxwell!" Singer yelped.

On the screen the crowd had surged back from the center of the room.

Mama hit the backscan. When the recording started forward again, Cruz laid down the reports, the four of them concentrating on the screen. Janna watched hands in particular. The needlers ought to appear soon. She glanced at the counter on the player. Any second now.

The camera focused on a high-breasted woman in a shimmering lavender dress with a neckline plunging to the waist in front and a skirt slit to the hip on the side.

Cruz groaned. "Forget the bibi; we need a long shot of the entire room."

The camera lingered on the woman, however, zooming in on breasts threatening to slip out of the dress's precarious restraint.

Singer howled. "Pan, you lightwit toad! Pan!"

Too late. Above the roar of voices came the crash of breaking class and a growing murmur of dismay. Janna swore. Now, finally, the camera pulled back its focus and swung in search of the commotion.

It found guests already in retreat, backing away from a ring of six scarlet-tuxed men braced with needlers held in two-handed grips. Except for their needlers and a gold hoop in one man's ear, the men looked conservative, unmemorable . . . average in height, weight, and coloring. They wore similar medium mustaches and hair short over the ears and caught in a pigtail at the nape of the neck.

In the center of their circle, oddly enough, stood a waitron. Its empty shelves and the glasses littering the carpet around it explained the breaking glass.

"Ladies and gentlemen, may I have your attention?" said a loud voice with a slight flatness of inflection. *The waitron*! "Quiet! Please."

Though less than a minute had passed since the first crash of glass, by now everyone had seen the needlers. The confused babble died into frightened silence.

The waitron's voice lowered to a more normal tone. "First, please notice that the hallway doors are closed. They are also locked. Don't attempt to leave. Mr. Salmas, the waiter in front of them, is with us. That said, I must ask that those of you with cameras to shut them off and lay them on the floor."

"Clever," Mama said. "The waitron does all the talking. There are no voices to analyze and compare to suspect voices later."

A man on the front edge of the crowd scowled. "What the hell do—"

The nearest gunmen aimed the long barrel of his weapon at the man's feet. Carpet exploded in a small geyser of gold fibers.

Janna ran a hand up her thigh boot, over the flat silhouette of the needler inside, and touched the Starke's butt with a stab of resentment. While the bad guys used explosive needles and old-fashioned bullet shooters, the government muckies had decreed that to prevent "excessive force" and "the abuse of power" leos could carry only needles with paralyzing percurare.

Faces in the crowd went ashen. Another gunman aimed at a videographer.

"Lay the cameras down, please," the waitron repeated. "That was the only warning shot. The next needle will be aimed at someone's face or chest."

The screen went snowy.

Cruz sighed. "So much for real evidence. Now we have to rely on witnesses."

The statements all varied, sometimes wildly, but general facts remained constant. Some witnesses even managed real observation. The robbery began at 1910 hours, according to one guest who noted the time while he still had a wrist chrono. Hotel personnel identified the waiter accomplice as one Cristo Salmas.

A statement read, "One of the waitrons started spinning around, throwing glasses everywhere. When it stopped and I looked up, there stood those men with needlers."

"After he locked the doors, the waiter handed plastic bags around," a woman's statement said. "The waitron ordered everyone to put all personal valuables into the bags and pass them forward. The waiter asked people for any vending or transport tokens we had, too."

Janna blinked. Tokens? How many tokens would there be in a room full of castlerows, who must rarely use public transport or the few other conveniences that could not be paid for with the Scib Card, that all-purpose social care/identification/bank card. Taking tokens seemed petty.

The woman's statement continued: "The waiter was a little taller than I am with slicked back auburn hair and the largest, reddest mustache I've ever seen. It looked like wings."

Another statement said, "The bags came forward. I was on the front row and when I'd dropped my chrono and a valuable sash pin in the bag, the waitron ordered me to put the bag in a hole in its side."

Still another statement read, "While the man next to me put his bag in the waitron, the gunman who moved aside for him came straight at me and stuck his needler almost in my eye. When I flinched, he grinned before backing away. Others threatened other people. They all seemed to enjoy it."

The riffers had left through the service door at the rear of the ballroom, the waiter leading, followed by the waitron, still surrounded by the gunmen. Hotel security reported that the security camera on a ground level service door out of the building malfunctioned at 19:18 hours and the door alarm had activated at 19:21 hours.

Singer looked up, frowning. "The guards claim they noticed nothing suspicious? What about the two in the service corridor? The riffers had to pass them."

Mama said, "I have their statements. 'A waiter with a huge red mustache came out of the ballroom. He tripped just after he rounded the corner past us and fell flat on his face. My partner and I helped him up and he went through the door to the stairs. Then this waitron came by and damned if *it* didn't go into the stairs, too. I never knew waitrons could use stairs. I'd have gone to watch it but just then someone came tearing out of the ballroom yelling for us.''

Singer pursed his lips. "Would there be time enough for the gunmen to slip out while the guards had their backs turned helping Salmas?"

Cruz snorted. "Six men? No, the guards had to be in on it. Something else, too." He pawed through the stack of statements. "Here it is . . . a statement by hotel security. After the riff they played back the recordings from all the door cameras and none of them showed any men of our riffers' descriptions leaving. They had to go out that service door with the disabled camera."

"At least they made a mistake coming in. Being guests means names of some kind are on the door list."

They thumbed through the printouts. Mama came up with the guest and victim lists. He handed them to Singer. "You'd think they'd be aware of the door list and plan for it. I'm wondering how they brought guns past the guards. Did you see the poor fit of their tuxes? Obvious cheap rentals. The guards had to see that, too, and showing up at this kind of affair looking like an outsider means an automatic thorough search."

"The carry went into the waitron. Maybe the guns came out of it," Janna said.

Singer groaned.

"Found something, Dan?" Cruz asked.

"A problem. There are just five more names on the door list than on the victim list. Three are marked 'no show' and two have noted: 'left—will return.' ''

Mama tapped the reports into a precise stack, folded down the VC player's screen, and returned the chip to its case. "So our riffers entered unrecorded into an area with front and rear entrances guarded. Maybe more hotel staff than Salmas are involved. We'd better check out both the hotel and security personnel.''

Janna dug in the cache pocket inside her thigh boots for a vending token. "Let's flip for it."

Cruz and Singer won Beria. Janna and Mama headed for the hotel. She could hardly believe the vehicle they used, however . . . an Ashanti, low and broad and so aerodynamic that even crouched on its parking rollers it seemed to be hurtling toward the sound barrier. "Since when does the department own a car like this?"

Mama grinned. "It's a loaner for an undercover operation that just ended. It goes back to the dealer tomorrow, but Perera thought we'd enjoy driving it today."

Successfully defending Sergeant Angel Perera's uniformed daughter against disciplinary action last month had made the usually dour motor pool chief her partner's devoted buddy. A situation with its rewards. Department cars were Datsun-Ford and Chrysler road cars, all dependable workhorses but without flash. Unlike the Ashanti.

The Ashanti had no radio, of course. Only their ear button radios and the built-in transponders let Dispatch communicate with them and track Mama's and her positions.

Janna's ear button muttered: "Alpha Cap Eleven, see a Mr. Tarl Braman, 1314 Kansas, reference vandalism of after-hours shopper keypad."

The deluge outside did not faze the Ashanti, which sailed smoothly, even through the spray and turbulence kicked up by the big airfoil fans of the buses and trucks on Topeka Avenue. Janna did not envy the drivers of the light little runabouts around her, though. At least with this weather the bicycle lanes were almost empty.

"It's interesting," Mama said. "Historically, countries entering the world market have competed first with low-priced mass market goods. But the African nations are specializing in limited-production luxury items. I wonder if it's the example they saw set by the diamond industry when Whites had the power there."

"Capitol, Beta Cap Seven," Dispatch murmured in her ear button, "investigate report of runabout driving through yards in area from Jewell to Boswell between Fifteenth and the Washburn Campus. No license number. R.P. thinks vehicle is possibly a Hitachi Bonsai or Chrysler Elf.''

The arch of the skyway from the Sheraton to the grounds of the Expocentre across the avenue appeared ahead. Mama swung the Ashanti left on the turn light and set it down under the covered entrance at the front doors.

Inside the hotel a plant-filled atrium made a jungle of the lobby. An attractive Afro-Asian woman commanding the register of the restaurant off the atrium gave Mama directions to the ballrooms and he started across the atrium for a broad corridor beyond it.

"Shouldn't we be asking the way to the personnel office?" Janna asked.

Mama shook his trench coat into careful folds and laid it over his arm. Where had he found one in such a brilliant shade of scarlet? It made her and her gray one fade into near invisibility. "There's something I want to check first."

The corridor stretched back through the building, flanked on the left by a sunken bar in another atrium and on the right by meeting rooms and wide stairs leading downward. At the far end, doors led to a rear parking area and another corridor intersecting on the right beyond broad double doors. Along its thickly carpeted, wood-paneled length they found a coatroom, rest rooms, and the Rotunda and Konza Ballrooms.

Mama pointed back at the double doors. "That has to be where the front guards were."

She agreed. There they could control access and check identification, yet let guests move freely once past the entry point. Call the distance fifteen to twenty meters from the ballroom doors.

"Go back to the doors," he said. "Let's see how much they could hear." When she reached the doors he spread his arms and launched into a new song by Heylen's Comet. " 'You ask do I think you're beautiful . . .' "

Whatever else about Mama might frustrate and irritate her, his singing never did. He sang beautifully, his voice the rich, trained product of theater arts classes. However, now Janna heard little more than a whisper, even with her ear button tapped off to reduce interference.

"That's enough," she called. Her own voice fell short around her, swallowed by the carpeting and accoustical ceiling. She tapped her ear button back on and joined him by the ballroom doors. "A small bomb could have gone off in there without the guards here hearing it."

"Now let's see about the pair in back."

Janna tried the doors. Locked. They returned to the main corridor and a door marked: *Employees Only* that opened into a service hallway.

The base leg of the T-shaped hallway ran down behind the ballrooms, with the elongated crossbar servicing small meeting rooms and connecting to the service elevator, stairs, and kitchen. Tile replaced carpeting here and sprayed vinyl the wood paneling. However, the hallway had an accoustical ceiling and accoustical backing on the doors, and the tile gave under Janna's boots with a familiar resilience she felt every day in the hallways at headquarters . . . shock and sound absorbent semicolloidal tile.

Standing at the corner, Mama said, "This is where I'd station guards."

Janna nodded. That point controlled access to the service area behind the ballrooms and commanded an unobstructed view of all the entrances along the other leg. Like the door guards, those here had the excuse of distance and poor acoustics for not being aware of what was happening in the ballroom, but the riffers should not have been able to walk unchallenged past them.

Mama headed down the service hall to the Rotunda Ballroom door. Janna followed. Together they stood studying the hallway. Mama pointed at a long, shallow alcove stretching most of the way behind both ballrooms on the rear side of the hallway. "What if the gunmen ducked in there until the guards went into the ballroom, then rabbited?"

Equipment for the ballrooms filled the greater part of the storage space: stacks of chairs and round tables with legs folded, rectangular platform sections, speaker's stands, and two idle waitrons.

Janna eyed it. "They'd be gambling the guards wouldn't look that direction."

"Not really." Mama pushed his glasses up his nose. "They knew the guards' attention would be focused on the ballroom." He frowned. "They pulled this off with split second timing. Every move had a purpose. So I wonder why they disconnected the door camera. The alarm alone would reveal which exit they used. Help me with one of these.'' Moving across the hall he caught one of the waitrons by its upper shelf and tipped the robot sideways.

She held the waitron at a 45-degree angle while he dropped his trench coat and knelt down to peer at the robot's bottom. It weighed less than she expected, brass-colored plastic and not metal. ''What are you looking for?''

''How it moves.'' He prodded underneath. ''Like that guard, I've never heard of a waitron using stairs.''

Janna considered the idea, then shrugged. ''There's no reason they couldn't. The department swatbots do.''

''How many waitrons are built like swatbots?'' He sat back on his heels, pushing his glasses up his nose. ''This one isn't. The treads aren't flexible enough to climb anything more than a shallow riser.''

She raised a brow. ''Meaning they used their own custom model and didn't just reprogram one of the hotel's.'' That gave them another lead. ''Therefore they had to bring it into the hotel somehow. We can check the hotel records to see who made what kind of deliveries this past week.'' She righted the waitron. ''After we check on hotel per—''

''May I help you?'' a steel-edged voice asked.

They turned around to face a lean man whose coppery skin and high cheekbones suggested Amerind ancestry. ''I'm Captain Keleman, chief of hotel security,'' he said, and when they showed their identification, added, ''I'm always happy to assist the police . . . when asked.''

Mama smiled as though not hearing the reproof. ''Thank you. We need directions to the personnel office. I'm also curious if anyone's determined yet how our riffers disabled the door camera.''

One of the other man's brows rose. *You don't know?* his expression said. ''My office sent out a service tech last night while your Criminalistics people were still here. He found a timed charge on that camera's wiring inside the hotel. What's left of the device should be at your crime lab.''

His obvious satisfaction at knowing more than the ''real'' leos sent a flash of irritation through Janna. She pushed it aside to focus on what he said. Timed charge? First they had the waitron and now something else which needed technical know-how, and not only for building the device but familiarity with both the hotel layout and the security system to know where to plant it. Salmas might have given all the necessary information to the engineer, of course, and been given the charge and timer with instructions where and how to set it. Of the group as they knew it so far, the waiter was the one who could come and go in the hotel without arousing suspicion.

"How do employees enter?" she asked.

Keleman folded his arms. "One rear door is equipped with a biometric lock programmed to clock in employees as they enter, making it mandatory that they enter through that door. Employees insert their Scib cards in the card slot, which activates the retinal scanner. On confirmation of the retinal pattern, the door opens and records the employee's entrance. The lock is programmed to open only for authorized personnel and only at the time of their shift."

"That sounds secure," Mama said. "How long have the guards who worked security for the fund-raiser been assigned to the hotel?"

Keleman's eyes narrowed. "You think one of them was involved in the robbery? Beria chooses its personnel carefully. We run a background check as extensive as the one your police candidates undergo. And our officers are bonded."

"But can we afford not to check them out anyway?" Mama asked.

The security chief eyed him for a moment, then said abruptly, "They aren't assigned to the hotel; they work only special assignments, such as the fund-raiser. The personnel office is up the steps by the front desk and to the left." He wheeled and strode away.

A little pouter pigeon of a woman superintended Personnel. She moved like a bird, too, in staccato steps and gestures.

Handing back their identification, she fluttered over to the computer. "You've set yourself quite a task, investigating all our employees."

"Yes, ma'am." Janna grimaced. "To make it easier, we'll start with just those on duty last night."

In her ear the radio murmured: "Capitol, Beta Cap Fourteen.

Investigate 10-97 at 812 Hampton, upstairs apartment. R.P. advises one co-husband is threatening the other with a knife."

The pouter pigeon pecked at the keyboard. "I can give you the names and addresses of the hotel employees. That doesn't include anyone working up in Diversions, however. The club is independently managed. You can probably disregard its employees anyway. They're all under close surveillance, and not just the dealers and croupiers . . . also the barmaids and barboys."

That figured. "The club doesn't want to miss collecting its commission on any tricks the boys and girls turn."

The pouter pigeon looked up at Janna, eyes piercing as a hawk's. "Why should it, when it's paying for the house license?" She punched a key and the printer hummed to life. Frowning at the pages feeding out the top, she went on, "Mr. Salmas is not the most sterling of employees but I'm surprised that he's involved in this robbery."

Janna saw Mama regarding the woman with interest. "You know him?"

She shrugged. "I know his employment record. And while it is one of intermittent lateness and absenteeism—though to his credit, Mr. Salmas is apparently efficient enough on the job— it seems to me inconsistent that he would call in sick yesterday afternoon if he were planning that robbery."

"Called in sick?" Mama frowned thoughtfully.

Janna said, "But he came to work."

The plump hands fluttered impatiently. "Yes, yes. That's because he called back about fifteen minutes later and said he thought he could make it after all. But why would he make the first call if he was one of the thieves?"

"Why indeed?" Mama said. Behind his glasses his eyes gleamed. As soon as the printer stopped he scooped up the hard copy and headed for the door. "You've been very helpful. Thank you very much. Come on, bibi, we've got to go."

"Go where, and why the hurry?" She stretched her legs to keep up with him back through the hotel and out to the car.

"1930 Makepeace Road."

"The Soldier Creek area? What's there?"

"Salmas's address."

She slid the car door closed and settled back under the safety harness. "Salmas? You really expect him to be fool enough to be there?"

"Call it a hunch."

The speed of their run north had to trip every automatic speed monitor along the way, but they arrived in the Soldier Creek area in one piece. The house at 1930 Makepeace, a modest duplex, sat in a clipped, now soggy, yard. Mama did not knock at the door but walked around the house, peering through the windows. He checked the thumb latch on each.

Janna huddled in her trenchcoat and glanced over her shoulder. Maybe the downpour hid them. "You're considering breaking and entering in broad daylight and in front of god knows how many neighbors?"

"Of course not," he replied. "We're officers making a welfare check. Ah." A window slid sideways. He put a leg over the sill and eased through. "Come on, bibi."

Against her better judgment, she followed. Inside she stared. Lengths of glass tubing stuck up out of bins on one wall. More tubing lay on a large table beside a gas torch. In several corners tangles of glass tubing in varying colors rose glowing out of broad bases.

"Neon sculpture," Mama said. "Not bad." He pointed at a fan-shaped one with light pulsing out and back through the yellow, green, and blue spokes.

Janna hissed in exasperation. "For God's sake. We're breaking and entering and you're taking the time to be an *art critic*!"

"Sorry." He glanced around. "Let's find Salmas."

They found a man answering his description sprawled fully dressed on his back on the bed in the bedroom. Under his nose spread the most spectacular mustache Janna had ever seen, a fiery set of wings indeed.

But he lay very still. Too still. Janna could not hear him breathing. "Mama!"

He was already beside the bed, feeling for a pulse. "He's alive, but we'd better call an ambulance."

She eyed the limp man. "Odd he'd try suicide over a robbery."

"He didn't." Mama looked up at her. "I think he's been here since he called in sick."

She stared. "You think someone else went to work in his place? Impossible! You heard Keleman. That door takes not only a Scib card but an r-scan. Someone else might take his Card, but how could they pass the scan?"

"I don't know." Mama pushed his glasses up his nose. "Bibi, I have a feeling this case will be complicated."

TWO

Janna brooded at the foot of the emergency room bed. Salmas's breathing had improved and he moved from time to time, but . . . he still slept. She glanced at her wrist chrono. Two hours since they brought Salmas in.

"You're sure there's nothing we can do to wake him up?" she asked the E.R. doctor beside her.

The doctor, a young Hispanic with a name tag on his blue scrub shirt reading *Muñana*, shook his head. "I can't give an antagonist until the blood analysis tells me what he took. Even then I'd feel better if we also had the medical history from his Scib Card. You're sure you couldn't find it?"

"Someone stole it."

Muñana blinked. "Who'd steal a Scib Card? No one else can use it."

Supposedly. But who could be sure any longer, though? Janna grimaced. Once thumbprints had been thought to be foolproof identification with a Card purchase, then a way had been found to fake them. Now everyone believed as fervently in retinal scans, but maybe retinal patterns could be counterfeited, too. She glanced at her chrono again. "I don't want to nag, but it's important we talk to him. Would you check on the blood again?"

He sighed and headed for the door. "You do nag, Sergeant, but I'll check on the blood."

The radio murmured in Janna's ear, "Ten-nine, Alpha Cap Seventeen? Your unit is where?" After a pause, the dispatcher continued in a voice with laughter leaking out of it, "Your Twenty is confirmed on the map. Do you need assistance off the roof or are you close enough to shore to swim?"

As she had many times, Janna wished Communications did not use a duplex system. Most of the car radios had been rigged to receive both bands, despite the official opinion that such a clutter of traffic distracted the ear from Dispatch calls, but the ear buttons received only signals from Dispatch at headquarters and the division stations. Too bad. The unit's side of that last exchange would certainly have been interesting to hear.

Mama strolled in. "The doctors haven't managed to wake him up yet?"

"Not without an ID on the drug from a blood analysis machine that appears to operate on the same time scale as our Records computer on a Priority Three search." She glanced sideways at Mama. "Where did you come up with that hunch about finding him at home?"

"To start with, that business of calling in sick, then calling back to say he'd be there after all." Mama polished his glasses on his tabard. "Also, we have statements by several of the other waiters saying he came and hardly said a word, just fussed with the glasses on the waitrons. It all suggested someone arranged to take his place. I just didn't know if Salmas consented or not."

Salmas twitched an arm. Janna frowned. "But the other waiters swear it was Salmas."

Mama put his glasses back on. "If someone the right size and coloring and with that mustache showed up when you expected Salmas, would you give him a second look?"

"Probably not. Did you find the name of Salmas's bank and how soon will we have a warrant?" If purchase trails meant anything now. Would the bank record of Salmas's Card transactions tell them what Salmas had been doing . . . or only where his Card had been?

"He's at Bank One and thanks to the weight of Paget's personal interest in this case, Judge Escamilla not only processed the warrant at light speed but I've already used it." Mama pulled a printout from an inside pocket of his trenchcoat. "Here are his transactions for the last forty-eight hours."

Janna scanned them. The record showed three transactions yesterday: a roll of transport tokens from a machine at Vail and Makepeace at 12:45, a Glo-crystal pendant from Terra Crystallos at 14:17 hours, and two drinks at The Planetfall at 14:45.

"You see the drinks, bibi?" Mama pushed his glasses up his nose. "Two, purchased at the same time."

She handed back the printout. "So he had a companion."

He nodded. "And after that, no more transactions. Something else . . . how many tokens did we find in his pockets?"

Tokens? Her neck prickled. "None." No Scib Card, no tokens. Only keys, a handkerchief, a pocket knife, and a mustache comb.

Mama nodded again. "But he bought a new roll that day and I checked the phone book for the location of that shop and bar. They're both in the Granada Mall. Even two bus fares out there and back wouldn't use the whole roll. So . . ." He raised a brow. "Where's the rest of it?"

The waiter accomplice had a fondness for tokens. Janna eyed Salmas in frustration. "Mama, we've got to get him awake."

"Immediately, bonita," Muñana said from the doorway. He came in carrying a spray hypo. "It turns out we're not dealing with anything exotic, just Superdream on top of alcohol."

Janna frowned. Superdream, a cocktail of perfectly legal Dreamtime and nonprescription strength antihistamine . . . the formula recreational pilgrims claimed strengthened and extended the effect of Dreamtime, but which straddled the edge of legality since the combination had produced some fatalities. She glanced at Mama. "He could have taken it himself, after the robbery. Celebrating."

"Then what happened to his Card and the rest of his tokens?"

On the bed, Salmas sucked in a deep breath and opened his eyes. They widened in obvious disorientation. "Where am I?"

"Stormont-Vail Hospital," Muñana said. "How do you feel?"

"Stormont-Vail!" Salmas's forehead furrowed. "I must have hallucinated more than I thought. I could have sworn Kruh took me home."

"Who's Kruh?" Janna asked.

"Oh, God." Salmas's mustache vibrated like insect antennae. "I hope I didn't hallucinate calling in sick at work, too. I'm supposed to serve at a big banquet toni—" He focused on Janna. "Who are you?"

"Sergeant Brill, and this is my partner Sergeant Maxwell. We're with Crimes Against Persons."

Salmas licked his lips. "I've had some bizarre dreams. Did I . . . go off my tick and . . . do something?"

"We're trying to find out," Janna said. She reached in the breast pocket of her jumpsuit and tapped on her microcorder. "First, for the record, can you tell us your name?"

"Cristo Alexander Salmas."

Muñana straightened, touching the pager button in his ear, left the room.

"What do you remember about yesterday?"

Salmas hesitated. "Should I be talking to you without a lawyer?"

"You're not under arrest, Mr. Salmas," Mama said.

The waiter looked anything but reassured.

Janna prompted, "You took a bus out to Granada and bought a crystal pendant."

Salmas stared. "How—oh, Kruh told you, I suppose. Shit." He sat up, mustache twitching in even more frantic semaphores. "If I didn't go home, then where's the pendant? Is it with my clothes? It's a present for my mother's birthday."

"I expect it's safe at your house. That's where we found you and decided you'd better come here."

Salmas's expression had become one of total bewilderment. "If Kruh didn't tell you about the mall and the pendant then how—" He broke off, fear replacing bewilderment. "What's going on?"

Mama said, "Why don't you tell us who Kruh is."

The waiter eyed them warily. "His name's Tamas Kruh and he's a shuttle pilot with Frontier, waiting out the turnaround time for his bird. I ran into him outside the store where I bought the pendant." Salmas shook his head. "It was the strangest experience of my life. There I was face-to-face with someone who looked just like me . . . same eye color, same hair, even same mustache." He drew his fingers out along the mustache, fluffing it at the ends. "And I thought I had the only one of these in the world. After staring at each other for a while, we started talking.

We went and had a drink together. About then I started feeling strange. The room went strange colors and I started seeing things that couldn't possibly be there. Kruh called a cab and took me home.'' Salmas frowned. ''I can't believe he's involved in anything serious. What is it you think he's done? Some industrial espionage?'' He grinned. ''Helping smuggle corporate secrets down from the space platforms?''

''Something a little closer to home,'' Janna said dryly. ''For starters, he appears to have stolen your Scib card. Do you know what cab company he called?''

''I think it had a yellow flower on the door, but—my Card?'' Salmas blinked. ''Why?''

Janna glanced at Mama to see if he wanted to say anything. He folded his arms, their signal in this situation for: *go on; you play it*. She said, ''Someone of your description reported to the hotel last night for work, and if your story is true, it had to be Kruh.''

Salmas gaped. ''That's impossible! The door has an r-scan— *Last* night! How long have I been out?''

''Almost twenty-four hours. If you're telling the truth,'' Janna said. ''As you say, it's supposed to be impossible for someone else to use your Card. Also, your colleagues identify you as the waiter who helped six armed men rob the Democrat's fundraiser.''

Any doubt about his innocence disappeared watching shock, horror, and terror take turns on his ashen face. Emotion could be faked; Janna had seen that often enough. However, she had yet to meet even the most accomplished actor who could go pale at will.

''Don't worry, Mr. Salmas.'' Mama moved in to where he could pat the waiter's shoulder. ''Sergeant Brill and I believe you. That's the good news. The bad is we have to prove your story because the other waiters identified you and the hotel computer says you clocked in. So we have to hold you—as a material witness—and we need you to tell us every detail you can remember about how Tamas Kruh looked and what he did and said.''

Salmas peered from one of them to the other for a long minute. Looking for some sign in their faces that they might be tricking him? As though he had any real choice but to cooperate. After a bit, he nodded.

* * *

Before they left the hospital Janna called the Sunflower Cab Company, the only one in town with a yellow flower on the door. The cab company confirmed that at 15:30 hours, they drove a double fare from the Granada Mall to 1930 Makepeace Road, and gave her the name of the driver. Punching off, she turned to Mama, "Who finds him and talks to him?"

"Perera assigned the car to me," Mama said. "Also there are a few Ears I want to visit, to see what they've heard about this riff. You check the bar, and while you're out there, visit Frontier's offices at Forbes and see if they know Kruh."

He dropped her at the Granada Mall. Clouds still hung leaden overhead as she trotted in through one set of the tall front doors, but at least the rain had stopped.

"Beta Forbes Twelve," her ear button murmured, "Granada Mall security would like to speak with an officer, reference a subject being held for attempting to buy drugs at Stambaugh's Drugs with an expired addict's card."

As always the mall awed her . . . one and a half square kilometers of shops, theaters, restaurants, gardens, and sport and recreational facilities beneath a single transparent roof, all presided over by the luxurious tower of the Holiday Inn with its spectacular view of the Forbes Aerospace Center across the highway. And somewhere among the maze of concourses crowded with Saturday shoppers, street performers, and display holographs lay the bar Salmas claimed to have visited.

Down the concourse to her right the word DIRECTORY glowed in midair. She wound her way to the computer terminal beneath it and punched in the name of the bar.

A cheerful female voice said, "Welcome to Granada Mall. It is a pleasure to help guide you. You will notice that each walkway is named. The names appear in the floor every twenty meters. To reach The Planetfall, follow this walkway, Sigma Draconis, to your right as far as the green slidewalk. Board the slidewalk." A map appeared on the computer screen and as the computer talked, a red line marked the route. Not a long distance . . . just across this corner of the mall. "If you wish a printout," the computer said at the conclusion of the directions, "push the button marked PRINTOUT, and should you have further difficulty, please do not hesitate to consult me again through another terminal. I am always at your service.''

Holo ads for shops and services crowded the space along and above the slidewalk, too. One of a young man in a skin tight snakeskin-patterned bodysuit appeared to lean on the guardrail of the slidewalk, a hand reaching out as though to catch at her. For a moment Janna mistook him for a real person, but as she neared him a telltale translucency at the edges gave away his true nature. She swung her own arm through him as she passed. The engineers tried, but while holos looked three-dimensional, they never appeared quite solid.

Moments later she forgot him in the scramble to make her exit.

The Planetfall sat just inside an eastern exit of the mall, sandwiched between a luggage shop and a beauty salon whose window advertised scalp and body painting—temporary or permanent—in addition to complete hair care. The bar's circular door dilated for her, then snapped closed after she stepped through. Leaving her in darkness and a fog of alcohol, tobacco, and drug fumes.

The ceiling fixtures, suspended globes painted to look like planets and moons, illuminated only themselves. All real light came from a glowing strip of something floating horizontally off to her right and similar discs clustered across the room. As her eyes accommodated to the gloom, the strip and discs proved to be the bar and tables. Music played on the threshold of perception, five flute notes endlessly repeated, with a counterpoint of ringing and tinklings.

She groped her way toward the bar and a figure behind it. "Cute door." The figure wore a stylized version of a shuttle pilot's flightsuit. Another scent reached her through the others. Hamburger? Her stomach growled, reminding her that she had eaten nothing since toast and caff this morning. "Do you serve sandwiches in here?"

The bartender held a book. She looked up from the glowing screen. "Honey, we serve anyone over eighteen."

Janna considered suggesting the bartender eat that book. "Do you serve them sandwiches?"

The bartender pushed MARK on the control pad down the side of the book's screen, closed the cover, and shoved the book in a thigh pocket of her flightsuit. "If it can be snorted, drunk, absorbed epidermally, or eaten, we serve it. We aren't licensed for anything intravenous or for sex, although . . ." She looked Janna over with interest. ". . . you and I might work out a private arrangement."

"What are the sandwich choices?"

The bartender shrugged. "Hamburger or tuna, chicken, or egg salad."

Hamburger sounded the least lethal. The bartender pulled a vacuum pack from a cupboard behind the bar, broke the seal, and popped the pack in a little microwave. Eating the result minutes later, Janna wondered what decade the hamburger had been sealed in. Her stomach welcomed it, however, and it washed down well enough with the help of excellent, slightly cinnamon-tasting caff.

While she ate, Janna glanced around the bar. Just half a dozen patrons sat scattered across the room. Or maybe eight. Two of the forms, each sitting in near-blackness at a back table, might be embracing couples. "Is this your average afternoon business?"

The bartender had returned to her book. "Just about. Are you interested in buying the place?" She thumbed the DN pad to advance the page.

Janna laid her ID on the bar. "I'm interested in if you'd remember someone who came in here yesterday afternoon."

The bartender eyed the ID calmly. "If I'd seen him." She extended an arm toward the anonymous shadows across the room.

Good point. Well, she could hope. "A jon about a hundred sixty-five centimeters tall, medium build, slicked back hair." Forget color in this light. "A mustache like wings."

"Oh, them."

Them. Janna let out her breath, and only then realized she had been holding it.

The ghostly light from the bar showed a wry smile on the other woman's face. "I had two jons in here with mustaches like that. They came together. Which one do you want to know about?"

Janna reached into her trenchcoat pocket to tap on the microcorder. "Both."

* * *

She played back the chip for the others late that afternoon in The Lion's Den. The four of them sat drinking caff and comparing information from the reports they had just finished, talking while it was still possible to carry on a normal conversation. Vernon Tuckwiller's bar sat uncharacteristically quiet. Janna could even hear the newscanner over the bar covering presidential candidate Edward Rau's arrival at Forbes for a Humanitarian Party fund-raiser. The influx of leos coming off duty at headquarters up the street had not yet begun; they were still in debriefing, that end-of-shift session to talk out the job stress. Most of the customers at the cardboard tables and chairs and in the colloid plastic booths remained civilians, some accompanied by half-dressed boys and girls from The Doll's House upstairs.

"They left with one leaning on the other," the bartender's voice said.

Janna tapped off the microcorder.

Cruz pursed his lips. "So it looks like Salmas is telling the truth about meeting Kruh and being sick."

"About the cab, too." Mama flipped open his notebook. "I talked to the driver and he says he couldn't forget one man with a mustache like that, let alone two. One of the men seemed near-comatose. The driver says he asked the other man if they needed to go to a hospital, but the man said his brother had only tried some designer smoke too strong for him."

"Then the conscious man paid the fare?" Singer asked hopefully. Janna could almost hear him thinking: *Scib card.*

"Yes, but . . ." Mama shrugged. ". . . he paid in transport tokens, not by Card."

Janna blinked. Under the circumstances it would have been brainbent to use a Card. Still . . . pay a *cross-town cab* fare entirely with tokens? "Which explains what happened to Salmas's tokens, but his alone wouldn't be enough."

"No. And if Kruh could make up the difference, it meant he brought along a good supply. Because he knew he'd need them, do you suppose?"

Cruz shook his head. "You have to admire the deek's planning."

"He scares the hell out of me." Singer tugged at his mustache. "Most of it's simple enough . . . track Salmas, make up to look like him, and arrange a meeting. Drug him and steal his Card. But . . . how did he *use* it? If he's found a way to fake an r-scan . . .'' His voice trailed off.

"We've got to wrap him as fast as we can," Cruz said grimly. "It'd help if we knew what he looks like. Has anyone checked with the lab about the enhancement of the news chips?''

Mama said, "I did. It'll be tomorrow at the earliest. I also prodded under some rocks to see if anyone's heard about something like this in the pipe." He frowned. "No one's heard a whisper.''

Cruz said, "You'd think the riffers would at least have sounded out possible fences.''

"Maybe they plan to wait for cool weather before cashing the carry." Singer glanced at Janna. "What did Frontier have to say?''

"That Kruh lied to Salmas about his job." Need they have asked? "Their office at Forbes checked with the main computer in Denver and it has no record of ever employing a Tamas Kruh, either as a shuttle pilot or in any other capacity. What did you find out about the guards?''

Cruz answered. "Keleman told the truth. None of the four are on permanent assignment to the hotel, though they've all worked events there. Unfortunately their personnel files didn't give us anything in their lives that suggests they're vulnerable to subversion.''

Bank records might, but a warrant required more probable cause than existed at this point. Oh for judges like the ones who gave TV detectives bank warrants by the fistful. Instead, she and her colleagues were stuck with talking to neighbors and friends to learn who had excessive debts or a bad gambling habit or a taste for expensive designer drugs or illegal drugs . . . or maybe some socially repugnant perversion one of them would do anything to hide.

Though Janna had difficulty imagining what perversion a person could be blackmailed for these days.

"Bring on the nuclear waste!" a male voice boomed from the bar's door.

A group of five men and women swept in, all talking.

". . . couldn't tell the difference between the road and the river?" one woman asked.

"It was pouring," the man beside her protested. "Do you

look at the road when you're chasing a speeder? You just follow, right? And this deek went off the road, down a hill, and kept going over this wet-looking area. How'd we know the deek was driving a damned amphib vehicle?''

The woman just snickered and called at Tuck, "Double toxins for Captain Nemo here. He needs them.''

Tuck mixed drinks, his bulk sliding along behind the bar with an agility that made his thinner assistant seem sluggish by comparison.

The hour of the lion had arrived, the *real* end-of-shift therapy session. Janna watched the civilians fade toward the door, as Singer and Cruz left.

By pairs and small groups, more leos drifted in. Abandoned by the civilians, Fleur Vientos's boys and girls sidled up to them. Without missing a beat at the bar Tuck bellowed at them in a voice that still carried the authority of his Vice Squad days, "You don't peddle that down here!"

"We ought to think about going home, too, bibi," Mama said. "I'll bet you haven't eaten today. Let me fix you something.''

Something? In his vocabulary, that meant a banquet. "I'm fine. I had a sandwich at The Planetfall.''

He pushed his glasses up his nose, frowning. "That isn't adequate nutrition. And don't forget you have a test coming up in your Problems In Law Enforcement class next week.''

Mama indeed. Call him a mother hen. Janna opened her mouth to remind him she had been of age and looking after herself for some years now, then spotted Dale Talavera, half of the Alpha Cap Five watchcar team, among a new group coming in. He beckoned to her. So she told Mama only, "I'll study later.'' Besides, at home the couple downstairs would likely be at it again. How could she study above a cat fight?

Without waiting to see what Mama did, she strode over to join Talavera's group. "How was the shift?''

Talavera put an arm around her shoulders and while she reflected on the pleasure of being around a man tall enough for her to fit under his arm, he said with a grin: "Aside from arresting a dog that invaded a school lunchroom, making a couple of welfare checks on people who didn't answer when Carephone called, and hunting a lost child who turned out to be hiding in the laundry hamper because he didn't want to go to school, we took the initial call on our candidate for Bizarre Murder of the Month.''

From the far side of him his partner Tarla Koskow said, "This jon apparently toxy on drugs or alcohol was shouting insults and lewd suggestions at passengers waiting at the bus stop across the street from him. Just before the bus arrived, one of the passengers, a middle-aged, distinguished looking man, removed a machete from his briefcase. He crossed the street and hacked the toxy jon several times on the neck and head. When the victim went down, he returned the machete to the briefcase, recrossed the street, and boarded the bus with the other passengers. It wasn't until the bus had left that a bibi waiting for another bus thought to call us.''

"Let me tell you about a call we took last week," a lion said.

That started everyone trotting out stories involving the endlessly amazing behavior of the human animal. Several drinks and sandwiches later, the subject had still not run out. The stories, however, had grown increasingly bawdier and bloodier. Then Tuck's voice boomed through the roar, "Brill! Phone!"

The supposed soundproofing of the kiosk to the side of the bar worked as long as she leaned her head close to the speaker. The face of Lieutenant Christine Candarian, night watch commander in Crimes Against Persons, looked out of the screen at her. "Brill, during this case, maybe you'd better wear your radio around the clock so we can find you fast. Get out front and wait for your partner to pick you up. Your riffers have hit another fund-raiser, the Humanitarians'. And this time they've killed someone.''

THREE

A second robbery so soon could be good strategy, Janna agreed
. . . a strike while the police were still sorting out the first crime
and before the castlerows had time to harden security in reaction.

Mama turned his MGE runabout off Gallardo Street through
a crowd of media people and past a Sherwood Division watchcar
guarding the gates—two gates, one ten meters inside the other
—of the Lincoln Yi estate.

Why on earth had they chosen this target, though? Even if
they felt confident about evading the estate's security systems,
surely the riffers saw the difference in difficulty between containing and controlling victims isolated in a single room and
those scattered throughout a private home.

Inside the gates a parking area spread the width of the property,
featureless except for the stone block paving, still damp from
the day's rain, garages at the far right end, and a massive rivet-
studded wooden door in the sandstone wall ahead. A uniformed
officer guarded the door, the iron gray and red sidestriping of
her bodysuit vivid against the creamy tan of the stone, the white
of her helmet gleaming in the light from iron-bracketed lamps
on either side of the door.

Mama set the car down in front of the door between the ME's
modified station wagon and the Criminalistics' van—both white

over black with red sidestripes like the watchcars—and climbed out grinning. "Now we see why these areas are called castle-rows."

The wall had the look of a fortress.

The she-lion at the door pushed it open for them as soon as she inspected the ID's hung on their breast pockets. "Sergeant Cruz asked me to tell you that he and Singer are already here."

A second courtyard lay beyond the door, this one much smaller, with benches and islands of vegetation in the paving.

Another uniform straightened from studying a flaming spear of blossoms. "You're Maxwell and Brill? This way."

Following him, Janna discovered that the house incorporated a series of courtyards, some covered by clear domes, some open with broad roof overhangs providing a sheltered walkway around the edge. And everywhere people dressed in the same elegant clothing Janna had seen on the news chip that morning stood in tense, bewildered clusters.

"A hell of a house," the uniform said. "It takes up the whole property except for a security corridor between the inner and outer walls. Not much furniture, though, is there? I wonder if that's to give Mrs. Yi plenty of room. She's blind."

Mama quirked a brow. "Or it could be oriental simplicity."

That matched what Mama had told her about Lincoln Yi on the drive out. Son of a banker who came to the U.S. from Indonesia in the forties to escape the Dokono regime's perse-cution of the Chinese minority. Owner and president of the Sunflower Federal Banks in Kansas and the Great Plains Air-ways. All those dirigibles flying commuter hops between small towns from North Dakota to Texas belonged to him.

While elegant, however, the house presented a major difficulty for a riffer. The spacious, spartan rooms with their white walls and open-beamed ceilings often lay between several courtyards each, and the glass panel walls pivoted open, making courtyards and rooms, in effect, a single space.

Janna frowned. "It doesn't make sense to stage a robbery here. You can't hope to control the area. Anyone who plans as carefully as our jons did the hotel robbery ought to see that."

Mama polished his glasses with a corner of his tabard. "What makes you think they didn't?"

His thoughtful tone caught her ear. She eyed him. "You have an idea?"

"Maybe." He put back on his glasses. "We'll see."

The uniform led them through a covered courtyard where buffet tables surrounded a swimming pool. Though partially depleted, plenty of food remained, and the tantalizing scents of beef and barbecued chicken filled the courtyard. Everything sat ignored now, however, avoided by guests and unattended by servants. An ice sculpture of the White House settled into a puddle.

At the far end, Dr. Anne Cordero, one of the night assistants in the ME's office, appeared out of a breezeway, a bag of sensor probes slung over her shoulder. Behind followed two blue-tunicked attendants with a stretcher.

Seeing Mama and Janna, she stopped. "You want a look at the victim before I take him away?"

"Please," Mama said.

An attendant opened the pressclose down the middle of the body bag with a rip of Velcro. Guests watching them from a huddle on the far side of the pool stared even harder, obviously curious but trying not to be obvious.

Cordero lowered her voice. "There's nothing very exciting to see. As a body, he's as tidy as they come."

Whatever the explosive needle had done to him internally, none of the damage showed outside. Not even a blood spot marred the rich perfection of the wine velvet and gold lamé of the victim's tuxedo. His face, a strong face rather than a handsome one—clean shaven, square-jawed, straight browed—stared up at them with little expression except, perhaps, disbelief. Dying had been the last thing he expected of the evening.

"Who is he?" Janna asked.

Cordero shrugged.

The uniform said, "His name's Carel Armenda."

The name sounded familiar to Janna though she could not place it. Mama evidently did. He winced.

"Was he important?" Janna asked.

Mama sighed. "Bibi, Carel Luis Armenda, is president of Armenord Industries and two-time winner of the Cushinberry Award for philanthropy. His companies are known for offering minorities and handicapped people jobs and advancement opportunities they don't find in many other corporations." He glanced at Cordero. "Is Criminalistics still going over the scene?"

"Oh yes. Measuring and sampling, photographing and recording. Headed by the King himself tonight."

Kingsley Borthwick had left his computers and everything-meters to visit a crime scene personally? "What happened?" Janna asked.

"I think he heard someone sixty-oned the mayor and he came to make sure."

Janna grinned.

Mama said, "Lindersmith isn't so bad. He just isn't Libertarian. Thanks, Doc. Lead on, Macduff," he told the uniform.

The uniform headed for a sliding glass door. Through it Janna saw a man leave a seated group inside to answer their knock. Cruz.

He slid the door open, grinning. "Welcome to the party."

Singer hurried over to join them. "Lord, am I glad to see you two. The Sherwood Division has given us plain janes and portable dictypers to help take statements from witnesses to the actual crime, and we're having uniforms talk to the other guests, but Yi says there's almost five hundred of them. We'll be here all night. And the mayor's here, too—not a witness, thank God—and a gang of media people, of course, and we've got to keep them all away from each other."

For a moment the room distracted Janna from Singer's jeremiad. Behind the group of formally dressed civilians in deep reading chairs, shelves of printed books filled the entire length and height of the wall. The most impressive private collection Janna had ever seen. A bank of library cabinets stretching along the adjoining wall dwindled to insignificance by comparison, though the narrow drawers must hold thousands of book chips in their slots.

Cruz's voice pulled her back to business. "We also have six men in tuxedos with a waitron for the talking and a servant to collect the carry . . . a woman this time."

A woman? Janna frowned. A change of accomplices? Or . . . maybe not.

Mama must be thinking the same thing. He asked, "How tall a woman?"

Cruz blinked. "You're thinking they ran another substitution?"

"Has she been identified?"

He nodded. "Chrysanne Wald, one of the caterer's staff. We

have an Attempt to Locate out on her." He paused. "But if you're right, maybe we ought to try her home."

"I'll find her address," Singer said. He hurried out.

Janna asked, "Why did they kill Armenda?"

"We're just finding out." Cruz nodded toward the civilians.

Janna eyed them. "You're talking to them in small groups?"

"No . . . these are high muckies. Though I think Mr. Yi brought them here more to make sure they're protected from the media than to separate them from the common herd. There isn't much common herd."

Mama's eyes gleamed behind his glasses. "Were any of the videographers—"

"Not this time," Cruz sighed. "Yi had barred media from the courtyard where it happened, reserving it for off-the-record meetings between the ambassador and his supporters."

Ambassador? Janna glanced at the civilians again. Now she recognized faces among the four men and two women . . . the pleasant, no-nonsense features of Senator Barbara Kassebaum-Martin and a distinguished middle-aged man with a complexion several shades lighter than Mama's and a dark green tux with collar and upper diagonal of the tunic iridescent white. Edward Rau . . . once ambassador to China, more recently ambassador to Kenya . . . a leading candidate for the Humanitarian Party's nomination.

"The others, about thirty of them, are over in the game room on the far side of the pool giving statements to division janes. Except Armenda's wife. A doctor is with her in one of the bedrooms."

Cruz led the way to the civilians. "Ladies and gentlemen, sorry to keep you waiting. This is Sergeant Maxwell and Sergeant Brill. They'll also be working on the case."

He introduced the civilians: Rau, the senator, her husband Wyatt Martin, a lean man with oriental eyes that Janna knew must be Lincoln Yi even before Cruz told her, the county party chairwoman Maranne Hejtmanek, and a husky nordic blond whose watchful eyes and the needler showing inside the open front of his tux announced his profession even before Cruz introduced him as Rau's bodyguard.

"Mr. Yi," Cruz said, "please continue telling us what happened."

Yi spoke in a clear, measured voice. "As I said, the men

appeared around the waitron. I don't remember seeing them before that minute. Perhaps they came into the court earlier and hid in one of the bedrooms until ready to move. The waitron instructed everyone to line up on the side of the court farthest from the breezeway. One man kept watch on the breezeway while the others covered us.''

From that point on the story sounded like a repeat of the hotel robbery, including the threat displays.

"The men were very aggressive," Yi said. "They pressed forward until someone cringed, and only then backed away. The one with a gold ring in his ear evidently pulled the trigger by accident. I—"

"Why do you say by accident?" Mama asked.

"When the needler fired, he leaped backward looking very startled," Senator Kassebaum-Martin said.

Yi nodded. "I didn't understand why until Carel collapsed. It took several moments to realize he'd been shot. Needlers fire almost silently, I know, but one expects an explosive needle to . . . explode." His mouth quirked wryly. "An impression created by television and the cineround, no doubt."

"Then what happened?" Cruz asked.

"The waitron ordered the maid to leave immediately while the men covered her, and after she had, told the men—"

"Just a minute," Mama interrupted. "The *waitron* ordered the retreat? Not one of the men?"

The civilians exchanged glances. Rau said, "That is odd, isn't it? At the time I didn't notice, possibly because I was preoccupied with self-preservation and memorizing the appearances of the men." He smiled wryly. "And I thought politics would be safer than foreign service."

"Someone obviously built an AI unit into that machine," Wyatt Martin said.

Mama pushed his glasses up his nose. "A remarkably sophisticated one to possess that level of situation recognition and reaction."

"I wish we had him working for us."

The senator's husband did something in Intelligence, Janna recalled. She sucked in her lower lip. With the waitron giving orders, it sounded more and more to her as though whoever built the waitron was not merely an accomplice but the tickman, the brains, behind all this.

She missed the next question and pulled her attention back barely in time to hear the bodyguard reply to it. ". . . about the men, but the maid and waitron went out the rear gate. I drew my weapon and pursued them the moment the danger to Mr. Rau appeared past. By the time I reached the pool court, they'd all disappeared, so I asked people by the buffet tables about them. The only one who remembered seeing any of them was an attendant at the buffet tables who asked the maid to bring another bowl of melon balls. She headed for the kitchen, he said. When I reached there, I was told she had taken the waitron to the caterer's van in the service court." The body-guard shook his head. "I found the van, but no maid, and no waitron."

Mama eyed Yi. "I assume your security system includes a panic button. Couldn't you reach it from the courtyard?"

The banker straightened in his chair. "Of course. Our system uses remote triggers so that every member of my family and live-in staff can carry one." He pulled what looked like a pen from the inside pocket of his tux.

Most of the systems Janna had seen used hardwired buttons, but the principle here must be the same. A twist activated the trigger, sending the signal that locked all the gates and phoned an alarm to the police.

"I activated it as the thieves left the courtyard," Yi said. "I can only suppose they knew the override code for the ga—" He broke off, sighing. "My apologies. I've become absentminded this evening. We don't have to suppose. Come with me."

He led the way to the end of the library and slid open a door. The control console for an automated security system lined one wall. While the three followed Yi in, the civilians clustered in the doorway.

Yi sat down at a computer keyboard and began typing. "The computer records all activity in the system, including the times the gates open and whether they were opened from the inside by keypad or the outside by Card and r-scan." The printer beside the computer hummed. Paper fed out. When it stopped, Yi ripped the printout free. "This is all the activity since midnight last night, and, yes, there it is." He pointed to an entry near the end of the sheet. "Here I hit the panic button and here, thirty-five seconds later, the override code was entered on the rear gate keypad. No doubt they all left then, though I'm not sure how the gunmen reached the service court without going through the kitchen.''

"At least we can track them through the guest list," Hejtmanek said. "We mailed tickets out to persons requesting them and took all donations at the door by Card, so we have the names and addresses of everyone here tonight."

Cruz looked doubtful.

Mama said, "I wonder." Leaning over Yi's shoulder, he pointed at an earlier entry. "The computer records dialogue, too?''

"Whatever's said by someone pushing the call button outside either gate.''

"At four-thirty the caterers announced their arrival at the rear gate and at six-thirty a keypad code opened the front gate, for the first of the guests, I assume. What's this keypad entry for the rear gate at six-fifty? No one pushed the call button. Did someone leave?''

"We'll see." Keys clicked as Yi typed. "Watch the main camera monitor.''

It sat at the far end of the console, surrounded by smaller screens. The image of the caterer's van appeared on it, the time and date along the bottom of the screen. The numbers raced in fastscan. Cars on the street outside sped by in a blur. Then, at six-fifty, motion flashed at the edge of the camera's field. A moment later the screen went black except for the date and time.

Yi started, then frowned. "It couldn't have malfunctioned; that triggers an alarm.''

From the doorway, Rau said, "Maybe the maid disabled the camera before letting in her accomplices. That's one way to avoid being on the guest list.''

Mama glanced back over his shoulder at the presidential candidate. "Why disable the camera? If our perpetrators knew enough about Mr. Yi's system to have his override code, they'd know what that camera recorded wasn't likely to be played back until after the robbery, by which time what does it matter if we see them come in?''

Singer's voice spoke from behind the group in the doorway. "Maxwell, you were right about the Wald woman.''

The leos slipped through the civilians in the doorway to join Singer in the library.

The red-haired investigator lowered his voice. "The apartment manager unlocked the apartment for the watchcar uniforms. They found her in bed, drugged. She's been taken to St. Francis Hospital and someone from CAPer is going to be there when she wakes up. Oh, and one of the Criminalistics techs just stuck his head into the pool court. He says they're finished.''

Mama pushed his glasses up his nose. "Then let's take a look at the scene.''

"You go,'' Cruz said. "I had a peek before Borthwick ran us out. On your way, will you ask one of the janes in the game room to bring a dictyper over here so I can finish with these people's statements?''

They left Cruz and Singer in the library and hailed a uniform outside. While he went after the jane and dictyper, they headed for the breezeway. The moment Janna entered the court on the far end, sidestepping the Criminalistics team loading instrument cases on their hand truck, she saw why the riffers used it. Here they had control. Only the breezeway connected the courtyard to the rest of the house, and the area had no obstacles like a swimming pool or trees. Only a few rocks, pieces of driftwood, and bonsais decorated the edges of a small fish pond near the breezeway. A chalk outline near a wooden bench in the far corner marked where Armenda had fallen. Kingsley Borthwick stood over it with his back to them, hands clasped behind him.

"Finding something interesting?'' Mama called.

Borthwick turned, ramrod straight, blue striped jumpsuit impeccable, and stared down his roman nose at them. No mean feat from a height of a hundred and twenty centimeters. "You should be well aware, Sergeant Maxwell, that I never draw conclusions in the field.'' Ice edged every syllable. "My report, when finished, will find its way to your desk.'' He circled the fish pond toward them, managing a very good stalking stride for someone with such short legs. "If you have questions, I shall of course answer them as best I can without complete data.'' He paused. "*Do* you have questions?''

"Not at this time. Good night, sir,'' Mama said.

"Good evening.''

They retreated through the breezeway. "Arrogant bastard,'' Janna said.

Mama shrugged. "Self-defense. How many people would take him seriously if he were genial? Have you ever watched a new defense attorney cross-examine him? They always start by equating 'dwarf' with 'diminished capacity.' Five seconds later they're running for their lives. If there's a scrap of evidence in that courtyard, Borthwick will find it, and document it irrefutably. Let's hunt up the kitchen.''

It lay beyond another courtyard or so, filled with every modern convenience, the house staff, and the caterers in their elegant black-and-silver bodysuit uniform. They all denied opening the rear gate just before seven o'clock. None of them had even gone into the service court then.

The cook said, ''I think that woman who helped rob Mr. Yi did, though. She said she had to get something from the van.''

That left a perfect opening. Janna turned to the catering staff. ''Did Wald seem different today?'' She could understand the mustache blinding people to other differences in Salmas's case, but how could no one notice the substitution for Chrysanne Wald?

''She wore more makeup than usual,'' a woman said, ''and she had her hair down around her face.''

''No, you lightwit,'' a man said, ''they mean did she act different? Yes, she did. She hardly spoke. At the time, I thought she was just in a bad mood.''

So they saw a change and ignored it. Janna sighed. ''You're sure it *was* Wald?''

They blinked at her. That it might not be had obviously never occurred to them.

''She clocked in at work,'' the woman said. ''That takes a Card, so how could it be anyone else?''

Smiling his thanks, Mama led the way out the backdoor. As it swung closed behind them, he said, ''I wonder if we've created a trap with the Scib card? We tell everyone it's foolproof, so they accept the Card as proof of identity no matter what they might see and hear that contradicts that.''

The caterer's van sat at the back door, its sides lettered: *Holliday Catering, Holliday Square*. Beyond it sprawled the court, paved in the same stone as the front parking area, and large enough for a good-size truck to turn around. A double set of sliding barred gates, one set ten meters inside the other as the front gates were, restricted access from the street. High on one side of the inner gate, a plastic bubble housed the tiny security camera . . . originally copper tinted, probably, but now splattered with black paint.

"I think the motion we saw was a shooter firing a paint capsule," Mama said.

Inside the gate below the camera bubble, a metal box set in the stone opened to reveal the keypad.

Mama pointed at a plate on the inside of the door. "Beria Security installed Yi's system, too."

Janna eyed the engraved logo, address, and phone number. A link between the two crimes? Beria provided security at both scenes, security that had not worked. On the other hand, it might be coincidence. As one of the largest security firms in the city, Beria had probably installed half the systems around the neighborhood.

Closing the box, Mama turned to look up at the roof. "That roof's low enough to reach from the top of the van."

Which could explain how the riffers bypassed the kitchen, but . . . it still baffled her why they had bothered to rob the fundraiser at all. "Five hundred people here and they settle for robbing a mere thirty? Why go to so much trouble for so little profit?"

"Maybe profit wasn't what they wanted."

She frowned. "What else could they be after?"

"Power." He folded his arms. "Consider: they've defeated good security to strike two political events. What if our jons are making a statement, saying: you politicians are vulnerable?"

Cold ran down Janna's spine into her gut. Terrorism during the British elections last year had resulted in injuries to nearly four hundred people and the deaths of thirty, including two candidates. Was this a prelude to the same horror here?

FOUR

Coming into the pool court, Janna noticed that all but one small group of the guests previously gathered there and in the living-room opening off the far end had gone. Interviewed and released by the uniforms if they had seen nothing. Were the people left witnesses or yet-to-be-interviewed? A uniform stood talking to them.

Then she spotted the craggy face of Mayor Jordan Lindersmith among the group. At the same time, the mayor noticed Mama and her. He said something to the uniform and headed for them, followed by another man in the group.

"Inspectors? I need to speak to you." Catching up to them, he lowered his voice. "I tried stopping the red-haired detective earlier, but he claimed he didn't have time for me then. This is Mr. James Molinero, Ambassador Rau's campaign manager. He and the other members of the ambassador's staff over there need your help."

One guess what kind. Janna stiffened her back to give herself another centimeter or two of height above the polished Mr. Molinero.

Mama said, "You want to know how soon Mr. Rau can leave."

Molinero smiled. "You've read my mind . . ." He peered at

the ID on the pocket of Mama's tabard. ". . . Sergeant Maxwell. While this is a tragic incident which I'm sure concerns the ambassador deeply—strengthening law enforcement is one of his aims in running—"

"Then you understand the importance of his testimony," Mama interrupted.

Molinero hesitated. "Of course, and even without having seen the ambassador I know he wants to cooperate fully. Still, there are other witnesses, at least some of them, I feel confident, who must have been standing closer than the ambassador to the murdered man. Theirs is much more significant testimony, while the ambassador has many other commitments important for him to keep. Surely you see that, Sergeant."

Janna saw a man less concerned about a crime and its victim than about the inconvenience that crime caused him. "Mr. Rau wouldn't be leaving here for several more hours even under normal circumstances, would he? He must have been scheduled to give a speech and then mingle some more after that."

The campaign manager frowned at her. "Yes." He sounded unhappy at having to admit it. "Under normal circumstances he would catch a nap on the plane, too. But this kind of experience is very exhausting. He'll need time for more than a nap."

"I have every confidence in his strength," Mama said.

Now the mayor frowned. "You're missing the point. You can't treat the ambassador like your average—" He stopped. Remembering that few of the witnesses tonight, and almost none in the library with Rau, could be considered average citizens? He resumed in a sharp voice: "We can't penalize the ambassador for being in the wrong place at the wrong time."

Mama said, "Mr. Armenda was," and walked away while the two men stared speechless after him.

Janna caught up with him. "Shouldn't we warn Molinero about possible terrorists?"

"And send him into a panic before we're sure there's any danger?" Mama glanced sideways. "Once we've said the words, bibi, how long before they're on the newscanner?"

Where if they were not true already, some wickertick or extremist group would make them so. She eyed him. "If we tell anyone, we run the same risk."

He paused with his hand on the door of the game room. "So let's not say anything."

Keeping possibly vital information from other members of their team, not to mention their superiors? Hardly proper procedure. Lapses like that earned reprimands and suspensions, and did not help promote an Investigator II to Investigator III.

Yet, Mama was right. Once they said *British elections* or *terrorism* aloud, where would the reverberations stop?

He slid open the door.

The game room occupied one side of the pool court. Depressions in the carpeting running at right angles to the poolside wall indicated that the glass panels normally stood open, letting the two areas flow into one another. Now, however, the panels had been pivoted closed, making the room a world of its own. A hushed world, where the people standing or sitting in small groups spoke in whispers if at all. Janna did not count heads, but at first glance the number of people seemed almost equaled by the pieces of play equipment . . . TV, table and holo games, exercise equipment with holo projectors to create the illusion of other scenery around the machines. Three janes had set up portable dictypers on a large round card table and two holo boards. Janna nodded a greeting to the jane at the card table, but picked up the stack of statements already printed out without interrupting his current interview. Mama collected the statements from the janes at the holo boards. Leaning against a billiards table, the two of them read through the eyewitness versions of the theft and murder.

For the most part the accounts agreed with Yi's.

Differences appeared to be no more than the normal perceptual variations. And one striking similarity leaped out at Janna.

"Mama. Tokens again." The maid accomplice had demanded that each victim hand over vending and transport tokens.

Mama nodded.

None of the property reported lost was extraordinary, however, none of spectacular value . . . nothing to suggest greed accounted for taking so much trouble to rob these few people. Janna rubbed the prickling hairs on the back of her neck.

"Excuse me."

At the voice Janna looked up from the statements to a dark-haired bibi whose face looked vaguely familiar, and so tight it seemed ready to shatter. "How can I help you?"

"You can answer a question." Dark eyes measured Janna. "I'm Sydney Armenda. Hoards of leos have been scurrying around here talking to everyone and measuring and recording, but are any of you actually *doing* anything to find my father's killer?''

Now Janna recognized the face. The coloring, the shape of the eyes, the square jaw and firm mouth all echoed the dead man's. As her gold bodysuit and the wine velvet of her ankle length tabard echoed his tuxedo. If her presence in this room meant she had been in the courtyard and seen her father killed, no wonder she held herself with such rigid control.

Mama said, "First we have to find out what happened and collect information that will help us identify the persons responsible."

The bibi frowned. "One of them is already identified . . . a maid with the caterers . . . about my height, a hundred seventy centimeters, medium build, honey blond hair worn down on her shoulders. The caterer will have her name and address and if you hurry, surely you can catch her before she leaves the city. She'll know the names of the others."

"We're hunting her now," Janna said. "If you've given your statement, perhaps we should ask the doctor who's with your mother to give you—"

"Stepmother," a voice interrupted. It came from a young jon fingering the controls of a skiing machine. "The houseplant is our father's fourth wife."

"C.J.!" Sydney snapped.

He gave her an insolent salute, then turned a dazzling smile on Janna. "Carel Junior at your service."

Only their father's square jaw marked them as siblings. The boy, the obvious younger of the two, was as fair as his sister was dark . . . a beautiful boy with golden chestnut hair pulled back in a pony tail and eyes of a turquoise blue so vivid they had to be tissue dyed.

"Is there anything either of you can tell us that might help?" Janna asked. "Anything in particular you noticed? Anything one of the thieves did or said?"

"Nothing that isn't in our statements already," Sydney said. "One thing, though . . . does Aida, our stepmother, have to give a statement tonight?"

Mama shook his head. "If the doctor think she's too upset, no. We can come by tomorrow when she's feeling better."

Sydney gave him a tight smile. "I'd appreciate that. Then

will you please escort me while I collect her so the lions at the door will let us out? You'd better come, too, C.J."

Her brother frowned as though about to protest, but when she repeated his name in a sharper voice, he turned away from the ski machine and followed her.

Janna read through the rest of the statements and listened to the three janes interviewing more witnesses.

One jane pointed to four people seated down by the wall-size TV screen. "Those are guests not at the murder scene but the watchcar teams think they might know something useful."

Talking to them, Janna quickly established that their information consisted of having seen the waitron and maid leave the breezeway.

"Did you see which direction the men in tuxedos went when they came out of the breezeway?" she asked.

A bibi said, "I don't know about *men*. I saw one man, big and blond, carrying a needler. He went the same direction the maid and waitron did."

Rau's bodyguard. "You didn't see any others? They all had similar mustaches and brown hair in a braid in back."

After a hesitation, the four shook their heads. A jon said, "But I wasn't paying much attention before the blond man with the needler."

The others echoed him. After taking their names and addresses, Janna let them go.

Only one witness remained when Mama reappeared.

"What did you do, escort them all the way home?" Janna asked.

"The doctors have managed to wake up Chrysanne Wald."

She arched a brow. "Ah. You stopped by St. Francis on the way back."

He grinned. "The call came for Singer while I was helping Mrs. Armenda to the car. He was still on the phone to the jane at the hospital when I stopped by the library on my way back in."

"And?"

Mama took the time to hold his glasses up to the light and start polishing one lens with a corner of his tabard before answering. "It looks like a repeat of Salmas's experience. Wald told the jane that while running errands before going to work, she met another bibi who looked enough like her to be a sister. They started talking and went to have a cup of caff together. The bibi called herself Vesper Harmon. When Wald began feeling ill at the restaurant, Harmon took her home in a cab. And took her Scib card.''

A phone sat on a table near the television. Janna flipped up its screen and punched the number of the Records computer at headquarters. It answered on the first ring but murmured: "Hold, please," and kept her waiting nearly four minutes before coming on again to ask for identification and access and priority codes.

Was the computer really that busy at this time of night, she wondered, reciting her badge number for voice ID and punching in the access code, or did it have some cybernetic equivalent of a secretary putting a caller on hold and going off for coffee? "Priority two." They did not need the information tonight; on the other hand, it would be nice to have in the forseeable future. "Search: subject approximately one hundred seventy centimeters tall, medium build, male or female. Key words: robbery, disguises, takes tokens. End search." She punched off and folded down the screen.

"I'd like a look at the person who showed up here as Wald," Mama said. "Let's see what the media people have."

She raised a brow. "You think they'll show us after we've kept them shut away from the action?"

He smiled. "We'll say please."

With directions from a uniform they found the group sequestered in the music room, located in another secluded courtyard.

A dozen media personnel descended on them. "What's happening? Is the group involved in the robbery and killing tonight the same one that robbed the Demos last night? Are Senator K-M and Ambassador Rau all right? How is this affecting them?"

Mama said, "Sorry. No statements yet."

The protests went up. "You can't do this to us."

"We have a right to report what's happening."

"But we haven't been allowed to talk to anyone or see anything. We can't do anything except sit here."

Nothing, Janna reflected, except sit there with cameras on playback, reviewing the chips and planning where to edit so they could have the stories on the air minutes after they reached their stations.

"The phone's even been taken out of this room," one of the jons complained.

With good reason. She gave him a sugary smile. "You know we need to make sure the line stays free for official business. And speaking of business, we need your help."

"I can guess what kind," a female videographer said sourly. "You want our chips, just like last night."

"Not necessarily," Mama said. "We need to see what's *on* them, yes, but if you play them back for us now, you can keep them until you've turned in your stories, then send a copy of each chip to our lab."

The group hesitated, expressions thoughtful. "How about telling us what you're looking for?"

Janna ticked her tongue. "Don't push too hard."

Mama held up a hand. "It's all right, bibi. We've established that the waiter involved last night and the maid tonight are not Cristo Salmas and Chrysanne Wald, but someone posing as them. Both were drugged a few hours before reporting to work and their Cards stolen to provide the impostor with identification."

Astonishment and disbelief spread across the group's faces. One jon began, "How could their Cards—"

"We further suspect that a single individual is responsible for both masquerades," Janna interrupted. No sense letting the media know the leos had no idea how the riffers managed to use the Cards.

Mama said, "To prove or disprove that, we need images of the maid to enhance and compare to images of the waiter. We'd also like pictures of the gunmen, of course, so we'll be looking for them among the crowd, too."

After another hesitation, the group set their cameras for playback. Mama held one up to his eye. Janna peered into the eyepiece of another and pressed the scan button.

Rau dominated the chip. The videographer had concentrated on the candidate, following him as he moved through the house at Senator Kassebaum-Martin's elbow . . . raced through, on fastscan, smiling, shaking hands, chatting with people she introduced him to. Janna had to look past him for anyone else. No one fitting the description of Wald or the gunmen appeared in the background, however.

Rau remained central in the second chip she watched, too, though the videographer had also used some of her chip to catch other snippets of action. Such as Armenda on the receiving end of apparent angry words from an elegant, middle-aged woman.

"Who's the woman with Armenda?" Janna asked, holding out the camera to the videographer it belonged to.

The bibi peered into the eyepiece for a few seconds. "Ydra Trexler, formerly Ydra Armenda, wife number one. I had to get that scene. Every time they meet, they fight."

As Janna's parents had for years after her mother cancelled their marriage contract. She concentrated on the chip to shut out memories that still left her gut knotted. After a moment she recognized Trexler's face as one of those in the game room. So Armenda's ex-wife had witnessed his death, too?

"Usually it's quite a show, with her screaming and throwing things . . . food, drinks, blunt objects. They had a sacramental marriage, so they had to divorce and it wasn't at all fr—"

"Bibi, I've got her!"

Janna lowered her camera to see Mama holding his out to her. She took it.

"She's in the background, almost behind a tree."

Janna saw her . . . a flash bibi in her black-and-silver bodysuit, honey blond hair curtaining her face. Could that really be a man? Or had a woman played at being male last night? Janna back-scanned, then ran the chip forward again, trying to see Wald's hands, which ought to reveal the sex. But intervening objects always hid them.

Someone pulled the camera away from her. "Sorry, leo, but I need that." The cameraman ejected the chip, shoved in another, and settled the camera down over his eye.

Around Janna the other videographers did the same. She quickly saw why. In the courtyard outside, Edward Rau circled the fish pond and trees toward them, flanked by his campaign manager and bodyguard. Everyone poured out of the room into the courtyard, cameras to eyes.

Rau looked at Mama and Janna, however, not at the cameras. "Sergeant Maxwell, Sergeant Brill . . . Sergeant Cruz is sending the senator and me on my way. I wanted you to know, though, that I've left a number with him that will let you reach me if there's anything more I can do to help you find Mr. Armenda's killers. His death is a tragedy and a great loss to Topeka. Good luck on catching his killers." He extended his hand to each of them.

Shaking it, Janna saw sincerity in the dark eyes, but could not help thinking that Rau must be as conscious as she of the cameras recording the event.

Then he was gone. Minutes later a sleek whisper-bladed heli-ocopter rose from a distant part of the house and glided away southeast toward Forbes.

"A Condor," Mama murmured. "Cruz has to be in lust and itching to be at its controls."

"Yi's private chopper," one of the videographers said.

As though the candidate's departure were a signal, the oper-ation at the house folded. After a short conference with Mama and Janna, Cruz gave the media a statement and released them. Uniforms and plain janes followed. Soon Janna found herself and her three colleagues alone with the Yi's, Hejtmanek, and the servants and caterers cleaning up the pool court.

"Thank God your children weren't here," the county party chairwoman said.

Yi nodded.

Mrs. Yi touched a platter of cheeses. "So much food left. I wish it didn't have to go to waste."

"Why not send it to the East Topeka shelter?" Mama sug-gested.

She turned her head toward him. "Of course. Thank you."

Janna eyed her with interest. Except for the fixed focus of her eyes, the red-haired Maeve Yi hardly seemed blind. She looked straight at people talking to her, reached for objects without fumbling, and never hesitated in negotiating the obstacle course the pool court had become as the caterers packed. Since Mrs. Yi used no dog or cane, the gold filigree ear wraps curving around and into her ears must be an EchoVision system.

As though feeling Janna's gaze, Mrs. Yi turned toward her.

The fixed stare gave Janna the uneasy sensation of having her mind read. She found herself blurting out the foremost thought. "Your sonar units are beautiful."

Mrs. Yi's face lighted. "Thank you. They're an anniversary present from Lin. He had them custom made, because, as he said, there's no reason crutches can't also be objects of art." A puzzled frown crossed her face.

Mama asked, "Is something wrong?"

After a hesitation the woman shook her head. "I guess not.

For a moment I had a sense of déjà vu, then I realized it's just because I said almost the same thing to a waitron earlier tonight.''

Singer blinked. ''To a *waitron*?''

Mrs. Yi's smile went sheepish. ''Initially I didn't realize it wasn't a person. The signal came back from something tall and thin without the hard echo of dense surfaces like metal and even though the male voice sounded a little flat, he seemed to know me.''

The hair rose on Janna's neck. At the corner of her vision she saw Singer and Cruz stare.

Mama drew a breath. ''What did it say?''

Mrs. Yi frowned in concentration. '' 'You're looking top dink tonight, Mrs. Yi. I've never seen those ear wraps before. Are they new?' I gave it the same answer I did Sergeant Brill. When it left, the hum of its treads told me I'd been talking to a machine.''

Cruz said, ''A waitron that sophisticated had to be the one in the robbery.''

Behind his glasses, Mama's eyes gleamed. ''Yes . . . and that's our good luck.''

What blue sky was he flying now? Janna wondered. ''Why?''

''Because its chat with Mrs. Yi tells us the waitron isn't controlled by AI, bibi. No AI unit would be programmed to call attention to itself with un-waitronly behavior.''

Hejtmanek frowned at him. ''I don't understand.''

The significance hit Janna, though, and from the expressions around her, she saw it occurred to her colleagues and Yi, too. If the waitron were not an AI unit, it had to be operated some other way. Janna could think of only one that explained everything the robot's behavior. ''Remote control, Ms. Hejtmanek.''

Mama beamed at her the way her father had when she brought A's home from school. He turned to Yi. ''Did you have anyone watching the street outside tonight?''

Yi nodded. ''Of course, to provide reasonable security for the cars that couldn't be parked inside the wall. I hired two off-duty officers from this division to patrol the area.''

''Not the people who maintain your security system?''

The banker regarded him in surprise. ''Their personnel wouldn't be familiar with who lives in the area and what they drive, nor could private security officers ask for a license check on cars they wondered about. But surely if the leos noticed anything suspicious, they'd have reported it to you."

"The person controlling the waitron would be careful not to appear suspicious. However, he had to be close. We need to know everything that team saw tonight."

"I'll get them." Yi headed for the front of the house.

Cruz and Singer moved close to Mama. Cruz said, "Even remote control doesn't explain why the waitron spoke to Mrs. Yi."

"Human error." Mama glanced toward Mrs. Yi and lowered his voice. "She said he sounded as though he knew her. Maybe he does, and when he saw her, he spoke without thinking."

Singer took a breath. "One of their friends?"

"He called her Mrs. Yi, not Maeve. But it has to be someone who's been in the house and had the opportunity to study the security system."

Janna remembered the label inside the keypad cover at the back gate. "Such as the people who installed the systems here and at the hotel?"

Cruz said, "Tomorrow someone better visit Beria again."

FIVE

Pass-the-Word Morello was bursting with so much chop he had
no time to build suspense before blurting it out. Director Paget
had spent the night being called by anxious castlerows and politicians. This morning a commentator on KTNB hinted that the
robberies might be only a taste of things to come, after which
the committee setting up a Libertarian fund-raiser scheduled in
several weeks called the department to beg for police protection.
Paget had ordered a major case squad into operation.

"His chop runneth over," Maro Desch said, grinning.

Thinking about the KTNB commentator, Janna grimaced. She
supposed she should have expected it; if Mama saw significance
in two political events being victimized, other people, even those
without quantum leaping minds, could, too. She could have done
without hearing about it this morning, though, after spending
half the night writing reports and the rest trying to sleep over
shrieked accusations and crashing ballistic objects downstairs.

"Don't they ever wear out?" Mama had asked as the two of
them finally reached home and heard the battle. He picked up
Janna's trench coat from where she tossed it on the divider
between the entryway and dining nook and hung it in the entry
closet.

Resentment flared in Janna, fueled by exhaustion and annoyance at the neighbors. She had had enough of his compulsive neatness! "You could move; then you wouldn't hear them!"

He froze for a moment, then closed the closet door quietly. "I'm looking for a place."

The hurt in his voice pricked her conscience. But not enough to drain off her anger. "Meantime, you might try going down in uniform and telling them to be quiet."

He just sent a look over his glasses and turned away.

Janna had had to grin. Not even Mama was brainbent enough to voluntarily walk into a 10-87. "Maybe they'll kill each other."

Unfortunately, the women had not and Janna fought back yawns as Vradel reviewed the overnights.

The lieutenant, who looked as though he had not slept much, either, confirmed the major case squad. "The two teams currently assigned to the case will be joined by Weyneth, Showalter, Zavara, and Threefoxes from Crimes Against Property. The east end of the room is yours."

"Next to the caff urn, of course," Babra Cardarella whispered to Janna. "You'll probably need it."

"Cruz is senior officer and coordinator. Commander Vining in Public Information is your media liaison and will be here shortly for briefing."

After roll call they pushed their desks to the end of the room while they waited for the other teams to arrive.

Singer sighed. "I can't believe the lions patrolling around Yi's place don't remember any vehicle our waitron operator could have been using. It had to be large enough to pick up everyone and the waitron."

"Large vehicles don't necessarily attract notice," Mama said. He plugged his phone into the wall jack beside his new desk position and swiveled the screen to precisely parallel the rear edge of the phone. "Everyone might fit in a stretch limo, for example." He punched his phone on. "I hope the lab has those enhancements. It'll be easier finding those jons when we know what they look like."

The squad room swung open. A courier glided in on whispering wheels and threaded its way to Pass-the-Word Morello's desk. "Priority three requests: Hurtado, Roth," it intoned, its arm depositing a stack of papers on the desk. "Priority two requests: Kazakevicious, Calabrese, Cotterhill, Brill."

Her Records search.

Janna went after the printout. Not a long one, she quickly discovered. The computer had come up with three males and a female in the height/weight range who used costumes and impersonations as part of their M.O. But a quick scan established that none of them habitually took tokens along with other property. Janna sighed. Maybe the tokens were a new habit. In any case, the four would have to be checked out.

She returned to her desk in time to hear Mama saying, "But we need those enhancements."

"I'm sorry, Sergeant," a face on the screen said. "The program takes time to run. We'll tell you the moment we have something."

Mama sighed. "Thank you." He stabbed the disconnect button.

"We can't do anything at Beria today, either," Cruz said. "Only service technicians are at the office."

Janna dropped the printout on her desk and gave way to a yawn. "So until our colleagues show up, I think I'll have a cup of—"

A phone buzzed.

"It's for you, Maxwell," Cardarella called moments later.

Mama tapped his connect button. "Sergeant Maxwell."

Kingsley Borthwick's face appeared on the screen. Janna stared. What was he doing here at this time of day?

"Sergeant, we have a problem. Dr. Kolb and I would like you and your colleagues to join us in the morgue. Promptly," Borthwick added.

Mama snapped to his feet. "We're on our way."

"I'll wait for the others and Vining," Cruz said.

What would Borthwick consider a problem? The three of them speculated about it on their way down through the building. With Borthwick and the medical examiner himself collaborating, it must involve autopsy findings.

"We'll know soon enough," Mama said.

As always, the smell of death greeted them as the entry door slid back . . . pervasive, persistent, despite air scrubbers and shining cleanliness. Yet the odor bothered Janna less than the impression the monochrome blues of floors and walls, scrub suits and gurney drapes gave of having stepped into twilight.

The woman at the receiving desk pointed them toward the

autopsy room and returned her attention to the newscanner behind
her counter, watching an interview with the Russian jivaqueme
flutist Alexei Mir. Janna eyed her as they passed. Did the M.E.
choose desk personnel for their hair? At night the wild maned
orderly Kolb called Blue Hair presided. Today they had platinum
and red curls in a frothy tower Janna would have thought impossible to maintain outside of zero-gee.

Blues persisted in the autopsy room . . . blue plastic sinks
and tables, blue-gray corpses. The smells of death became more
pungent and individual—putrefaction, old blood, intestinal
contents—mixed with sounds whose combination had become,
to Janna, forever associated with autopsies: the drone of dictating
voices, a bone saw's whine, the gurgle of running water.

On Monday the week end's crop of death would fill all the
tables, but for now only two were occupied. The hiss of opening
doors had distracted the assistant M.E. at the first table from
opening the chest of his subject. He looked up at the investi-
gators, causing the overhead camera slaved to him to focus on
them, too, and follow them with a glassy cyclops stare as they
headed toward the other occupied table.

As always Kolb looked as though he had worn his jumpsuit
for a week. Uncombed hair framed his head in a wild gray halo.
For all that, however, Kolb's face showed no beard stubble. He
bent over the body, tall and slightly stoop-shouldered, murmuring at Borthwick, who stood on a chair beside him, and at
assistant M.E. Sid Chesney across the table.

Gravity furrowed Sid's forehead, an expression that almost
accomplished what his glasses and thin mustache could not, bring
maturity to his baby face. Janna blew him a kiss. Until Sid
married last fall, he had shared the apartment with her.

Borthwick turned on his chair. "Ah. Commendable prompt-
ness."

"What's the problem?" Mama asked.

"The angle of the entry wound," Sid said.

Borthwick turned a glacial stare on him.

Kolb said mildly, "Dr. Chesney, the man has spent most of
the night at his computer and sacrificed going to bed in order to
see if the autopsy findings corroborate his. Don't upstage him."

To Janna's surprise, Borthwick let pass the implication he was
a prima donna and turned to them. "Dr. Cordero's initial examination of the body revealed that the needle had penetrated

deep enough into the victim's thorax to leave two and a half centimeters of the tract intact after detonation.''

They all nodded. Only in TV and the cinearound did needles explode on contact, spraying bystanders with blood and flesh.

"She inserted a probe and we recorded and measured the angle of entry. This morning I asked Dr. Kolb to do likewise. He has, as you can see, and verified that we were correct last night.''

They crowded around the body. The probe, a piece of metal like a skinny knitting needle, jutted from between Armenda's lower right ribs.

"What's wrong with the angle?'' Singer asked.

"If he were standing the probe would be almost parallel to the floor. It also angles forty degrees to his right. Consider: Armenda stood one hundred seventy-five centimeters tall. The perpetrators were a similar height, according to the statements I had the Records computer route to me as soon as you'd entered them. Also according to the statements, they held their weapons thusly.'' He extended both arms straight in front of him, one stubby hand clenched into a gun shape, the other supporting it. "I ran computer simulations based on information in the statements and all my entry wounds angle distinctly downward and less than fifteen degrees to the right.'' He lowered his arms. "I cannot fire the alleged murder weapon from its reported position and reproduce the victim's entry wound.''

No one spoke, but meeting Mama's eyes, Janna knew he had to be thinking the same thing she was: if Borthwick were correct, the riffer could not have killed Armenda.

So who did?

Back in the squad room, groans of dismay greeted Mama's briefing on the autopsy finding.

Cruz grimaced. "What do we have, then, other than double shit . . . one crime or two?''

Singer said, "I don't see that much difficulty. Suppose Armenda was turning to his left. That could account for the lateral angulation.''

The copper beads strung in Devon Zavara's cornrow braids clicked as the CAProp investigator nodded. "He has a point.''

Singer sank into his chair as though melting. A common reaction to Zavara, Janna had noticed, and today even more understandable as the other she-lion displayed her dark honey skin and hard, rippling muscles in a snug bodysuit the same color as her complexion. Small wonder Zavara's partner Trane Threefoxes wore a perpetually bemused expression.

"The lateral angulation," Mama said, "but we know how the riffers held their weapons, so how ever else killer and victim stood relative to each other, if the riffer fired the needle, it had to result in an entry wound with a downward angle. Now, I asked Borthwick to rerun his simulations and—"

"You asked the King . . ." Samanda Showalter began, lavender-dyed eyes wide.

". . . to repeat work?" her partner Marion Weyneth rumbled.

Popular opinion held that the two from Crimes Against Property, better known as Thumbelina and Mt. Weyneth, had been partnered because averaged together they made a normal-size team. Whether the averaging required them to share sentences, or they simply liked the effect, remained a matter of debate.

Mama shrugged. "He isn't an ogre."

"More of a troll," Zavara said.

Janna bit back a grin. What a skin. Far from voicing any doubts about the simulation, Mama had put on a grave expression and said, "Sir, it would help me a great deal to visualize this if I could see those simulations. Did you by any chance also work out a range of possibilities for a source that *could* have produced that entry wound?"

Knowing that of course Borthwick would have.

Mama pushed his glasses up his nose. "He had simulations shooting from various heights and firing positions. No one taller than 145 centimeters could have fired that needle from a shooting stance."

"The entry angle falls in the range of a taller person firing from about waist level, though," Janna said.

Threefoxes' expression became thoughtful. "Someone standing to Armenda's right."

Zavara looked skeptical. "Someone who just happened to come armed? Was it even possible to bring in a weapon? We know they were verifying identification at the door, but did they search the guests?"

Cruz rubbed the back of his neck. "We need to find out. We also need to find out who stood around Armenda and who might want him dead."

The image of Armenda's ex-wife yelling at him replayed in Janna's head. Had the argument led to the ultimate violence this time? She had worked several cases where one person appeared to walk away from the argument, only to return armed some time later and attack the other combatant.

Mama nudged her. "You've thought of someone?"

She told them, adding, "Mrs. Trexler was in the courtyard at the time of the murder."

Mama pursed his lips. "I wonder if Yi kept a needler in the house, and if Mrs. Trexler knew them well enough to be familiar with that fact."

Showalter nodded. "That would be a more logical source for the weapon than . . ."

". . . bringing it to the fundraiser."

"So, we need to talk to the witnesses again," Cruz said. "Brill, you and Maxwell take the Trexler woman. Also check her out as a possible suspect and see who else might have a motive for killing Armenda. I'll talk to Yi and ask about needl—"

"Brass alert," Zavara interrupted.

Janna looked around. Commander Gifford Vining strode between the desks toward them. His folksy face wore the grin that had been disarming and charming the media for eight years. "Good morning, lions and she-lions. Well, Sergeant Cruz, what can we tell the media today?"

Janna lost all impulse to smile back. What could they tell the media . . . not how was the case going or how were they doing. That certainly made his priorities clear.

The others appeared to read his question the same way. No one moved from where they sat at or on desks, but their silence had the feel of people standing at attention.

As Cruz briefed him, the information officer's smile faded, too. "Christ! First possible political terrorists, then people who can apparently fake a retinal scan. Now this . . . if this *is* real, and frankly, it sounds blue sky, Borthwick's simulations or not. You're supposed to be finding answers, Sergeant, not more questions."

Cruz met his gaze. "Yes, sir. We will."

"I hope so." Vining's mouth thinned. "Meanwhile I'll think of something to feed the media that won't create the circus this development would. But they won't accept bullshit for long, and neither will the Director, so let me know the minute you have something I *can* report.''

He walked away.

Zavara's lip curled. "Brass."

Cruz shrugged. ''At least we have someone between us and the media. Let's go to work.''

They divided up the chores and scattered.

After the Ashanti, their Meteor sedan felt very mundane indeed, despite its metallic blue finish. Though even the Ashanti might have seemed dull beneath the morning's threatening overcast. The light meter on the dash indicated barely enough light for the Simon cells on the car roof to run the fans on solar power.

Mama headed south rather than west toward the Trexler home in the Cedar Crest area. A phone call before leaving the squad room had already established that the Trexlers were not home.

''They're at the gallery,'' the maid on the screen told Mama.

He nodded and punched off, obviously knowing what she meant, but Janna asked, ''What gallery?'' as they slid through the light Sunday morning traffic.

''The Trexler Gallery.''

She rolled her eyes. ''That's a big help. I've never heard of the Trexler Gallery.''

The car radio and her ear button crackled once and went silent again. Radio traffic ran light today, minutes at a time passing between messages.

''You've just never paid attention when we passed it.'' Mama dialed up the magnification on the dash's rear scanner.

''Passed it where?''

''In the Expo Center Mall.''

The mini-mall south of the Sheraton? She raked through her memory, trying to recall an art gallery among the gift, clothing, and sundries shops catering to guests at the Sheraton and Expocentre. Only one possibility came to mind, however, and that seemed unlikely. ''You don't mean the place with the purple cow in the window?''

Mama beamed at her. ''You noticed after all.''

Five minutes later they passed the cow during the walk to the mall doors from Sheraton parking lot where they left the car. It grazed in the streetside show window below glowing white letters on the combed concrete wall: *Trexler Gallery*. Painted white and royal purple in the same color pattern as a Holstein, the cow appeared to be cut from four sheets of wood, one for the body, with horns, front, and hind leg sections slotted in at right angles . . . like some full-size replica of a child's homemade toy.

This was art? More incredible yet, the cow had the edge transparency betraying it as a hologram, which meant that the gallery considered the object too valuable to put the original on display outside.

"People actually pay good card for something like that?"

They pushed through the doors into the mini-mall's short, skylighted concourse.

"For a Dvorak sculpture?" Mama grinned. "Not good card. *Gold* card."

The gallery's entrance, a broad arch supported by Grecian columns, lay on their left. At the moment, however, glass closed the arch, a seamless sheet with the faint internal glitter of imbedded monofiliment mesh. Peering through the door into the gallery, Janna tried not to touch the glass. Logic said it must be a heavy double thickness with the mesh sandwiched between the layers but gut reaction cautioned her to avoid even the chance of breaking it. Monofiliment once snared her ankle during her patrol days and she still went cold remembering how effortlessly the fine-chain molecular structure sliced through her boot, and how easily it could have amputated her foot.

"I see someone, bibi."

Janna did, too, a woman in a baggy dark coverall and a thigh-length fall of jade green hair, disappearing behind a partition beyond what appeared to be a precariously balanced stack of metallic cubes.

Mama rapped on the glass.

The woman peered around the partition, frowned, and came toward them as far as the metallic cubes. *We're closed*, her lips mouthed. She pointed at an easel just inside the glass.

A placard there read: OPENING TODAY, GLASS FANTASIES BY LYMAN KINTICH, Hours: 1:00 P.M. to 8:00 P.M.

"Police!" Janna shouted. They pulled their badge cases from under their trench coats and held them up.

The bibi came to the door and studied the ID's. Though not beautiful, all rawboned angles, in fact, the woman had the most perfect complexion Janna had ever seen. The porcelain translucency of it made the jade of her hair and slanted eyes all the more striking.

She continued frowning but presently pulled a sonic key from her overall pocket and punched a combination on the keypad. Something clicked in the door. The woman slid the glass aside enough to make an opening at the left end of the arch. "How may I help you?"

Mama smiled. "We need to talk to Mrs. Trexler. About last night," he added when she did not react.

She hesitated a moment longer, then sighed. "Come in." When they had, she closed and relocked the door. "I'll get her."

"Being wanted gives me such a warm feeling," Janna murmured to Mama as the woman disappeared beyond the partition.

Off to the left of the entrance stood the original of the holo display. Janna strolled around it. In "person" it still looked like an oversize toy.

Her ear button muttered, "Alpha Cap Nine, investigate a report of a vehicle driving on the lawn of the Capitol building. Vehicle is blue, possibly an Hitachi Bonsai or Chrysler Elf."

"Sounds like the one north of the university yesterday," Mama said.

A moment later the radio continued, "Alpha Cap Nine, Beta Cap Seven advises the vehicle is a Bonsai with amphibious modifications. Do not follow it into any body of water."

Janna grinned, then noticed another sculpture and forgot the Bonsai. A metal shaft with a wide base thrust up through the middle of spiraling metal vanes. The central shape reminded her of a waitron.

She walked over to it. The vanes begged to be touched. When she ran her hand down them, they gave and sprang back, setting off vibrations that spread along the rest of the spiral in a pinging chorus.

Mama eyed her. "Don't tell me you've suddenly developed an appreciation for art."

She stroked the vanes again. "I'm appreciating the fact that we're just across a parking lot from the Sheraton and that one way to hide a waitron quickly might be to trick it up with something like this in place of its shelves."

The middle-aged woman on the video chip came around the stacked cubes. Ydra Trexler raised her brows at them. "Sergeants Maxwell and Brill?'' she asked in a husky voice. "My assistant said you wanted to see me?"

Mama smiled. "Yes, ma'am. We're sorry to bother you, but we have a few more questions about last night."

Mrs. Trexler sighed. "So he might win after all."

Janna kept her face expressionless. "I beg your pardon?" Who? Armenda? Win what?

Mrs. Trexler shook her head. "Nothing. Will this take long? We're behind schedule getting ready for this showing because we had to spend much longer at the fund-raiser last night than we intended and even working since dawn hasn't caught us up."

"We can talk while you work, if that's any help," Mama said.

Mrs. Trexler nodded. "This way."

She had the carriage and good bones that maintain elegance even when age has thickened the waistline and wrinkled the skin. Not that Mrs. Trexler's skin had wrinkled. Though she must be near fifty, it remained smooth, and no gray showed in the sleek upsweep of wheat-blond hair.

Nor did she seem alarmed by their presence. Which indicated what? A serene conscience . . . or supreme self-confidence?

They followed her past the stacked metal cubes and around the partition. A long, narrow room with white walls and a parquet floor stretched away on the far side, scattered with display stands. Most held an object each . . . a bowl or a vase, a tree, an animal . . . all made of glass.

A distinguished, gray-haired man looked around, frowning, from setting a fairy castle of spiral crystal towers and lacy battlements on an internally lighted stand. "Ydra, this is no time for visitors!"

Mrs. Trexler smiled at him. "They're leos, not visitors. This is my husband Loudon Trexler," she told Mama and Janna, "and you've already met Arianna Cho, my assistant."

The jade-haired woman nodded at them from where she knelt by a small crate and thumbed on a palm-size depolarizer. She ran it down the plastic strips sealing a crate the way a wrapstrap restrained a prisoner's wrists, by the charge in the strip making it adhere to itself. With the charge neutralized, she peeled the strips loose and released the latches on the crate.

Mrs. Trexler reached into the plastic foam pellets filling the crate. "What are your questions?"

Mama said, "We need to know peoples' positions at the time of the shooting. Was Mr. Armenda facing directly at the gunman who shot him, do you recall?"

Out of the crate came what Janna at first took to be another castle, only black, then recognized it as some kind of horned animal head. Mrs. Trexler looked up with it in her hands to smile wryly. "I have no idea. The only thing in the world I saw just then were those guns. If you're interested in an opinion based on experience, however, yes, he faced the gunman. Pride would have made him stand his ground until the last possible instant of safety. Carel backed away from things but he never backed down."

Her tone did not make that a virtue.

"Where were you standing at the time? Left of him, right, behind him?" Janna asked.

Mrs. Trexler set the head on a display stand. "Right of him."

Janna kept her face expressionless and her focus on Mrs. Trexler, though she wanted to exchange glances with Mama. "About how far away?"

Mrs. Trexler opened her mouth, but Arianna Cho sat back on her heels and spoke first. "That's a strange question."

Janna gave her a bland smile. "It's just routine."

Cho sent back a thin one. "Really? To ask where Ydra stood in relation to Carel, maybe, but . . . how far away?" She stood, jade eyes boring into first Janna, then Mama. "I could almost think there's doubt about who killed Carel."

Both the Trexlers started. "Arianna!"

Janna felt her smile freeze. She tried to catch Mama's eye. Did they admit the truth when their media liaison wanted to keep it quiet?

She might have known such a question would not bother Mama. He eyed Cho with a thoughtful expression. "You're very perceptive. There are facts which suggest that, yes."

Cho's lips thinned, hardening the angular face. "So you came looking for someone who might want him dead. Why do you think that's Ydra?"

"Me!" Mrs. Trexler gasped.

Janna met the woman's shocked eyes. "One of the videographers last night has a chip showing the two of you fighting not long before Mr. Armenda died. She told me that you always fought, often violently."

To Janna's astonishment, Mrs. Trexler laughed. The warm huskiness of it echoed in the gallery. "Those weren't fights, Sergeant. They were scenes, spectacles, and if they suggest anything, it's that I have every reason to want Carel alive. I threw those fits to embarrass him, which they always did. Killing him would end my fun."

"Fun?"

"Don't talk to them, Ydra," Cho said. "They'll use it against you."

Mrs. Trexler shrugged. "I have nothing to hide. Sergeant, Carel Armenda stole control of my father's company from him, then when I inherited it, he stole the whole company from me, changed the name from Nord to Armenord, and discarded me in favor of more passive houseplant consorts. Of course I hated him and attacked him. But the bitterness was before I married a man who truly cares about me and wants me to share his life as well as his bed." She spread her arms to the gallery. "After a while I only despised Carel, but the scenes had become a habit, and a game . . . a way to remind him who he really was under the façade that won him Cushinberry Awards."

Mama pushed his glasses up his nose. "He never asked for an injunction to stop you?"

"He couldn't." She smiled. "No more than he could run away from the scenes I made or cringe in front of that gunman. It would be admitting his lack of control. Carel always had to be in control, of everything . . . of his employees, his children, his wife. He suffered when he wasn't; he didn't feel like a man."

Understanding gleamed in Mama's eyes. "So you took control away from him."

She nodded. "He put up a calm front, pretending to patiently weather the hysterics of an unreasonable female, but I could always smell his fear that everyone around us was thinking: 'What's the matter with Armenda? Is he so weak he can't rid himself of that virago?' It was very satisf—oh, Lord, look at the time!" she wailed. "Loudon, why did you let me rattle on? We've got to get the rest of these pieces uncrated, and the crates put away. When is the Sheraton delivering the wine and cheese?" She hurried out the door at the far end of the room.

Trexler ran a hand across the top of his hair and back to the pigtail at the nape of his neck. "My wife's telling the truth; she doesn't hate Armenda enough any more to kill him. She wouldn't anyway; despite all the sound and fury when she's putting on a show, she isn't a violent person.''

"Were you in the courtyard at the time of the killing?" Janna asked pointedly.

He hesitated, then shook his head. "No. We have an agreement . . . she can make the scenes as long as I don't have to watch."

"There's also a little problem of what she could have killed him *with*," Cho said. Anger edged her voice. "The tickets came with a statement that everyone must agree to be scanned for weapons at the door."

Well, that answered one question. Janna asked another. "How well do you know the Yi's?"

Trexler shrugged. "We've met at social functions and they're regular customers."

"Have you been in their house before?"

"Yes. To deliver and help hang paintings." He eyed the two of them. "Are you arresting Ydra?"

"Not at this time," Janna said.

"Then while I don't wish to seem hostile, I wish you'd find another time to ask your questions. We're—"

"Of course," Mama said. "In the meantime, ask your wife to see if she can remember who was near her and what their positions were. Come on, bibi."

Cho followed them to the door. Unlocking it, she said, "You want to know who else was standing by Carel when he died? When Ydra told me earlier this morning what happened, she mentioned talking to Carel's wife and children in that courtyard. So they had to be close. If you're looking for someone with a motive for killing Carel, talk to them." Cho slid the door open to let them out. "C.J. likes his pleasures and hated being on a restricted allowance. Sydney is her father's daughter, right down to wanting Armenord. Carel felt C.J. should take over but I've heard Sydney say that she intends to have Armenord, no matter what she has to do to get it."

SIX

Like other houses in the Lincolnshire Estates area, the Armenda house sat behind a tall wall and heavy gate, though from the bottom of the winding drive the house's low profile of buff limestone and coppery glass had struck Janna as surprisingly modest. Inside, however, modesty disappeared. Armenda had just built his sprawling house underground and down the back side of the hill, the skylighted open-beam ceilings, stone walls, and rough-plastered walls giving it an elegant cavern appearance.

"Alpha Sherwood Five," Janna's ear buttom murmured, "attempt to locate a loose horse on the Wrexham Road bridle trail, west of Bristol Place. Described as a gray American Warmblood gelding, wearing an English saddle and bridle."

A side glance caught Mama grinning. Janna grinned back. "The trials of working a castlerow division."

The servant they followed descended an arc of stone stairs to a room with heavy drapes on one wall partially drawn and another wall devoted to a bank of library cabinets.

Sydney Armenda stood with her back to the window, hands shoved in the pockets of a faded denim jumpsuit. "Sergeants Maxwell and Brill, isn't it? My stepmother will be down in a minute."

Beyond the drawn drapes lay a grottolike swimming pool.

Janna noticed Junior's chestnut hair showing above the edge of the steaming whirlpool.

"Interesting architecture you have," Mama said.

"My father built it for Indra, his second wife . . . inspired, I suspect, by the living quarters of James Bond villains."

Who?

"The movie versions of Hugo Drax and Scaramanga, you mean," Mama said.

Sydney's brows arched. "Old cinema is your bob, too? It's —". Her voice faltered. "It was my father's. We have chip copies of around six thousand movies made over the past hundred and fifty years." She waved at the library cabinets.

Janna stared. "Six thousand!"

A covetous gleam came into Mama's eyes. "Sometime I would enjoy seeing what you have."

"Be my guest."

"Unfortunately . . . while we wait for your stepmother, we need to ask you a few questions, too." He pushed his glasses up his nose. "Can you remember the names and exact positions of the people around your father at the time he was shot?"

A line appeared between her eyebrows. "Why do you need to know?"

Janna and Mama had discussed answers to this question on the way from the gallery, discussed it with some heat on her end. "What were you trying to do back there," she had demanded, "give the suspects a sporting head start by warning them we know what happened?" Now, as the question came, Mama looked at Janna. *Your turn,* his eyes said.

The bastard. Janna gave Armenda's daughter a bland smile. "We're just clearing up routine details."

Several seconds passed while Sydney eyed them. "Of course," she said in a flat voice. Obviously not believing Janna. "I was standing behind and a little to Dad's right. On his left was a state representative whose name I can't remember but who wanted Dad to appear at a committee meeting to support proposed state legislation easing restrictions on work permits for aliens. Aida was clinging to his right arm."

His wife had been closest? Janna sucked in her lower lip. If she had indeed been clinging, it would have been easy to put a needler against her husband's ribs and pull the trigger. But the question remained of where the weapon could have come from. And what might her motive be? This many wives down the line, Armenda surely had clauses in the marriage contract that limited any material profit from the marriage. Still, it gave them questions to ask her.

"Where was your brother?" Mama asked.

Sydney hesitated before replying. "Standing to Aida's right."

"Do you remember your mother being anywhere close?"

Now the dark eyes narrowed. "Ydra? Yes . . . just beyond C.J. Is she the reason for your questions?"

Mama pushed his glasses up his nose. "Was her behavior unusual in any way?"

Sydney leaned back against the glass. "She followed us into the court when we went to meet Ambassador Rau. I wouldn't have expected that since she'd already made her scene for the evening." She paused. "Have you heard about those confrontations yet?"

They nodded.

"On the other hand, she loves embarrassing Dad and making another scene in front of a presidential candidate might have been too tempting to resist. She certainly had Dad sweating for fear she would. I doubt he heard half what the legislator said, he kept so busy watching her."

Which hardly upset the daughter, judging by the satisfaction in Sydney's voice, Janna reflected.

Mama said, "You find that amusing?"

Sydney's hands came out of her pockets. She pushed away from the window to stand up straight, feet braced apart, arms folded. "Suppose we stop the bullshit and come to the point. Am I a suspect, and what am I suspected of?"

Mama raised a brow at Janna. She shrugged. All right, let him do it his way.

He focused back on Sydney. "The angle the needle entered your father makes it impossible for the gunman to have shot him."

She took a minute to digest that, then gave them a thin smile. "I had my differences with my father. However, I didn't kill him. How would I have smuggled a weapon into the fundraiser?" When they did not answer, she continued, "In any case, I'm not the only person with motive to kill him."

"You mean your mother?"

Sydney snorted. "That's an old, cold hate. Besides, she has her revenge embarrassing him."

"What about your brother?" Mama asked.

"Impossible." As though worried that she made the denial too fast, Sydney continued hurriedly, "Not that in his pleasure-loving greed he has no motive, but his style is impulsive . . . the blunt instrument at hand in a moment of anger . . . a push out a window. My brother is a creature of the moment. I was thinking of the men whose companies my father has taken over." Her gazed shifted past them. "Aida, you remember Sergeant Maxwell from last night, and this is his partner Sergeant Brill."

"I remember," a soft voice said. "Thank you for helping me to the car."

They turned. A loose black jumpsuit and cape of brilliant copper hair hid most of the woman descending the stairs. At the bottom, though, she tossed the hair back over her shoulders, revealing a face so perfect it remained beautiful even with her emerald eyes swollen and bloodshot. She looked no older than Sydney.

"Do you feel up to telling us about last night?" Mama asked gently.

Aida Armenda glanced at Sydney.

"The sooner you do it, the sooner it'll be over," Sydney said. "And it's not as though you're a suspect." The comment carried the faintest emphasis on the pronoun. "If it's too upsetting, you can always stop."

The room's chairs had deep seats and high backs that curved around to enfold the sitter. Aida curled up in one, leaving little of her visible again except bare feet, eyes, and copper hair.

Sydney headed for the stairs. "You probably prefer talking to her alone, under the circumstances. Don't forget to ask her where everyone was standing."

Aida watched her stepdaughter climb the stairs. When the door at the top closed, she sighed. "She's so smart. It's really a shame that—"

"That what?" Janna prompted as Aida broke off.

The red-haired woman shrugged. "Nothing. I just don't understand why my husband insisted that only a son could take over from him, especially when so many of his employees are women."

Mama said, "I'm surprised he has a daughter at all, then. You'd think he'd sex-select for sons."

"He did." Aida looked up, eyes wide. "But the process isn't foolproof. What did Sydney mean about asking where everyone was standing?"

Sitting down, they gave her the story about routine details. Aida answered carefully, taking time to think, and sometimes to fight back tears. Her version of the robbery told them nothing new. She had focused so tightly on the gunman in front of her, in fact, that she saw even less than most of the other witnesses. However, she did corroborate her stepdaughter's statement about people's positions around Armenda.

Janna settled back in her chair, enjoying the velvety softness of the upholstry. That corroboration meant Sydney could not have fired the weapon that killed her father.

But Aida could have. Perhaps the marriage contract had almost expired and Armenda was not going to renew it. Aida might be bitter at being discarded. Or perhaps Armenda provided better for his widow than his ex-wives.

Or Aida could be a tool, conspiring with Sydney.

Obviously thinking the same thing, Mama asked, "If it isn't too personal a question, what happens to you now?"

Tears gleamed in the emerald eyes again. "I'll be leaving after the funeral. Carel's death voids the marriage contract. Sydney says there's no hurry and I'm sure she means it—she's always been tolerant and polite, and even kind in her way—but without Carel, I . . . can't be comfortable here." She huddled deeper in the chair.

"Does his will leave you anything?"

She shook her head. "The only profit in marrying Carel is staying married to him. I leave with my clothes, jewelry, car, and the dividends from some investments Sydney's made for me with birthday checks and gambling winnings and the like."

Janna sent a glance at Mama. They ought to check that portfolio for how much "the like" Sydney had invested. Large, frequent amounts might mean payments.

The door at the top of the steps opened. Junior appeared, wrapped in a bath sheet and grinning down at them. "I feel left out. Everyone's being interrogated but me."

As though it were a game. Did he care that his father had

died? "Interrogation is for suspects," Janna said. "Should you be a suspect?"

He bounded down the steps. "Isn't everyone guilty of something?"

From the corner of her eye, Janna saw Aida huddle even deeper in her chair and recalled the red-haired woman's remark about feeling uncomfortable in the house. Now Janna suspected why. She decided she did not like Armenda's son.

Especially not the way he looked *her* over . . . like someone inspecting a cut of meat. He smiled. "Why don't you and I discuss it over dinner, kitty? What time do you get off?"

The toad. Janna sent back a sugary smile. "Way past your bedtime, muffin."

He stiffened, anger flashing in his eyes. For a moment Janna expected him to deliver some scathing retort, but he wheeled away, pausing in passing Mama to point at the glowing orange of the jumpsuit showing beneath Mama's scarlet trench coat and say, "You certainly light up a room," before focusing on Aida. "I think you've been subjected to enough questions. You look exhausted. Let me take you to your room."

"If she's tired," Sydney's voice said from the top of the stairs, "she's perfectly capable of finding her own way."

The blaze in his eyes suggested that if his sister had been within reach, Junior would probably have struck her. A crime of passion man, as his sister had said.

Aida stood. "I do have a head ache. Are there any more questions?" she asked Mama.

"Not right now . . . though we do have a question or two for you after all, Mr. Armenda," he added when Junior took a step after Aida.

Junior turned. "I hear on the newscanner all the time about leos being hurt stepping into the middle of domestic situations."

Mama shrugged. "A risk of the job. Why don't you sit down?"

From the top of the stairs Sydney said, "Before you tell them anything, C.J., you'd better know that the gunman didn't kill Dad."

He flung himself into a chair. "Well, they certainly don't have to look far for a good suspect, do they, dear sister? Eventually you were bound to get tired of trying to please the old man and realize it doesn't matter how smart and capable you are; he was never-going to forgive you for being born female.'' He smirked at Mama and Janna. ''Even when she graduated summa cum laude from the KU law school, the old man wouldn't attend the ceremony and Edde, the houseplant in residence at the time, even got in trouble for going with our mother.''

The door above them clicked shut.

Junior scowled. ''You'd think just once she'd slam it when she's mad, but no, she's like the old man . . . no tantrums, no tears, always in iron control. Someone like that can plan and commit a murder, don't you think?''

Janna shoved her hands in her raincoat pockets to keep from grabbing the little bastard by the neck and knocking him into orbit. ''You don't seem grief-stricken yourself about your father's death.''

He pulled the bath sheet tighter around him. ''You wouldn't be either if he had been your father. Sydney would have sold her soul to make the old man notice her, but I'd have given anything to trade places with her. The bastard never let me alone. Why wasn't I getting better grades? How could I be so lazy and not want to work twenty-four hours a day? What did I mean, I wanted to go skiing; we had stock to buy up and another company to take over.''

''So . . .'' She smiled at him. ''. . . his death frees you . . . and frees your finances.''

The flurry of panic she hoped to see never came, however. Junior just shrugged. ''You're welcome to try finding a way I could have known that robbery would happen so I could shoot my father during it. Any more questions?''

She made sure they had some, including one about people around his father. His answer matched the women's.

In the car, headed back for headquarters, Janna said, ''I hope that little toad's involved.''

Mama grinned. ''What? Am I really hearing this from By-the-Book-Brill, the she-lion who keeps criticizing me for operating on gut feeling instead of objective facts and the rule book?''

She stared out at the traffic along Southwest Boulevard. ''I'm not accusing him; I'm just saying what I'd like to be true. Hey! Those look like nice apartments.'' She pointed at a *Now Leasing* sign on the wall around a new complex.

Mama barely glanced its direction. ''It'd make too long a drive downtown every day, even if I could afford the rent.''

Too long a drive? Last week he had dismissed apartments near the Statehouse as too close to central city noise and traffic. Every place was always too something. "Just what the hell *do* you want in an apartment?"

"Let's worry about the case first. You realize that unless the Armenda gang is all lying, Aida is the only one who could fire from the right angle to have made that entry wound, and I can't see her pulling a firing button."

Neither could Janna, nor see Sydney depending on her stepmother for the task. Even less did she see Aida conspiring with Junior. "The needle had to come from somewhere, though."

Mama's expression went thoughtful. "From somewhere."

"What about Sydney's suggestion we check out the men who lost their companies to Armenda? Mama?" she prodded when he did not answer.

He glanced at her. No, she decided, not at her, just her direction. "One of my law school buddies in corporate law is an encyclopedia of corporate chop. I'll ask him what companies Armenord has absorbed."

Mama called his friend from the squad room. Janna used the opportunity to visit the rest room. Pushing open the door, she heard sobbing, and came around the screen wall to find a woman huddled against the wall at the end of the sink row, head down on updrawn knees, her whole body shaken by the sobs. With a shock, Janna recognized the sleek dark helmet of Babra Cardarella's hair.

"Cardarella?" She dropped to her knees beside the other woman. "What's happened? What's wrong?"

Cardarella lifted her head and leaned it back against the wall, streaming eyes closed tightly. "The Gelfand boy, the missing juvenile Norm and I were assigned to last week? We found him. In neat packages in the family freezer."

Janna's gut lurched. "Dear God," she whispered. "Who—"

"His mother." Cardarella opened her eyes. They stared blindly toward the ceiling at the far end of the room. "That sweet, shy little woman who spoke barely above a whisper to us and who seemed so frantic when her son didn't come home from soccer practice." Her fists clenched. "He was eight years old. How could she do that? My Taura isn't much younger; I

know how maddening kids can be, but . . . how could she do
. . . *that* to her child?''

Janna put her arms around the other woman, fighting a con-
striction in her throat. ''Have you talked to Dr. Venn?''

The head buried against Janna shook *no*. ''I thought I was fine.
We booked her and I came down here before I started the reports,
then when I went to wash my hands . . .'' Her shoulders shook.

''Come on.'' Janna pulled her to her feet. ''You don't want
to go home to Taura like this.''

They climbed the stairs to Venn's office, avoiding civilians
who might be in the elevators. Walking back down after turning
her colleague over to the tick tech, Janna thought about Cardarella's sweet little butcher mother. Every once in a while
someone came along to remind them that appearance had no
relationship to what a person was capable of doing. Maybe she
shouldn't be so quick to discount Aida Armenda as a killer.
Maybe contrary to Sydney's assessment, an artful schemer lurked
inside Junior, too.

Back in the squad room Mama sat frowning at a set of doodles.
He glanced up as she dropped into her chair. ''I was beginning
to wonder if you'd fallen—what's wrong?''

She told him about Cardarella, then asked, ''Did you reach
your friend?''

He nodded. ''That'll teach him to carry a phone on the golf
course. He says Armenda engineered six takeovers, all small,
privately owned companies . . . two here in Topeka, one in
Wichita, three in Kansas City.'' He stretched across the desks
to hand her a sheet of paper, then sitting back, resumed frowning
at his doodles. ''Those are the companies and the ex-company
heads. Several of them, male and female, were vocally bitter at
the time. It's been up to ten years since some of the takeovers,
though—a long time to hold a grudge.''

Some people smoldered for a long time before exploding. He
knew that. Why did he sound indifferent, then?

Scanning the list told her why. ''I don't remember any of
these names on the list of people in the courtyard.'' She dropped
the list, sighing. Another dead end.

''They aren't. I checked. But maybe . . .'' He drummed his
fingers on the doodle. ''. . . they just weren't there in person.''

She eyed him. Excitement edged his voice now. Suddenly she realized Mama had not been indifferent, only preoccupied. She waited for him to go on.

In the corner above the caff urn, the newscanner announced that a Russian shuttle had crashed into the Sea of Japan as it attempted to land at Vladivostok.

Mama sat listening to the entire announcement before saying, "Mr. Andrew Kiffin in the list there used to own Servitron, Inc."

Janna found the names. Servitron . . . one of the K.C. firms.

"Servitron makes service robots, including waitrons. That started me thinking."

Always a prelude to trouble. Janna stretched her neck, trying to see the doodles. It appeared to be nothing but a group of circles.

Mama pushed his glasses up his nose. "We've been guilty of tunnel vision, saying only Aida was in the right position to produce that entry angle. There's another possible source of the shot." He shoved the doodles toward her and leaned across his desk to point. "If this circle represents Armenda, these three Aida, Sydney, and Junior, and this line of circles in front the gunmen, then if we draw a line pointing forty degrees to Armenda's right . . ." His finger traced a dotted line already drawn and stopped on a circle behind the gunmen labeled *W*.

Janna frowned at it. After a moment the meaning became clear. She stared. "The waitron? That's im—"

"Swatbots carry weaponry," he reminded her.

A tingle slid down her spine. "Mama . . . shooting Armenda with a needler rigged in the waitron means—"

"Someone intended Armenda to die in that riff," he finished grimly. "The robberies were just camouflage for the real objective." His eyes gleamed behind his glasses. "That's why the riffers settled for thirty people out of five hundred. And that's how Junior or Sydney could be responsible."

The theory met mixed reviews with the squad members who drifted in over the next hour.

"It explains the angle of the entry wound," Cruz agreed. "However—"

"That's a lot of trouble to go to . . ." Mt. Weyneth rumbled.

". . . to kill someone," Showalter finished.

Cruz eyed them, frowning. "We'll get along better if you let me finish my own sentences." He turned to Mama. "These people had to circumvent two separate security setups. Very risky. One slip on the first job and they'd never have the chance to kill Armenda."

"Challenge appeals to some people," Mama said.

Cruz shook his head. "What about the risk of hiring seven people, maybe eight if your perpetrator wasn't the person controlling the waitron? That's at least seven chances for leaks, seven chances of being tied to the crime."

Showalter nodded. "It'd be much simpler to hire a . . ."

". . . professional killer. And safer," Weyneth said. "The average person's daily routine offers . . ."

". . . any number of opportunities for fatal accidents." ·

Mama pushed his glasses up his nose. "When we find who killed Armenda, maybe he, or she, will explain the rationale behind choosing such an elaborate charade. Cruz, did you find out if Yi has a needler in the house someone could have used?"

The pucker of Cruz's forehead suggested he wished Mama had not asked that question. "The only weapons Yi has are some ancient Chinese swords and stuff."

"Making it difficult for anyone in that courtyard except the riffers, and the waitron, to be armed."

Janna admired Cruz's self-possession. After a moment of eyeing Mama like someone feeling the onset of a headache, he shrugged. "You're right; at this point, we can't afford to overlook any possibilities. Have you come up with anything else today?"

Janna said, "We spent a chunk of department funding on long distance calls to locate the ex-heads of companies Armenda took over. Only Russell Brashear, who used to own Konza Holotronics, is still here in Topeka. Morgan Wiedower moved to Kansas City after Armenda took over his security firm."

Cruz's expression went thoughtful. "Someone like Wiedower knows security systems well enough to neutralize them."

Which pushed Wiedower up the suspect list next to Kiffin. Janna went on, "Also in K.C. are Andrew Kiffin; Rebecca Voelker and Miles Green, of Voelker & Green, manufacturing biometric security devices; and Lewis Pritchard, who had Videoscribe, Inc."

"Pritchard lost only ownership, however," Mama said. "He

still manages the business, which transposes movies from film and videotapes to chips.''

''He could still hate . . .''

''. . . Armenda's guts.''

Janna looked up from her notes. ''We can forget about Corelle Bruckerhoff in Wichita, at least. After losing BruckerJet, her charter air service, she bought into a colonial company. Their ramjet's been headed for the stars for the past ten years.''

''That still gives us six possible suspects, if we go along with Maxwell's gunslinging waitron.'' Cruz pursed his lips. ''Maxwell, since it's your theory, tomorrow you and Brill drive up to Kansas City and talk to the five subjects there.''

Mama nodded.

''Maybe you'll get lucky and find that Wiedower and Kiffin teamed up, Weidower masquerading as the waiter and maid to take care of security and Kiffin handling the waitron.''

Weyneth nodded. ''And the enhancements will show the rest of the suspects . . .''

''. . . among the gunmen,'' Showalter continued, ''the whole plot suggested . . .''

''. . . by the son and daughter,'' they finished in unison, and grinning, slapped each other's hands.

''Speaking of enhancements,'' Janna said.

Cruz nodded. ''Even as Lieutenant Applegate's CAProp comedians perform, Dan is down in the lab . . . begging and threatening, whatever it takes to light a fire under the computer fundis.''

''Fast bargain.'' Mama's gaze focused up the room.

They turned to see Daniel Singer coming in with a bulging manila envelope.

He threaded his way back to them and dropped into a chair, sighing. ''Well, I had to promise them your firstborn children, Em, but here the enhancements are.'' He turned the envelope upside down. Colored computer prints spilled onto the desk. ''The markings in the lower left corner of each photo are for the purpose of comparing them to the original if you want. One-A and One-B are the waiter and maid.''

They scrambled for the prints. Each showed four faces. Mama's long arms snaked by Weyneth's bulk to capture one of each print. Janna waited for him to sit down, then peered over his shoulder.

Though the frame chosen for enhancement caught the waiter at a different angle than the maid, both were the same face . . . androgynous . . . male but marginally, equally believable as female. Janna knew enough about the enhancement program to understand that the computer chose hair and eye colors according to skin tones. In their waiter's case, the computer had suggested light brown hair on both the waiter and maid photographs, but light brown eyes on one and blue eyes on the other. The face looked pleasant but unremarkable to the point of disappearing instantly from memory.

Janna grimaced. No one would ever remember seeing him.

The gunmen's enhancements seemed more promising. All were male . . . four of them lean, two stocky; one red-haired and freckled, one sandy blond, two of average coloring, two olive-skinned. A small gold hoop gleamed in the ear of one of the olive-skinned jons. A scar cut the eyebow of another, gleaming white in the black hair. Another scar sprawled lividly across the back of the blond jon's hand.

"I wonder if those are real." Singer tapped the scars.

Weyneth rumbled, "Records should . . ."

". . . tell us." Showalter raised a brow at Singer. "You did . . ."

". . . take them by?"

Singer sighed. "Am I a rookie? I had the Criminalistics computer call the data directly into Records, Priority One, and Communications send it to NCIC. The local results should—"

Singer's phone buzzed.

Cruz pounced on it, and grinned as the Records computer's voice said, "Investigator Daniel Singer, Priority One request results." But the grin faded as the enhancements ran up the screen to the computer's accompanying litany of: "Subject One-A, negative; subject One-B, negative; subject Two, negative . . ."

Singer stared in disbelief. "They can't all be negative."

They were. Not one photograph matched any one in their files.

"Outside talent." Mama pulled off his glasses and polished them with a tissue from his desk drawer. "As long as we're going to K.C. tomorrow, we'll take a data chip of the enhancements and ask the KCPD to run it through their computer."

"Might as well," Cruz said. "NCIC won't be back by then. The FBI's computer is good but a file search for seven subjects by photograph alone is going to be a long job even for it. Meanwhile, we do have leads to follow here. We can't let the others do all the work.'' He picked up several copies of the prints and headed for the door.

The rest of them followed.

SEVEN

No morning could have been better for traveling. Janna relaxed in her seat. The temperature remained cool enough to require a coat, but warm enough that they let their trench coats hang open, and the sky arched in a flawless bowl of cobalt, the last clouds cleaned away by rain last evening. Against it overhead shone the east-flying silver of a dirigible's ball-like balloon and the manta ray gondola clinging to the bottom. Turnpike stretched away across the hills in an undulating ribbon, scattered with the looming bulk of trailer trucks. The rare road cars darted like minnows among whales.

Sometimes very fleet minnows.

Janna avoided looking at the speedometer as Mama skimmed the Meteor past one behemoth after another. She made conversation instead. "Where did you disappear to yesterday evening?"

Mama shrugged. "Salmas's place."

"Salmas's place?" Janna knew the waiter had been released to house confinement under his material witness status, but what sent Mama back to talk to him again? "Did we forget to ask something?"

"I went there about his sculptures, not the case."

Janna blinked. "His sculptures? You really think they're good?"

"Absolutely." He sailed around a big Aeromac. The Meteor bucked over the turbulence of the truck's fans. "Arianna Cho thinks so, too."

"Cho?" Listening to herself, Janna grimaced. She sounded like a damned echo.

"I talked her into coming with me," Mama said. "I thought Salmas might like a professional opinion. Today she's asking the Trexlers for permission to exhibit a couple of Salmas's pieces at the gallery." He paused. "She's a bright and interesting woman. We had dinner after leaving Salmas."

At least dinner. According to the bedside clock, when Janna managed to pry one eye open to read it, he came in sometime after one in the morning.

"Did you study?" he asked.

"I tried." She grimaced again. "Witch and bitch were at it again . . . this time fighting over separating trash for the pickup today. Bitch accused witch of throwing recyclables in with bio-degradables and witch countered that last week bitch didn't sort the recyclables correctly." She sighed. "I wonder why they ever married?"

A corner of Mama's mouth twitched down. "Sometimes, bibi, even a witch or bitch is preferable to living alone."

Janna eyed him. Maybe the reason he had not found an apartment had less to do with location and rent than with the lack of a roommate.

But surely that was nonsense. In her experience, people unable to bear solitude were insecure, and she could not imagine anyone more secure than Mama.

Belatedly she realized that he had continued talking. "What?"

He grinned. "Earth to Janna. I said the idea of everyone being guilty isn't that outré. It happened in a movie called *Murder On the Orient Express*." His eyes went thoughtful behind his glasses. "I wonder if that movie is in Armenda's collection."

Janna frowned. "You mean someone with access to the movie could have taken the idea, gone to a group of Armenda's ene-mies, and suggested they gang up to kill him?"

Mama smiled. "It's an interesting possibility." The toll gates appeared ahead. "Where do you want to start, after we've been polite and let the KCPD know what we're doing in town?"

She pulled their list of names and addresses out of her trench coat pocket. "Since you mentioned movies, why not with Pritchard at Videoscribe?"

Mama nodded. "What's the address?" Before they left Topeka, Communications had given them a Kansas City map chip but when Janna gave Mama the Broadway address, he blocked her reach for the car computer. "I can find that."

And after swinging by the Locust Street HQ building to announce their presence to the KCPD and leave the enhancement data chip at the Records section, he drove back toward I-70 and straight to Videoscribe.

The company occupied the top floor of a twentieth century brick building dark with age. Mama insisted on walking up the old fashioned open staircase but Janna took the elevator—modern despite its antique grillework car—past a party supply wholesaler, the editorial offices of a balloon enthusiasts' magazine, an architectural firm, and a colonial company outfitter. Videoscribe's reception area looked like something straight out of the building's period: leather arm chairs, potted plants, and antique movie posters in cases on the walls.

Most were unfamiliar to Janna, but Mama's eyes gleamed with enthusiasm. "*Citizen Kane, The Rocky Horror Picture Show, Icrade 16:42, The Dream Maze*. This is a cinema bob's idea of paradise."

The reception desk had been built with a raised front edge to hide the word processor and communications system phone on top, and a small newscanner. Nothing, however, hid the anachronism of the incense-scented receptionist in his waist-length purple ponytail and spray-fit copper bodysuit.

After examining their identification and calling Pritchard on the phone, he sent them through the double doors behind him, then returned to watching a newscanner story on whether the Russian shuttle had crashed accidentally or been shot down by the Chinese.

Beyond the doors, all antiquity vanished. The electronic equipment they glimpsed through workroom windows wore the gleam of leading edge technology.

Until they reached Lewis Pritchard's office. In it, flat metal canisters, videotape cases, and video chip cases sat stacked everywhere . . . around the videocassette player and video chip player on the battered L-shaped desk, filling half-open drawers of metal filing cabinets, cluttering the floor, the straight wooden chairs, the window ledges, even the top of the computer on the desk ell. Long rolls of paper that might be more movie posters made a pyramid on a worn leather couch.

The tantalizing smell of coffee filled the room. Coming from a steaming mug between the cassette and chip players on the desk. Real coffee. Janna savored the scent.

"Shove that stuff off the chairs," the man behind the desk said without looking up from the chip player's screen.

Mama stared at the canisters. "Shouldn't these films be in some environmentally controlled room?"

Pritchard glanced up. "What? Oh. Don't worry; the cans are all empty."

They cleared the chairs. Sitting down, Janna eyed Pritchard. A man in his late thirties or early forties, he looked pale and soft, filling his jumpsuit like marshmallow. Dark wisps stuck out all over his beard and hair. No stretch of the imagination could match him to any of the enhanced photographs.

After a minute Pritchard folded down the screen, picked up his mug, and leaned back to sip from it while he eyed them across the players with apparent puzzlement. "You're Topeka leos? What can I do for you?"

Mama said, "We'd like to talk to you about Carel Armenda."

Pritchard set the mug down. "God, wasn't that terrible? His daughter called me yesterday to tell me about him."

"You're shocked by his death?" Janna watched him.

His eyes widened. "Of course. What's going to happen to Videoscribe now? That boy doesn't give a damn about movies, let alone appreciate their historical or entertainment value. The only thing I ever saw him look at was a piece of *Dying Thunder*. That's the Paul Kendig film about the last Le Mans run with wheelers." Pritchard drank from his mug again. "Sydney would be all right. She at least appreciates what we do, even if she's not the cinema bob her father was."

"How was Armenda to work for?" Mama asked.

Pritchard shrugged. "Fine. He let me run Videoscribe the way I wanted as long as he saw the books regularly and I notified him when interesting new property came in, so he could have a copy if he wanted."

"You don't mind that he took the business away from you?"

The pale eyes narrowed. "Why do you ask that? Sydney said one of the thieves killed her father."

"We thought so at first. We were wrong," Janna said.

The marshmallow body shifted. "Well, if you're looking for suspects, you're wasting your time here. I couldn't have asked for anything better than having Armenda buy up my loan notes and foreclose. I always hated all the tax and social care paperwork. Now his accountants take care of that and I'm free to just transcribe movies and books—we also do video chip facsimile reproductions of books in danger of being lost due to paper deterioration. Corporation backing gives me more credit to negotiate for transcription rights. And every year Armenda gives me a bag of pure Colombian coffee beans that he somehow brings into the country outside the trade armistice quotas." He wrapped both hands around his coffee mug and pulled it against his chest. "I wonder if the girl knows how he did it."

Pritchard sounded anything but bitter. Though of course he could be lying. Janna asked, "You were never afraid of being fired?"

Pritchard smirked. "The licenses for access to the movies in the Turner Libraries and other depositories belong to me personally, not Videoscribe."

Mama toyed with one of the film cans. "You said Armenda liked to be kept informed of new properties in case he wanted a copy. What kind of movies did he like?"

"War movies, adventures, mysteries, thrillers. A few comedies. No heavy drama. He liked entertainment."

"What movies, specifically? How about *Murder On the Orient Express*?"

Pritchard scratched at his beard. "I expect. He collected all the movies made of Agatha Christie's books. I told you he liked mysteries and thrillers. He wanted anything with Steve McQueen or Sean Connery or David Teman. He collected directors, too, Robert Altman, Ridley Scott, Paul Kendig, Isas Cilombo."

None of the names meant anything to Janna, but Mama nodded at each. He pulled a copy of the enhancements from an inside pocket of his trench coat and handed them to Pritchard. "Have you ever seen these people around Armenda or either of his children?"

Pritchard studied the photos, then shook his head.

"Do you know anything about Armenda's other companies here in Kansas City?"

"Do they have to do with movies?"

Obviously he did not know. A short time later they left, leaving a copy of the enhancements and their card, in case Pritchard remembered the faces after all.

"Next stop?" Mama asked as they climbed back into the car.

She activated the car computer and recited the addresses into it. For each, the city map flashed on the dash screen and by successive enlargements, zoomed in on the block with the requested address. That gave her not only routes to the addresses but their relationship to each other. "Kiffin's office in North Kansas City looks closest."

The office, a sales and service center for IBM's robotics division, might be. Andrew Kiffin was not.

Leaving the service section, where Kiffin worked as an engineer trouble shooter, Janna shook her head. "He's been on the IBM space platform for two months? That eliminates him as a suspect."

"Maybe not."

She glanced sharply at Mama as she slid the car door closed. "Maybe not how? When you're on a platform, you don't casually drop groundside for a few hours."

Mama switched on the power. "They said he's working on the Sunbath II project."

Project Sunbath, she remembered from Modern History in college, had been a disaster. The dome over an experimental mining operation on Mercury failed, killing all four hundred people under it. It also set back for over a decade plans for any new mining projects requiring life supports, such as proposed sea bottom operations. Did this mean IBM wanted to try Mercury again? "What does this have to do with our riffers?"

"The plan," Mama said, "is to use robots this time, robots that can be controlled from the safety of a space station."

Janna took a breath. "You think Kiffin controlled the waitron from the IBM platform?"

"He has the capability."

Except it needed more than capability. "Whoever controlled the waitron knew Mrs. Yi," she reminded Mama. "Does Kiffin?"

"That's something to find out when we're home again."

* * *

Miles Green at Voelker and Green, Inc. came next on their list. Like Pritchard, he remained at the company he used to own, but as an employee. Like Pritchard, too, the small, wiry man, who talked to them in a spacious office with the title *Chief Engineer* on the door, showed no resentment of the takeover.

"Mr. Armenda's death is a tragedy. He did a lot for this company." Gadgets and electronic bits and pieces everywhere made the office look like a workshop. Green paced down a narrow path through the clutter to a windowed wall looking down on the assembly floor. "We have credit for research and development." Still talking, he paced back to the desk and picked up a caff cup. After a sip, he set it down again and headed back for the window. "We've developed three new models of our biometric locks, doubled our floor space, increased automation, and quadrupled our sales since Armenda bought us out. I only hope that before he died Armenda had the sense to leave control of the corporation to his daughter."

Another vote for Sydney.

"Junior doesn't impress you?" Mama asked.

Green grimaced. "The boy never comes by here except with his father, and then he's obviously bored blind." Returning to the desk, he picked up the cup again, but set it down without drinking. Janna decided that even if Green had resembled any of the enhancements, which he did not, or been tall enough to be one of the riffers, which he was not, he was incapable of standing as quietly as the riffers had. "Sydney never comes with her father but she's here several times a month . . . visiting with management and employees, asking intelligent questions about what we're doing, inviting suggestions for improvements."

Leaving the plant, Janna told Mama, "Sydney sounds like a campaigning politician."

Mama pursed his lips thoughtfully. "Doesn't she. Give the computer Servitron's address. Let's see if she visits there, too."

A stop at the assembly plant, located in a refurbished twentieth-century brick warehouse north off I-70, and a conversation with the plant manager confirmed that Sydney did make regular visits.

"Does she go down to the assembly line?" Mama asked the manager, a stout man of apparent mixed Asian-Hispanic ancestry whose jumpsuit sleeves rolled above the elbows gave the impression of a willingness to work on the line, too.

The manager frowned at them. "What does that have to do with finding the thief who killed Mr. Armenda?"

"Nothing," Mama replied with an innocent smile. "We've just heard personnel in several Armenord subsidiaries express pleasure at Miss Armenda's interest in their businesses and I was curious whether that's typical of her."

The frown faded. "I don't know if it's typical, but she seems interested in not only how many service robots we produce but how we build them and if the employees are happy working here."

Back in the car, Mama said, "She's making friends and allies everywhere. Building support for taking over Armenord, do you want to bet?"

Janna nodded. "The question is, did she know when she'd have this chance?"

Their next interview, Rebecca Voelker, said, "Someone killed Carel Armenda? That's the best news I've had today." Small and wiry with burr-cut platinum hair tipped lavender, she eyed them across the desk of her spice-scented office off the Plaza.

Mama leaned back in his molded foam chair and crossed his legs. "You still hate him after four years?"

Iridescent lavender nails rapped the desktop in one staccato roll. "He's a bastard." Voelker pushed to her feet. "He *was* a bastard." The lavender lips curved in a smile. "Never has the past tense sounded so sweet." She paced toward the windows overlooking the Plaza. Sunlight gleamed silkenly on the fabric of her beige bodysuit and ankle-length tabard. "If you're looking for people who wanted him dead, I'm one, but I didn't kill him." She turned to face them, smile drawn thin. "I wasn't anywhere near the scene at the time."

"We haven't mentioned where or when he died," Janna said.

The iridescent nails drummed the glass at Voelker's back. "It doesn't matter. Whenever, I was probably here." She circled the room, straightening pictures. The spicy scent eddied around Janna and Mama. "I'm almost always here. I have a business to run."

"The Meal Deal." Mama raised a brow. "Catering?"

"No." Voelker rearranged articles on a shelf of art glass. "Although it's a service we can extend to subscribers."

Subscribers. "You're a subscription meal service?" Janna asked.

Voelker swung to face them. "With a difference. We tailor our service to each subscriber's individual needs. A week's worth of one, two, or three meals a day chosen from a menu is only the start. If you're a shut-in, we can deliver every day instead, to check on your welfare. If you're diabetic or have an ulcer or are a recovering cardiac patient, or you just want to lose weight, we provide meals within your dietary limits. If you suddenly have ten people coming to dinner, a phone call provides food for all of them."

"It's an excellent concept," Mama said. "How is business?"

Voelker's smile answered the question. After a moment, the smile twisted. "I could have done as well or better with Voelker and Green, if Miles had given me a chance. But I'm afraid my cousin is a born wage slave." Voelker paced back toward the windows. "I had to talk like hell to convince him to go into business for himself and not just sell his designs to one of the companies already manufacturing biometric locks, then when Armenda came slithering into our lives, he couldn't wait to jump camps and throw away everything I'd worked to build." Her hands clenched into fists.

"What did Armenda do, buy up your loan notes and fore-close?" Janna asked.

"We didn't have any loans," Voelker said with pride. "We started small and built slowly. Armenda extorted V & G away. He started as a client, buying our locks for his security business. Then when he'd made friends with Miles, he informed my cousin that I hired slighs."

Janna straightened in her molded foam chair. Hiring slighs, unidented citizens, was legal. The government urged, even pressured, citizens to be idented, but no one *had* to be . . . however brainbent it seemed to forfeit bank accounts, legal schooling, free medical care, and social care just because of moral objections to being numbered, digitized, and computerized. However, because unidented employees must be paid in barter, having no bank account, they turned the employer's tax and social care paperwork into hell. So most employers did not bother filing on slighs . . . which *was* illegal. Also, slighs usually being unskilled labor and always leery of calling official attention to themselves, employers felt safe paying them a fraction of what an idented employee earned.

As though reading Janna's thoughts, the small bibi's voice went defensive. "We needed slighs to save money. I tried to be fair, though." She paced between her desk and the window. "We provided a noon meal, and only the slighs knew they didn't pay for theirs and that I let them take home what was left each day, plus teas and caff and occasional bottles of wine when I came across something decent in bulk at a bargain price. I bought them clothes at the better quality discount houses. I arranged for visits to doctors and dentists I found who would slip slighs in among their registered patients. I even located teachers willing to teach an evening or week end session to sligh children."

"Yet you didn't tell your partner what you were doing," Mama said.

Voelker spread her hands. "The more people who know a piece of information, particularly worriers like Miles, the bigger the chance of letting it slip to someone we'd rather not have know it. He certainly worried enough after Armenda told him . . . until Armenda said he could protect us if we'd let him become an equal partner." Her jaw tightened. "Of course, as soon as the bastard had a third, he wanted all the slighs fired. Miles voted with him. Then he bought Miles's share. I'd rather starve than be his employee, so I sold him my share, too. Only I made him pay a hell a lot more for it than he'd paid for Miles's."

But not enough. Janna eyed Voelker's hands. The slim fingers had clenched into fists. Maybe no amount of credit could be enough.

She saw Mama watching, too. He handed Voelker a copy of the enhancements. "Do you know any of these people?"

Voelker looked over the photos. "No." She could be telling the truth. Interest and curiosity showed in her face, but no flicker of eye or expression that indicated any recognition. "I take it you believe they're involved in killing Armenda?"

"Possibly."

She returned the enhancements, shaking her head. "Bad planning. That's too many people. If I were killing someone, I'd be the only one who knew what I'd done."

On the sidewalk a short time later, Janna said, "The number of riffers may be the best break we have going for us."

Mama pushed his glasses up his nose. "All we have to do is find them."

Their last interview, Morgan Wiedower, worked in the Plaza area, too, as director of the Kansas City branch of Personal Security Services. The security firm occupied a floor in one of the terraced sections of the Burnham Building's twin towers. Wiedower's office opened onto the terrace itself, overlooking the Plaza and Ward Parkway. Janna admired the view beyond the open drapes as she and Mama sat down in deep, contoured chairs. Nice work, coming to that every morning.

The ruddy-haired ex-owner of Shawnee Security smiled at them across his desk. "What can I do for the Shawnee County PD this afternoon? I assume you're not here applying for a job. Although," he added, looking them over, "we could use both of you. We always need personnel who don't look like bodyguards."

He matched the gunmen in weight and height. Janna pulled the enhancements out of her trench coat pocket and casually glanced at them.

"If you ever think you'd like to be better paid for risking your life, let me know."

If she added his ruddy brush of a mustache to the red-haired riffer, would the two of them look more alike? "Mr. Wiedower, tell us about Carel Armenda."

He leaned back in his chair. "Depending on who you talk to, he's either a pirate or one of Topeka's sterling citizens. I favor the former, but then, I walked his plank . . . which you must know or you wouldn't be here."

Janna exchanged glances with Mama. Wiedower used the present tense when referring to Armenda. By design, or was he unaware of Armenda's death?

"Haven't you seen the newscanner story about him?" Mama asked.

Wiedower's eyes narrowed. "All I've seen since I got back in town last night is reports on the Russian shuttle."

"Back from where?"

"First," Wiedower said, "suppose you tell me why you're asking."

Janna handed the enhancements across the desk to him. "Saturday night Armenda died during an armed robbery perpetrated by these individuals. They didn't kill him, however."

For several seconds Wiedower sat frowning at them, then his eyes widened in comprehension, only to narrow again for a moment before crinkling at the corners in amusement. One end of his mouth quirked. "Neither did I. Aside from the fact that I gave up brooding about Armenda a good four years ago, PSS had a management meeting at the home office this week end. I was in San Francisco from Thursday night until Sunday afternoon."

Which gave him a good alibi, although he could still have hired the group, and the man controlling the waitron. Except that he struck Janna as too relaxed to be hiding the deep, bitter anger Armenda's killer must feel to go to so much trouble to kill him.

"Whoever arranged the killing knows security systems," Mama said. "Could one of your former employees be so loyal to you he or she would harbor a grudge? Maybe one of them who now works for Beria Security?"

Wiedower frowned in thought. "No one comes to mind. Have you—"

The telephone on his desk buzzed.

He punched it on. "Yes, Chandra?" The phone must have focused sound. Janna caught only an indistinct murmur. "When he arrives, send him in." Punching off, he raised his brows at Mama and her. "There's a leo coming up from the lobby looking for you. While we wait for him, I started to ask if you've checked out the rumor I heard that someone in another company Armenda acquired tried to sue him for theft but never got to court because, so the accusation went, he bought off the judge."

They straightened in their chairs. "Which company?" Mama asked.

Wiedower shrugged. "I don't know. There may not even have been—"

The door slid open. Through the opening past Wiedower's elegant secretary strode a man in the gold-sidestriped turquoise bodysuit of a KCPD leo, turquoise blue helmet tucked under his arm. He headed for Mama and Janna. "Sergeants Maxwell and Brill? Did you know there's been an ATL out on you for the past three hours? Luckily I spotted your car going down into the building garage and the guard in the lobby remembered which elevator you'd taken, so I had only one tower of offices to call to locate you. You're to contact Sergeant Diosdado in Robbery.''

Wiedower swiveled the phone screen toward them. ''What's the number?''

A succession of lion faces on the screen stopped at one with the classical beauty of a Greek statue, albeit a statue of someone approaching middle age with a puckish cant to his eyebrows. ''Those are some interesting individuals on your data chip,'' the Greek statue said. ''Records fed them to our computer and passed the results to me. You're in luck, and maybe I am, too. We have a positive ID on one of your suspects.''

EIGHT

Squad rooms all over looked alike, Janna mused . . . rows of desks, many back-to-back; buzzing phones and overlapping voices; lions and she-lions talking to phone screens or civilians; dictyper screens glowing in a row against one wall. They even smelled the same, of caff, fast food, and a musty accumulation left by the decades of humanity who had sweated, fretted, and worked here.

Sergeant Diosdado leaned forward in his chair, spreading hard copy across his desk. "Your suspect is an old acquaintance of ours. Righteous name, Antony Howath Kushner. Street name, Tony Ho. Licensed in Missouri as a joyeur."

Tony Ho might actually sell his sexual favors, but he had probably bought the license to provide an easy explanation for converting large amounts of carry to credit. Even with sex being a legal commodity, many clients paid in carry to avoid having their bank records show that they paid for sex.

"Here's what we have on him locally, plus information obtained from Chicago and St. Louis the first time he was arrested here in Kansas City."

Janna studied the photograph with the hard copy. It matched the enhancements of the waiter. Janna grinned at Mama. If she had to choose just one of the riffers to identify, the waiter would have been her choice.

Mama glanced down the copy. "He cross-dresses and likes to wear disguises, bibi."

Reading over his shoulder, Janna saw that, and something else even more significant. Tony habitually took any tokens his victims had. "He sounds like our jon."

"Arrests in St. Louis for theft and fraud," Mama went on. "Two convictions, one year of community service for the first one, a year and a half at Phoenix Hill for the second." He glanced across the desk at Diosdado. "How's that project working?"

The sergeant shrugged. "It shows the lowest recidivism rate in the state. But whether that's because of its methods and the fact that it's privately run, or due to the class of prisoners sent there, I don't know."

Phoenix Hill had not rehabilitated Tony. Janna saw more arrests in Chicago for theft and fraud, none resulting in convictions. Then came a conviction for armed robbery. He had been one of five people involved in the robbery. A group effort. She pointed at the entry.

Mama nodded to indicate he saw.

Sentenced to Joliet, Tony made parole in two years. After which he moved to Kansas City, where he had been the subject of numerous field interviews as both the primary subject and a companion to the primary, had been questioned five times in relation to fraud complaints, two resulting in arrests, and been questioned half a dozen times more by Robbery, with no arrests. Charges had been dropped on both fraud arrests.

"What happened?" Janna asked.

Diosdado grimaced. "Once Tony's out of whatever role he played during the skin, he looks completely different. See the narrative info on the FIF's? He looks male; he looks female; the field interview officer wouldn't have known who he was without seeing his Scib card. Fraud told me the witnesses in their complaints were so unsure about identification, the fraud charges wouldn't stick. The same thing happened to my partner and me." The spring on his chair squeaked as Diosdado leaned back. "We suspect Tony of being involved in two jewelry store riffs we've been investigating. Specifically, we think he's the individual who provided diversions—a pregnant woman going into labor one time, an old man having a heart attack the other—that drew security guards away from their posts long enough for his accomplices to enter the stores without resistance. Except we've had no better luck than Fraud in finding a witness to positively identify him.''

"Do you know who his accomplices are?" Mama asked.

"We think so, but . . ." Diosdado shrugged. ". . . so far there's nothing solid to—oh, I see what you're getting at. Our others can't be your others. We have records on several of those deeks, and none of your enhancements look like any of them. The M.O. doesn't match, either." Teeth flashed in the handsome face. "Finding Tony may give us two sets of riffers."

Something else struck Janna. Tony's record showed no indication of violence. He had never been identified as carrying a weapon, even in armed robberies. Considering that and the reported startled expression of the riffer who thought he shot Armenda, maybe none of the group expected a murder. And if that were the case: "He might give them to us on a platter if we'll guarantee no prosecution for felony murder."

"What's UDMT?" Mama asked, pointing at the letter combination in a list of dates and alphanumeric designations on the first page of the hard copy.

Janna presumed the KCPD's Records section did the same as the SCPD's, record the access codes of officers calling up files, in order to keep track of what criminals interested which sections. And if that were the case, the access code must indicate not only the officer calling up the file but also his section. The UDMT designation, two entries before today's, stood out sharply among the succession of LVRB and IVFD codes.

"That's someone in Metro patrol." Diosdado smiled. "A uniform on an independent safari, I expect."

Possibly because Tony had victimized a friend or relative, Janna reflected, though more likely a lion or she-lion hoping for a wrap that would open the way to Investigations. City to city, leos remained the same. "May I use the phone? I'd like to call home and start warrants through the pipe."

Diosdado pushed his phone toward her.

Reaching Vradel, she reported what they had and gave him Tony Ho's name and bank. Vradel smiled out of the screen in grim satisfaction. "If you feel you're close to catching this deek, stay up there. The Russian shuttle has made most of the media forget our riffers, but the director, his father-in-law, and the mayor haven't.''

Punching off, Janna sighed. ''I should have brought my tooth-brush along.''

Mama sent her a quick sideglance, but before she could wonder at the meaning, he said, ''Since we have our suspect's last known address, let's go visiting.''

''You did hear me mention how different he can look, didn't you?'' Diosdado asked, then he shrugged and grinned. ''On the other hand, it isn't much fun here alone with my partner home on paternity leave, and we might get lucky.''

One way or another, Janna mused. The grin made him look gleefully wicked. And even more attractive . . . more Pan-like than ever. She smiled back at him.

Luck did not start, however, at Tony's home address, the second floor of a Victorian house in the Westport area. Mama volunteered to knock on the door because he looked the least lionish. Diosdado climbed out of the car around the corner to cover the back of the house while Janna waited across the street by the car, soaking up the spring sunshine. Fifteen minutes later Mama came back shaking his head. ''No one's home,'' he said, and erupted into a string of violent sneezes.

''You all right?'' she asked.

He nodded, sniffling.

She reached in through the car window and tapped the horn three times. No Tony. That hardly came as a surprise, but it was still frustrating. Missing him here meant legwork hunting for him.

When Diosdado appeared around the house to rejoin them, they gave him the bad news, too. He shrugged philosophically. ''We want some challenge in the job, don't we? Are you catching cold?'' he asked as Mama sniffled some more.

Mama shook his head. ''Spring pollen, I think.''

Or any of the other numerous plants and animals he reacted to, Janna reflected. Fortunately for him, new treatments coming down from research labs on the space platforms kept his allergies under control most of the time.

''We may not be totally out of luck, though,'' Mama said. ''I found a little more probable cause, if we need it. I talked to a teenage girl home downstairs. According to her, Tony left

Wednesday. He told the girl's mother he would be home Sunday afternoon, then came back just after midnight Sunday morning. Around Sunday noon he left again and hasn't been back since."

Diosdado grimaced. "Gone into hiding, or rabbited out of the state."

Mama reached under his glasses to rub his eyes. "Not necessarily."

The confident tone set off warning bells in Janna's head. Suddenly she wondered what had Mama been doing there at the house. Fifteen minutes seemed a long time for the conversation he reported . . . and why should he react to spring pollen now when he'd been exposed to it all day?

But when Diosdado raised a questioning brow, Mama gave them both an innocent smile. "He didn't cut cloud after your robberies, did he?"

"They didn't involve a killing, either."

"Call it a hunch, but I think he's around." Mama slid open the driver's door and swung in. "After all, he did come home, and not leave again for a number of hours. That doesn't sound like someone in a panic. We just have to hunt him without letting him know it."

Diosdado climbed into the back seat. "That won't be easy in the places he frequents, looking the way we do. On the other hand . . ."

Janna lost the rest of the sentence in circling the car to the passenger side, and regretted not having waited to hear it out. He must have said something amusing for Mama to be grinning that way when she slid into the car. "On the other hand what?"

"With the right clothes, I think we can make Maxwell look like mincemeat—or are you ho already?" he asked Mama. On receiving a negative shake of the head, Diosdado focused on Janna again, eyeing her appraisingly. "And if you'd use more cosmetics and wear something feminine and sexy, you could pass as a female impersonator."

Janna frowned at Mama. So he found it amusing that she needed to look more feminine in order to pass as a man pretending to be female? She wondered how amusing he would find being turned into a pretzel.

Diosdado leaned his forearms on the backs of the front seats. "I have friends at Metro Division. I'll see if I can talk them into giving us access to their decoy wardrobe."

Mama switched on the car. "We don't have to bother Metro; we have everything we need. I packed clothes for both of us."

Now she understood that side glance in the Robbery squad room. Outrage flared in Janna. "You pawed around in *my room*?"

The car rose off its parking rollers. Mama sighed. "Don't get so upset, bibi."

"Upset!" she gritted her teeth. "Who the hell's upset! You're dead, Maxwell!"

"Wait until I get out of the car so I don't have to be a witness," Diosdado said.

"Bibi," Mama said hastily, "it's just that the New York City Ballet is here this week, and I thought that as long as we were in town, it'd be a pity not to see them. There's more to life than police work. You know you enjoy these things when I drag you to them, but if I'd said anything to you beforehand, you'd have refused to consider it. We just need somewhere to change," he told Diosdado over his shoulder.

The K.C. detective sat back with a bemused expression. "How about Metro Division? We need photographs of Tony's friends anyway. Go south to 63rd and turn east."

They changed in the station locker room while Diosdado called Records for the photographs. Mama's bodysuit fit as though it was sprayed on and changed color with every shift of light, from gold to blue to a red that matched his over-the-knee boots. But why the hell had he chosen what he did for her . . . just because he'd talked her into buying it? She liked the metallic blue color and even the wide, latticed opening up the sides of the pantlegs, but she had never worn the jumpsuit. At home away from Mama's enthusiasm, the neckline plunging to her waist in front and back left her feeling threatened with imminent exposure. It still did.

She frowned at her reflection in the mirror above the wash basins while wiggling her feet into matching stiletto-heeled ankle boots. "What female impersonator would wear something this revealing? It'll slide off my shoulders the moment I relax, or I'll fall out of it, anouncing to all the world that I'm female, and we'll be blown."

"No." Mama rolled his eyes. "In the first place, the sleeves keep it from sliding off your shoulders. In the second, what do you think double-sided tape is for?'' He tossed her a roll of it and returned to painting his fingernails gold with a polish pen he had bought on the way to the division station. ''A strip down each side of the décolletage will keep it flat against you and hide the fact that that's you under the fabric, not padding. Be sure to use plenty of makeup, and jewelry. I brought several necklaces. Put them all on, and the ear wraps.''

She sighed and opened her cosmetics kit on the shelf under the mirrors. He would choose the most uncomfortable jewelry her father had ever designed. The support wire cut painfully into her ear with the weight of those silver leaves dangling from the lobes and curling down into the ear from the top. She began drawing on eyeliner. ''This better be worth it. I'll take it out of your hide if I endure this suit and these wraps and find Tony's left town after all.''

The polish pen's foam tip gilded his nails in sure, practiced strokes. ''His closet and dresser drawers didn't look as though he'd packed anything, and with all night to do it, he would have if he were cutting cloud.''

Closet and dresser drawers! She whirled on Mama, lowering her voice so one one coming into the locker room would hear. ''I knew it! Shit. You broke into his apartment.''

Mama blew on the nails. ''I did not break in. The women downstairs have a key so they can feed Tony's cat when he's away.''

''Cat? No wonder you were sneezing.''

He continued smoothly, ''I just convinced the girl that I'd heard the cat crying and we ought to go up and check on its welfare.''

''And while she did, you looked around.'' Janna shook her head and went back to applying makeup. The man was incorrigible. ''Mama, one of these days you are going to drop us in shit too deep for even you to swim out of.'' But as long as he had gone there . . . ''Did you find anything interesting?''

Grinning, he capped the pen and gingerly picked up his glasses from the shelf. ''The man has excellent taste. Furniture, jewelry, clothes—both men's and women's—are all top card, quality with understated elegance, nothing gaud—bibi . . .'' As the glasses settled in place, he frowned at her. ''. . . if you want to look like a man, you *have* to use more cosmetics than that.

You're trying to cover a beard, remember." He reached for the kit on the mirror shelf. "I'd better do it for you."

She let him, and let him press on the long silver false finger-nails he bought along with the nail polish pen. It made her feel like someone being made up for a play, which was essentially the situation, come to think of it.

Diosdado came in while Mama fussed over her hair, frizzing and backcombing it into a bush. He held up a sheaf of paper. "Cohort photos fresh off the telscriber. Well." The puckish brows climbed. "You two dink up nicely. But now I don't know if I ought to let you run around the city. We don't need ho jons throwing themselves off the AT&T building in despair when after you've dazzled them, they find out you're female and you're heterosexual."

She glanced toward the mirror to see exactly how she looked, and gaped at the flash stranger staring back.

Mama smirked. "Now maybe you'll listen to your Mama's advice on how to dress."

"When your wardrobe stops being fluorescent I'll think about it. Meanwhile, let's figure out where we're going and go before these wraps amputate my ears."

They spread the hard copy of Tony's file out on a massage table and studied the FIF's for the locations he had been seen and the names of his companions on those occasions. Fraud's reports yielded a few more names as well as the locations where the skin games occurred. Diosdado had still more names in connection with the suspected robberies.

They lacked photographs of those friends without police files, however . . . many of whom were artists and musicians. The general impression Janna received was that fit with Tony's pre-ferred territory, Westport to the Plaza, an area Janna knew by reputation from hearing Mama talk about his own theater and artist friends there.

"Where to first?" she asked.

Diosdado pursed his lips. "Not the clubs yet. The meat walk won't be in full parade for another couple of hours and the people we're interested in like action. Let's try some of the gallery cafes."

Topeka had none of the breed, but Janna had heard about them from Mama, who claimed Westport, rightly or not, as the birthplace of the first ones. The idea sounded pleasant . . . a café-cum-gallery, somewhere people could enjoy artwork with their food and drinks.

It sounded informal, however. She eyed Mama and herself. "Aren't we overdressed?"

Diosdado grinned. "Yes, and no. You'll see."

The Glass Dragon was their first stop. She and Mama arrived first . . . without Diosdado. *Too many people down there know me*, the detective had said as they planned their itinerary. *Coming in with me would tag you as lions, too*. Despite the still-chilly April temperatures, a number of fashionably dressed patrons sat at tables on the sidewalk. At their feet, or in one case, stacked in a squatty porterbot, sat bags imprinted with the names of area shops, identifying them as shoppers resting before heading home, taking the opportunity to renew their energy with a cup of caff, perhaps laced with amphetamines.

Janna envied them their jackets, wishing, shivering, she had not let Mama convince her that no female impersonator would cover this outfit with a gray trench coat. True he had also left his coat behind, but his bodysuit did not bare his back and chest.

A young woman at a table by the door gave them a measuring stare and began sketching on the pad in her lap.

Mama caught Janna's hand. "Get in character, bibi. Put some swing in your hips. Strut."

He himself, Janna noticed, had been swishing from the moment they parked the car. Passing the artists, he made it even more theatrical. She felt more like jogging, to keep warm.

In the Glass Dragon, the rich scents of coffee and cinnamon enveloped them. Coffee. Janna's mouth watered. It felt like an eternity since the sandwich lunch in Servitron's break room.

Mama made a pleased sound. "Solange is doing African subjects now."

He pointed at a long, oval glass panel etched with the detailed image of a Maasai warrior. It hung on the walls with paintings and other panels of stained or etched glass, above display cases containing small sculptures and pieces of art glass.

Surrounded by the art sat a diverse assortment of people that explained Diosdado's remark about being and not being overdressed. More shoppers occupied tables next to men and women in business clothes, and dancers still in the leotards and leg warmers of their practice costumes. Another artist sat sketching and glancing toward a table of young men and women wearing the baggy floral-patterned jumpsuits Janna noticed were popular with university students at home. She also spotted several male and female prostitutes, and individuals dressed much as she and Mama were.

The two of them stood inside the door looking over the room, and making no attempt to hide the fact. After all, Mama had reasoned in the car on the way, what was more natural than for someone coming in to look for familiar faces?

No one Janna saw matched any of the photographs they studied at Metro division. Unfortunately, there might be any number of people here useful to them, but she and Mama, unfamiliar with the territory, had no way of identifying them.

Mama apparently had the same thought. "Let's find a table and wait for Diosdado."

They headed for an empty one. A businessman, catching Janna's eye as she passed, raised his brows inquiringly and tilted his head toward an empty chair at his table. She swept by him, shaking her head in disgust. Wonderful. Her reward for suffering killer jewelry and clothes that invited hypothermia was a toad who mistook her for not a female impersonator but a joyeur.

A waiter barely out of his teens materialized to hand them menu cards. "Are you looking for someone?" A white dragon crawled over the left shoulder of his hip-length green tabard, the head end of the dragon stretching across the tabard's front, its hind legs and long, elaborate tail curling down the back.

"Tony Ho," Mama replied, and when the waiter raised a brow, described their suspect, adding, "Sometimes he cross-dresses."

The waiter gave them a polite smile. "He doesn't sound familiar. What would you like?"

"Coffee," Janna said promptly. "Very hot."

"The same for me," Mama said. "Are you new? Tony comes here all the time."

"Sorry." The waiter repeated the smile, more mechanical this time. "I don't know him." He backed away from the table.

Janna grimaced. "Too bad we can't badge him. Maybe he'd try harder to help."

"And maybe he can't; Tony might prefer not drawing attention to himself."

Possibly. From the corner of her eye Janna watched the door for Diosdado. He had still not arrived by the time their order did, and Janna, savoring the coffee sip by rich, scalding sip, found herself torn between wondering what was keeping him and hoping he would not appear until she finished. She fought to keep from tearing the wraps off her ears.

Pieces of conversation drifted from the surrounding tables, fragments about classes, about dancing, an argument on the merit of a painting hanging near them. The table with the businessman who showed interest in her discussed the election as they sipped their wine. Janna listened to distract herself from the pain in her ears.

"What we need," a woman's voice said, "is another Neva McLeish."

"Another Velvet Hammer?" a jon came back. "God help us."

"Are you trying to make us think you're old enough to remember McLeish?" The woman's voice scoffed. "Lipp is charming, but what have charming Presidents brought us? A worldwide trade war, near-collapse of the ecology, catastrophic pollution, and the biggest energy crisis of all time. Since we still suffer from runaway self-indulgence, we desperately need someone else with the guts to say, 'You've had enough candy; now sit up at the table and eat your spinach!' "

From the corner of her eye, Janna saw Diosdado come in the door and forgot the political discussion. As she and Mama had, he looked over the patrons. Then he headed for a table to spend a minute talking to a pair of male joyeurs. After drifting on to chat with the artist, he turned and left.

Janna stiffened. "That isn't what he's supposed to do." The plan had been for him to come by their table next, to tell them what he saw and learned.

Mama frowned but shrugged. "He can do what he wants. It's his territory."

"And our suspect!" What were they supposed to do, sit with their thumbs up their noses watching him? Not her!

She gulped down her coffee and headed for the cashier. By the time the register ran her Scib card and r-scan and she reached the street, the K. C. detective had disappeared. They could only continue down Pennsylvania to the next café.

No one in the Encore looked familiar, either, and it did not even have waiters; patrons placed orders electronically from the table and waitrons brought the food. When Diosdado had still not appeared after twenty minutes, they went on to Conundrum.

Etched mazes decorated the oval glass in the café's doors. On the wall of the entry vestibule hung a long mirror of the same oval shape. As the two of them passed, it lighted inside. A smiling face appeared in the glass. "Welcome to Conundrum," an echoing voice intoned. "This week we have five exciting new neon sculptures by Wathena Kroll. The wine list has added three new varieties from the Phoenix Hill winery. The Phoenix d'Oro is particularly excellent with tonight's special, shark fillet."

They pushed through the inner doors.

Diosdado stood across the room talking to a wizened old man with lanky hair hanging to the waist of his shapeless jumpsuit. No sooner had they spotted him, however, than he and the old man headed for the kitchen doors.

Son of a bitch! Janna clenched her fists . . . and quickly opened them again as the artificial nails stabbed her palms. She held up the fingers. "I always wondered why any woman encumbers herself with these talons. Now I can think of a use for them."

Mama grinned. "Come on. Let's see what he does at Downstairs at the Upstreet."

She grimaced. "What's upstairs?"

"The Upstreet Gallery, of course."

The Downstairs, too, had sidewalk tables. Janna slowed, approaching them. Diosdado's little man sat at one playing pan pipes. Appropriately enough. She nudged Mama.

"I see him."

They separated and closed in on him from two sides. Janna sat down in an adjacent chair. "You're quick on your feet. We just saw you at Conundrum."

The old man looked up from the pipes. Amusement glinted in his eyes. "I'm old, not crippled." He eyed her. "You better get a shawl or something, apple, before you catch pneumonia." He returned to playing the pipes, something slow and haunting.

Janna bared her teeth. "We saw you talking to Diosdado. We're interested in talking to him, too."

The music stopped. "He said you would be."

"What else did he say?" Mama asked.

The old man shrugged. "That he isn't trying to avoid you. If you go to The Jewel Tree and sit near the dance floor, he'll join you."

He had better be there. She was tired of being cold and in pain and not knowing what she was doing.

Oddly enough, as soon as they walked into The Jewel Tree, she felt on familiar ground again. They might have been in the Satin Rocket or the Janus Club back home. Around her milled the same patrons, air thick with the same smells of perfumes, alcohol, and drugs. After buying drinks at the bar, she and Mama pushed through an already thick crowd to claim the last tiny table by the dance floor. Janna remembered to swing her hips.

Around them everyone wore high dink, many with light tape inserts in the fabric of their clothing . . . whether men dressed as women, women as men, or straight-dressers. Lights spun and pulsed in time to jivaqueme music more felt than heard, reverberating in the bones. Though any music would be difficult to hear in the roar of voices. Clothes glittered; light tapes gleamed and twinkled; jewelry flashed. In the strobing light lovers touched each other affectionately. Singles eyed each other with measuring gazes. A few tried each other out on the dance floor, bodies glued together, hands exploring. The meat walk had begun.

Janna leaned closed to Mama's ear, shouting so he could hear her. "He sure as hell better find us, because we'll never recognize anyone here!"

"Dance?" a voice boomed.

They looked up. Above them towered a bodybuilder mountain of male with ebony skin. His suit gave them plenty of chance to see his color and muscles, too, for while it sheathed his lower trunk, right leg, and left arm in iridescent white sidestriped in blue light tape, his chest and remaining arm and leg bore only decorative spirals of twinkling blue and white light tape baring more skin than it covered.

Janna hesitated. Would the mountain take *no* for an answer?

Then she saw he looked at Mama, not her. He smiled. "Hi. I'm Marcus."

Mama smiled back, an arch, provocative smile. Playing his role to the hilt.

But neither of them could afford to leave the table until Diosdado showed up. She slipped her arm through Mama's, baring her teeth. "And he's taken. Trail time, choomba."

The mountain hesitated, then shrugged and turned away.

Mama pouted into his drink. "What a possessive bitch you are."

The lights blinked three times. The dance floor cleared. A spotlight came on and a female impersonator, gorgeous in a brief tuxedo, strutted into its circle. "Welcome, gentlefolk. It's show-time."

The show, too, consisted mostly of female impersonators, the best of which were a stripper, who took off only slightly less than he would have if he were female, and a pastel-haired trio called Raw Sugar. Janna enjoyed them despite the torture of her ear wraps and her irritation with Diosdado.

As the show ended, the dance floor filled again. Janna's impatience returned. She drummed the talons on their tabletop. Where the hell *was* the bastard?

"Dance?"

Another one? She looked up with a scowl.

Diosdado smiled down at her, his plain jumpsuit drab and out of place.

"Save my seat, Mama," she said grimly, and followed Diosdado onto the dance floor. A dozen acid comments came to mind, but she discarded them in favor of keeping the detective friendly. The object here, after all, was finding Tony. "What've you got?"

He pulled her against him. "Such impatience. Try to act like we're a normal part of the crowd." His breath tickled her ear.

The touch reminded her how much her ears hurt, short-circuiting any pleasure in the contact between them and putting an edge on her voice. "If people here know you're heat, should you be holding me so close?"

"You have to be able to hear me." He spun her between two other couples. "It's a necessity, strictly business."

"Then that's a gun I feel in your pocket?"

He laughed but loosened his grip. "I have a lead on our man."

For that she could forgive him everything. She pulled back to look him in the face. "What lead?"

He whirled her on across the floor. "My sources say Tony came here yesterday and went home with a friend."

"What friend?"

"One Donald Kossay, stage name Salome . . . the pink-wigged singer in Raw Sugar." He stopped and stepped back from Janna. She found herself at their table again.

Mama looked up, brows raised. Quickly, she repeated what Diosdado told her.

Diosdado said, "Let's go talk to Salome."

Mama pushed his glasses up his nose. "Let Jan and me go first and arrange to be invited in. Then you join us."

Janna eyed him. "Invited in?" What was he up to now?

He grinned at her. "Just follow my lead."

Five minutes later they stood in Raw Sugar's dressing room. A sandy-haired man in a bathrobe sat at the dressing table holding the slip of paper Mama had sent backstage. "I'm Jade. Which of you is Mr. Sumner Maxwell?"

Mama held out his hand. "I am, assistant manager of the Velvet Garter in St. Louis, as I say in my note. This is Hat-shepsut." He touched Janna's arm. "One of our dancers."

Hatshepsut! Trust Mama to come up with a bizarre name like that.

Jade looked her over. "Wonderful legs! Once you loosen up your spine so you walk more like a woman, honey, you'll look fabulous!"

She put on a sugary smile. The next person making a remark like that would earn a very close view of these fancy nails!

"Your act is absolutely fabulous." Mama strolled over to peer at a group of photographs on one wall. "Do you ever go out of town for gigs?"

Jade sat several centimeters taller. "Sometimes. Are you interested in bringing us to St. Louis?" Despite an obvious effort to keep his voice nonchalant, eagerness ran through it.

"Very. These are nice photographs of your group." Mama turned around smiling to face Jade. "Where are the others, Salome and China? I'd like to meet them."

"Down the hall in the john. I'll get them." Jade jumped up and hurried out.

Janna said, "We're in, but I don't think they'll like us when they find out we lied about being from the Velvet Garter."

"They don't have to." Mama turned back to the photographs. "I think I've found what we came for."

She blinked. "What?"

"These aren't the three people who performed tonight. The one in the blue wig is different. During the show, I kept thinking the blue-haired one looked familiar. Now I know why."

Her pulse jumped. "We couldn't be that lucky."

But he nodded.

"Here they are," Jade's voice caroled from the doorway. He stepped aside as they turned. "Jade and China. My pets, may I present—"

"Shit!" one of the two robe-clad men in the doorway yelped. "Lions!" He flung himself backward.

Janna tossed her shoulder bag to Mama and leaped in pursuit, shoving aside the second, gaping, man.

"Sic him, bibi!"

The running man raced down the narrow hallway. Janna pounded after him. "Tony! Running won't do you any good!"

He crashed through the fire door at the far end. Its alarm whooped.

Janna banged through after him. Outside a dim alley stretched two directions. The street lay up it to her left. She paused a second, breath held, listening. The slap of running bare feet faded to her right. Deeper into the alley. Janna charged that direction, too. But while her reflexes carried her along, her head wondered what she was doing chasing the deek? He probably knew every rat hole in the city. There could be dozens of traps laid this way, even monofilament. Hit that at neck height and she would slit her throat to the spine and be dead before she even felt the wire.

On the other hand, if she let Tony elude her, how long before they caught up with him? Changing his appearance and depending on friends so he did not have to use his Card could mean months before they found his tracks again.

The slapping footsteps veered left. She heard them just in time to avoid running into a wall as the alley changed direction. Seconds later they came out on a street. Spotting her quarry was easy enough . . . the only man in sight in a bathrobe. She stretched her stride. While she wore heels, a handicap, he was barefooted, and she had longer legs. She gained steadily.

His glance back showed her a grimace of . . . desperation? He dashed into the street, dodging cars. Heading toward the alley mouth she saw on the far side? She plunged after him. Fans screamed into braking mode. Drivers swore. She ignored them all; Tony could not be allowed to reach that alley. As sure as she breathed, she knew what he would do. He would reach the dark and stop running. He would pull into a hole, muffle his breath, and cut off his trail.

He reached the far sidewalk. The alley lay just strides away. But a truck bore down on her, too big, too heavy to stop in time. She dropped to the pavement, rolling. The turbulence from the truck's fans kicked at her, battering her, pushing her aside. The thin lattice on the pantlegs ripped. Pain lanced up her leg, and down her back where her bare spine scraped the pavement. Janna ignored it, rolling once more and using the momentum to somersault onto her feet and launch into a last dive after the fleeing man.

The tackle hit him at the waist just as he reached the alley. They slammed into the wall with a bruising smack of flesh against brick. The breath whooshed out of Tony. He collapsed wheezing. Almost on the sidewalk already, Janna slid the rest of the way, rolled over on her back, and lay panting beside him.

"Wasn't that . . . invigorating?" She no longer felt cold, she noticed. "As soon as . . . we catch our . . . breath . . . we'll go somewhere . . . more comfortable . . . and chat." Also, both ear wraps and half the fake nails had come off somewhere along the way. Janna grinned. Every cloud had a silver lining.

NINE

"Talk to us, Tony," Diosdado said. "Tell us about Friday and Saturday night."

Tony glanced from Diosdado standing over him on one side, arms folded, to Janna and Mama leaning against the interview room table on the other. Then he looked down. He did not, despite Janna's silent urging, look at the wall ahead, where a hidden camera focused on his face to record pupil response to their questions.

They needed that camera's information; Tony gave them no help otherwise. Fussing with the sleeves of his jumpsuit, he repeated the same apologetic answer he made to every question asked during the walk back to The Jewel Tree and the ride downtown. "I'm sorry; I have nothing to say."

Janna swore silently. That answer left them with no grip on him, nowhere to dig. If only he would say *something*, even a lie. Preferably a lie. Lies provided a good toehold for tripping him.

Diosdado sighed. "Come on, Tony. You're lion meat and you know it. You panicked and ran from these officers. No innocent man would have."

"They startled me." Tony gingerly touched the purpling swell where his forehead met the alley wall.

That reminded Janna of her own abraded leg and back, smarting under her jumpsuit.

"Jade said we were meeting nightclub people from St. Louis and would I keep on pretending to be China so we could have a gig at their club to tell the real China about when he came back from his uncle's funeral." He glanced sidelong at Janna and Mama. "I didn't expect to see the leos from a newscanner story about a riff in Topeka."

"Do you remember everyone you see on newscanner stories?" Janna asked.

Tony looked down and said nothing.

"So you realized they'd lied to Jade," Diosdado said. "That doesn't explain why you ran."

"I'm sorry; I have nothing more to say."

Diosdado's lip curled. "Tony, you certainly know your right to remain silent, but then, you've had plenty of practice. Except this isn't like being brought in for fraud, or even robbery." He unfolded his arms and leaned down until his face came within centimeters of Tony's. "This time, choomba, someone died."

Janna noted with satisfaction that sweat gleamed on Tony's upper lip. She gave him her grimmest smile. "So the charge will be felony murder. Kish? Everyone involved in commission of the crime can be tried for murder, whether or not he personally killed Armenda. In Kansas, conviction for felony murder carries a mandatory death penalty."

Mama pulled up his legs so he sat cross-legged on the table. "And it's only fair to warn you, Tony, that the legislature is now in the process of passing an organ harvest law like the one in California." He pushed his glasses up his nose. "Instead of receiving a lethal injection, you're anesthetized in a surgical suite. Your blood is drained and bagged for transfusions, and every useful organ removed. That includes muscle sections, lengths of blood vessels, bone, and bone marrow, digits—whatever the organ banks need—until there's almost nothing left but brain to cremate. It's execution by disassembly." He drew out the final sentence, pronouncing every syllable separately, making the last word a long hiss.

Of all the case law and legislation they invented to bluff suspects, playing off the California law had to rank as one of Mama's best efforts. It made even her shudder.

Tony went white. They said nothing, just let him sit with his imagination working on him. At the end of the long, strained silence, however, he whispered only, "I'm sorry; I have nothing to say."

Janna shoved her hands into her pockets to keep from smacking the table in frustration.

Diosdado sighed. "I'm sorry, too, because you know, Tony, I like you. I hate thinking of you as scattered component parts."

Tony huddled in the chair. "First you have to convict me."

"You think we won't?" Janna said. "The media went to those fundraisers. We have video chip recordings of you at both of them."

He focused on her. "Impossible."

"You were disguised, of course, but from the video chip recordings, we made these." She pulled a copy of the enhancements out of a thigh pocket and handed them to him.

He returned them after a glance. "You can't take those to court as proof. The right program can make those faces out of anyone's. Enhancements are just computerized guesswork."

Tony knew computers and the law. Did he know juries? Janna returned the enhancements to her pocket with a shrug. "We can still present the enhancements as our probable cause for arresting you, and do you think the average jury believes the computer is just guessing? Do you think they'll care, if you're the only one available to try for this premeditated murder?"

He stiffened. "Premeditated! It was—the newscanner said the killing was. . . ."

Mama interupted, "The media hasn't been told yet that someone rigged the waitron with a needler." He unfolded his legs and slid off the table. "The killer used you and the others, Tony. The robberies were just a cover for killing Armenda. He's still using you. Do you want to stand trial and be executed for what he did?"

Tony sucked in his breath. "I want to call my lawyer."

Two hours later he sat in the interview room again, looking much happier, even smug, beneath the wing of his attorney, a plump baby doll of a woman of multiple dimples and a breezy smile. Flint glinted in her eyes and voice, however. Janna had first noticed that when the attorney negotiated with the KC and Topeka district attorneys' offices on the phone. She drove a hard bargain, too . . . Tony's cooperation in Diosdado's armed rob-

beries and the Armenda murder in return for immunity in the
KC robberies and a guilty plea in Topeka to robbery only, with
the Topeka D.A. recommending a minimal sentence in a min-
imum security facility similar to Missouri's Phoenix Hill. "Ask
him your questions, leos."

Janna opened her notebook. "Who are the six gunmen and
the man controlling the waitron?"

The satisfied quirk at the corner of Tony's mouth vanished.
"I . . . don't know."

So much for cooperation. Janna snapped the notebook shut,
shaking her head at Mama and Diosdado.

"I don't!" Tony bounced forward onto the edge of the chair.
"That's the way the tickman set it up . . . no names, no contact
between us except during the riffs. The tickman's the only one
I met!"

"Where and how?"

Tony hesitated, but it appeared to be a pause for thinking
rather than reluctance to answer. He sat back in his chair. "A
letter came to the house two weeks ago, not signed, no return
address on the envelope. The writer said he needed someone
good with disguises and I'd been recommended. He said the job
paid well."

"He?" Mama asked. "The letter gave the writer's gender?"

Tony frowned. Annoyed at being interrupted? "No, but he
was a jon when I met him later. The letter said if I wanted to
know more, he'd phone at eight o'clock that night. Money always
interests me so I waited for the call. It came exactly at 8:00."

Janna made a note of that. "What did the caller look like?"

Tony spread his hands. "He had his screen covered. He
wouldn't talk about the job, either, just said to meet him at the
Crown Center Hotel, room eight-twenty, within the next hour."

"And you did." Mama raised his brows. "You weren't worried about it being a sting?"

"I thought I'd look at the offer." He grinned. "A sting doesn't
work if you walk away from the bait. When I knocked, this
voice said come in, the door was open."

Janna poised her pen over her notebook. "Describe the man
you met."

Tony licked his lips. "All I saw was a shadow by the window.
The room was dark except for the light inside the door. The jon
ordered me to stand under it."

A very cautious tickman. "You can't tell us *anything* about his appearance?"

"It was a tall shadow."

"What did he sound like?" Mama asked.

Tony shifted in his chair, crossing his legs. "Average . . . not raspy or high-pitched, nothing special to remember. No accent. He said don't bother asking his name just listen. He had two riffs planned, both political fund-raisers out of town. If I joined the team, I'd be one of seven, but I wouldn't know anyone's names and they wouldn't know mine. I wouldn't even meet them before the riffs and we'd leave separate ways afterward."

At the edge of Janna's vision, Mama started, then grinned. She glanced around in surprise. "What is it?"

"We had the wrong movie."

Tony's lawyer frowned. "I don't understand."

Mama smoothed his face. "It has to do with recognizing the M.O. is all."

Janna straightened. She saw Diosdado perk up, as well. "Who uses it?"

He sighed. "No one who can be involved here. Go on, Tony."

Tony crossed his legs the other direction. "The jon asked was I interested. My gut reaction was anyone that careful about hiding his identity wasn't a lion so I said sure. He said look in the ice bucket by the bathroom sink. I found some unset gems. Earnest money, he called it. Then he said my instructions would come by mail and had me close the door on my way out."

"You must have discussed what the job would pay sometime in there," Janna said.

Tony glanced up at his attorney.

She dimpled. "I believe that's irrelevant, Sergeant Brill. We will specify, however, that Tony was to receive half after each job."

"That was two weeks ago?" Mama asked. "What day, exactly?"

"Monday before last, the eighth."

"When did your instructions come?"

"Last Tuesday . . . big thick envelope with pages of instructions, a timetable, a one-month bus pass, and photographs. I was supposed to buy transport tokens and acquire some drug that could be given in a drink without the drinker realizing it and would keep him asleep the better part of twenty-four hours. The instructions also gave me a number sequence for a sonic lock and said I needed to buy a key and have a locksmith tune it to the scale the instructions gave me the code for.''

Mama pursed his lips. ''Do you remember the code?''

Tony grinned. ''Why care when I can tell you which lock the key opens? Wednesday I took the bus to Topeka and went to an address he gave me. Apartment fourteen-forty in the Terracrest Apartments out on Lockwood,'' he added before anyone asked. ''According to letters and things there, it belongs to someone named Katura Murane.''

Janna wrote down the name, not bothering to exchange glances with Mama. Of course Tony searched the apartment. So would she under the circumstances. ''And then?''

Tony rubbed his eyes. He winced as that touched the bruise on his forehead. ''Then I stayed in the apartment studying the timetables and plans and using wigs and makeup left for me to practice making myself look like the photographs of the two people I was supposed to impersonate.

''Salmas and Wald.'' Mama's scalp furrowed. ''You didn't follow them except on the day you approached them?''

''I didn't have to. Everything I needed to know about their habits was in the instructions.'' Tony shook his head, grinning. ''That's one thorough tickman.''

Other accomplishments bothered Janna more. ''How did you use Salmas's Scib card to clock in at the hotel?''

Still grinning, Tony shrugged. ''Just the way I'd use my own, fed the card into the slot and looked into the r-scanner. I don't know why it worked.''

The attorney's dimples vanished. She stared down at her client. ''You used someone else's—'' She bit off the rest of the sentence, mouth setting in a grim line. ''Go on with your questions, Sergeant Brill.''

''As the inside man, did you bring in the needlers?''

''No. I don't handle weapons, ever. The gunmen brought them in themselves.''

''Did you bring in the waitron?''

''It was already at the hotel. And at the caterer's ahead of me, too.''

''You had no trouble passing the scan to clock in at the caterer's either?'' Mama asked.

Tony snorted. "They didn't have an r-scanner. No real security at all." He shook his head. "I just walked in through the front door past a receptionist and back to the time clock. Can you believe that? Anyone could have come in. The time clock is just your basic shove-your-Card-in-the-cardslot type, too. Someone needs to have a serious talk with that manager about proper security!"

His disapproving tone made Janna grin.

Mama's forehead furrowed. "Do you know why someone disabled the security camera at the service door you used to leave the hotel?"

Tony blinked. "That's lightwitted. Why bother when the door alarm would tell Security which way I'd left?"

A dark eye rolled Janna's direction said: *see?*, reminding her that Mama had expressed the same thought. "After you and the others and the waitron went out the service door, what kind of vehicle picked you—"

"The others didn't follow me out," Tony interrupted. "I told you, we all left separately."

Janna frowned. They had to leave together. The security cameras had not picked them up at other exits. Unless . . . they had *not* left, not immediately? They wore disguises, after all. Could they have stripped off the wigs and mustaches and been drinking caff in the restaurant or enjoying gambling and sexual favors up in Diversions while the police swarmed through the hotel?

"No one picked me up outside, either. The waitron led me across the parking lot to the mini-mall there and told me I'd find my first payment in a bag taped under the biodegradables dumpster there. I collected the bag, threw my wig and mustache into the dumpster along with the waiter's coat, and took a bus back to the apartment."

"Leaving the waitron and all that carry?" Diosdado asked in a skeptical voice.

Tony grunted. "Absolutely. The instructions said the waitron was wired to defend itself with electric shock. I didn't try to see if it was true."

Wise. In light of what happened at the Yi house, electric shock might have been the least consequence of trying to rob the waitron. "Tell us about Saturday night."

He rolled his eyes. "It all fell apart. We were supposed to riff five of those courtyards, leaving one of the team behind each time to keep the group under control until we finished in the last court.'' He paused. ''But the tickman lied, didn't he? He never intended us to clean more than that first group.''

''Back up,'' Mama said. He paced toward the door. ''You arrived with the caterer's van and set up the buffet. Then at six-fifty you went into the service court, shot paint at the monitor camera lens, and opened the rear gate for the gunmen, is that right?''

Tony straightened in his chair. ''How did you know—oh.'' He sat back, nodding. ''The security system log. Mr. Yi has a top card system. I opened the gate, yes, but not for the rest of the team. They came in with the other guests, just like they did Friday night.''

Janna met Mama and Diosdado's eyes. The gunmen could *not* have come in with the other guests. Either Tony lied, or there was another way through the security screen into the house.

Mama asked, ''Why open the gate, then?''

Tony shrugged. ''My instructions said to blind the camera and test the override code.''

Across the room, Mama's face went thoughtful. ''Did the others leave through the back with you?''

''No. It was just the waitron and me again. Don't know how the others got out.'' Tony glanced down at his wrist chrono and smothered a yawn. ''It wasn't my job to worry about them.''

''How did you leave the neighborhood?''

Tony grinned. ''The tickman picked me up. And before you ask, it was too dark inside the car for a good look at either him or the little jon driving. The driver told me the waitron had two sections, bayonetted together. He had me break it down, put the pieces in the back of the car, and climb aboard with it. He handed me the second payment when they let me off at a bus stop about a klick away.'' He grimaced. ''I was supposed to stay at the apartment until Sunday, but the killing scared me shitless. I wiped the place clean and headed for the bus station.''

''Describe the vehicle,'' Janna said. How had it sat around the neighborhood all evening without Yi's leos noticing it?

''A Triton wagon in some dark color,'' Tony came back promptly. ''Green.'' He paused. ''Or blue, maybe. I'm not sure of the year, either, seventy-six or seventy-seven, whenever the Chryslers ended up looking like Datsun-Fords. The rear seat had been taken out and a computer desktop with a multifield screen set up in the cargo space, but without the desk, just on short legs. Probably for controlling the waitron.''

Mama frowned. "A desktop? A laptop should have been . . ." His voice trailed off.

Janna frowned, too. Nothing about Tony's description of the car helped explain how it escaped notice.

"Since Chryslers and D-F's looked so much alike that year, how can you be sure it was a Triton and not a Monitor wagon?" Mama asked.

Their prisoner gave them a wry grin. "Because I've been FI'd in Tritons too often not to know them. The KCPD likes those wagons for its watchcars, right, Diosdado?"

After Diosdado had his turn and Tony had given the K.C. detective names from the jewelry store riffs and been sent up to the holding cells for the night, they headed for the Crown Center Hotel. Mama glanced around at the late twentieth-century decor of the lobby in obvious delight. "So they've finished the restoration. It's beautiful, don't you think, bibi?"

Janna looked it over as they leaned on the registration desk waiting for the clerk to punch off the phone . . . small couches and tables around a bar in a sunken center, thick columns supporting a mezzanine, a ceiling soaring three stories above them, and a waterfall tumbling down a terraced wall from high up past the registration desk. She had never seen the hotel before, but it did look nice now, if wastefully difficult to heat and cool, a restful echo of a prosperous, simpler time when life moved more slowly and resources seemed endless.

The clerk folded down the phone screen and turned toward them. "May I help you?"

Diosdado showed her his badge. "We need to see to know who had room eight-twenty on April eighth."

"Just a minute." She typed on a keyboard down behind the desk.

Diosdado turned his back to the counter. "Do you suppose this will do us any good? Chances are he borrowed the room from a friend."

"Even that name will give us a place to start hunting," Janna said.

"If the friend will talk." The dark eyes followed an ascending rectangle of lights that framed the glass back of an elevator.

"It's like something out of an historical movie, isn't it? And speaking of movies . . . ." Diosdado turned to eye Mama. ". . . what did you mean, you had the wrong movie?"

Grinning, Mama told him about their speculation on murder à la *Murder On the Orient Express*. "But we were wrong. The M.O. for setting up these riffs comes from another movie entirely, *The Thomas Crown Affair*."

Diosdado glanced sideways at Janna. "Did anyone ever tell you you have a strange partner?"

"A strange partner?" Janna arched her brows. "Mr. Somewhere Over the Brainbow, you mean? The Wizard of Odd? How can you say he's strange?"

"*The Thomas Crown Affair*," Mama said with the slow care of someone speaking to not-too-bright children, "was made in the last century and starred an actor named Steve McQueen."

The name reverberated in Janna's head. She whipped toward Mama. "Isn't that one of the actors Pritchard said Armenda collected?"

Mama nodded. "So that movie ought to be in his collection."

Where Junior or Sydney could have seen it.

The clerk looked up. "I'm sorry, Sergeant, but eight-twenty was unoccupied on April eighth."

They frowned at each other. "Maybe he had the date wrong," Janna said. "We can try Sunday."

"No mail deliveries that day," Mama pointed out.

"Maybe Tuesday." Diosdado leaned on the counter. "See who had it the evening of the ninth."

More keys tapped, then the clerk looked up again. "Tuesday that room was part of a block reserved for Governor Hershey's party."

Janna vaguely remembered the newscanner covering the Libertarian presidential candidate's campaign stop in Kansas City earlier in the month. Could their tickman have a friend among the governor's staff and aides?

"But the party didn't check in until nearly eleven that night," the clerk went on.

Leaving the room effectively unoccupied that night, too. Janna swore under her breath.

But Mama smiled at the clerk. "What kind of locks do you have on the rooms these days?"

"Key operated, of course, to fit the decor." The clerk held

one up. Instead of a serated edge, however, the heavy key shaft carried cone-shaped indentations on the edges and sides.

As they walked away from the desk, Diosdado said, "You're thinking our jon broke into the room? You don't pick those locks without a fight, and you don't copy those keys at a hardware store."

"True," Mama agreed, "but someone who can learn a private home's override code and arrange for Tony to pass an r-scan with Salmas's Scib card could probably manage to copy one."

Maybe he knew how to walk through walls, too. Though Janna would never admit such a thing to Mama, their killer's blithe contempt for locks and other security measures was beginning to make her feel as though they were chasing ghosts.

TEN

Lieutenant Vradel leaned back in his desk chair. "Our suspect is tucked safely away in a cell?"

Mama and Janna nodded.

"Very pleased with himself for coming out what he considers best in our deal." Janna grimaced. "He may be right. Diosdado got more concrete information than we did. Anything happening here?"

"Oh, a lot of activity." His mustache twitched. "Not much in the way of results." He leaned forward to peer at the notes and sketches covering his desk blotter. "Cruz and Singer went to the Armenda funeral this morning. A well attended affair, Cruz says, with everyone appropriately solemn but no one prostrate with grief. Junior kept leering at his stepmother. Daughter behaved very decorously, then went off with a group of company managers after leaving the cemetery.

"The FBI sent back a list of possible matches for our enhancements, though Cruz told me this morning that the first two they traced are in prison." His pencil circled a sketch of two interlocking gears. "Zavara and Threefoxes talked to the man who owned one of the local companies Armenda took over."

"Russell Brashear, Konza Holotronics," Mama said.

Vradel nodded. "He has nothing friendly to say about Armenda but doesn't appear bitter. The new company he started is doing well. Some of the employees at Konza quit after the takeover, apparently in protest. One even filed a lawsuit, but later dropped it. Brashear hired most of the protesters at the new company. Threefoxes is getting their names from Armenord to check out. Oh yes.'' He tapped a sketch of a mustached face. ''The Sheraton says they took delivery on a waitron Friday morning. No one thought anything about it at the time, but checking their records yesterday at Showalter and Weyneth's request, they found that none of their waitrons had been sent out for repairs. A small male with a mustache made the delivery, driving a van with the logo of G & B Cybertronics on the door. G & B normally services the hotel's waitrons and porterbots. On playback of security camera recordings for that day, they found the camera at the loading dock had caught the delivery van's license. Showalter ran the plate. The vehicle is registered to G & B but they deny sending any delivery to the hotel. They claim that particular van was on their lot out of service that day.''

So the small jon with a mustache possibly ''borrowed'' it to deliver the waitron? Janna exchanged glances with Mama. Could that be the same jon who drove the car picking up Tony Saturday night? ''Did anyone check with Holliday Catering to ask about waitron deliveries there?''

''Cruz didn't say.'' Vradel checked his blotter again. ''He did say that so far, our informants still have no information on the riff . . . not a murmur. That's about all the update I have. Nothing's turned up on Beria and hotel personnel we've checked so far. Maybe you'll have better luck. We need some results before the media loses interest in that Russian shuttle. Before you sail, however . . .'' He looked up, tone going dry. ''. . . I've been asked to mention that the department is not happy about receiving a traffic citation on an Ashanti 667 bearing plates assigned to the SCPD, which five separate speed monitors recorded traveling north Saturday on Topeka Boulevard at excessive speed.''

Janna winced. She knew it!

But Mama's eyes widened innocently behind his glasses. ''That was a emergency run to check on the Salmas man's welfare.''

Vradel's mustache twitched. ''I explained that to Traffic. Captain Bernard reminded me in return that official vehicles, which officers are expected to use, have signals which activate with the light rail and/or siren, causing the monitors to disregard such vehicles so Traffic doesn't print out citations on them. I've been asked to urge, however strongly I think it necessary to make the point, that you do drive official vehicles hereafter." His voice hardened. "I don't know how you talked Perera into assigning you that Ashanti, Maxwell, but I'd better not hear about a stunt like that again. Ever. Kish?"

Mama stiffened. "Yes, sir."

"And I'm very disappointed you went going along with him, Brill," Vradel added.

Heat crawled up her neck. "Yes, sir." Damn Mama. Damn *her* for being a fool. The knot in her gut wiped out the last lingering warmth of Diosdado's lovemaking last night and his good-bye kiss this noon.

"I expect a better exercise of judgment from you. If anything happened to that vehicle, not even both your salaries for the year would cover the department's liability."

"Yes, sir." Ears burning, Janna slunk out of Vradel's office.

Mama followed. "I'm sorry, Jan."

"What do you have to appologize for?" she said bitterly. "I'm the lightwit who lets you talk her into these stunts."

He patted her shoulder. "Speaking from a vast experience in being on commanding officers' shit lists, I can assure you Vradel will forget all about this when we wrap Armenda's killer. And toward that end, let's go talk to Yi's lions."

They caught up with Martin Surowski and Sheila Inge on patrol. Lake Sherwood spread out from the overlook where the four of them leaned against their parked vehicles, soaking up the afternoon sunshine.

The radios murmured in Janna's ear and from inside the cars. "Beta Sherwood Nine. Vehicle with 10-46 or Signal 3 driver is headed south on Oakley from 31st Terrace. Vehicle has struck three parked vehicles and a power pole. R.P. reports power is out in the area."

"An unmarked car?" Inge echoed when Janna asked. "Yeah, there was one near Yi's that night."

Janna shrugged deeper into her trench coat, glad she had not taken out the lining yet. The sun's warmth did not quite compensate for the chill of the breeze off the lake. "Are you sure?"

Surowski snorted. "It wasn't a D-F, true, but when was the last time you couldn't recognize an unmarked car?"

"Besides," Inge said, "we approached it once to find out what was in the pipe. The black glass made it hard to see more than a vague shape on the passenger side. When I rapped on the window, this little jon wearing an ear button slides the rear door open a crack and sticks his head out. 'Get away before you blow us,' he says, then pulls back in and slams the door. We stayed clear the rest of the evening."

Janna sent Mama a glance. The little jon again. "Can you describe this jon better?"

"We didn't have much more than a glimpse of him." Surowski frowned in concentration. "You're out of luck on exact height or clothing. Slight build, brown hair short over the ears and pulled back behind them, ordinary mustache."

"Brown eyes," Inge added. "Why the interest in him and the car?"

"A dark blue or green seventy-six or seventy-seven Chrysler Triton wagon driven by a small male picked up the waitress and waitron after the robbery," Janna said.

The two watchcar officers stared at her while from inside the watchcar came a radio voice high with excitement. "Beta Sherwood Nine, Sherwood. Request backup, Oakley and Twilight Drive! That Signal 3 driver has left his vehicle and gone into a house and is throwing things out the windows at us!"

A moment later all their radios crackled to life as Dispatch broadcast the request.

Inge glanced at Surowski, brows raised.

Her partner sighed. "By the time we can get there, the fun will be over." He focused on Mama and Janna. "The car we saw was a dark green seventy-seven Triton. You mean we had two of those riffers right there and just walked away from them? Shit."

His partner expressed it more strongly. Janna sympathized with their frustration.

"I'd have done the same, under the circumstances." Mama gazed out over the lake. "When did you first notice the car?"

"It was there when we went on duty at eighteen-thirty," Inge said.

"Located where?"

"The corner of Shriver Circle, one block from the rear of the Yi house." Inge sighed. "And we just let them sit there."

But Surowski grinned. "We can make up for it. I remember the license number."

Mama lifted his head. Janna pushed away from the car.

"It used my wife's initials . . . K-J-S-five-two-six."

Janna tapped her ear button. "Indian Thirty, Capitol, requesting a ten twenty-eight on King John Sam five-two-six." Then she stood chewing a knuckle waiting for the reply.

Shortly, her ear button and their car radio said, "Indian Thirty, your ten twenty-eight shows on a twenty seventy-nine Smith Sundowner . . ."

"A runabout!" Inge spat in disgust. "The bastard must have sto—"

Janna waved her to silence as Dispatch continued, ". . . registered to a Jordan or Irene Minshall, 2428 Colorado. Have you seen those plates? I have an alert on them as reported stolen."

"Hah!" Inge slapped the roof of her unit.

"When was the report filed?" Janna asked.

"Sunday, April twenty-first."

"The day after the riff," Surowski said.

Mama took his hands out of his trench coat pockets and pushed away from the car. "Let's talk to Mr. Minshall, bibi."

No one answered the bell at the Minshall house, but a neighbor working on the flower beds in her yard knew where he worked: as a law clerk for Kettering, Kettering, and Axthelm. They tracked him down at the law office. He reported he had left work around eight o'clock, as usual. The car was parked in the Sunco parking lot at 13th and Jackson, in his stall on the reserve levels.

"The tags had to be stolen there," Minshall said. "At home I keep the car in the garage."

"You didn't notice the plates missing then?" Janna asked.

He had not . . . not until the next morning, when the family was preparing to leave for church.

Back in their own car, Mama said, "Our riffers knew Minshall's habits."

"That or they just happened to steal plates from someone who works late enough that the earliest he could report the theft would be after the riff."

So did that mean they were looking for someone with a connection to Armenda, the Sheraton, Yi, the Murane woman, *and* Minshall?

They drove back across town west to the Terracrest Apartments next.

But as Mama reported to Cruz in the Gage Zoo parking lot after calling in a request to meet with him, the trip yielded only one useful fact. "Katura Murane is a behavioral psychologist at the Menninger Foundation. She's been up on one of the space platforms doing some kind of research for the past month and isn't expected back until the end of May. We have a request in to Menningers for the platform name and phone number but the manager says as far as he knows, Murane isn't in the habit of loaning her apartment to friends or giving out the tone sequence of her lock."

"So what's the useful fact?" Cruz asked.

Mama pushed his glasses up his nose. "Beria installed and services the security system at the complex."

"Someone at the agency *has* to be involved," Janna said. "And they either have to know Murane or been at the apartment complex within the last month and heard she's away."

In the distance, a lion roared, a deep, hollow sound. Cruz glanced the direction of it. "We're already checking everyone."

"Service technicians as well as guards?" Mama asked.

Cruz sighed. "Of course service technicians. Everyone. And it looks as though most of the service techs, *all* the day people—five techs, four on duty at any one time—have made calls on every client sooner or later. Only some of the evening and night techs haven't. So far, though, we haven't turned up a connection between Armenda and anyone at Beria."

A peacock strutting inside the tall chain link fence around the zoo turned to peer at them and scream a high-pitched *aaah*!

"My feeling exactly," Janna told it. "Mind if we go down to Beria and poke around?"

Cruz shrugged. "*I* don't. I presume the agency people won't, either. They've been very cooperative. Naturally Beria and son are anxious to either find the rotten apple or prove their agency can't possibly be involved in robbery and murder." He paused. "Did you learn anything more from this Tony Ho on the drive back than what you phoned in to Vradel this morning?"

Janna shook her head.

"Have you found how the riffers slipped that waitron among the caterer's?"

"Maybe." Cruz pulled his notebook out of a thigh pocket. "Holliday hasn't had a waitron come back from servicing, but . . ." He grinned. ". . . Friday night around nine, workers cleaning up in the kitchen heard a sound on the loading dock. They checked and found the rear door open and a waitron halfway through it . . . and footsteps outside running away. They brought the waitron back in and relocked the door."

" 'Back' in." Janna shook her head. "Sly . . . slip it in by pretending to be trying to steal it. Is Holliday another of Beria's clients?"

"No." Cruz slid the notebook back in a thigh pocket. "They ordered their alarms direct from a manufacturer and had a local electrical firm install them. I looked at the system. It's very basic . . . barrier-and-alarm, nothing tricky, nothing for recording or trapping an intruder. Anyone with some expertise in security systems could walk right through it."

Mama said, "Vradel mentioned that an employee at Konza tried to sue Armenda for taking over the company. Do we know anything more?"

"Zavara and Threefoxes are checking it out now." Cruz glanced at his wrist chrono. "If you want to do anything at Beria this afternoon, you'd better go. I'll see you at the end of the shift."

Beria's offices occupied the two floors above their security equipment store at the corner of Third and Kansas. At the top of stairs narrowed by the wheelchair lift built along one side spread a reception area as spartan as a gallery. Like a gallery, too, scattered display stands held samples of small security devices and models of larger ones.

The sleek amerasian woman behind a black glass desk raised her eyebrows at their identification. "More of you? Just a minute." She picked up a handset on a screenless phone and murmured into it. After listening, she told them, "Go on back," and pointed to the door behind her.

It slid aside at their approach, then whispered closed behind them. Before them stretched a corridor with clerical offices opening off the right side and a left-hand turn at the end.

Around that turn came a gray-haired but fit looking man in a dark green bodysuit with diagonal slashes of gold and peacock blue. "Sergeants Brill and Maxwell? I am Arkady Beria." He spoke with a faint Russian accent. "How may I help the police this time?"

Mama eyed the bodysuit. Thinking how it might look on him? "We're after more of the same, I'm afraid . . . still trying to find someone who knows the various security systems relevant to the crime. At the moment, it appears that individual must be one of your service personnel."

Beria's heavy brows dipped. "I thought your colleagues already determined so, and that most of my technicians qualify in such respect."

"But now it seems likely that only one with contact in the last month is involved," Janna said.

Beria sighed. "Perhaps that helps. I hope. I would like this resolved, you understand. This way."

He led them around the corner to another sliding door. Several seconds passed before it opened, however.

"A scanner confirms I wear a transponder emitting a proper signal before opening." Beria touched a pin with the Beria logo on the turtleneck of his bodysuit. "You will need someone authorized to let you out, and out to reception area as well. Listra, we have more detectives," he said to a plump afroam woman at the computer keyboard inside. "Help them all you can."

Mama watched the door slide closed behind him. "Nice outfit. The color's a little conservative, but it's a very nice design."

The afroam woman eyed him . . . and the orange-and-purple diagonal striping of his jumpsuit, visible through the open front of the scarlet trenchcoat. "I'm Listra Wassman, queen of chips. What do you need, leo?"

Mama smiled at her. "Is the law firm of Kettering, Kettering, and Axthelm one of your clients?"

Wassman typed. Mama leaned on the desk, peering at the monitor.

Janna's ear button murmured, sending Beta Cap Twelve to investigate a man who had been sitting on the curb in front of a residence all day.

Wassman looked up from her screen. "Sorry. There's no file with that name on it."

"Then may we have a list of the service calls made to the Sheraton, the Lincoln Yi house, and Terracrest Apartments in the past month, and we need to know what service technician took the calls?'' Mama asked.

"Terracrest? That's new.'' She typed in the information. Janna bent down to peer over her shoulder, too. A service log scrolled up the screen, giving the date, time, nature of the call, charge, and personnel involved. "The Sheraton's had several service calls in the past few weeks. Spring thunderstorms can play havoc with alarm systems.''

Janna nodded. When she rode watchcars she had answered a number of bank alarms set off by lightning-caused power surges.

Wassman kept typing. "Mr. Yi's done better. One call to us, one initiated by us to check his system after a power outage in the area. And now, Terracrest. Lordy.'' A long log scrolled up. She shook her head. "Either the spring storms hit them hard or their tenants are hell on the property.''

Janna read the log. Damaged window alarm circuits. More window alarm circuits damaged. Inoperable door lock due to sonic key being out of tune. A security camera out of service. Debris jammed in the cardslot of the entry gate. That must have been fun fixing in the middle of the night so tenants did not have to abandon their cars on the street. Key inoperable due to spouse changing the tone sequence. Another camera out of service.

"Which technicians have taken calls all three places?'' Mama asked.

"Aschke and Spelts had the Yi calls. We can check for their names on the other service logs.''

Janna watched the listings come up on the screen. Both technicians had taken Sheraton and Terracrest calls, Spelts one at the hotel, two at the apartments, Aschke one each place. "Are they male or female?''

"Both are men.'' Wassman's fingers played across her keyboard. "I'll call up their personnel records. But I have a hard time imagining either one of them involved in something like this.''

The phone chirped. The Amerasian woman's face appeared on the screen. "An Officer Morello is looking for either Sergeant Maxwell or Sergeant Brill.''

Janna stood closest to the phone. She moved in front of the screen. "I'll take it.''

A moment later Pass-the-Word Morello's foxy face replaced

the receptionist's. "Menningers called. The Murane woman is on the Russian's Mir platform. I have the phone number."

· She copied it down, all sixteen digits, then with Wassman's permission, punched the numbers into the afroam woman's phone, followed by the eleven extra digits that charged the call to the department.

Wassman grinned. "You can die of old age punching in that number."

That and waiting while the screen flashed and spat, and while the cheerful female who answered, speaking Russian that switched instantly to flawless English when Janna spoke, put her on hold to contact Katura Murane. Janna sighed. "In bed? It never occurred to me they'd be on Moscow time. She's going to love us."

Wassman left the room on some errand. Janna stood staring at the phone, wondering what Earth-to-platform calls cost per minute, while Mama read through the printout of the two service technicians' personnel files.

Finally a dark-haired bibi came on the screen, groggy but apprehensive. "I'm Dr. Murane. You're from the police? What's wrong?"

No need to take time telling her about the robberies and murder. "We have in custody an individual who's admitted to entering your apartment while you've been gone."

"Broke into my apartment!" Outrage wiped away the last trace of sleepiness. "Shit! Will he, or she, tell you what was taken? It's impossible for me to come back right now and no one down there can tell—"

"Don't worry, Doctor." Janna gave her a reassuring smile. "He didn't take or damage anything. And strictly speaking, he didn't break in. He had a key."

The dark hair bounced as she flung up her head. "What! That's impossible."

"You didn't tell a friend your tuning code and tone sequence, or give someone permission to use the apartment while you were gone?"

Murane's mouth thinned. "I did not."

Mama laid down the printout to move over in the screen's range. "Do you know a Marion Spelts or a Jason Aschke?"

The doctor frowned, then shook her head. "Not by name."

"Before you left, did you have trouble with your lock that necessitated calling the security firm out to service it?"

"The lock's been just fine. However this person came by my key, I assure you *I* didn't give it to him. Talk to the manager. The office has a copy of my lock tone sequence."

"Thank you," Janna said. "That's all we needed to know." She punched off.

The door hissed open. Instead of Wassman returning, however, in trotted a small bibi with dark hair pulled up in a topknot and a Beria shoulder patch on her green jumpsuit. She stopped short. "Where's Listra?"

"Gone to the john or something," Janna replied.

Intelligent dark eyes looked them over with obvious curiosity. "I'm Karis Sandoz. That's Karis with a K." She edged toward the printout lying beside Wassman's keyboard. "Are you more detectives working on those fund-raiser robberies?"

Janna picked up the printout. "I'm afraid so."

"Good luck." Sandoz grinned. "The rumor I've heard is Republicans did it, thinking that if they take the other parties' campaign money and use it for themselves, they can become a major party again." She headed for the door. "Tell Listra I'll be back. I need to see the service log from Striker Import Auto for the past four months."

Janna read through the printout. To her disappointment, nothing in either file helped them. Both men appeared to be ideal employees. Marion Spelts, age forty-two, employed at Beria for fourteen years, had been chosen Beria Employee-of-the-Month three times. Jason Aschke, age thirty-three and employed for eight years, was awarded a bonus three years ago for devising an improvement in the security camera placement during one system installation. "I guess we need to talk to them." She glanced at her wrist chrono. Past 15:00 hours. "Here, maybe, if we hurry."

The door opened again, this time for Wassman. "Did you finally get through?"

"Finally." Janna folded up the printout. "A Karis—"

"Karis with a K, remember," Mama interrupted.

"Anyway, she said she needs the Striker Import Auto service file."

Wassman grinned. "Karis with a K. Yes. God forbid we should spell it with a Ch and realize it's short for Charisma."

Janna shook her head. Another unfortunate named after Charisma Nairobi? Agosta in their squad was, too. All through her childhood, with Charismas abounding in the classes behind her, Janna had given thanks she was born before everyone went crazy over the cineround movie made from Elizabeth Chilombe's book *The Dream Maze*. "Where might we find Aschke and Spelts, if they're still here?"

"They are," Wassman said. "That's where I went, to have Mr. Beria ask them to stay. I thought you'd probably want to talk to them. I'll take you up to the service department. This way." She headed for the door.

Janna pulled her jaw back into place and followed. When Beria said help them in every way possible, he meant it. He obviously wanted very much to resolve this.

One look at Marion Spelts, however, suggested *he* would not resolve it. Janna understood Wassman's reluctance to believe his involvement. Even standing up, the rotund little jon's head barely reached her shoulder, and he wore a gold cross prominently displayed on a chain around his neck.

He sat on the edge of a plasic bucket chair in the employee lounge, feet barely touching the floor and hands folded together across his chest. "What was I doing Friday and Saturday nights? The Lord's work, Sergeant. Members of my church and I held prayer in front of The Fantasy House. Such places defile our city. We hope that publishing pictures we took of people going in will shame the citizens degading themselves there into—"

"What time was that?" Janna did not bother giving him a smile to soften the abruptness of her voice. His group had a right to disapprove of prostitution and fight it, but not by violating other citizens' civil right to privacy.

If Spelts noticed her tone, he showed no sign of it. "From six o'clock until midnight."

"The whole time, straight through?" Mama asked. "You didn't take a break?"

"Of course not." Spelts looked offended by the idea. "We can't accomplish our mission unless we're persistent in the task."

They sent Spelts on his way and asked him to send in Jason Aschke.

A prickle ran down her spine as the second technician came into the lounge. His height equalled hers. More than that, his eyes ducked theirs when she and Mama introduced themselves. He folded into the bucket chair Spelts had vacated and slumped back.

"I already told the detectives here yesterday that I spent Friday and Saturday night at home," he muttered toward his knees. "Do you want to hear about the TV shows I watched?"

"That depends." Janna eyed him. "Do you own a video recorder?"

Aschke glanced up, then down again. He licked his lips and wiped his palms on his thighs. "I didn't have anything to do with those robberies."

Alarms rang in Janna. But he had not watched TV, she would swear to that. He recorded some programs and scanned through them later.

Mama smiled at the service technician. "We have to check all the possibilities."

"But why—" He bit off the end of the sentence.

Mama eyed him. "Why what?"

Aschke shook his head. "I wouldn't do anything like that. My job is protecting people."

Janna glanced at Mama. Evasions. "Did you know Carel Armenda?"

"The man who died?" Aschke shook his head.

"Do you live with anyone?" Mama asked.

Aschke hesitated a moment before answering. "Not anymore."

"Did you see anyone at all those evenings?" Mama pushed his glasses up his nose. "Maybe someone called you?"

"No one." He scowled. "But I was home."

"Just like he was watching TV," Janna said after they let him go. She stood in the doorway of the lounge, arms folded, watching Aschke hurry down the wide central hallway of the service section.

At her shoulder, Mama shrugged. "Lying about the TV doesn't means he's lying about everything. I have a hard time seeing him as our tickman. He doesn't sound the way Tony described the hotel interview."

"He could be acting. He's hiding something, Mama. That is definitely a man with a guilty secret."

"Not the robberies," another voice said.

They looked around. Karis Sandoz stood in a doorway behind them.

She gave them a sheepish smile. "I'm sorry; I couldn't help overhearing." With a quick glance around, she moved close to them. "I know this is none of my business and that all I know about the robberies is what I've seen on the newscanner. And Jason did swear me to secrecy after I accidentally found out about his project."

"But . . ." Mama said.

Sandoz grimaced. "But he's such a private person, and probably a little afraid of looking brainbent, I doubt he'll tell you on his own, even when it's to his advantage."

Janna frowned. "Tell us what?"

Sandoz lowered her voice. "About his robot. His passion is robots and artificial intelligence. At home he's developing a sentry robot . . . something that would be semiautonomous, a hybrid of waitron and swatbot. That's usually what he's doing when he claims to be watching TV."

The hair prickled on Janna's neck. "Developing it at home?"

The small bibi nodded. "He has a workshop in his basement. I saw it once. It's beautifully equipped."

Janna glanced at Mama. A security technician with a workshop at home for building robots? Aschke might not sound to Mama like the man Tony Ho met in that Crown Center Hotel room, but he certainly deserved further investigation.

ELEVEN

"You mean we finally have a suspect for the tickman?" Commander Vining asked.

Janna would have given anything for him not to have walked in on the case squad's morning discussion just as she and Mama were arguing over Aschke. Or for him to be asking Cruz. But his gaze obviously focused on her.

She settled back in her desk chair and shrugged. "Maybe." Damned if she would commit herself, no matter how much she liked Aschke for a suspect.

Vining frowned. "Do you suppose you can manage to be a little more specific, Sergeant?"

Janna told him about Aschke's connection to the two crime scenes and the Terracrest Apartments, and what Sandoz said about his home workshop. "We went to his house last night to check out the workshop. No one answered the door, so we talked to his neighbors, using the pretext of investigating reported prowlers in the area. They can't confirm or disprove the workshop. He hasn't invited anyone into the house in five years, not since his wife died. They saw lights on Friday and Saturday evening, but one neighbor's daughter, who went around Friday night selling high school band concert tickets, didn't get a response when she rang his bell."

"Which proves nothing," Mama said. "According to the neighbors, his lights can be on when he's gone, or he may not answer the door even when he's there."

"Have you checked with DMV to see if he owns a Triton wagon? Is there any connection between him and Armenda, maybe concerning his wife's death, that might give him a motive for murder?"

Did he think they were rookies? "We ran him through DMV last night. There's no vehicle of any kind registered to him. We haven't had time to hunt for a connection between him and Armenda, but there doesn't have to be one. He could have been hired for the job, in which case, maybe the tickman furnished the Triton."

"Do any of—" Vining began.

"Today we'll be cross-checking registrations of seventy-seven Triton wagons against a list of people associated with Carel Armenda." If only they had enough probable cause for a bank warrant. That would tell them if Aschke had gone to Kansas City on the eighth, a point she considered more important than Mama's concern over how the man Tony met gained access to the hotel room. After all, Aschke knew locks, and even those using drilled keys must be pickable.

Vining glanced around at other members of the squad. "Any luck finding the gunmen?"

"No," Cruz said, drawing the syllable out. "Tracing from last known addresses, we've located five more of the possibles from the FBI photo file. One is dead, three on parole with whereabouts confirmed those nights, and one confined to a wheelchair. We've distributed copies of the enhancements throughout the department here and sent copies to departments in major cities in the surrounding states. Brill and Maxwell left copies with the KCPD. So far, there's been no response."

The information officer shook his head. "There have to be records on these jons somewhere. They worked too smoothly to be beginners. What have you found out about the lawsuit that employee filed against Armenda?"

Zavara straightened in her chair with a sinuous ripple. "It was against the corporation, not Armenda personally, and it never reached court."

Threefoxes consulted his notebook. "May of seventy-eight, a Lesandra Santos sued for the rights to a miniaturized projector she built. Armenda claimed the projector belonged to Armenord since she was an employee and had used research company facilities for working on the projector. Apparently Santos decided they were right; she withdrew the suit."

"That doesn't mean she forgot about it. Have you talked to her?"

"No. She resigned and left the area, according to people at Konza. There's certainly no local phone listing for her. We went to Armenord's personnel department for a forwarding address but the computer had eaten Santos's file."

"In other words, we have four teams plugging away without anything to show for the time and expense?" Vining shook his head. "That won't impress the Director and the media."

Cruz stood, bringing him to eye level with the information officer. "I'm sure Paget understands these things take time. Give the media Tony Ho."

"Tony Ho." Vining shook his head again. "One small fish, who's obviously an outsider, meant to be thrown away, and no help finding the others."

Janna caught Mama's eye, thinking of his *Thomas Crown Affair* theory that everyone was an outsider. If Vining had not been there, she might have mentioned it.

"We were the subject of Hollis Dunne's eleven o'clock commentary last night." Vining glanced toward the newscanner. " 'People ought to be asking what kind of security the police are providing the general public when they can't find men who rob and kill our most important citizens, even when given video recordings of the event.' He showed segments from the news chips of the Demo fund-raiser and invited viewers to call in if they have any knowledge of the crimes. 'Maybe the People can accomplish what those hired for the job appear unable to,' he said."

Zavara's lip curled. "Hollis Dunne is an asshole."

Vining turned a cold stare on her. "His four daily broadcasts are seen by better than a hundred thousand people each. If he suggests protesting trash pickup fee hikes by dumping non-recyclables on the mayor's lawn, people will. We don't need him focusing that kind of attention on us."

Janna kept her face pulled smooth over the flare of resentment in her. So honey the bastard. What did he think the department paid its Public Information section for?

At the far end of the squad room Vradel came to the open door of his office and stood gazing in their direction. "Commander, before you leave, may I see you in my office?"

"I can come now," Vining said.

Mama, who, remarkably, had not moved in several minutes, sat up on the corner of his desk. "Just a minute, sir. I think we do have something interesting for the media."

Janna grinned inwardly. Behind his glasses, Mama's eyes glinted, and for once, she waited with relish for the results of his brainbent thought processes.

Vining beamed. "Excellent, Sergeant. What?"

Mama crossed one zebra-striped leg of his jumpsuit over the other. "According to Aschke's neighbors, he became a loner after his wife died. She was one of the fatalities in the city bus that went off the Topeka Avenue bridge into the Kaw in seventy-five. I believe he's been brooding about it ever since, blaming the city government at first, and by generalization, eventually hating all government and politicians."

He believed? Janna forced herself not to roll her eyes. That had been *her* postulation in the debate last night. Allow him creative borrowing, but how did he plan to turn such a sad scenario into a punchline that would leave them laughing behind Vining's back?

Vining pursed his lips. "So you think he built a robot and set up the robberies for revenge? That might be a possibility, except for one thing . . . why kill Armenda?"

"You're right; he wouldn't have reason to under those circumstances. However . . ." Mama pushed his glasses up his nose. "What if the perpetrators are people who also hate government and merely used Aschke's feelings to recruit him to help them circumvent the security measures at those two fundraisers? When they found out about his interest in robots, they used that, too."

Janna frowned at Mama, and all around her, faces had gone grim, especially Vining's. He shook his head, however. "No. It would help explain why we can't identify the gunmen, but Armenda's death still doesn't fit. Political terrorists would have killed Rau or maybe Senator Kassebaum-Martin."

Leaning toward Vining, Mama lowered his voice. "Not necessarily. Choosing Armenda is potentially even more effective." He ticked off points on his fingers. "First, of course, the mere fact of violent death generates fear. Then as the investigation progresses, there's confusion. Is it one crime or two? Who's responsible for each and if Armenda's death is a murder, who wants him dead? We go running off in all directions. At some point the perpetrators can contact individuals like Hollis Dunne and ridicule us through them. Can't we even decide what crime we're investigating? That causes the public to lose confidence in us, which increases their terror as the perpetrators promise more violence. Killing Armenda also places control of several companies, including a jet charter service, a construction company, and a firm which manufactures locks and other security devices, in the hands of a boy susceptible to manipulation by someone who knows how to exploit his love of physical pleasure.''

Janna regarded Mama with horror. Maybe he dreamed up that rationale for the information officer's benefit, but it echoed in her with the icy ring of possibility.

In Vining, too, apparently. His mouth thinned. "Thank you, but I won't give that to the media. I'll play up Tony Ho. And hope to God you're wrong, Sergeant.''

After he left, Janna realized that the usual voices and buzz of phones continued at the far end of the room, but everyone near the case squad's grouped desks had turned to stare at Mama. The newscanner's latest update on the Russian shuttle situation carried clearly through the near silence. Even odors seemed sharper . . . the scent of caff from the caff urn, the spicy sweetness of the perfume Zavara wore. Vradel marched their direction.

Cruz ran a hand through his hair. "Jesus. Why didn't you mention this before, Maxwell?''

Mama blinked at him. "Surely you didn't think I was serious?''

Now it was Cruz's turn to blink. "What?'' He sounded torn between anger and relief.

"Think!'' Mama slid off the desk and turned, holding out his hands to everyone. "Terrorists wouldn't need Tony. They have people just as expert as disguise. They'd also have killed Salmas and Wald and hidden the bodies so we'd be wasting time hunting them . . . one more thing to ridicule when the time came to reveal themselves. Vining would see that if he weren't so damned anxious to cater to the media.''

"Maxwell . . ." Vradel said on a rising note.

Mama faced him. "Look at it this way, sir; from now on he'll be so relieved when we don't find terrorists, he'll be happy with whatever progress we make."

Vradel's mustache twitched. "Then I won't need to remind him he isn't the squad commander. But, Maxwell . . . while I understand your reason for this skin, I don't agree with it. Vining isn't the enemy. So if he finds out he's been skinned, you're on your own with him."

"Mama, what the hell are we doing here?" Mama was incomprehensible. At the elevators he had caught her sleeve and dragged her on past to Records. "I thought we wanted to identify the owner of that Triton."

"We do. This is faster than going over to DVM. Good morning." He beamed at the clerk behind the counter. "That green looks lovely on you. Hey, Liliedahl," he called. Back beyond the counter, a thin woman with an awkward posture betraying a twisted spine looked up from her computer keyboard. Mama clasped his hands over his heart. "I need you."

Miranda Liliedahl arched a wry brow, but after a minute, pushed out of her chair and limped up to the counter. "But will you respect me in the morning?"

"Respect?" Mama said. "I am in absolute awe of your finger technique. Can you help us?" Last night they had made up a list of people involved one way or another with the crimes. He laid it and a list of Beria employees on the counter. "I need you to download a file from DMV and run these names against it."

She studied the list. "Why not have DMV do it? They have faster access to whatever file it is you need."

"But their data processing technicians are user hostile."

Liliedahl grinned. "All right." She picked up the lists. "I'll see what I can do."

By the time they went through the gate at the far end of the counter, Liliedahl had reached her terminal and was running the lists through the computer's reader. She phoned DMV. Shortly, the modem light flickered and a list of names scrolled rapidly up the screen. At the front counter, the clerk flirted with a uniformed lion. A bank of printers across the room hummed, dropping hard copy into their catch baskets.

"We want the intersects," Mama said.

Long fingers tapped keys. "Somehow I suspected that. There's the end of the file. Intersects coming up."

The screen flickered . . . and two words sat in the middle of the blue field: *Not Found.*

Janna stared in disbelief. "Not one of those people owns a seventy-seven Triton?"

Liliedahl shrugged. "Sorry."

Mama leaned down toward the screen, hands clasped behind his back. "Let's check the corporate registrations, too . . . Armenord Industries; Beria Security; BruckerJet; Custom Electronics. That's Russell Brashear's new company, bibi. Images Unlimited; Konza Holotronics; Midstates Construction; Nord Electronics; Servitron, Inc.; Shawnee Security; Videoscribe; Voelker & Green, Inc."

Liliedahl's fingers raced across the keyboard.

A clerk picked up the hard copy from the printers and began sorting it into a courier robot.

Liliedahl sat back with a last tap of a key. "Cross your fingers."

The computer's drive lights flickered. The screen blinked. *Not Found.*

Janna swore. "You'd think all those companies would have at least one seventy-seven Triton in their fleets. What now?"

Mama shrugged. "We can try car rentals, or go to Armenord and ask for a list of the employees in all their companies and check those against the registrations."

She groaned.

"So I'd like a printout of the whole file, please," he told Liliedahl.

"As long as you understand I don't provide a cart for carrying it." Liliedahl resumed typing. "This may take a while."

Janna used the time to start checking out the car rental agencies by phone. Which saved them travel time, as it turned out. Only one agency handled older model cars.

Older indeed. Standing in the office of Oedipus Wrecks Rentals, Janna peered out the window to confirm what she glimpsed as they turned off Kansas Avenue onto the lot. One row of cars toward the back still had wheels.

"Do people really rent wheelers?" she asked.

The agency owner, a stocky man who had introduced himself as James Oedipus Jaax, wiped the grease from his hands and shoved the shop towel into a thigh pocket of his red coveralls. "Oh yes . . . especially after some period movie with screaming-tire car chases plays on TV or at the cineround. The internal combustion models are all converted to electric, of course, but they're still fun to drive. That's why I keep them around."

"The upkeep must be difficult, though," Mama said.

From beyond a door connecting to the shop came a ring of metal and a female voice, swearing. Jaax winced. "Labor intensive. If one of those kids needs a part, I usually have to make it myself. But the challenge of seeing if you can do something is half the fun, isn't it." He pulled a printout from under the counter and laid it on top. "After you called I checked my inventory file. I have ten Tritons, three of them seventy-sevens. These are their rental logs for the past month. What are you looking for?"

Janna forgot the wheelers. Leaning on the counter beside Mama, she fastscanned the logs. "One of these vehicles may have been used in the fund-raiser robberies Friday and Saturday nights."

Jaax grinned. "One set of crooks cleans another. There is justice in the world."

Justice for Carel Armenda, too, perhaps. Janna caught Mama's eye and grinned. Two of the Tritons were wagons. One went out two weeks ago to a Leda Bondank and had not been returned. The other had been delivered to the Billard airfield Friday morning, where the client, Willem Edmiston, picked it up at eight-thirty in the morning. Monday morning he left the vehicle at Billard again.

Her ear button murmured. Janna barely heard. Edmiston took over the car well before noon. Giving him plenty of time to install the desktop for controlling the waitron. Janna looked across the counter at Jaax. "How easy is it to remove the rear seat in the wagons?"

"It took us less than five minutes to pull the one out of T-77-30 after the bibi requested it." Jaax tapped the log of the wagon rented by Leda Bondank.

Janna exchanged glances with Mama. His eyes gleamed. "May we see the contract for that vehicle?"

Jaax brought the contracts for both wagons. After reading them over, Janna carefully wrote Bondank's address and phone number in her notebook.

Mama copied down the information on Willem Edmiston of Omaha, Nebraska. Who listed himself as "self-employed," Janna noticed. "May we see this vehicle?"

Jaax led them outside and down a line of parked cars. Which seemed dominated by Datsun-Ford and Chrysler road cars.

"This row looks straight out of our garage at headquarters," Janna said.

Jaax grinned. "It should. Most of these used to be police cars. I buy my stock when the new-car agencies and your department auction off their old vehicles. Leo cars are a good buy if they haven't been wrecked . . . reinforced bodies, heavy duty fans and circuitry, Simon cells operable in very low light levels. Here's the car."

Janna eyed it. The Bondank bibi's removal of the rear seat in her vehicle made her look good as a suspect, but this wagon came in the right color. And the rental timing fit well, too.

She and Mama went over the vehicle, Mama in back checking under and behind the rear seat, she examining the front seats. Neither yielded any objects that might have been left behind by the tickman and his driver.

"We clean the cars after each rental," Jaax said.

Mama sat back in the rear seat, glancing around him. "If someone had removed this seat and replaced it, could you tell?"

Jaax frowned a moment, then pulled a mini-light from a breast pocket of his coveralls and stretched across the airfoil skirt to lay flat on the car floor. He shone his light under the seat. "There's no dust around the clamps or in the floor slots but that could be from a thorough vaccuming." He backed out and stood up. "I'd have to pull the seat completely out and take a close look before I could say for sure if it's been moved."

Janna exchanged glances with Mama. "Lab?"

He nodded and slid out of the car. "Mr. Jaax, we may want our Criminalistics people to go over the car. Please don't rent it again until you hear from us."

The car radio and Janna's ear button kept up a continuous stream of traffic while Mama drove north toward the address Bondank gave. It looked genuine, on the north fringe of the city, but was it really Bondank's, and if so, would she be there or long gone with whatever jon—husband, lover—she rented the car for?

The rural mailbox at the end of the driveway provided no help. It said: *Prairie Hill Pet Hostel*. Nor did a Triton wagon sit on the drive curving up by the brick house and low, sprawling barn. Mama set the Meteor down at the barn, by a door marked *Lobby*.

With the car's fans silent, Janna became aware of muffled barking. It became louder as they entered the "lobby."

The fragrant scent of cedar filled the room. Deep arm chairs covered in deep-pile fabric sat against walls paneled in wood and hung with inscribed photographs of dogs and cats. Janna read the inscriptions in one group, several with a pawprint in a lower corner.

Thank you for taking such good care of me, Leda and Clell. Thank you for a wonderful visit.

Next to Max and Tori, you're my favorite human, Leda.

And on the photograph of a sleek, coppery-red dog: *To Leda and Clell. Though I'll never see you again, across the light years I will always remember you. Tsar the stardog.*

Janna pointed out Leda's name to Mama. Bondank did seem connected to this address.

A door at the far end of the room hissed open. A smiling young man with short white-blond hair appeared through the opening. "May I help you?"

"Interesting inscription." Mama pointed at the copper dog's photograph.

The young man nodded. "Tsar was a lovely boy, amazingly mellow for a Vizsla. I don't blame Dell and Zanandra for taking him along on their colony ship, though I was surprised when they told me you have to buy pets a share in the company, too. And it costs the same as one for a person."

"Every sleeper uses a separate capsule," Mama said, "so the cost per individual is the same no matter what the age, size, or species."

One more miscellaneous fact out of that bottomless grab bag of data in Mama's head. Janna eyed him. Was there nothing he did not know something about?

Mama smiled at the young man. "Are you Clell?"

"Clell Van Hoose. Are you looking for a place to leave your pet while you're away? We pride ourselves on being a home away from home for our guests. Dogs and cats each have a large run, the cats' furnished with climbing posts and platforms and boxes for lounging and hiding. Birds enjoy the freedom of a flight cage. Reptilian and rodent pets' cages are kept in our garden atrium. We make sure all the guests are played with and petted, and dogs exercised. If they're on a training program, we continue it, as well as maintain medical and physical therapy regimes. We groom and clip, and we keep a copy of your itinerary, so you can receive regular reports of your pet's welfare. May I show you around?'' He paused with an expectant smile.

Janna almost regretted having no pet to board there. "We're looking for Ms. Bondank."

"I'm sorry, she's out right now." The smile never wavered.

"When do you expect her back?" Mama asked.

"I'm afraid I don't know."

A howl rose above the barking.

"Excuse me." Van Hoose disappeared through the door.

Janna looked at Mama. "What do you think we've got . . . he doesn't know when she'll be back, or he doesn't expect her back?"

Mama pushed his glasses up his nose. "Doesn't know when she'll be back. He doesn't act like someone covering up her absence."

The howl stopped. Van Hoose returned carrying a small dog with a foxy face and bright eyes peering out of its fluffy reddish fur. "It's all right. Brutus here just decided he'd had enough of being alone." Van Hoose scratched the dog behind its ears. "You're a spoiled brat, you know that?" He looked up at them again. "I started to tell you that Leda's out picking up some new guests. We also provide ferry service if you're unable to bring your pet to us yourself. Are you sure I can't help you?"

Janna shook her head. "We—"

"Maybe you can," Mama interrupted. "We're from ARCA, the Association of Rental Car Agencies."

Janna grinned inside. More Theater.

"We're surveying rental customers. According to our information, Ms. Bondank is presently driving a car from . . ." Mama pulled his notebook out of a breast pocket and flipped through it. ". . . from Oedipus Wrecks Rentals? Is she satisfied with it, do you know?"

Van Hoose nodded, still petting the dog. "It's a lifesaver while her own car's being repaired."

"Very good." Mama made a note. "What kind of driving does she do? I mean, how far and where on any given day . . . say last Friday afternoon."

The dog squirmed so it turned over on its back in Van Hoose's arms. He rubbed its belly. "She left around noon to stop at Socrates Zupancic's vet's office for a bag of the prescription dogfood he eats, then bought some other supplies various places, then drove out to Lake Sherwood for Shogun and Samurai Gallardo, a really nice pair of Akitas." He rubbed the dog under its chin. "That must have amounted to fifty klicks or better by the time she came back here."

When she came back would have been more useful information. Janna put on a smile. "Did she go anywhere in the evening?"

Van Hoose shook his head. "We exercised dogs until dark."

That did not sound promising. "Are you the only two who drive the vehicle?"

"*She's* the only one who drives it."

Mama nodded and made another note. "What about . . . oh, Saturday evening?"

The dog started squirming again. Van Hoose turned it back upright. "She didn't drive anywhere at all. We worked the dogs until dark again, then played with the cats for another couple of hours."

Janna sighed. Unless blondie here were lying, and her instincts said he was not, or someone had sneaked the Triton away without him seeing it, this could not be the vehicle they wanted.

So now they checked out Mr. Edmiston of Omaha.

A call from the squad room to the number on the rental contract reached only to a machine. A foxy face reminding Janna of Pass-the-Word Morello's appeared on the screen. "I'm sorry I'm unavailable just now. When the menu appears on your screen, please choose an option and leave a message."

The choices started with an invitation to punch in an access code, the kind which typically put the caller's message in a priority file and/or rang the phone, as the initial connection in such systems did not.

Jana raised a brow at Mama. People had any number of reasons for screening their calls. Including illegal businesses, which used possession of the access code, obtainable only through the right contacts, as an endorsement of the caller. "I wonder if the Omaha P.D. knows Edmiston."

Mama grinned. "My thought exactly."

After choosing *Urgent Message Requiring a Return Call ASAP* from among the remaining options and leaving their names and number, Mama broke the connection and called Information for the OPD's phone number.

Edmiston's name meant nothing immediately to the detective in Central Robbery who drew their call, but she promised to run him through the OPD computer and telescribe the information to them.

Edmiston's name came back negative from NCIC in Washington, too. How much did that mean, though, Janna wondered. NCIC had nothing on any of their riffers.

They spent the rest of the day talking to Jason Aschke's co-workers at Beria, bringing up the subject of his wife. Everyone agreed, he had been devastated by her death.

"He changed completely after Corenne died," Listra Wassman said. "He never laughs or jokes anymore, never goes drinking after work with us, never attends parties. And if her name happens to come up, he either looks through you or walks away."

"Do you know how he feels about politicians?" Janna still liked the theory that he blamed the city government for the accident and had been recruited for the riffs by someone playing on that bitterness.

Wassman shrugged. "He doesn't talk about politics. For that matter, he hardly talks about anything."

No one else had any more to offer on that subject. No one knew if he had gone to Kansas City on the eighth, either.

After the squad's end-of-shift conference, Mama dropped Janna off at Washburn University before going home to cook dinner for Arianna Cho.

"Dinner. Of course." She snickered and climbed out of his little MGE.

"There are people in this world who appreciate food, bibi," he called after her, "people to whom dining is more than an action that stops one's stomach from growling."

The comment set Janna's snarling. She headed for the student union and wolfed down a sandwich while looking over her class notes one last time before the test.

Only to have her concentration interrupted by the sound of Tony Ho's righteous name on the newscanner in one corner of the snack bar. "The case has city officials worried. Not only did armed guards and the most modern security technology fail to prevent the robberies and the death of Topeka businessman Carel Armenda, but the revelation that Kushner used the Scib card stolen from waiter Cristo Salmas to enter the Capitol Sheraton Hotel in his place has raised concerns about the accuracy of identification procedures currently employed in the use of the Cards."

Janna covered her ears to muffle the sound, but she could not shut out thoughts about the case. Even during the test, the churning questions about real problems in law enforcement kept running over the hypothetical ones on the page.

Aschke finished work early enough that on any given day he could catch a commuter dirigible from Billard to K.C. Municiple airport. Great Plains Airways' records showed no Aschke taking any flight on Sunday the seventh or Monday the eighth, true, but that did not clear the service technician. He could have borrowed a car. Beyond that . . . was Edmiston involved, and if so, how had he connected with Aschke? Had Junior or Sydney gone to Edmiston and then he in turn set up the robberies? That made a long, involved chain, and long chains sprang leaks. This one showed no signs of leaks.

Janna walked home from campus still chasing questions in her head.

Which stopped abruptly at her front walk. She halted, staring. Broken furniture and shredded clothing spread across the lawn from the front porch to the street. A bookcase lay smashed at the foot of the steps, the book chips in it scattered down the walk in a spray pattern. On the porch, the front door stood wide open. Something pale fluttered on the jam. When Janna picked her way through the wreckage and up the steps, she found a marriage contract, ripped in two and spiked to the wood with a kitchen knife.

She raced up the side steps to her apartment. The garlic scent of Mama's baked marinated chicken enveloped her at the door. "What happened downstairs?"

"The final battle." Mama and Arianna Cho sat cross-legged on the living room couch, holding wine glasses and listening to a recording of something brassy and baroque. "I don't know the details—I found the same mess down there when I came home—but the ladies have lost their lease." He leaned forward to pour wine into a third glass on his round oak dinner table cut down to coffee table height. "After making sure there were no bodies downstairs, I called the landlord and invited him over for a look. Have some rosé and let's toast peace."

Amen to that. Janna tossed aside her trench coat and lay back in the molded-foam easy chair, sipping the wine. Warmth spread through her. So did an idea. She caught Mama's eye. "An eviction means an empty apartment . . . one very easy to move into from here."

Mama twirled his wine glass. "I thought about that. Unfortunately, not fast enough."

Cho shook the jade cape of her hair back over her shoulders. "I've already spoken for it." She smiled at Mama. "Meeting Mama has been a wonderful stroke of luck. In less than a week he's introduced me to a delightful new sculptor, fed me the kind of homecooked meal I love but have no time to cook, and solved the problem of the impossible escalation of my present rent."

Lucky for Arianna Cho, maybe. Janna took another swallow of wine and sighed. It left Janna Brill with Mama still in residence.

The phone chimed on the end table between the couch and easy chair. Being closest, Janna leaned sideways and flipped up the screen. "Yes?"

On the screen, puckish brows hopped. "My very favorite answer."

Diosdado! Warmth spread through her. She smiled. "To what question?"

He grinned. "Several come to mind. This evening, however, it's: do these people look familiar? I had copies of your enhancements posted in all the division stations. A call came from Central a few minutes ago. A patrol officer there thinks he knows a couple of your gunmen."

TWELVE

More rain. Janna wiped the steam from the inside of the passenger window and eyed the drenched streets of Kansas City outside. With luck, though, this would keep people under cover where they could be found. She turned in her safety harness to glance back at Averill Kinderman, the Central Division patrolman Diosdado mentioned on the phone and then introduced to them in the Robbery squad room a few minutes ago. "We really appreciate you giving up your free time to help us."

"How could I stay inside on a top card day like this? Or miss the chance to be a pretzel." The K.C. leo twisted sideways in the seat and stretched his legs by extending them toward the far door. "Sitting back here with a prisoner must be fun; you're both as leggy as I am."

Janna looked down at the enhancements in her lap, two of them circled in red: one stocky and red-haired, the other with a gold ring in his ear. "These jons call themselves Dragon and Tsunami, you said?"

He grimaced. "They sound like gangers, don't they? I remember when slighs had names like Mouse and Liberty."

Slighs. Yes. Janna sucked in her lower lip. The big surprise of the day. They had not expected to hear that about their riffers when Diosdado introduced Kinderman. If he were right, it ex-

plained the lack of records on these two. And made her wonder
. . . if two did prove to be slighs and no records had surfaced
on any of the six yet, could the other four also be?

Behind the wheel, Mama frowned. "I can't believe slighs are
involved. The jons we saw on the news chips are very aggressive,
and enjoy terrorizing people."

"You think slighs don't?" Kinderman grunted. "They're
changing. No more silent shadows slipping away at the edge of
your vision. These days when I stop them for an FI, they're so
fucking full of brass I can hear their balls clank."

Janna had noticed that among some young slighs in Topeka,
too.

Thunder rolled overhead. Kinderman said, "We need that
mandatory identation the legislature keeps talking about but never
gets around to passing."

A ripple across Mama's scalp stopped in furrows on his forehead. "We need to leave them alone. They aren't harming anyone. It's the threat against their life-style that's making them
militant."

"Life-style?" Kinderman's lip curled. "Don't tell me you're
one of the bleeding hearts who—"

"What we need," Janna interrupted, "is to find these jons."
Which alienating Kinderman with an argument would not help.
"I know you said back in the Robbery squad room that your
contact with them has always been at night, but you do have
some idea where they might be days, don't you? At home slighs
work places like stockrooms and in the kitchens of restaurants."

Kinderman continued eyeing Mama for a moment, then
shrugged. "Here, too. Dragon and Tsunami hang around the
River Quay, and since we have a few restaurants and clubs down
there that manage to stay in business, I thought we'd check them
out. The city market is close, too. Take a right on Main to the
intersect with Delaware and follow Delaware over I-70 into the
Quay."

A short time later Mama set the Meteor down on its parking
rollers at the curb in front of a building Kinderman indicated.

Janna stared. Only the walls stood, a shell of blackened bricks
with rubble visible through the empty arch of the doorway. "I
thought you said there was a club here."

"The Levee, yes." Kinderman grinned. "The entrance is in

the alley. We can shortcut through the building; most people do."

They climbed out of the car, Mama taking off his glasses and tucking them inside his trench coat out of the rain. From deep inside the hood of her trench coat, Janna stared around as they followed a winding path through the dripping remains of fixtures and interior walls. She stepped over a puddle and around the pieces of a broken urinal. "Aren't the owners planning to rebuild?"

Ahead of her, Kinderman nodded. "Probably, but it usually takes four or five years and it's only been three since the fire."

"Usually?" That implied previous disasters.

Behind her Mama said, "Over the last hundred and fifty years, the clubs and restaurants in this area have all suffered periodic bombings and fires in disputes between crime families, or been the site of family leaders being gunned down. When I was at UMKC, the River Quay had been redeveloped for the umpteenth time and these were top dink places to party and eat. No longer, it appears."

"For the umpteenth time. Watch the step down." Kinderman led them into the alley.

Across it like a skyway stretched an aging holo, faded and patently transparent, of a riverboat churning up and down beside a pier. Narrow stairs beneath the near end led down between the burned building and the next one. Janna eyed them with distaste. Such daylight as existed barely penetrated the stairwell and the smell seeping up generated mental images of sewers. She followed Kinderman down holding the handrail all the way, and carefully stepped from the last tread across the murky pool below it to the raised sill of the door the K.C. leo opened. "Welcome to the Levee."

The Underground would be more appropriate. The club stretched out in a series of barrel vaults. Smoke layering the air, thick and stale and heavy with drug fumes, gave it the faded blue appearance of a cheap holo, too. Last night's smoke, Janna guessed, shaking the water from her trench coat, since only the bartender and a woman with a pushbroom occupied the club. Mama put his glasses back on.

The bartender looked around from sliding glasses into overhead racks. "We don't open until noon."

"We're not customers." Kinderman pulled his badge case out of a hip pocket. "Do you know a couple of slighs calling themselves Tsunami and Dragon?"

At the corner of Janna's vision, the woman with the pushbroom stiffened.

"Who knows what their names are?" the bartender said.

Janna laid the enhancements on the bar. "Here's what they look like."

The bartender studied the pictures briefly. "Sorry. No jogs."

Mama sidled toward the woman. Her fingers tightened on the broom handle. Fighting the urge to run? Slighs tended to react that way to leos. And this was a sligh; Janna's every instinct swore to that. Mama whispered to her, bending his head to her level.

Kinderman rapped the bar with his badge case. "I've seen them here, jon." Accusation edged his voice.

"I haven't," the bartender came back calmly. "But then I don't pay much attention unless the customer's a troublemaker or a regular."

The woman murmured something back to Mama.

"The slighs are regulars," Kinderman said.

"Not paying regulars." The bartender turned back to his glasses. "I don't know them, leo."

For a moment Janna wondered if Kinderman were going to lean across the bar and grab the bartender. His body swayed that direction. Then he turned and crooked a finger at the woman. "You. Talk to me."

Mama stepped in front of her. "I've been talking to her already. She suggests we try the city market." He tucked his glasses back inside his trench coat and headed for the door.

Janna followed. After a moment, Kinderman did, too.

Up in the alley again, he said, "She's one of them, you know."

Mama nodded.

"So you have to be careful. Slighs will say anything to protect each other."

Janna frowned. They stuck together, yes, as any minority did, but not always, and except in the case of blindly loyal friends, not when it threatened the welfare of the entire group.

Mama, however, reacted with only a myopic squint and a

mild: "It won't hurt to try the market. Besides, Jan ought to see it."

Shit. She rolled her eyes. "Mama, we came up here to track riffers, not play tourist!"

He ticked his tongue. "One should never waste an opportunity to expand one's horizons, bibi."

The expansion of horizons remained to be proven, but the city market did widen her eyes. Suddenly, art studios and apartments that had probably started life as warehouses gave way to a four-block plaza. In sharp contrast to the square solidity of the surrounding brick buildings, low, interconnecting domes covered the better part of it, rising in airy grace from multiple open arches and gleaming gold even in the rain.

It looked like a piece of a fantasy city.

But reality settled back in place as soon as they set the car down in the perimeter parking area and hurried in through the nearest arch. Close examination showed her the domes had been constructed of Mylar, supported by air-filled ribs.

In the unbroken space beneath stretched row upon row of plastic crates and baskets sitting on the ground or in the open backs of trucks, filled with fruits and vegetables and flowers. Hand lettered signs by many of the produce stalls promised products organically or hydroponically grown, or from ground with soil and water certified free of contamination. Men and women in jeans or coveralls presided over the stalls, each with a lap computer and Card/retinal reader for recording sales. Buyers prowled the rows towing shopping baskets or porterbots, or drove vans lettered with the names of local restaurants and hotels. The turbulence from their airfoil fans flattened Janna's trench coat against her legs in passing.

Kinderman made a sound of disgust as they passed a pair of winos shuffling past in the opposite direction. "Welcome to gandie land."

Janna spotted trippers, as well . . . thin, dressed almost uniformly in grimy clothes grown too large for them, their shaved heads decorated with blurred tattooes. Looking for a place out of the rain and, with luck, a handout of food. Except they were more likely to trade it for drugs than eat it themselves.

Lacking a hard ceiling to reflect sound, the market seemed

strangely hushed for the number of people and vehicles in it.
Even the rap of rain on the dome sounded distant and muted.
But scents made up for the quiet. Odors swirled around Janna
in a thick tide . . . the sweetness of flowers and herbs, the sharp
tang of citrus, fishy smells. The source of the latter became
obvious when she spotted iced tanks of catfish and trout on trucks
bearing fish farm logos.

Watching a brawny young man load a carton of fish into a
hotel van, she also saw the potential for sligh labor. They had
to love it . . . an environment with an informal structure but a
need for laborers, where wages could be taken in food and either
eaten or bartered elsewhere for clothes and housing.

Mama took a deep breath. "I always liked coming up here.
Right after dawn is best, when it's bustling while the rest of the
city sleeps. The commercial customers make their big buys then.
There used to be an old man who showed up a couple of times
a week with coffee beans. He'd take only barter and he'd be
gone in half an hour with enough fruit and vegetables to feed
an army. I've always wondered what he did with it all."

"Trader Jon," Kinderman said. "I think he fed slighs and
gandies. I'd almost forgotten." He smiled. "It's been a while
since I've been here this time of day."

"With both of you intimately familiar with the place, then, I
hope one of you knows an easy way to locate those slighs in
here," Janna said.

"There's only one way, bibi." Mama pushed his glasses up
his nose, grinning. "The old heel-toe heel-toe."

So they walked, covering the market row by row, stall by
stall, studying each face. With no luck for a long while. Then,
at a wheeled truck displaying baskets of hydroponic tomatoes,
the arm of a jon counting tomatoes into a bag in a porterbot set
off an alarm in Janna's head. A scar crossed the back of the
hand. Unfortunately, the jon stood with his back to them.

She nudged Mama. He dipped his chin to indicate he had seen.

Moving casually, Janna crossed the aisle to the tomatoes.
"Excuse me. Are these vine ripened?"

Scar-hand looked around and she barely heard his answer.
The lean face with its light complexion and sandy hair matched
one of the enhancements. One Kinderman had not circled. Her
hand slid on through the inside of her trench coat pocket to her
thigh boot, to the wrap strap down inside it.

But she did not take it out. Instead, she thanked Scar-hand and rejoined Mama, memorizing the stall's location.

"You're going to come back later and hope he's still there?" Kinderman asked after they walked on.

"Better that than wrap him now and risk warning the other two we're after them," Mama said. "Do you know him?"

"Not really. I've just seen him around." The K.C. leo glanced back at the stall, frowning. "He's another sligh. Calls himself Rebel, I think."

Another of those names, so un-slighlike, so . . . Janna hunted for a word to characterize them. Aggressive? She found her hand reaching through her trench-coat pocket again to the top of the wrap strap in her boot. Maybe Kinderman was right about slighs changing. It had to be more than coincidence that three of them with names like that appeared to match enhancements of the riffers.

And if three of them worked here, what about the others?

As they kept searching the market, she watched for faces to match the remaining three enhancements.

She saw none of those, but in the next dome, approaching a stall selling cucumber and squash, Kinderman murmured, "There's Dragon."

She saw him, too . . . stocky, freckled, carrot-red hair pulled up in a ponytail. But he might easily have been overlooked. His faded denim jumpsuit/coverall matched those worn by many of the vendors, including the middle-aged woman sitting at the front of the stall with a newspaper laid open on the computer in her lap.

Kinderman said, "Hello, Dragon."

The sligh turned from combining the squash from two baskets in one. He moved not as most slighs would, with the rigid control of someone forcing himself to stand his ground, but leisurely. An insolent smile spread across his face. "Well, you do walk around in daylight, leo. And we though you spent it in a locker, sleeping on a bed of parking tickets and report forms."

Kinderman sent back a smile as thin as a blade. "That's only when I haven't drunk enough deek blood. Speaking of 'we', seeing you solo is new and different. Where's Tsunami?"

The vendor looked up from her newspaper. "Is there a problem, Officer?"

"Not if I learn where Tsunami is." He watched Dragon as he said it.

Frowning, the woman opened her mouth as though about to respond, but Dragon snorted and spoke first. "What's the matter, leo?" He tossed the emptied basket into the airfoil pickup parked behind the stall. "You can't stand leaving the 'Companion Information' section of your FI form blank?"

"I have people who want to meet him." Kinderman gestured at Mama and Janna.

Looking them over, the sligh went still. A moment later he snorted again, but not before a hint of worry lines showed on his forehead. "Maybe he isn't interested in meeting more lions."

Two strides took Kinderman around the produce baskets. He caught Dragon under the elbow. "Hard card. Let's find him, choomba."

The sligh's lip curled. Janna sighed. Forget a quiet wrap of the two. If Dragon had not connected this visit with the robberies and killing before, it must have occurred to him by now, and the universe could die its heat death before he led them to his friend.

Beside her, Mama shook his head. "Forget it, Kinderman. You were right; for all the swagger, around lions they turn rabbit just like other slighs. We might as well let him hop away."

Dragon stiffened. He jerked his arm out of Kinderman's grip. "Rabbit? Fuck you, puss." Putting his thumb and first finger in his mouth, he blew three shrill, rising notes. "I'll show you rabbit."

A minute later a lean, dark-haired jon came loping between stalls, the gold ring in his ear gleaming. Janna blinked. Then Dragon had not realized why they were here. Either that or he had brassier balls than even Kinderman realized.

The whistle attracted the attention of other vendors and passing citizens, who turned to look at them.

Reaching them, Tsunami grinned. "Well . . . if it isn't Officer Children-Man. Et al," he added, glancing across the produce baskets at Mama and Janna. "Is troikas the new fashion in lion country?"

"What's going on here?" the vendor demanded.

"Just some routine questions, ma'am." Janna moved around the baskets and behind Tsunami, where she could grab him if he tried bolting.

Mama followed. "Sergeant Brill and I are from Topeka."

Incredibly, both slighs looked back at them with no reaction except *so-what* expressions. Uncertainty stirred in Janna. She caught Mama's eye. Maybe Kinderman's identification was wrong after all.

She pulled the enhancements out of her trench-coat pocket and handed them to the slighs. ''What do you think about these?''

They glanced over the pictures. Tsunami shrugged. ''Someone took 2-D's of us.''

''And of a sligh called Rebel,'' Kinderman said.

''It looks like him.'' The ponytail swished as Dragon pulled in his chin. ''Who took these?''

Janna moved a step closer to the slighs. ''First tell us about the other three. Do you know them?''

Tsunami handed the enhancements back to Janna. ''Why do you want to know?''

He knew the others. The expression in his eyes told Janna that. And he finally suspected something. That showed in his voice. She turned toward the vendor, who had stood up and was watching them with a frown. ''Are you here every day?''

''Except Sunday.'' The woman spoke slowly. ''We farm hydroponically, so we always have fresh vegetables to bring in.''

''And how many of those days does Dragon work for you?''

The woman hesitated before answering. ''He doesn't really work for me. When I need a hand with something, I whistle. He or his friend or one of the others floating around come and help. Or sometimes one of them will stop and ask if there's anything they can do.''

''Was he here last Friday and Saturday?'' Kinderman asked.

Her forehead furrowed in thought. ''I'm sure he was. They always are.''

''But do you *remember* seeing him, or his friend?''

She hesitated again, this time longer, glancing back and forth from the K.C. leo to the slighs, furrows deepening.

''Of course we were here,'' Dragon said in an impatient voice. ''Remember the bibi who wanted two dozen squash but said they all had to be the same size and shape, so you had me go through every basket to find a matched set?''

The vendor's forehead smoothed instantly. She smiled. ''Of course.''

''Which day was that, ma'am?'' Janna asked.

Dragon answered for her. "Friday."

The woman nodded. "Friday morning. I remember because after she left, I took a break for lunch."

"And was he here in the afternoon, too?" If they left around noon, they could have reached Topeka with time to spare before the fund-raiser.

Again a hesitation. Above them, rain thundered on the roof of the dome.

Kinderman said, "There isn't much need for them in the afternoon. Is there, ma'am? The quantity sales, the ones where you need someone to carry baskets to the buyers' vehicles, are mostly in the morning." He eyed the slighs. "Where did you go in the afternoon, and evening?"

In unison the slighs folded their arms. Tsunami said, "Where I damn well wanted to. Leo, I don't know whether you can't get enough of harrassing us when you're on duty or you're just showing your country cousins how the boys in the big city do it, but I've had enough." He started to turn away.

Kinderman reached out an arm to block him.

The sligh stopped. "What're going to do, hit me? Commit police brutality in front of witnesses?"

Mama circled to where he faced Tsumani. He smiled. "We're just asking where you were Friday and Saturday night."

"And I'm telling you that's none of your fucking business!"

A citizen looking over the produce at the stall across the aisle turned to stare at them.

Uncertainty nudged Janna again. She heard anger and defiance in the sligh's voice, but no defensiveness, no fear, nothing that said to her: *guilty*.

Kinderman's knife blade smile appeared again. "Oh yes, it is, choomba." He kept his voice low. The citizens and vendors turned back to their own affairs. "Because those photos weren't taken of you here in K.C. They're from news chip recordings of six perpetrators who riffed two political fund-raisers in Topeka and killed a guest at one of them."

The slighs gaped.

Kinderman's smile widened. "So . . . I think we ought to continue this discussion at the station house."

Dragon started. "Wait a minute. Those 2-D's can't be us. They just look like us."

"And one just happens to look like your friend Rebel, too?"

Janna asked. That was too much coincidence to believe. She caught the vendor's eye. "Ma'am, we need your help." She handed the enhancements across the produce baskets to her. "Do you know the three individuals other than these two and the one with the scar on his hand?"

After a troubled glance at Dragon and Tsunami, the woman nodded. "This one with the scar through his eyebrow helps here, too. "I think he's called Swift."

Four of the six. That *was* too much for coincidence.

As though reading her thoughts, Kinderman nodded. "Let's go."

"But . . . we haven't been out of K.C.," Dragon protested. "How would we get to Topeka? Walk? You can't pay bus fares with cucumbers."

"Someone gave you tickets."

Tsunami's eyes narrowed. "Not us." He toyed with the ring in his ear. "You asked about Friday and Saturday night so that has to be when the robberies happened. What time?"

Mama told him.

His sudden grin dripped insolence. "I don't know about the other three, but Dragon, Rebel, and I can't possibly be your perpetrators." He folded his arms. "On Friday evening at seven o'clock Officer Gariana Bondini, the lion I dream of being shut in the back of a watch car with, was FI'ing the three of us outside the Waterloo Club. Check your records. I just hope she noted under 'Narrative information' how cooperative I was, offering to let her strip search me."

From the flare in Kinderman's eyes, Janna wondered if he wanted to hit the sligh, but his only move was to reach into a thigh pocket and pull out an ear button. "We'll see, choomba." Without taking his eyes off the sligh, he screwed the radio into his ear and tapped it on. He murmured too softly to be heard but lip reading, Janna saw him ask for a records check.

They stood in silence, waiting for the results, while rain contined hammering the dome overhead and from around them came the murmur of vendors' and customers' voices.

Presently, Mama looked at Dragon and Tsunami. "We're going to find out the names of the other two slighs sooner or later, so why don't you tell us now and let us spend the time it would take us to find them checking out their alibis for the times of the robberies."

The two exchanged glances. Dragon smiled. "You're the detectives. Detect."

"Shit!" Kinderman swore.

They all looked at him.

He pulled the radio button out of his ear, scowling. "I don't know how you three did it, because we all know damn well that's you in those photos, not jons who look like you. I intend to find out, though, and when I do, we'll have another discussion."

"You mean they're telling the truth?" Janna asked.

He sighed. "According to Records, Officer Bondini did file an FIF on them for Friday night, just where and when they said. If we believe that, they couldn't have been in Topeka."

THIRTEEN

Despite a closed door, the raised voices leaked out of Lieutenant Vradel's office and the squad room had fallen silent, listening. Cruz even turned off the newscanner's sound.

"They spend two days up there, and what do they come back with . . . nothing . . . just a few names!" Commander Vining paced inside the windows. "It's been a week since Armenda was killed. What am I going to tell Paget?"

Vradel did not pace. He sat motionless behind his desk. Motionless, that is, except for the twitch of his mustache and the twirl of the pencil in his hands. "*You* don't have to tell him anything." He did not shout. Janna had to strain to hear. The biting edge on his words, however, suggested that only iron will kept the volume under control. "Facing the director is my job. You just worry about the media."

"You'd better worry, too." Vining frowned through the window in the direction where Janna and Mama sat on their desks. "That pair had four good suspects in their hands and they let them go! The media will be asking why."

"If they learn about it, I suggest you point out the lack of evidence. That FI report gives three of them an iron-clad alibi for one riff."

Janna sighed. Yes . . . although the slighs had offered it too glibly in her opinion. Rebel, whom they rounded up as soon as Records informed Kinderman about the FI, used almost the same words Tsunami had. As if they all practiced the story together.

It baffled her how they could have faked the FI, however. Certainly not by having friends pose as the three of them. When she and Mama talked to Bondini at the beginning of the evening watch, the she-lion assured them she knew the trio too well to be skinned that way. Her thinly concealed contempt for slighs convinced Janna that Bondini was unlikely to have filed a false report for their benefit.

Besides, if the slighs had arranged alibis, surely Swift, whom Kinderman had located before leaving the market, would have someone more credible than other slighs to swear to his presence in Kansas City. And why had none at all been given for the last two, York and Shadow, after their pictures were identified by Central Division officers?

She and Mama found no proof the slighs took the bus to Topeka those afternoons, either. The bus line did not record who bought tickets, just the date and destination of each. Besides which, the tickets could have been bought elsewhere or days earlier, or like Tony Ho, the slighs could have been given passes. In any case, the enhancements failed to ring any bells with the drivers on those runs.

On the other hand, none of the four interviewed could prove their whereabouts Friday and Saturday afternoons. They refused to name their other jobs, claiming—probably with justification —that their employers would not only deny hiring slighs, but be so nervous at being asked that they would fire all sligh employees.

"All we have against the slighs," Vradel continued, "is their likeness to the enhancements."

York and Shadow might be the key. The inability to locate the two, even with the entire KCPD on the watch for them, made Janna wonder if they were being hidden for fear they would give something away.

"If that's all we have, we'd better come up with something more." Vining pulled the door open. "Or the heat being generated on the third floor by media crucifixions and scared high muckies will start cooking gooses down here."

Now Vradel stood, but only to follow Vining as far as the office door. From there he watched, deadpan, as the information officer stalked out of the squad room. Then he looked over his squad, who had suddenly become very engrossed in papers on their desks. "All right, I hope everyone's ready for roll call . . . and will continue being as attentive and quiet as you've been the past five minutes."

At the end of the briefing, Cruz gathered the case squad for their own additional briefing. He ran a hand back through his hair. "Vining's right, unfortunately. Unless we start producing results, life is going to be hell."

At the caff urn behind them, Maro Desch reached up while his mug filled and tapped the sound control on the newscanner.

". . . in Beijing assured Moscow the missile firing was accidental and after expressing profound regret for the tragedy, announced his government has begun a full investigation of the incident. Campaigning in California, Humanitarian presidential candidate Earl Lincoln said—"

"So they finally admit shooting it down," Desch said, overriding the former Secretary of State's comment.

Cruz waited until Desch left before continuing. "Maxwell and Brill, the Omaha PD called. They have nothing on any Willem Edmiston. I had the lab check that Triton at Oedipus Wrecks."

Janna crossed her fingers. A little luck, please. "Had the backseat been removed?"

He shrugged. "Sometime in the past month or so, they say, based on the clean condition and smooth operation of the locks, but they can't be more exact. Taking out the seat, which was the only way to check the floor slots, put new marks over all the older ones."

Janna swore.

"It looks as though only your Mr. Edmiston can tell us if he took out that seat."

"Speaking of Edmiston." Mama pushed his glasses up his nose. "Did he ever return our call?"

"In a manner of speaking," Zavara said. She stretched in a ripple of shoulder and abdominal muscles that set several male members of the squad drooling. "I took a call from him Thursday afternoon. But he claimed to be unable to say what he was doing in town last week end, but promised he'd call us back at a more . . . 'convenient' time." She bared even, white teeth. "I advised him to find a convenient time by this week end."

Janna rubbed her forehead. The mysterious Edmiston and his

rented Triton, the slighs, people with possible motives for killing
Armenda, Aschke's service calls to the crime sites and apartment
complex where Tony stayed . . . all pieces floating around but
none connected to each other. They needed connections.

Mama moved around the desks to sit beside her. He murmured,
"I wonder how Aschke, or Sydney or Junior, would react to the
enhancements and Edmiston's name."

Connections. Janna grinned. "Let's see."

After Cruz finished updating everyone on the case's progress,
she and Mama headed for Beria's office.

The receptionist located Aschke in the service workshop on
the building's third floor. Passing the open door of the employee
lounge on their way to the workshop, they saw Listra Wassman
and a young man standing on chairs hanging a computer-gen-
erated banner on the far wall. *Congratulations, Karis. Best of
luck always.*

Wassman waved at them.

"Congratulations on what?" Janna called.

"Her new job. After a year of filling out forms, she's been
accepted for an electrical engineering position at the American
dome on Mars."

Where Janna's brother worked. Too bad Sandoz was not at
work now, Janna reflected, following Mama on toward the workshop. She would have suggested Sandoz look Andy up.

In the workshop they found Aschke hunched on a stool before
a computer with the face of the monitor case divided horizontally
between the rectangular screen and a panel with groups of per-
forations. As they came in the door, he picked up one of several
small circuit boards lying on the table beside and him and plugged
it into the panel.

"Good morning," Janna said.

He did not look up. Long fingers continued tapping the keys.
Colored lines zigzagged across the monitor, some angling up,
some dropping, several stopping short of the far side. Aschke
sighed . . . tapped more keys. A different set of lines appeared.

"We'd like to talk to you."

A new key combination, new lines. "The last time I talked
to you, Mr. Beria took me off service calls."

The implication was clear: talking to them brought him trouble;
he wanted no more.

Mama smiled. "We just need you to look at some pictures."

Out came the circuit board. In went another. Aschke frowned at the new lines on the monitor. "I don't . . . know . . . anything . . . about . . . those . . . robberies."

Janna reached out to block the monitor with her hand. She hardened her voice. "We'd like you to look at the pictures anyway."

For several moments he continued staring ahead of him, as though seeing the monitor through her hand, then his shoulders hunched still more. Sighing, he turned on the stool. "Where are they?"

Mama handed the enhancement to him.

At least he spent more time looking them over than anyone else had the past few days. Janna watched closely, waiting for a flicker or twitch, something to indicate recognition. But Aschke handed back the pictures with no change of expression. "I don't know them."

That could be true even if he were involved. His part might have been only providing the information on bypassing security at the hotel and Yi's house. He must have had contact with the tickman, however . . . the jon from Omaha? Janna pointed at Tsunami's photo. "Have you heard the name Willem Edmiston?" He might be ready to pretend convincingly that he had not, but she hoped associating the name with the wrong person would startle him into an incriminating reaction.

Aschke only shook his head, without even a flicker of suprise.

Maybe he was telling the truth.

A twitch disturbed the smooth gleam of light on Mama's scalp. He smiled at Aschke. "What do you think about the party this afternoon? Listra Wassman says your friend Karis plans to dance nude on the table."

What! Janna gaped at Mama.

"May I go back to work?"

Then she understood the reason for the preposterous statement . . . to see if Aschke would react to anything they said. Since he had not, his lack of response to the enhancements and Edmiston's name proved nothing.

Time to get tough. She moved close, hopefully violating his personal space, and put a hiss in her voice. "Aschke, suppose you—"

"Go back to work," Mama finished. "Come on, bibi." He caught her sleeve and pulled her with him toward the door.

They reached the corridor before she recovered enough from surprise to jerk loose. She whirled on him. "What the hell are you doing?"

He backed out of reach. "Saving us wasted effort. He isn't giving us anything, either because he won't, or he's innocent and he can't. Why badger him until we're sure it's a case of the former?"

Glass comprised the upper half of the partition between the workshop and corridor. She frowned through it at Aschke. "We need a bank warrant."

"Maybe Junior or Sydney will give us a connection that makes probable cause."

Provided, of course, either of them were involved . . . and would talk.

A phone call to the Armenda house gave them the information that Sydney had gone to Nord Electronics. They drove to the plant in the Soldier Creek division, and found her behind a copper glass desk in a wood-paneled office that smelled of lemon oil and saddle soap. She waved them to leather chairs.

"You look comfortable," Mama said.

The leather squeaked as she leaned back. Her hands ran down the chair arms in a caress. "I've always loved my father's office. Now it's mine."

Janna raised a brow. "Despite the fact your brother inherits control of Armenord?"

A corner of Sydney's mouth quirked. "Correction. He inherits *Armenord*. Control is another matter. Not that he'll fight me for it. If he cared about anything except the toys our profit can buy him, he'd be asserting leadership right now. Instead, he wants to go to Rio, and being denied that until the matter of Dad's death is settled, he's consoling himself with whatever pleasures he can find in town."

"I take it he's no longer on a restricted allowance since your father died," Mama said.

She gave him a bland smile. "I want my brother to be happy. How may I help you today?"

Janna shoved the enhancements across the gleaming desk top. "Do you recognize any of these people?"

The radio button in Janna's ear murmured, "Soldier Alpha Ten, home detention unit requests enforcement aid. HDU computer locates the transponder on detainee Adara Staats at Green Hills Mall, in violation of detention limits.''

Sydney looked over the enhancements. ''Other than these two of the man the newscanner says you have in custody, none of the faces look familiar. Are they the men who carried the needlers?''

''Possibly,'' Mama said. ''We think the red-haired man is named Jason Aschke and the one with the earring, the one who fired at your father, is a Willem Edmiston.''

Excitement shot through Janna as Sydney shook her head. ''No . . . Edmiston's shorter than the men in that courtya—'' She broke off, eyeing them. Her face congealed. ''From your expressions, you already know that. What's this about?''

''Connections.'' Janna gave her a bland smile. ''Tell us how you know Willem Edmiston.''

''I don't.'' Sydney pushed the enhancements back across the desk at them. ''My father did.''

Janna collected the enhancements. ''They were friends?''

''Business associates.''

''Associated how?'' Mama asked.

The dark eyes narrowed. ''Why do you want to know? How did his name come up?''

Janna shoved the enhancements inside the top of a thigh boot. ''Edmiston was in town last week end . . . driving the kind of car seen parked in the area of Lincoln Yi's house the night your father was killed.''

The other woman went so still she might have turned to stone. She appeared even to have stopped breathing. Shocked? Or dismayed at their discovery of Edmiston's name? After a long silence, she said slowly, ''And you believe he's involved in my father's death?''

''It's a possibility.'' Mama pushed his glasses up his nose. ''Unless you have information to the contrary.''

Sydney leaned back in her chair. ''Edmiston deals in information, not blood.''

Now why did that phrase set her spine tingling again? Janna raised her brows. ''What kind of information?''

''Market research.''

''Also called industrial espionage,'' Mama said.

Janna straightened. Of course. That explained the screening on Edmiston's phone . . . so only bona fide clients could reach him. It suggested answers to other questions, too. That kind of "market research" often included burglary . . . which involved knowing how to defeat security systems. "Can you be sure there's a limit to how far he'll go to obtain information for a client?"

Sydney stared steadily back at them. "Murder isn't the same."

"But can you be sure he can't be bought for murder, too?"

Not a flicker showed in the dark eyes. "I suppose anyone can be bought if the price is high enough." Sydney stood. "If I hear from him, shall I give you a call?"

They took the hint and stood, too. "Please," Mama said. As they headed for the door, he pulled off his glasses and slipped them in his trench coat pocket.

Janna stared. What the hell was he up to? Without his glasses, how did he expect to find the elevator and avoid running into walls?

Outside the office door, sure enough, he tripped and went down on his knees.

"Fine. I—damn!" He squinted. "I've lost a contact lens." And sighing, he groped around on the carpet.

One foot, Janna noticed, held the office door open a crack.

Understanding came. So that was his plan. Kneeling, she pretended to help with the search. In the course of it, she worked her way back to the office door.

From inside came the sound of Edmiston's recorded phone greeting, followed by Sydney's voice, reciting a number sequence, and then, steel-edged: "Mr. Edmiston, this is Sydney Armenda. We have to talk. Today."

Southbound on Topeka Avenue, a Chevy ZRX-30 tried to cut across the front of the Meteor's airfoil skirt into their lane. Pretending his vehicle was the Ashanti its body design aped? Janna shoved her steering wheel forward, revving the police-package fans into thunder. The Meteor gunned past the ZRX, clearing the vehicle by millimeters and forcing the driver to swerve back into his original lane.

Mama winced. "And you accuse me of rock jock driving."

Her mouth tightened. "We should have gone back into the office, Mama."

His sigh said: *I suspected that's the problem.* "For what purpose? She didn't say anything incriminating, such as warning him to be careful because we're getting close. If we'd gone in and she claimed her intent was to ask him if he's involved, and if so, what will it cost to buy the name of the person who hired him, how do we prove otherwise?''

"We have to start pushing sometime." She dug her fingers into the wheel. "How else will we get answers that tie everyone together?''

He sighed again. "What if they aren't tied together?''

Christ. She rolled her eyes. "Mama, they *have*—''

"Do they?'' His scalp furrowed. "Bibi, working this case is like catching shadows. We're riding off in all directions at once . . . after riffers, then political terrorists, then a murderer, now an industrial spy. Not to mention that we have a city full of suspects: the ex-wife, the current wife, the son, the daughter, Aschke, slighs, embittered corporate victims, disgruntled former employees, and Edmiston. With so little solid on any of them . . . just enough that we can't dismiss anyone. And about the time we think we have a hold somewhere, it's gone; they were being FI'd at the time or they can't be positively identified.''

Maybe that was why she longed for an excuse to throw someone, anyone, into a wall.

"Let's check out the lead Sydney gave us,'' he went on.

Lead? "What lead?''

He grinned. "You mean you missed it? She mentioned that Edmiston is shorter than the riffers.''

So he might be the small jon involved? She waited for him to go on.

"Inge and Surowski said the small suspect spoke to them from the rear area of the Triton. That suggests he had at least part control of the waitron. Certainly the voice. I can't see Aschke being that chatty.''

Nor could Janna. And the waitron had spoken to Mrs. Yi with familiarity. "So does Edmiston know the Yi's?''

Mama's grin broadened. "I think she's got it. Shall we ask them?''

They found Yi at his bank.

When they asked him about Willem Edmiston, however, the banker shook his head. "The name isn't immediately familiar.

I deal with a great many people throughout the year, though. Just a minute." He tapped a key on the computer/phone console built into his desktop.

Mama nudged Janna and pointed at its screen. She nodded. It had caught her attention, too. The back side of the wafer-thin rectangle appeared to be a screen, as well, enabling Yi to display information or a phone call to both him and someone on this side of the desk simultaneously. At the moment, though, colored lines and abstract shapes chased each other around and across the screen, turning it into a piece of electronic art.

"Directory," the computer said.

"Search. Willem Edmiston."

"Visual display?"

"Yes." Yi leaned back. "If I've dealt with him, the directory should have an entry. I like to include relevant facts, also: in what capacity I've met him, names of associates, spouse, and children, that kind of thing." He smiled. "Sometimes I feel like a cyborg, with half my brain in my desktop."

Mama said, "In Roman times, important men had a slave called a *nomenclator*, whose job was to accompany him and recognize the hundreds of people the poobah knew. When they met one of those individuals, the nomenclator whispered information about the person in his boss's ear so the poobah could sail up and say things like, 'Hail, Julius, how's your wife Olivia? Congratulations on your son Marcus being made legate in the army.' "

Yi smiled. "Really? And here I thought I was being clever and original."

The computer beeped. "Willem Edmiston not found."

Yi spread his hands. "I'm sorry."

Mama said, "Maybe you've met him using another name. May I make a long distance call on your phone if I charge it to my department?"

"If this helps find who killed Carel Armenda, I don't mind standing the cost of a call." Yi paused. "As long as it's to somewhere here on Earth."

Mama came around the desk and punched in the number. "To Omaha."

Janna grinned. She should have thought of that.

Moments later Edmiston's voice was reciting the message it had when they called.

Mama raised his brows at Yi. "Does the face look familiar?"

Yi studied the screen. After a moment, he shook his head. "I'm sorry, no. For something like this, you'd probably do better talking to my wife; she has a wonderful memory for voices." His face went thoughtful. "It's possible, of course, that I haven't actually met him. There've been several attempts to buy my airline. Maybe he researched me looking for leverage his clients could use."

Janna considered that possibility while driving out to the Yi house. "Would ear jewelry be anything he'd be familiar with in that instance?"

"He'd certainly have learned that Yi's wife is blind. Let's just hope he didn't study them from a distance."

Maeve Yi received them in the airy livingroom overlooking the pool court. Not surprisingly, Edmiston's name meant nothing to her, so they called his number again, and set the phone on Record.

"Listen closely to this voice, please," Janna said.

Mrs. Yi unwrapped the sonar units on her ears and settled herself in a bucket chair with her eyes closed. Her forehead furrowed in concentration while the message played.

When the menu came on the screen, Mama punched off. "Have you heard it before?"

"Play it again, will you?"

Mama tapped the replay button.

After three replays, she said, "It isn't the waitron."

"We know that," Mama said. "The waitron's speaker was probably designed to reproduce whatever its controller said, but in a voice of its own. We need to know if the voice is one you've heard anywhere else before."

"Play it again." After listening several more times, she sighed. "I'm sorry; I don't know. It isn't one I'm familiar with. But it's a very ordinary kind of voice and I could have heard it only once or twice. That wouldn't be enough to make it familiar."

"Still, you *might* have talked to him before?" Mama's tone coaxed.

She slipped her sonar units back on. "I can't swear to that, but . . ." She shrugged. "It's *possible*, yes."

Mama grinned. "Thank you very much."

He continued grinning all the way out to the car. Janna eyed him. "What was that about? A possibility doesn't help us. It just means we can't definitely include or exclude him." Her fingers closed on empty air. "As you said . . . shadows."

"Maybe not." He settled back in the passenger seat. "You say bank warrants can help us. I agree. And now Mrs. Yi has said she possibly talked to Edmiston before. We can use that."

Janna switched on the Meteor, grinning. "Ten-four."

Vradel looked up at them from across his desk. "This seems to be the day for bank warrants. Showalter and Weyneth just asked for one on your service technician from Beria . . . Aschke."

Janna caught her breath. "What did they turn up against him?"

"A ticket clerk at the bus station and a driver on the K.C. run who both ID Aschke's photo as that of a jon traveling to Kansas City several times in the past month." The outline of a bus emerged under the doodling tip of Vradel's pencil.

Janna grinned. The shadows were starting to solidify!

He looked up. "What's your probable cause for this Edmiston?"

She expected Mama to reply, but a sideglance found him staring glass-eyed past the lieutenant. Rather than drag him back from outer space, Janna answered. "As we indicate on the warrant form, he generally fits the description of the small male involved in the robberies. He was in town during the robberies, driving a car of the same make and model seen near the scene Saturday night. He arrived early enough Friday to have stolen the van from G & B Cybertronics and used it to deliver the waitron to the hotel. We learned today he's an industrial spy, which means he probably knows security systems. He's had past dealings with Armenda that have brought him into contact with one and possibly both of the Armenda offspring." She told him about the call she overheard. Encouraged by Vradel's nod, she added, "Looking at Sydney and Junior's bank records would be helpful, too."

"Bring me probable cause." He glanced over the warrant. "Good; you already have Edmiston's bank listed. From the IRS?"

Grimacing, Janna nodded. Phoning a name into the IRS computer always made her feel lilke someone reaching for a bone under the nose of a large dog, no matter how many times the proper access code and law enforcement identification promptly brought back the subject's bank.

Vradel scribbled his signature on the warrant. "Morello can take this over to the courthouse in a few minutes."

She reached for the paper. "We'll take it ourselves. Who's sitting? Mama . . . Earth calling!"

His eyes snapped back into focus.

Vradel shook his head. "Judge Kendig. Good luck."

They jogged out of the office and down the stairs to the garage. Good luck indeed. Not only did Judge Kendig have to look on them sympathetically, she had to sign the warrant soon enough for them to phone the Omaha bank before its bookkeeping department shut for the rest of the week end.

Mama halted at the edge of the garage, however. "Bibi, I have something to do here. I'll see you later." And he disappeared back into the stairs before she had time to ask about his errand.

She headed for the car, sighing. Over the brainbow. She could only hope he was not up to something the brass would frown on.

At the courthouse, Janna discovered that Kendig had recessed her court at noon and was in chambers . . . occupied. Janna paced the corridor outside, eyeing her wrist chrono. After twenty minutes, she stopped a bailiff strolling by. "Are there any other judges around today?"

"On Saturday?" Then his expression went sly. "Pierce might be in his chambers."

She winced. So much for that idea. Experiences comparable to approaching Harlan Pierce included walking on coals and ingesting toxic waste.

Snickering, the bailiff disappeared around the corner.

Janna made herself comfortable against the wall.

An hour later the door of Kendig's chambers finally opened.

"Your client's guilty as hell, Ted," one of the men leaving said.

The other grinned. "You have to prove it, and if your arguments in there are any indication, you don't have the chance of a snowball in hell." They turned the corner out of sight. "How about a round of golf?"

Judge Kendig's bailiff invited Janna in. Where Her Honor insisted on reading the warrant over carefully and quizzing Janna about the case. Janna understood the necessity. Citizens' privacy must not be invaded cavalierly. Still, the judge's caution used time, and before she finally signed, three o'clock had passed.

Janna still smiled at the judge. At least this gave them a reason to look forward to Monday . . . and hope that then they would have some definite answers in the case, and hooks to catch those shadows.

FOURTEEN

At two in the morning the sound of the TV woke Janna for the third time.

"Quiet! Please," the waitron's voice commanded.

Her thought exactly. Wrapping a robe around her, she stalked out to the livingroom. "Mama, are you going to watch that damn chip all night?"

He sat as he had all evening, curled in one corner of the couch hugging updrawn knees and staring at the TV screen on the opposite wall. On it, gunmen surrounded the waitron. "Don't attempt to leave," the waitron told shocked guests. "Mr. Salmas, the waiter in front of them—"

"Mama!"

"Just a while longer."

Had he really heard? He never took his eyes from the screen.

This was the errand for which he sent her to the courthouse alone . . . talking the lab into making him a chip compiling all the news chip segments showing the gunmen. Earlier, on his third run through the chip, she had asked, "What do you hope to see?"

He had shrugged. "I don't know. But a ticket agent and driver remember Aschke taking the bus. He isn't that remarkable; so why can't others recall a much more memorable group of six young men?''

"Why memorable? They're slighs," she reminded him.

He just pushed his glasses up his nose. "I can't see them trying to be invisible the way most do. At least three of them swagger, remember?''

"Maybe not this trip, considering what they planned to do."

He shrugged. "Maybe. Even so, a group of six, slighs or not, shouldn't be that invisible.''

"So they boarded separately and pretended not to know each other." What was so difficult to understand . . . and why worry about it anyway? "They obviously managed it somehow, because there they are." She had pointed at the screen.

"And in K.C., Officer Bondini is FI'ing them." His scalp furrowed. "There must be something here that will tell us how they can be in two places at once.''

His reasoning sounded brainbent then—though what else did she expect from Mama?—and at this hour of the night, even more so. "Mama, if you haven't found something by now—"

"I have."

And he had not called her! "What is it?"

He frowned at the screen. "I don't know. Something wrong. It's there; I can feel it. I just haven't identified it yet.''

She sighed. Blue sky. She might have known.

On the screen, the scene had switched to a section from another news chip, the only one which actually caught the beginning of the action.

The waitron, just visible at the far right, began rocking and spinning. Its shelves emptied. The videographer swung to focus on the event, only to be repeatedly jostled off target by dismayed guests scrambling away from spraying wine and flying glassware. When the camera steadied, the gunmen had planted themselves in the space that opened around the waitron.

"Damn." Mama thumbed the backscan button on the remote control. Action reversed. The waitron sucked glasses back onto its shelves. Guests closed in on it, straightening their posture and smoothing their faces. After a pause, action resumed its normal forward motion and the guests ducked away once more. The gunmen appeared from among them.

Mama backscanned again.

After several more repetitions, the scene reminded Janna of

waves on a beach, rolling up across the sand then ebbing, leaving behind pieces of flotsam. In this case, sharks.

"I wish I could see where they come from." Mama slowed the action to a frame scan. The glasses floated outward in tiny jerks.

"No matter what you do," Janna said, "that camera isn't going to center on the waitron any sooner or hold any steadier."

"If I could only see them draw their needlers. Or figure out what it is I'm seeing that bothers me."

She might as well be talking to the wall. "I wish to hell you would, so you'd go to bed." She folded her arms. "If you'd spoken up faster, you could be moving downstairs, free to stay up as late as you want without disturbing anyone."

His eyes never left the screen. "You'd miss me."

"Oh, of course." Like an AIDS-C virus. "Why don't you admit the truth, Mama? You haven't seriously looked for an apartment because you can't bear the thought of living alone."

She could have sworn that he froze, but a blink later he grinned at her. "You need me here. I bring your life color."

Weariness dragged at her. Did he *ever* stop performing? She turned away. "Good night."

"Look at this place." His voice followed her to the bedroom. "The artwork and most of the furniture are mine, just as they were Sid's when he shared the place with you. You don't live here; you bivouac. Your life is the job. What kind of existence is that?"

Just what she needed in the middle of the night, advice on how to live her life! At the bedroom door she looked back. "You've successfully evaded my question. Now will you turn down your sound and the TV's and let me sleep?"

He went right on. "You're good at the job, granted . . . the best partner I've had. Though I wish you cared less about rules and more about people. But having all you want in life doesn't mean it's all you need. What if something happens to the job? What's left of you then?"

An icy hand squeezed her chest. She chased the cold with anger. "Just watch the goddamn chip! Watch it until you pass out. But don't come whining if I take my bicycle to work in the morning and don't wake you on the way out." For emphasis, she slammed the door.

His voice came through it, raised, yet gentler. "I care what happens to you, Jan. I don't want to see you hurt, and that doesn't mean just finishing each shift alive and whole.''

She leaned her head against the door, feeling anger drain away. The bastard. Just when she had hurled a bolt of verbal abuse, he came back with something like that. And meant it, damn him.

After a minute she opened the door and padded back out to the livingroom. Why not humor him in this thing about the chip. Curling up on the other end of the couch, she said, ''Okay, on with the show. Maybe two sets of eyes can spot whatever it is.''

By morning she wanted to kill him. Not because they had watched the chip until she knew every scene so well she could close her eyes and replay them from memory. Not because the effort was in vain; whatever Mama had seen earlier that had struck him as ''wrong'' defied identification. What infuriated her was that Mama showed no sign of having gone without sleep, whereas she, as one appalled glance in the mirror told her, looked like the walking dead.

In the squad room, nearly half an hour early for a change, Mama dropped into his desk chair and sat frowning into space. Janna homed on the caff urn, praying it was full and hot.

''My god. I thought we were the only shift who looked like that,'' Lewis Albino, one of the outgoing morning watch, remarked as she passed his desk. ''Would you like a waker?''

She halted. ''If you have something to spare.''

''Hold out your hand.'' He dug a blister pack out of a drawer and broke one bubble.

An oval blue-and-yellow tablet landed in her palm. She stared. ''You use FTL on *duty*?''

He shrugged. ''It's legal, and it keeps me awake.''

''For the next week probably.'' Still, she needed something with kick, and FTL had that. She gulped down the tablet dry. ''Thanks, Albino. I owe you.''

''Brill, Maxwell.''

Janna turned. Vradel stood at the door of his office with Lieutenant Susan Drexel, the morning watch commander.

''Nice to see you bright and early,'' Drexel said. ''There's something here already for the case squad. Since you two are first in, you can tend to it.''

''What is it?'' Mama asked.

Vradel's mustache lifted at one end. "A gentleman from Omaha. Interview room one."

Lieutenants enjoyed dramatics, too. Awake with a jolt, Janna jogged after Mama toward the interview rooms.

At the door Mama paused. "Why don't you run the camera?"

She nodded and continued past him to the observation room. Despite the stimulant and her adrenalin rush, he still looked brighter than she felt.

Inside the observation room, the camera dangled from the ceiling, aimed through the one-way viewing panel. She switched it on. Beyond the panel, slightly mottled by the accoustic tile design that from the interview room side made it blend into the wall, their suspect paced in measured strides. His feet made almost no sound, Janna noticed. In person he resembled Pass-the-Word Morello even more than he had on the phone . . . small, wiry, foxy-faced.

He swung around in a fluid motion at the sound of the door opening.

"Mr. Willem Edmiston?" Mama extended a hand. "I'm Sergeant Maxwell."

"Good morning." Edmiston shook the hand. "For the record, please note that I've come in voluntarily to talk to you. I would have been here sooner except I couldn't leave the project I was involved in." He sat down in the chair facing Janna's wall.

She slipped on the headset goggles, which slaved the camera to her and fed her the image coming through the lens, giving her the same closeup view of Edmiston's facial and pupil responses.

He stared straight at the wall. "I trust your camera is recording me." The pupils showed clearly in the pale blue of his eyes. "Let me save you the trouble of playing games, Sergeant. I've seen the newscanner items about Carel Armenda's death and I learned much of the rest talking to Miss Armenda yesterday afternoon . . . as least as much as she knows. I called her at her request. She wanted to know if her brother hired me to kill her father. I'll tell you what I told her . . . no, he did not. Nor, Sergeant Maxwell, did she hire me. No one did. I am not involved in Armenda's death. Assassination isn't one of the services I offer."

Janna sucked in her lower lip. Not once during the speech had his pupils dilated to indicate the stress associated with lying.

Several times he glanced left, but that meant nothing until Mama asked questions with known answers to establish how Edmiston's eyes shifted during lies.

"You were here those two days," Mama's voice said.

"Yes. I freely admit that. Why not?" A thin smile flickered across his face. "A check of the hotels will establish that I stayed at the Downtown Ramada. You already know about the Triton."

"An interesting choice of vehicles."

The smile flicked again. "I always choose something that looks like an unmarked police car. It allows me to sit parked for long periods of time without the inconvenience of lions stopping to ask what I'm doing."

"But you weren't parked near the Yi house?"

"I didn't even drive through that side of town." His pupil size remained constant. "My presence had nothing to do with Carel Armenda."

"Do you know the Yi's?"

"I know their address. I made a point of asking Miss Armenda about it, on the chance that my business had accidentally taken me into the area. Your witnesses did not see my vehicle."

"What *was* your business here?"

For the first time he hesitated. His eyes shifted left. Remembering? Or considering a lie? "I'd rather not say. It's . . . ongoing."

"We have a bank warrant. Tomorrow morning we'll know everything about you, including the names of any local people who've made payments into your account."

Now his pupils dilated. "That isn't necessary. At the time of Armenda's murder, I was having dinner at the Xanadu Club as a guest of Paul Adler of Smith Automotives, Inc. He'll confirm that. So should two waitresses named Amber and Aurora." A smile accompanied his leftward eye shift. "The Xanadu offers . . . unique table services."

So Janna had heard. To her disappointment, he gave no details. Had that left shift indicated memory or not, then? It maddened her not to be sure.

"After dinner the waitresses accompanied us up to the whirlpools. Judging by the camera blister I spotted on the ceiling, the club monitors their rooms, so they should have a video record of our visit."

Janna groaned. Another of *those* alibis?

"If you like, I'll wait here while you check."

"He was certainly cooperative," Arianna Cho said at the apartment that evening. She picked up the platter of bones, all that remained of the rack of lamb Mama cooked, and carried it into the kitchen.

Where did the two of them put it all? Janna wondered, following with more dishes. "Too cooperative."

Mama finished cleaning off the table. "That's just a man eager to clear himself so we won't be looking over his shoulder."

Cho shook jade hair back over her own shoulders before scraping the bones into the trash. "Did he clear himself?"

"That depends which of us you ask." He raised a brow at Janna. "Adler, club personnel, and video evidence all confirm his alibi. The club does have security monitors in every room, and each frame of the recordings carries the date and time. I don't know why you refuse to accept that, bibi."

Janna set her dishes in the sink. "If he's telling the truth, then we've not only lost him but Sydney and Junior. We're back to square one."

Mama shook his head. "What kind of attitude is that, hating to give up a suspect even if he's innocent?"

"What I hate is having another alibi so similar to the slighs' when like them, he looks so good as a suspect." She frowned. "I don't know how they've pulled this rabbit trick, but—"

Mama grinned. "Thanks for reminding me." He headed out of the kitchen. "Arianna, leave everything. I want you to look at something."

Janna groaned. "Not again!"

"You don't have to watch."

But she did anyway. Glancing sideways at the other two on the far end of the couch, Janna reflected that they made an interesting pair sitting next to each other . . . Mama in a pearlescent white bodysuit, Cho wearing a black one that emphasized the alabaster of her hands and face.

The sharp bones beneath the perfect skin showed even more clearly as Cho frowned in concentration at the screen. She pulled her legs up to sit cross-legged. "What are we looking for?"

"Inspiration . . . or anything that strikes you as odd," Mama said.

The familiar scenes played out. Janna found her eyes drooping. For a few minutes she fought, then surrendered to the drowsiness. Why bother watching? She knew it all by heart. The sound alone let her follow the sequences in her head.

Was Mama really watching it anyway? All he and Cho seemed to be talking about were clothes the guests wore.

She forced her eyes open. "Are we investigating a murder or attending a fashion show?"

"You could do worse than study these women, bibi. They know how to dress."

The smug bastard. "Et tu, choomba. Notice that not one of the men is wearing colors that glow in the dark?"

Cho grinned. "That's right; don't let him bully you into fuss and frills. Minimalism suits you. In fact, with your coloring, black would look—that's odd."

Suddenly Janna did not feel the least drowsy. "What?" she and Mama asked simultaneously.

Cho pushed her hair back over her shoulders. "Maybe I'm wrong. It could be just a trick of light and the artist in me. Play this part again, will you?"

"This" being what Janna had taken to calling the beach scene. Mama backscanned until the waitron appeared on the edge of the screen, then restarted forward play. Cho watched intently, leaning forward with elbows propped on her folded legs and her chin on her hands. The waitron spun. Guests retreated in a wave, leaving glassware and needler-carrying sharks behind.

"Well?" Janna prompted.

"What do you see?"

"It's what I don't see." Cho leaned back, looking from one of them to the other. "Your gunmen have no shadows."

Janna blinked at her, then the screen, disappointed. "No one does." Surely Cho saw that, and the reason why. "It's the lighting." The whole ceiling glowed, the illumination from each part cancelling out shadows thrown by other parts.

Cho shook her head. "Everyone else *does* have a shadow. It's small and immediately underneath so most of the time you don't notice it. But the gunmen are different. Excuse me, Mama." She took the remote from him, backscanned, and let the chip resume forward play. "Watch their feet. See when the one with the scarred hand starts to step sideways? There!" She hit Pause.

The gunman froze with one foot elevated above the carpet. The pile under his sole remained the same gold color as that of the surrounding area.

Mama let out a happy sigh. "I love you, Arianna Cho."

Janna frowned at the screen in disbelief. "How can he not cast a shadow?"

Mama took back the remote. The images reversed, bringing guests surging back around the waitron, swallowing up the gunmen. Action froze. And remained frozen.

"Do you see something more?" Janna asked. When Mama did not answer she turned to look at him. He sat staring the direction of the screen but with his eyes glazed. "Mama?"

Cho shook his shoulder. "Mama!"

He jumped to his feet. "Let's go. There is one possibility . . . but we need help to prove it."

The moment Mama swung his little MGE down the ramp into Headquarters' garage, Janna realized where they were headed. She considered sending him on alone. With Cho along, though, how could she admit to being cowed by a man half her size?

She thought she even managed to look calm when they walked into Criminalistics and Kingsley Borthwick turned from peering over a technician's shoulder to impale them with his stare. The acidic scent of the lab came from reagents used in chemical tests, Janna knew, but it was easy to imagine that it emanated from the night chief.

"A bit late for you to be around here, isn't it, Sergeants?"

"Yes, sir," Mama said. The respectful tone would have sent the brass who knew him into shock. "It's because we've discovered something perplexing and you may be the only person who can explain it." He held out the case containing their vid chip. "This shows scenes from the news chips recorded at the Democratic riff. The gunmen don't cast shadows."

"No shadows?" Borthwick's lips pressed into a disapproving line. "Your infamous imagination has been at work again, Sergeant."

"Actually, I noticed first," Cho said.

He swung on her, eyeing her hair, her visitor's badge. "You are a friend of the sergeant, I take it? Perhaps we have mass hysteria."

Mama continued to hold out the chip case. "Why don't you see for yourself, sir?"

Borthwick stared at the case. After a moment he took it and stood turning it over in his hand. "No shadows. Intriguing." A gleam warmed the chill of his eyes. "Let's have a look."

He trotted out of the room and down the hall to a computer room. The rest of them followed.

In the computer room Borthwick climbed onto a chair and inserted the chip into a player connected to a computer. "Do you have any idea why they lack shadows, Sergeant?"

"Yes, sir . . . but I don't want to prejudice you."

"Thank you." He tapped Play.

They stood silent behind him while the chip played on the computer screen . . . until the beach scene started. Then Cho began, "Watch this—

"I intend to, madam." His eyes never left the screen. "Without coaching, if you please."

Cho grinned. *He's wonderful*, she mouthed.

At the end of the recording, Borthwick leaned back, staring at the blank screen past tented fingers. "You are correct, Sergeant. No shadows." He sat up again and restarted the recording. When the gunmen appeared, he froze the image. "Let's have a closer look at the gentlemen, then."

His stubby fingers raced across the computer keyboard. He boxed one figure . . . enlarged it to fill the screen . . . enhanced. He boxed one ear . . . enlarged . . . enhanced . . . canceled that image for the previous one . . . enlarged and enhanced a hand. Edges appeared to interest him most.

After half an hour of studying first one gunmen, then another, he recalled the original image and leaned back, grunting.

Janna opened her mouth to ask if he had learned anything but Mama caught her eye and shook his head sharply.

Borthwick sighed. "The gentlemen themselves are no help. They appear quite normal. Except . . . they do lack shadows." He leaned forward again. "Let's examine their other interactions with the environment."

For the next hour he enlarged portions of the gunmen's feet and the carpet, first in one image, then skipping along the chip to another scene. The results apparently pleased him because he had the computer print out a number of the enlargements . . . of glasses lying on the carpet, of booted feet. One print documented the absence of a shadow, but Janna did not see the reason for the others.

"I could use something hot to drink," Borthwick said.

Mama looked around at Janna. She gave him the finger, then went for caff.

Only to find that the lab's urn had run dry, and the cabinet under it, which presumably contained supplies for brewing more, was locked. She set off in search of someone with a key.

By the time she finally brought caff back to the computer room, Borthwick had switched his interest to the gunmen's tuxedos. A stack of new computer prints lay on the desk. All showed the same thing, the area where the diagonal front flap fastened at the shoulder, pearly white meeting scarlet. A sixth print slid out of the printer while Janna set the caff mug down by the keyboard.

Mama snatched up the print. What did it show? Mama's face had become all teeth.

She peered around his shoulder, but saw only another view of the tux shoulder.

The lab chief picked up the caff mug and swiveled his chair to face them. "You were right to come to me, Sergeant."

"You can tell us why they don't have shadows?" Cho asked.

"Yes, of course." Borthwick sipped from the mug. "Is it as you anticipated, Sergeant?"

"Yes, sir." Mama turned to Janna and Cho. "They don't have shadows because our riffers—"

"Sergeant," Borthwick interrupted, "this is my territory. These are my toys. Therefore, I claim the privilege of showing off here. Sergeant Brill, please pick up the prints."

She did. When Cho moved beside her, she held them so the other woman could see, too.

"Exhibit A, a wine glass lying by the foot of one perpetrator." Borthwick sipped his caff. "Notice the reflections in it."

Janna studied the print. "Of the lights, you mean?" The unbroken glow overhead turned the entire surface of the glass the color of the ceiling.

"Precisely." Another sip of caff. "Yet your perpetrator towers above it. He does not, you notice, block any of the light to the glass. Exhibit B-1, a foot planted in the middle of a carpet section soaked with red wine. Exhibit B-2, the foot has moved to an unstained section of the carpet. Exhibit B-3, the foot has moved again and the carpet where it rested moments ago remains unstained.''

Janna blinked. When the riffer had stepped in the wine?

"Exhibit C-1, another glass," Borthwick continued. "Exhibit C-2, a perpetrator stepping on the glass. Exhibit C-3, the perpetrator's foot has moved and we see what remains of the glass.''

The hair rose on Janna's neck. The glass remained intact. Undamaged.

"The only logical explanation is that those men have no physical substance." Borthwick set down the mug. "They're holograms.''

Janna gaped at him. "That's impossible! Hundreds of people stood within meters of them, some within arm's reach. A holo can't pass as real that close, not even to people terrified by needlers in their faces.''

Borthwick nodded. "I agree, Sergeant; they seem perfect. I've examined them closely. Every edge is sharp and solid, without a trace of distortion or translucency. They are magnificent holos, but holos nevertheless." He peered at Mama. "Do you mind telling me how you deduced that? Surely not on the basis of the shadows. That is a quantum sideleap in thinking.''

"Mama's thinking is all sideleaps," Janna said dryly.

Mama grinned. "That's the nicest thing you've ever said about me, bibi. But no, sir, it wasn't just the shadows. I'd also been worrying about where they came from, because I couldn't see them in the crowd. They appeared out of nowhere. And while everyone saw the gunmen, the gunmen touched no one. Only Tony Ho had physical contact with the victims. None of the gunmen ever spoke, either . . . not a sound." He paused. "I also remembered that one of the Armenord companies is Konza Holotronics.''

Janna shook her head. "That doesn't add up to holos. And I still can't believe that's the answer.''

"Then consider Exhibits D-1,2,3,4,5, and 6," Borthwick said.

The tuxedo prints.

"See the stain on the upper corner, as though someone pressed the front flap closed with a greasy thumb?''

She nodded. It showed in every print, no matter what the angle of the shot. So?

Then it struck her. She held six prints of the same stain. Six.

Janna looked up. "Each of these prints is a different riffer?" She drew in a breath. "They're all wearing the same tux?"

Mama beamed. "I knew you'd get it."

Now she believed. Janna stared past Borthwick at the image still frozen on the computer screen. Holos. That explained so much. "Christ. We're killing ourselves trying to figure how they slipped through security and they never went through. We *have* been chasing shadows."

Mama nodded. "Why were the cameras at the hotel and Yi's house disabled? To keep us from seeing how many individuals actually entered and left. Holos is also why the Triton needed a desktop . . . for controlling the waitron *and* six holos."

And why the slighs appeared on the news chips when they never left Kansas City. Janna straightened. "Mama, we need to talk to those slighs again."

He nodded.

Cho said, "So the waitron went into its dance to make space for projecting the holos. But . . ." She pushed her hair back over her shoulders. ". . . it seems incredible to me that one waitron could carry all the projectors and the needler and the cameras and circuitry for remote operation. We have holo projectors at the gallery and to fit even one into a waitron you'd have to aim it straight up or down."

Borthwick spun his chair back to the computer. "We can see if your Armenord company offers something smaller." He began typing again. Modem menus flipped up on the screen in rapid succession. He kept typing until the menus vanished and the screen turned from blue to black. "Ah, here we are."

KONZA HOLOTRONICS spread across the screen in yellow and pale blue letters. A crawl strip slid across the bottom, its text accompanied by a pleasant female voice repeating the same information vocally. "Welcome. You have reached Konza Holotronics' on-line catalog."

Borthwick smiled, startling Janna. "Market by modem."

The sales voice offered menus of general categories of products, with the general categories broken down into lists of specific items, and then extensive information on each item.

One of those being Konza's newest holo projector, the Magus-1. "At four centimeters wide and high, and ten centimeters long," the cheerful voice said, displaying an image of the projector, "the Magus-1 is small enough to be mounted anywhere."

Even in a group of six in a waitron?

"Yet despite its size, the Magus-1 projects an image of higher quality than larger units."

High quality image. Janna drew a long breath. "I think we also need to talk to the Armendas again."

FIFTEEN

Mama wrapped his trench coat tighter around him and slid out of the MGE. Beyond the bars of the Armenda gates, the driveway curved up the hill, ground-level lights along its edge making it a glowing ribbon through the darkness of the grounds. One light showed in the portion of the house visible from the gate.

Janna frowned. "Mama, we don't have to talk to her tonight."

He leaned down to peer in through the window. "This is the best way to catch her off her guard." He headed for the call box on the gatepost.

"She could call knocking on her door in the middle of the night harassment," Janna called after him.

"It isn't that late." He pressed the bell.

"At least we ought tell someone where we are and what we're doing." She swore. Why had she let him talk her into this?

Because, she admitted, she wanted to catch Sydney off guard, too.

A face appeared on the gatepost screen, murmuring. Mama's answer reached her faintly. "Sergeants Brill and Maxwell to see Miss Armenda."

The face vanished. A minute later it reappeared, murmuring something more. This time Janna could not make out Mama's reply. The face spoke again, then Mama. It turned into a lengthy exchange. The face vanished again, this time for several minutes. Finally it reappeared, briefly, and when the screen went blank, the gate slid aside.

As they drove through, Janna said, "Had to talk a bit to get us in, didn't you? What did you finally say?"

He shrugged. "The truth, that we have important new information about Armenda's death and that discussing it here is much more informal."

A polite version of: *We can talk here or downtown*. Janna grinned.

During the trip to the house, she found herself wondering about Armenda security. Except for the driveway, the grounds lay dark, even near the house.

Lights came on in the entryway. Before the MGE finished settling on its parking rollers, the door opened. Sydney herself stood in the opening, barefooted and wrapped in a man's robe. The warmth in the house sent a faint cloud of mist into the chilly night air.

Janna nudged Mama. "You want me to dress like the castle-rows? I'll copy her."

"Don't you two ever go off duty?" The light tone of Sydney's voice did not quite hide the flinty edge on the words.

Mama slid his door closed and smiled at her. "It's a mark of our diligence, Miss Armenda. We care about finding your father's killer."

"I notice you keep looking here." She stood aside for them to come in.

After closing the door, she said loudly, "Reset house alarm."

"Alarm reset," an uninflected voice said.

She padded away down the stone-floored hallway to a set of carved double sliding doors. Inside lay what must have been Armenda's private study. A desk dominated the room, a massive antique with a top the size of a pool table, drawers everywhere, and a kneehole like a tunnel. It dwarfed the computer and stacks of wide printout on its top. Another set of doors opened in the stone of the far wall, revealing a bedroom beyond and flanked by a bookcase with drawers for several hundred chips and a newscanner tuned to a stock quotation channel.

Sydney waved them to deep, butter-soft leather chairs. She sat down down behind the desk, sipped from a steaming mug—which explained the scent of coffee in the room—and frowned at the computer screen. No light show played on the back of this one. "You'll have to ask your questions while I work."

Behind her lay the outside wall, coppery glass stretching floor to ceiling, wall to wall, undraped but with blinds sandwiched between the glass layers. Janna gestured at the darkness beyond. "I notice you have no security lighting outside. Is that wise?"

Sydney looked away from the screen only to pick up some printout. "Try walking around the grounds. The motion, your body heat, and the sound of your breathing and footsteps will turn on lights around you. The idea of darkness suddenly becoming a blaze of light with the intruder caught in the middle appealed to my father." She glanced across the desk at them. "Talking to you two offers something of the same experience. What's this new information on my father's death?"

Mama crossed one pearlescently sheathed leg over the other. "It appears that the gunmen were holograms."

Printout dropped back to the desk. "What!"

Janna bit her lip. If Sydney were acting, she deserved an award. Her double take was perfect. Could she not be involved after all?

"That's impossible! The jon who fired at my father came within less than two meters of me. At that distance—"

"On the news chips from Friday night they had no shadows," Janna interrupted. "One appeared to step on a wine glass, but it didn't break. Their tuxedos all have an identical stain."

Sydney sat back looking stunned. In the silence, the newscanner reported Uwezo, the African megacorp, up by eight and a half on the Tokyo exchange.

"How high *is* the image quality of Konza's new Magus-1 projector?" Mama asked.

She shrugged, shook her head, spread her hands. "Good, but . . . nothing like . . ." Her voice trailed off. A second later, she continued in a thoughtful tone, "Its image isn't *that* good. Unfortunately." She picked up the printout and resumed reading it.

Janna leaned forward. What happened in that pause? "You've thought of something?"

"Not really." Sydney flipped through the fanfold sheets to a new section . . . raised a brow . . . turned to the computer and pushed keys. "It just occurred to me that prerecording this action

of firing at my father and jumping back in surprise proves pre-
meditation beyond any doubt.''

That might have been her thought. It sounded reasonable,
except . . . instinct in Janna sang: lie! Protecting herself? Or
Junior? That would fit with asking Edmiston about her brother.

"Son of a bitch!" Sydney glared at the screen. "That isn't
shrinkage; that's mismanagement. Tomorrow I'll have you for
lunch, you incompetent toad!" With an abrupt shift of attention,
she focused back on them. "Ah . . . do you know who the
originals of the holos are?"

A casual tone. Too casual? Janna watched her. Lines around
Sydney's mouth suggested tension.

"We know," Mama said.

Sydney raised her brows. Waiting for him to go on? After a
few moments, the brows came down. She picked up her coffee
mug. "Then . . . you have some idea who made the holos?"

Definitely tension. Janna caught Mama's eye. Did he see, too?
"I'm afraid we're not free to discuss that right now."

The other woman eyed them a moment, then smiled. "Meaning you don't have the slightest idea." She leaned back, sipping
her coffee. Tension gone. Relieved? "There's nothing more I
can do to help you, then. If I knew where to find the person
responsible for those holos, I'd be out there negotiating a license
to manufacture his projector."

"Or hers," Mama said.

Sydney straightened. The newscanner quoted stock prices in
Manilla, Beijing, and Tokyo.

Prickles ran down Janna's spine. She glanced at Mama, wishing for telepathy. What was he thinking? Something good. That
comment had touched a nerve.

Sydney stood. "If you have no more questions, I'll let you
out."

Mama pushed his glasses up his nose. "As a matter of fact,
I do have another question or two." He smiled. "Tell us about
Lesandra Santos."

The name triggered memory with a jolt. Janna swore at herself
for being so slow. Of course! That lawsuit filed against Armenord
. . . a female employee at Konza Holotronics suing over ownership of a miniaturized projector. A miniaturized holo projector,
maybe?

"How good were the images from *her* projector?" Mama asked.

Sydney sat down again, mouth tight. "As I said, talking to you two is like walking in our grounds at night." She took a breath. "I don't know much about Santos. I never met her. At the time I was following the Grand Prix circuit with the Porsche team, convinced I loved Dieter Weiss. So I don't know what her projector could do, either, except that it impressed the hell out of my father."

"He'd seen a demonstration?" Janna asked.

"So to speak." Sydney arranged the stacks of printout parallel with the edge of the desk. The action reminded Janna of Mama. "One night on his way out after going over books with the new Konza company manager he noticed lights on in a workroom. When he went to investigate, he walked in on a test of the projector. C.J. told me he came home raving about it. Then he asked the company manager about the projector's production schedule and found out it didn't belong to Konza. The former owner let employees use some company space for private projects, providing they worked on their own time and paid a modest space and tool rental and for materials. In return, Konza received first refusal on production of the results, and I understand gave a good deal when it did buy." Sydney shook her head. "Dad should have done that. Look what we might have had."

Mama leaned forward. "He claimed that because she used company facilities for the work, Konza owned the projector?"

"Once in a while greed gets—" She caught herself. "—got in the way of my father's business sense. She filed suit, then later dropped it and handed over the plans. I don't know why; I think she could have made a good case. She quit her job, so she'd left before I came to my senses and left Dieter to his glitter girls."

Janna straightened in her chair. "You just said you don't have the projector."

"We don't." Sydney smiled wryly. "When we built the Magus-1 according to those plans, we had a tiny projector with only a slightly better image. My father went after the true plans, of course, but Santos had disappeared. She moved with no forwarding address. She changed banks. He couldn't bribe anyone for the name of the new bank and the courts wouldn't issue a warrant because he had no proof she'd given him altered plans. They matched the description of the projector as stated in the lawsuit. He couldn't even trace her through background information; her personnel file had vanished from the computer.''

"He never found her?" Mama asked.

"He gave up the hunt. Looking only kept her in hiding, he said. If he appeared to forget about her, however, she'd surface to sell the projector somewhere else. Then . . ." Her hands closed.

"You didn't hunt for her on your own?" Mama gave her a teasing smile. "That would have been quite a prize to bring home to him."

Sydney frowned. "Yes." She sighed. "Only I couldn't believe the projector was as good as he thought. He'd seen it operate just once, after all, and then late at—" She broke off, stiffening. "It's late now, too. I'm tired of playing your lion games. If you believe I found her and saw her holos and then decided to arrange—"

Janna gave her a thin smile. "We were wondering about your brother. You are, aren't you?"

Sydney stood and padded for the door. "Good night, Sergeants."

After letting them out the front door, she stood in the opening watching them slide into Mama's little runabout. As the MGE started, she called over the whine of the fans, "If you find Santos, let me know. I'll give her whatever she wants for the projector."

Janna shook her head in disbelief. "Santos is at least an accessory in Armenda's murder and the only thing about her that concerns his daughter is the projector." People never failed to astonish her.

Mama steered the MGE down the drive. "The priorities of business, bibi." He grinned.

Which made Janna wonder: maybe Sydney's relief a while ago had been less for her brother than because she thought she had a head start hunting Santos. Janna twisted to look back at the house. "It's too bad you didn't drop a contact lens outside the study window so we could learn if she's calling the pleasure palaces to ask Junior if he knows where to find Santos."

The car slowed. Mama glanced back at the house, too.

Considering the idea? Panic flared in her. "Mama, I'm only kidding!"

Ahead, the gate slid aside. To her relief, he sailed on through. She sighed. "So . . . back to K.C. tomorrow."

"Actually," Mama said in a bright tone that sent warning reverberations through Janna, "I thought we might head that way tonight."

"Tonight!" She sat up against the safety harness. "Mama, don't you think we ought to sleep sometime? We probably can't find those slighs before morning anyway. What difference will a few hours make? Besides, we need to tell Vradel and Cruz about the holos anyway."

"I was thinking of leaving them a note when we pick up the Meteor."

She snorted. "They'd love that. 'Dear Boss, the riffers are only holos; we're taking a field trip at our own instigation and will explain everything on our return.' No, Mama; let's not do that."

Riding east on the turnpike through the starry darkness, Janna reflected that she should know better than try telling Mama *no*. At least they left a full report, with Lieutenant Candarian reading avidly over their shoulders at the dictyper. That also meant that technically, a superior officer knew their whereabouts and activities, although the net effect would probably be the same as if they left only a note.

"We'd better bring home something good." She lay back her head and closed her eyes. Now was the time to rest. Once they reached K.C. and she swallowed one of the stimulants she bought at the Lion's Den on their way out of town, she would not be able to.

"Do you really think Junior's behind this, bibi?"

She sighed. Resting, unfortunately, depended on muffling the noise of Mama's mental wheels. Without opening her eyes she said, "Sydney seems to, and she knows him better than we do. He goes hunting Santos, sees the quality of the holos, and suddenly has this stroke of inspiration . . . he can be rid of Daddy harping at him and have even more money to play with."

"Why would he hunt Santos? I could see Sydney hoping to impress her father, but Junior didn't have that problem."

She settled deeper into her seat, lulled by the drone of the fans and rush of air past the car. "Maybe he went looking after the plot occurred to him."

"How would the idea occur unless he'd seen the quality of the holos?"

"His father told him."

"Armenda told Sydney, too, and she didn't believe they could be that good."

"So she says now."

"If she believed it, why wasn't she hunting Santos to bring the holos home to Daddy?"

Janna opened her eyes. "You don't like Junior for it?"

The glow from headlights in the westbound lanes silhouetted his shrug. "Casting him as the villain feels . . . weak."

What made a weak motive? People killed each other over separating the trash and forgetting to put down the toilet seat.

Exhaustion pulled her eyes closed again. The sounds of the car and wind wrapped around her, shutting out the world and pulling her down into warm darkness.

Some time later Mama's voice broke into a dream in which she chased red-tuxedoed gunmen down winding alleys, only to have each turn to smoke as she caught him. "We're almost there, bibi."

She struggled up in her seat. They came over a hill and down around a sweeping curve. Kansas City spread out in a glittering panorama along the bottomland below and up over the hills across the river. At this time of night, almost no traffic moved. They sailed alone through the yellow glow of the lights above the freeway.

In the city proper, they met little more traffic either swinging by headquarters to leave a message with the morning watch for Diosdado, or visiting the Central Division—a sleek structure of glass and stone replacing one leveled by a bomb fifteen years earlier. Lights shone down on deserted streets. The peace was an illusion, however, Janna knew.

After announcing their presence and business at the Central station, they headed for the River Quay. Mama circled the dark cave of the city market, then set the Meteor down on a side street. There they settled in to wait for their slighs.

Janna closed her eyes.

Mama said, "I've been thinking."

His tone of voice left Janna with no doubt he intended to discuss those thoughts. That left her with two possibilities: gag him, or let him talk.

She opened her eyes and groped in her breast pocket for the waker tablets. What did sleep matter? Sometimes his blue sky came solidly down to earth . . . and she did want to break this case, after all. "Thinking about what?"

"It's a who. Santos." The only working streetlight stood at the far end of the block. In the dim light it cast in the car, Mama frowned. "My mind keeps circling back to her. Bibi, why are we assuming she's involved because Junior or someone else dragged her and her projector in? Armenda's attempt to claim the projector gives her reason of her own to hate him, and no one knows the quality of the holos better than she does." He paused. "The height of the average woman is considered small in a man."

The last drowsiness vanished. Janna sat up straight. Santos in a mustache could be their small jon? An interesting idea . . . except for one fact. "Mama, Armenda didn't get the projector. She made a fool of him. From what we've heard about Armenda, that should put the most hate on his side. Or . . ." She turned toward him in her seat. ". . . do you think she'd kill him thinking that would free her to sell the projector elsewhere."

He shook his head. "There's no reason for that. In her place I'd just take the projector to another company and after showing them the holos, I'd tell the whole story and invite them to fight for the projector. Considering the facts of the case, the quality of the holos, and the free publicity the trial would bring, I'm betting they'd gamble on winning." He drummed his fingers on the steering wheel. "It's been two years, though, and in that time she apparently hasn't tried to sell the projector anywhere else. Why not?"

Janna had no trouble seeing what he thought the answer was. Another occurred to her. "Maybe she didn't think of your marketing strategy. I have a hard time imagining someone spending two years planning to kill someone she'd already made a fool of."

A watchcar passed them. At the intersection it made a U-turn. Mama ran down his window and put his arm out, badge case dangling from his hand.

The watchcar slowed to a hover beside them anyway, but as soon as he had established their reason for being there he grinned—"I saw about that fund-raiser riff on the newscanner. I don't envy you with castlerows breathing down your necks. Good luck."—and drove on.

They resumed waiting, and debating. None of it led anywhere.

The stars to the east had only begun to fade when the first trucks pulled in under the domes. She and Mama strolled down to the market and stood just inside one of the archways. More trucks arrived.

Janna quickly understood Mama's collegiate fascination with the place. Silence gave way to the thrum of truck fans. Lights appeared . . . battery lamps set on the hoods of trucks, on chairs and stacks of crates. In the cavernous darkness the first ones looked futile, pinpoints in a void, but as more lights appeared, the darkness became mottled by pools of light. In them, shadowy figures pulled crates and baskets from the backs of the trucks. Voices called out, laughed, occasionally swore. It all felt vaguely surreal.

More figures appeared from the darkness outside to help unload.

Janna nudged Mama. "Slighs."

He nodded. "Let's go."

They left the arch to head for the area where they saw their slighs on Thursday.

One of the farmers smoked a pipe while he worked. Its fragrant smoke curled around Janna as she passed. Passing another stall, she smelled hot caff. The scent set her stomach growling.

Then, ahead in a fan of light from a cordless fluorescent lamp sitting on the hood of a truck, Janna spotted carrot-red hair pulled back in a ponytail.

Mama called, "Hello, Dragon."

The sligh turned with the basket he had taken from the back of the truck behind the stall. Annoyance twisted his face. "You again?" Janna thought he also eyed the pearly white of Mama's bodysuit, visible beneath the open trench coat, with a touch of envy before setting down the basket and returning to the truck for another.

She leaned against the truck. "Us again. But this time it's a friendly visit."

He snorted. "Just what I need. Molidor will be back in a few minutes and expects the truck to be unloaded." Another basket of cucumbers joined the four already on the ground.

"Go ahead and work. All we need to know is when the holo recording of you was made."

Dragon stacked two baskets on top of each other and brought

them over with the others. "If this is 'friendly,' tell me why you want to know and give me one good reason for answering."

Janna frowned. A nice problem. They could hardly appeal to their friendship or his sense of civic duty.

Mama said, "I'll give you two reasons for answering. One, it won't harm you or any other sligh. Two, talk to us and I'll give you the suit I'm wearing."

The flare of yearning in Dragon's eyes reminded Janna with a jolt of a fact so easy to forget, that although forced by necessity to dress simply, even poorly, slighs could like expensive clothes, too. "Here, this morning?"

Mama nodded. "We'll find a place and trade clothes."

Dragon eyed Mama's bodysuit. "Which recording do you want to know about?"

Janna started. There had been more than one?

A quick glance at Mama caught his scalp crinkling. Surprised, too. He recovered almost instantly, however, and smiled at the sligh. "The recording with you in a red tuxedo."

Dragon sighed. "You've seen it? I'd like to. I thought we looked top dink. We spent the whole session taking turns in it and the mustache and wig, waving the needler around. Leo said, 'Even deeks dink up. Have fun. Pretend you're facing a legislator who advocates mandatory identation.' "

Leo? Janna sent another glance at Mama. That name had not come up before. Who was he, the tall man?

Mama remained focused on the sligh. "You did appear to enjoy being menacing. When was that?"

"Last month." He continued hauling baskets from the truck.

"And when did you first meet Leo?"

The sligh thought a moment. "Last summer. July sometime."

"Tell us about it."

Dragon grunted. "There isn't much to tell. Tsunami, Rebel, and I were playing Deathrace in the Waterloo Club with some vending tokens we'd gotten for collecting bottles and cans and this bibi challenged Tsunami to a game. She beat him, too, but then bought us all drinks and asked if we'd like to earn better carry than tokens. Of course we said sure. When she took us upstairs to one of the bedrooms I thought it was kinks time; she had lights and a camera and mirror set up. But she explained that all we had to do was follow some commands like point an unloaded needler and pretend to be shooting someone."

Electricity shot up Janna's spine. They had not met a man after all? "You mean the bibi is Leo?"

"Yeah." The sligh's quirked brows said: *of course*.

Excitement seeped up through her. "Is Leo short for Lesandra?"

Dragon blinked. "Lesandra?" He snickered. "Hell, no. You of all people ought to know what it's short for."

The connection came almost as he finished the sentence, plunging her into confusion. "A she-lion recorded you?" How could that be?

"Yeah." Dragon shuffled the cucumber baskets into a neat grouping. "She works in research and development. That's what the holos are for, a shoot/don't shoot training course. So if you want to know about it, why ask me? You ought to be talking to your lion buddies."

SIXTEEN

Questions churned in Janna's head. The holos were part of a police training program? Recorded by a she-lion? Then how had they ended up being shown from Santos' projector?

She caught Mama's eye. They needed to discuss this.

Just then a black van halted in front of the stall and set down. Janna stared at the woman who slid from behind the wheel . . . a study in black and white . . . black jumpsuit and black needle-heeled boots, white hands and face, sooty eyes and lips, a flat helmet of ebony hair. She bent down to feel the cucumbers. "What's your price per bushel?"

The mundane question turned an exotic creature into a mere customer. Janna lost interest . . . and discovered that the distraction had cleared her head. She sighed in displeasure at herself. Stimulants and the lack of sleep must be scrambling her brain. Explaining Santos's possession of the holos presented no problem if she and Leo were the same person. This might be where she disappeared. Which could also be the reason she had not tried selling the projector anywhere; using her holos for noncommercial projects like this would avoid attracting Armenda's attention.

Too bad they had no description of Santos. When they went back to Topeka, she would make sure they obtained one.

A gray-haired man in russet coveralls hurried around the front end of the truck. Molidor, Janna guessed. He frowned at Mama and her, and at Dragon, before switching on a smile he directed at the black-and-white woman.

Mama caught Janna's eye and gestured sideways with his head. "This jon doesn't look like the kind to pay off a sligh while people are watching." He whispered something to Dragon and left the stall.

Janna followed.

They moved slowly along the row and a short time later Dragon caught up, a paper bag with the top rolled shut tucked under one arm. Seeing them, his expression went from tense to relieved. "You meant it about waiting for me." The relief stripped the cockiness from him, leaving him looking young and vulnerable.

"We haven't forgotten our deal." Janna moved to one side to let a late-arriving truck pass. "But let's talk more first. What does Leo look like?"

"Small, dark eyes, dark hair down to her shoulders. Not flash, but not dog meat, either." The swagger came back into his walk. "I wouldn't have minded putting two with her but she only cared about her project. I told you, if you want to know about her, ask the leos."

"That's hard without knowing who to ask about," Mama said. "What's her name?"

Dragon shrugged. "She never gave it. Calling her Leo was good enough, she said."

The hair prickled on Janna's neck. "You mean she never showed you any identification? She only *told* you she was with the KCPD?" Leo could very well be Santos, and not in the department at all.

"You think I'd just take someone's word for that?" Dragon's lip curled. "We already knew about her when she came up to us. She didn't tell us; we told her, and she admitted she worked in research."

Mama asked, "How did you know?"

A carrot-red brow arched. "You see someone in watchcars all the time and coming into the clubs after the shift with lions, it's obvious."

Janna exchanged glances with Mama. Someone from R & D working on patrol? That seemed unlikely.

Mama toyed with one sleeve cuff. "Think of a place we can

use for trading clothes. You said she came into the clubs with other lions. Do you know any of their names?''

The sligh stopped short, forcing the driver of a restaurant van to swerve around them, shouting curses. Dragon glared at Mama. ''You can keep your damn suit. I just figured out what this is about. You aren't from Topeka after all. You're from Internal Affairs!'' He folded his arms around the bag of cucumbers. ''She's in trouble for using slighs, isn't she? Well, you go to hell! I'm not going to help you persecute her. She treated us like human beings. All of us will swear she didn't buy us clothes or anything else; we're volunteer labor. She came to us because the department didn't believe in her idea and wouldn't give her a decent budget to develop it.''

After such a passionate defense, Janna hated having to disillusion him. She handed her ID to him. ''Study that. We aren't KCPD and we aren't peeps.''

Mama said, ''I'm glad she treated you well. But she may also have killed Carel Armenda and tried to make it look as though your friend Tsunami did it.''

''That's a lie!'' Vendors and customers turned to look at them. He lowered his voice. ''I don't believe it.''

Janna took back her ID. ''We're looking for the person who killed Armenda. If Leo didn't, what can it hurt talking to her friends?''

''And the deal for the suit still stands,'' Mama said.

Dragon stared back and forth from one of them to the other. More hotel and restaurant vans passed them. Gradually, his scowl gave way to uncertainty. He sighed, and with obvious reluctance, said, ''I don't know their full names. All I see is what's on the name tags. But the one Leo rides with more than the others is a she-lion named Hazelton.''

They took the information to Diosdado.

His initial start on finding them at his desk when he came on duty turned to amusement on seeing the baggy jumpsuit Mama wore. A grin spread across the Greek-god face. ''Oversized neopioneer ersatz homespun is a new fashion statement for you, isn't it?''

Mama sipped the caff he had poured himself from the squad room pot. ''Always expect the unexpected from me.''

"It was the only thing in the used clothes stall at the city market in his sleeve and pant length," Janna said.

Lucky for them that one jon sold clothes alongside his herbs and spices. Dragon's jumpsuit had looked ridiculous, falling better than twenty centimeters short of reaching Mama's ankles and wrists. The sligh probably did not have so much to wear that he could afford to give up clothes appropriate for working in anyway.

"I hesitate to ask what happened to the clothes you presumably wore to Kansas City." Diosdado flipped up his phone screen and punched numbers on the keypad. Text rolled up the screen.

Sitting on the edge of the desk where she could look over his shoulder, Janna saw a list of cases, status, related persons and incidents, ATL's, warrants. "This is your morning briefing?"

"An anytime briefing." He tapped a number and stopped the text . . . made a note . . . let the text roll on. "The computer is constantly updating. Depending on the code I punch in, it selects for items relevant to Robbery, Homicide, or whatever, and items flagged as of general importance. Like this alert for a seventy-nine Cadillac Tracer. The vehicle, in the Denholm Body Shop for repair of damages from a hit-and-run on Friday was . . ." He paused, blinking, then grinned. "Breakers stole it during a burglary of the shop last night. They rammed the vehicle through the garage door and into a building and light pole across the street before escaping. I'm glad I didn't have to break the news to that owner." He cleared the screen. "So, what brings you to civilization this time?"

They told him.

The puckish brows bounced as Diosdado listened. "Tony was the only real perpetrator in the room?" He snickered. "One unarmed jon and a waitron riffed all those people?"

"And killed Armenda," Janna reminded him.

Diosdado sobered. "Right. So . . . you need Santos checked against our personnel file."

Mama finished his caff. "She did say she was in R & D, and development of an improved shoot/don't shoot program isn't a story you'd think would occur to the average civilian."

"You wouldn't think so." The K.C. detective punched a number into the phone. "While we don't have a research section as such, there are people attached to Information and Communications who can be considered in that category."

A female face appeared on the phone screen. "Personnel."
Diosdado talked to her. The face vanished.

He leaned back, face thoughtful. "Partying and riding along
with leos isn't your typical murderer-to-be behavior, either."

Janna agreed. That part puzzled her.

"Though if you need a thief," Mama said, "what better way
to locate one than make friends with people who can point them
out?"

Diosdado frowned. "Maybe. And maybe the number of recordings she's made could be to make sure she had images
appropriate for whatever occasion she found for killing Armenda.
However, it also fits with development of this kind of program
. . . and riding along is a logical way to collect scenarios for it.
So Leo could be legitimate." He grimaced. "It would be embarrassing as hell if she were, though, and we let our program
leak to a murderer."

The face reappeared. "We have a number of females named
Santos, but no Lesandra Santos, among either sworn or non-
sworn personnel."

"Try the name Hazelton. A female officer, uniformed division, assigned to Central."

The face looked off to her right. Shortly she said, "We have
a Donna Hazelton in Central."

Janna grabbed her notebook from her thigh boot and scribbled
down the name. "May we have her address and phone number,
too, please?"

The face read it off.

After Diosdado disconnected, Janna tapped the notebook with
satisfaction. "Now maybe we'll get somewhere."

"Farther than you think," Diosdado said. "If Leo isn't
with the department, she's riding along as a civilian, and that
can't be done without giving a name and other verifiable information."

Janna's pulse jumped. She leaned toward him. "Then she's
on record?"

He nodded. "Would someone with a guilty conscience allow
that? Could she?"

Mama pushed his glasses up his nose. "Right now I think
we're more interested in what happens to the information ride-
alongs give about themselves. Is it in the computer?"

Diosdado grinned. "Everything's in the computer." He

reached for his phone again. "There's a card the ride-along fills out that stays at the division station, but the information is fed into Records here. What do we want to know besides determining if a Lesandra Santos has been riding along?"

Mama galloped around the desk to where he could see the screen. "All the information possible on her."

But when Diosdado had punched in and recited all the necessary codes, and given the computer the search instructions, the screen flashed: NO CATEGORY ONE SEARCHES IN THIS FILE. CAT TWO?

Diosdado sighed. "Shit."

Janna stared at the message in exasperation. "What's this?"

"Files containing data the administration feels is unlikely to be urgently needed are locked out of priority searches so that time can be given to more important files." He stabbed the "2" button.

THANK YOU.

Amazing how two printed words could look so smug. "What's the wait for category two?"

He grimaced. "It might be faster checking the cards at the division station. Why don't you go ahead and contact Hazelton? Check back here later. I'll make sure that if the information comes in and I'm away from my desk, it'll still be passed on to you."

Janna used the phone to punch in the number Personnel had given her.

No one answered.

"Call Central Division," Mama said. "See when she'll be on duty."

A face at Central informed them Donna Hazelton was currently on duty.

"Will you have her call Sergeant Janna Brill in Robbery, please?" Janna asked. She gave Diosdado's number. After punching off, she sighed. "Now what? I hate sitting around waiting."

"Don't we all." Diosdado pushed to his feet. "They didn't tell us how much of it there'd be when we signed up. I wouldn't mind waiting with you now, though; this case is full of surprises. However . . ." He plucked two folders out of his IN basket. ". . . the captain holds the unreasonable view that I should be working on Kansas City cases. So I'll see you later." He brushed a kiss past Janna's mouth. "We'll think of ways for you to express your gratitude for all my assistance."

She stared after him, thighs tingling.

Behind her, Mama said dryly, "Have a cup of caff and cool off, bibi."

On her way back from the squad pot, Diosdado's phone buzzed. Mama punched on. Janna scrambled to peer over his shoulder.

A pleasant afroam face with a copper complexion looked out of the screen at them. "Sergeant Brill?"

"Sergeant Maxwell," he replied. "But we both want to talk to you." He held his ID to the lens at the base of the screen. "We're looking for information on a civilian woman who's ridden along with you. Small, dark hair and eyes. We believe her name may be Santos."

Janna held her breath.

Hazelton nodded. "Yes. Lesandra Santos. She's ridden with me a number of times. What do you want to know?"

Janna restrained an impulse to whoop and turn cartwheels. She did move out of the phone's range and raise clasped hands above her head. Confirmed . . . Leo was Santos!

"Where we can reach her." Mama's voice and expression remained matter-of-fact. "We'd like to talk to her."

Hazelton's voice brightened. "About her shoot/don't shoot program?"

From behind the phone, Janna tried to catch Mama's eye. So Santos used the story on everyone.

Mama kept his gaze on the phone screen. "We're interested in it, yes."

Janna straightened, frowning. Why answer that way instead of telling her the situation? "Mama," she began.

He ignored her. "What can you tell us about it?"

"That this program will null you." Enthusiasm bubbled in the she-lion's voice. "Lessa can give you all the details but basically it revolves around having a whole population of images available, any one of which may be projected from any station along the route of the shoot/don't shoot course. So the choices are infinite and never the same twice. And with the quality of these holos, holos like you've never seen before, believe me, you won't find a more realistic training exercise without using actual people."

Mama pushed his glasses up his nose. "I take it you've seen the program?"

A chuckle came from the phone. "Some of the images. One week end Lessa was staying with me and—"

"Staying with you?" Mama interrupted. "She doesn't live in the area?"

"No . . . in Topeka."

Topeka! Janna sucked in her lower lip. Santos had broken her trail by changing apartments and banks but never left the city? Interesting. Suggestive.

"I came home from my shift that night and a man armed with a knife lunged out of my kitchen at me. I had no time to go for a weapon, just throw my coat over the knife arm to foul it and jump aside. It was only when the coat fell through the arm to the floor that I realized he was a hologram. Even when she replayed the holo and I had time to study it, he looked real. I helped her set up similar tests on other officers." Glee crackled in her voice. Janna recognized the delight leos took in pulling practical jokes on each other. "None of them realized it was a holo until afterward, either. They each thought they had become involved in an actual situation. Can you see the potential for not just 'fun house' runs but training exercises in the field?"

What Janna saw was a terrible waste. Listening, she had found herself responding to Hazelton's enthusiasm. To remember that no such program existed, that Santos had squandered all that imagination and skill on murder, flooded Janna with disappointment and anger. Especially anger.

She scribbled: ADDRESS! on a notepad from Diosdado's desk and held the page above the phone screen. "Mama!"

This time he responded. His chin dipped. "It sounds exciting. However, it'll be difficult for us to see unless we contact Ms. Santos."

Hazelton's voice went apologetic. "Yes . . . sorry. I get carried away. I . . . can't tell you myself how to reach her. I'd think she'd be in the Topeka book."

Except Santos was not, Janna remembered. Not under her own name. Zavara and Threefoxes had already checked.

"But as long as you're here, contact Frank Grauer in Metro Division. He knows her best. She usually stays with him when she's in town."

* * *

Metro provided Grauer's address and phone number, and the information that he worked the night watch. When they called his number, a square face came on the phone screen with the fixed expression typical of a recorded response and recited a standard message. They declined to leave one of their own. Instead, they drove to his address, a brick house east of the UMKC campus, and parked across the street to wait for him.

While they waited, they checked Santos's name against the printout of '77 Triton owners they had been carrying around in the car since Miranda Liliedahl in Records obtained it for them. But of all the Santoses listed, none had the name Lesandra.

Janna hissed in frustration. "Where does that damn car come from?"

"We'll find it, bibi." Mama slid down in the driver's seat until his head rested against the back. "Lord, this street brings back memories. I lived two blocks from here when I was in college. A friend of mine roomed in the basement of that house on the corner."

He launched into a story about the friend but Janna did not listen. Sitting here felt a bit like a stakeout . . . an uncomfortable sensation given that they waited for a fellow leo. She found herself brooding, too, over how to approach Grauer. Asking questions without saying why they needed the information treated him no better than an average citizen.

"Why didn't you tell Hazelton the truth?"

Mama glanced sideways at her. "You think we should have explained the situation?"

"Didn't she deserve that courtesy? She's one of us and Santos lied to her. Santos betrayed her!"

He regarded her calmly. "We don't know that for certain . . . and would you talk to a couple of out-of-town lions who, with no proof to give you, claimed over the phone that someone you believe in used you in planning a murder?"

He might have a point. "Are we going to tell Grauer?"

"You decide." Mama closed his eyes. "You can talk to him."

She did not have long to think about it. Five minutes later a car rolled up the street and turned onto the steep driveway beside Grauer's house. She slapped Mama's shoulder on her way out of the Meteor. "A wheeler!"

He jerked upright.

Even with her head start, he managed to be on her heels by the time she reached the top of the driveway.

The coupe pulled into the garage attached to the house. Before the automatic door could close behind it, Janna called, "Good morning!"

The driver's door slid back. A broad-shouldered jon Janna's height swung out, the expression on his square face wary. That eased when she and Mama stopped well short of the garage and stood with hands at their sides, away from their trench coat pockets. A moment later his face relaxed. Spotting the subtle distinctions in movement and body carriage which stamped them as fellow officers?

"Good morning." Gravel rolled in his voice. He leaned back into the car to bring out a bag of groceries.

Janna strolled on toward the garage, holding out her ID. "I'm Janna Brill, Shawnee County PD. This is my partner, Mahlon Maxwell. That's quite an antique. What kind of car is it?"

"A Twenty-one Dodge Kobold."

"In original condition, it looks like," Mama said.

Grauer ran his free hand back along the top, smiling at the vehicle. "Aside from an electric motor out of a '57 Hurricane, yes." With a final pat on the top, he focused back on them. "What can I do for you?"

Her thoughts those last few minutes waiting for Grauer came rushing back to mind. Time to decide. Could she tell him the truth and still receive cooperation? Or was it better to be honest whatever the result? In his place, she would resent not being told.

She gave him a smile. "You might help a friend of yours. We're with our Crimes Against Persons squad. Lesandra Santos may be in trouble. If you have any information establishing her innocence, we need to know it."

Behind her, Mama murmured, "Nice approach."

Grauer's expression went wary again. "Innocence in what?"

"Murder."

Gray eyes stared into her for several seconds, expressionless, then he wheeled away. "Come inside."

Steps led up from the garage. The door at the top unlocked in response to the tones from the sonic key Grauer pulled from his jacket pocket, opening into a roomy kitchen. Another set of tones brought the garage door humming down.

"I'm home!"

A light flickered below the keypad and monitor screen on a panel built in between the refrigerator and microwave oven. A voice said, "Alarm disengaged. Shall I reset?"

"No." Grauer opened the refrigerator and began putting in items from the grocery bag. "Report."

"There have been no visitors. There was one phone call but the caller did not leave a message. The faucet in the upstairs bathroom is dripping. Shall I activate the newscanner?"

"No."

"I didn't know that housekeeper model comes with voice activation," Mama said, glancing around the kitchen.

"Les—" Grauer glanced over his shoulder at them. "I had it added."

By Lesandra Santos, Janna bet.

Grauer closed the refrigerator and turned around. "What's this about Lessa?"

A magazine called *International Horse* lay on the table. Janna pushed it to one side and sat down on the table edge. "A week ago Friday and Saturday, armed men riffed the Democratic and Humanitarian fund-raisers. A Topeka businessman, Carel Armenda, died during the second robbery."

"I heard about that." He leaned against the countertop. "How is Lessa implicated?"

"We've discovered that six of the seven men were holograms. Holograms Santos recorded—we've talked to the slighs who posed for her—and played back through a projector she developed at a company where she worked for the dead man." Briefly, Janna explained the situation with the projector.

Except for a start at mention of the holos, Grauer listened without expression, and without speaking, his arms folded. Only when Janna stopped talking did he ask, "How do you know these gunmen were holos?"

She explained the findings on the news chip. "And three of the slighs have alibis for Friday."

"Fortunately," Grauer said, "so does Lessa . . . for both Friday and Saturday. She spent the week end here." He crossed to a cupboard and put away the cans and cartons still in the grocery bag. "I picked her up at Municipal Airport Friday noon and put her back on the airship Sunday afternoon. In between she spent all her time with me, except during my duty shifts those nights and when she took my niece with her out making more recordings."

Mama picked up the magazine and opened it. "How did she happen to take your niece?"

"Brin asked to go along. She lives here; she adopted me after divorcing her mother, my sister."

Janna felt as though the floor had been jerked from beneath her. Santos spent those nights here? And came up by airship? She swore silently. Every good suspect in this case could produce a damn documented alibi!

Mama flipped through the magazine. "Santos always comes by airship?"

"More often by bus. She buys one-month passes." Grauer looked around. "Occasionally she indulges herself, though."

Suddenly Janna felt better. The tickman had sent Tony a one-month pass. How fortunate that Santos "indulged herself" on the one week end when the airship's passenger list and recording of boarding passengers would provide incontrovertible proof of her coming and going. Taking the girl along struck Janna the same way . . . convenient. As though Santos wanted to make sure she had someone to swear to her whereabouts. Had the girl really asked to go along, or had Santos managed to make it seem that way?

Excitement rose in Janna. Suppose Santos were the tickman . . . had planned everything, given her accomplices—Aschke and the small jon—what they needed, and sat back safe in her alibi while they carried out her dirty work.

"How does she haul her equipment around town?" Mama laid down the magazine. "Surely not on a city bus."

"She uses my car," Grauer said.

Really. Janna exchanged glances with Mama. A car could take Santos to Topeka without the inconvenience of commercial schedules or drivers who might remember her.

The same thought obviously occurred to Grauer as well. He went on, "She never drove it to Topeka. I always check my odometer readings when I get into the car. She drove less than thirty klicks each night."

Besides which, the car was not a Triton and Santos had companionship those evenings. Allegedly. "We'll need to talk to your niece, I'm afraid . . . and to Santos, of course. Do you have her address and phone number?"

"Of course, but it's on the paperwork she filled out for riding along."

"We would have taken it from there," Janna said, grimacing, "except your records computer is in no hurry to tell us."

Grauer sighed and nodded. "Housekeeper! Address search. Lesandra Santos."

"Searching." A short time later the housekeeper announced, "Lesandra Santos," and recited an address and phone number.

Janna wrote them in her notebook.

Grauer eyed her. "That's her home phone, best reached during the day. She works nights." Impatience flickered in his eyes and around the edges of his voice. "Look, I can see why Lessa's under suspicion, but isn't it a little difficult to believe that someone planning to use holos in a murder would spend a year and a half openly making recordings and telling everyone in sight what she's doing? Not to mention spending her days off running around with lions."

The response Mama made to Diosdado's similar comment came back to Janna. She repeated it. "If you're looking for a thief, though, don't you make friends with people who know where to find one?"

Grauer's mouth thinned. "She's never asked me to point out a thief."

Probably she never needed to. Listening to the conversation between any two or more lions as they watched the passing public would give her information enough.

"Did she ever ask about criminals who use disguises as part of their M.O.?" Mama asked.

"No!" Grauer scowled. "I think what's happened is that someone she knows here or in Topeka heard her talking and got the bright idea of using her holos."

The kitchen chair creaked as Mama leaned back, hands behind his head. "That's possible, yes. How long have you known her?"

"We met at a party in August or September two years ago." Grauer leaned against the counter, folding his arms. "She came with another Metro officer. We got to talking, liked each other, and she started coming down week ends to ride along with me."

"She's a lion buff?"

Irritation flickered across his face. "She was curious about the job. Then listening to some of us talk one night about training programs and the required annual 'fun house' run, she came up with this idea for the shoot/don't shoot program. In a way, her interest is professional since her job is private security."

Electricity shot up Janna's spine. At the corner of her vision, she saw Mama start, too, then go glass-eyed. Private security! "Did she tell you what agency?"

Grauer nodded. "Beria Security."

Beria! Janna clamped down on her urge to warwhoop. Connections! Aschke had to be their tall man. Everything was starting to fall into place.

"Everything about her is on record," Grauer said.

Mama looked up. "Maybe not everything. She goes by Lesandra Santos here, is that right?"

Grauer frowned. "Yes," he said slowly.

"She uses another given name at Beria."

Grauer's shrug dismissed that. "So? There's nothing sinister in that. It's her real first name, I expect. She told me she doesn't use it because she hates it, but she might use it there, to keep Armenda from finding her."

"Oh, I expect so. However . . ." Mama pushed his glasses up his nose, and focused on Janna. ". . . I do wonder why a person with a clear conscience introduced herself to us—"

"To us!" Janna stared at him. They had not met Santos. The only small, dark haired bibi they met was—

"—with a different last name as well."

Sandoz.

Through the dizzy clamor of thoughts in her head she heard Mama explain his comment to Grauer, and the K.C. leo's angry, "They're almost the same. You probably just misheard."

Had they? No. Thinking back carefully, she heard the voice again. *I'm Karis Sandoz.* Sandoz, clearly with a *d* and a *z*. *Karis Sandoz. That's Karis with a K.* God forbid, Listra Wassman had said, they should think the name had a *Ch* and was short for Charisma. A name hated by a number of the girls who bore it, including this one who, Janna suddenly recalled with dismay, was quitting her job at Beria this week in preparation for leaving for Mars.

SEVENTEEN

A fastener shaped like a stirrup held the chestnut hair back in a ponytail. A gold horse, arched in a jump with rainbow mane and tail flying, decorated one breast pocket of an otherwise plain blue shirt and breeches. Grauer's niece looked up at them from the chair beside the assistant principal's desk, hands folded in her lap, knee-booted legs crossed at the ankles and pulled back under the chair. "What did I do Friday and Saturday night the week end before last?" She glanced at her uncle.

"There's nothing to worry about, Brin," he said. "You aren't in any trouble. Just answer their questions."

Brin Terrill showed no apprehension at being pulled out of class for questioning. The glance at her uncle did not seem to be for reassurance, only confirmation that she should answer. An altogether unusually self-possessed thirteen-year-old. But then, a child who demanded legal separation from her parents would hardly be the timid kind.

"Of course, Uncle Frank." She smiled up at Mama, sitting on the edge of the desk. "A friend of ours, Lessa Santos, took me with her to record holos of people. She's collecting them for—"

Mama interrupted with a nod. "We know about her program. What time did you two leave and where did you go?"

"Friday Lessa picked me up from school about three. I asked to go along with her that night. We called Uncle Frank, he said yes, and off we went. Saturday we started early, nine o'clock. Both days we ended up in Westport."

"Where in Westport?" Janna asked.

The girl hesitated, forehead puckered in thought, then shrugged. "A gallery café. I don't remember the name. We went in the back door. The owner or manager let Lessa set up her camera and lights and mirror in a room upstairs. Then we went for a walk up and down the street and sat downstairs drinking coffee while Lessa looked over the people. We sat at the outside tables, too, Friday night, until it got too chilly." The girl's face and voice became more animated as she talked. Her hands left her lap to gesture in illustration. "She saw three people she liked. One was a transvestite dressed all in fringe. Lessa gave him a little shooter she'd borrowed from Uncle Frank and had him pull it out of the front of his dress and point it at the camera. Then there was a bibi with hair so short she was almost a skinhead. You could see scalp tattoos through it, rainbow stripes, like her bodysuit. Another bibi was really zone, though! Her hair came down to here." The girl drew a finger across the middle of her thigh. "Peacock blue. She looked nudie, just with some blue nebulas and stars painted on her and wearing a silver cape . . . except it turned out she had a transparent bodysuit. I'd wondered how she stayed warm. The best part was this big starburst pendant on her necklace with a little dagger hidden in it. Lessa had her pull it out and lunge like she was trying to stab someone."

Behind the girl, Grauer nodded.

"What about Saturday?" Mama asked.

The girl shook her head. "She didn't see anyone she liked. There weren't too many people in the cafe. Probably because of the rain."

Rain? That day in Topeka, Janna remembered, it stopped in the latter part of the afternoon. She caught Grauer's eye and raised a brow.

He nodded again. "It rained here until the middle of the evening, maybe twenty-one hundred."

"What time did you leave?"

The girl looked down at her wrist chrono. "I think we got home around eleven or eleven-thirty."

Mama smiled down at her. "You're sure this was the week end before last. You couldn't confuse it with some other week end?"

"No." She dimpled. "I got an A that day on my Russian test. I showed it to Lessa when she picked me up."

They let her go back to class.

Walking out to the Jacquot Middle School parking lot, Grauer said, "Brin did have a Russian test that Friday, and Lessa recorded those particular people. She showed me the holos when I came home. Saturday she complained about the rain keeping interesting people away. Now do you believe her alibi?"

Janna shoved her hands into her trench coat pockets. "The alibi, yes. Unfortunately, that doesn't clear her of involvement in the riffs and murder."

He rolled his eyes. "She isn't involved! I know her! Her temper is the kind that flares and is over with. She doesn't hold grudges like this killer has to."

"I hope you're right." Janna slid open the Meteor's passenger door.

Grauer stood frowning after them while they climbed in and drove away.

Glancing back as they reached the street, Janna saw him still standing by his car. "You think he's afraid we'll come back and ask the girl more questions?"

"We should," Mama said. "It was a mistake talking to her with him there. We wouldn't have allowed it if he'd been a regular citizen."

Janna straightened around in her seat, grinning. "Look who suddenly wants to go by the book." Then she sobered. "And speaking of the book, we ought to call home." If for no other reason than that Showalter and Weyneth must have been to Aschke's bank by now and learned if he had been to Kansas City on any relevant dates.

"Let's check out Crown Center Hotel first." Mama dug under his trench coat into a breast pocket of the jumpsuit.

When she saw the photo he brought out, Janna grinned again. Aschke. Their thoughts were tracking together.

For all the good it did them.

After introducing themselves to hotel security and being assigned someone to accompany them, they showed the photograph to staff members all over the hotel, from desk clerks and restaurant and bar personnel to maids, pool attendants, and security officers. Rather, Janna showed the photograph. Mama trailed along saying nothing, his face wearing a glassy-eyed expression he had acquired as the car set down on its parking rollers on the hotel drive. Janna considered tripping him to see if that would wake him up. Not that his participation would have changed the answers they received.

No one recognized Aschke.

"This doesn't mean he hasn't been here, of course," her escort said. Short-cropped peacock blue hair and an elegantly plain bodysuit-and-tabard made the security officer look more like a guest than a guard. "We don't remember everyone who comes through."

Janna frowned at her. "This jon had to do more than pass through. He was here at least long enough to locate a maid he could pay off to let him copy her key."

A master key made the most sense. With that in his possession, all Aschke had to do was pick an unoccupied room and invite Tony Ho to visit.

"There's no maid involved, bibi."

Both she and the security officer turned to look at Mama. So he had finally come back to Earth. "Who'd Aschke get the key from, then?"

"Aschke didn't." Mama pushed his glasses up his nose and raised a brow at the security officer. "Were you involved in the holographic recording here a short while back?"

While Janna started at the question, the security officer asked, "You mean the bibi with the leo training program?"

How did he know Santos recorded here?

The bibi said, "She used Jim Dalke and Evan March."

"May we talk to them?"

She tapped her ear button.

Five minutes later they met the two officers on the mezzanine by the waterfalls. They, too, wore civilian clothing. Only broader shoulders and a slightly more alert expression differentiated them from ordinary guests. Mama said, "Describe what happened when Ms. Santos recorded you."

The two exchanged puzzled glances. "Not much. She had us walk down halls and step out of doorways with and without weapons."

"Unlock doors?"

They shook their heads. One said, "One time she did have me hold my key up as though to put it in a lock at deadbolt height. She said that made it look almost like a small weapon, so some leo seeing the image from the corner of his eye would have to think fast to realize what it really was and not shoot."

Key! Janna grinned.

A short time later, on their way through the lower lobby, she said, "So Santos copied the key from the holo image and gave it to Aschke?"

Mama smiled. "She copied the key. She didn't give it to Aschke."

"You don't think he's the tall man?"

His smile widened. "You're forgetting, as I did until it hit me on the drive here from the middle school, who mentioned his robots and put him under suspicion. Santos. Why would she do that if he were really her accomplice? No, he isn't the tall man. There is no tall man."

Janna stopped short. What the hell had been happening in his head? "You've really gone over the brainbow, you know that, Mama? What about the man Tony met, and the one Surowsky and Inge saw in the Triton?"

"Why should she use holos for only the gunmen?"

Once the jolt from that thought subsided, it reverberated in her like a purr. Yes, of course. A holo worked perfectly in the hotel room. The figure told Tony where to find his advance payment. It never touched him. And the lighting prevented Tony from seeing that the figure did not talk. The voice was probably prerecorded through the same electronic apparatus that changed Santos' voice into the one emerging from the waitron. The figure Surowski, Inge, and Tony Ho saw in the Triton had not spoken at all. Only the small man had. "So all we have to do is find the small man."

"I know where he is. All I have to do is prove his identity. Let's make some calls." He headed back across the lobby for the phones, digging his notebook out of a thigh pocket.

The first one was long distance, she saw. Mama charged it to the department. "Who are we calling?"

A female face appeared on the screen. "Yi house. Who may I say is calling?"

That answered Janna's question.

Mama asked for Mrs. Yi. When she came on, he asked, "Sometime within a week or so before the robbery, did someone from Beria make a night service call without you requesting one?"

Maeve Yi's forehead creased in thought. After several moments, she nodded. "Monday night. Apparently there'd been problems with the systems of some clients in the area due to power fluctuations during the storms over the week end. So they were checking everyone."

"Do you remember which technician made the service call?"

"No. I'm sure she gave her name—they always do—but I don't remember.

She. Santos?

Mama made two more calls, to the Capitol Sheraton and the Terracrest Apartments, and asked the same questions. Santos had made "service calls" at both places within a week of the riffs, using the same excuse she gave the Yi's. Calls that of course went unrecorded on Beria's service logs.

It explained a great deal. Hacking into the Yi's security system gave Santos the gate override code. Doing the same with the Terracrest records provided her with the names and lock tones of absent tenants. But it did not tell them how Tony used the waiter's Scib card and passed the retinal scan at the hotel employee door.

They headed for the car. Coming out through the hotel doors into the covered entrance, Mama grinned. "It's so elegant. Aside from Tony, because someone had to be there for physical enforcement if necessary, there's only one person involved. Santos. She planned everything. She made the holos and controlled them. She delivered the waitron to the hotel and broke into Holliday Catering to leave it there. Simple, direct, no leaks because there's only one person who knows."

It could have been an elegant theory . . . except for one flaw. "Mama, there has to be someone else involved. Santos has an alibi, remember?"

"I have an idea about that." He pointed.

She turned to follow the direction of his finger. It aimed out of the covered entrance toward a large building located diagonally across the avenue intersection west of the hotel. "What's that?"

"The Pershing Equestrian Center, once the Union Station. Come on." He headed down the hotel drive.

She fell into step with him, leaning into the breeze that had stiffened since they went into the hotel. "What does a riding stable have to do with this case?"

His tongue ticked. "Kansas Citians would be insulted to have you refer to an historic landmark as a riding stable. They board horses and teach riding, yes, but . . . it's more than that. And Santos must have seen it when she visited the hotel." He halted at the corner to wait for the light. "Maybe it gave her the same idea for an alibi that it did me on our way in."

"Which is?"

The *Walk* signal flashed. Mama sprinted for the diagonal corner. Following him, Janna learned why he ran. The signal lasted barely two-thirds of their crossing, leaving them in a race against the wall of oncoming traffic.

On the safety of the sidewalk, Janna caught her breath, then repeated her question.

Mama just grinned and strolled up the drive to a long bank of doors leading into the stable.

Inside, Janna caught her breath. More than a riding stable indeed. She stared at a broad marble-floored concourse and a ceiling soaring above them like a cathedral's. Around the concourse lay a tack shop, a club called The Stirrup Cup, and a room with snack machines and clusters of molded foam chairs around a three-sided TV in the center. Signs reading: *Veterinary Clinic* and *Exercise Room* pointed to their left.

Following Mama on into the building, Janna discovered that the concourse was only the crossbar on a huge T, and the main leg had even more of the cavernous majesty of a cathedral. Except tanbark covered the floor of this "nave," a brown plain splashed with light shafting down from the high windows and dotted with jumps and the moving figures of horses. It reminded her of pictures of the Spanish Riding School in Vienna.

A spectators' gallery rose in steep tiers, separated from the riding ring by a chest-high wooden wall. A few people, some in street clothes, most in riding boots and breeches, sat in the gallery. Others leaned on the wall.

Mama moved up the ring. As Janna joined him, a horse cantered by, nostrils flaring, neck and shoulders damply dark, its rider, a girl in her teens, murmuring and clucking. In its wake, the sharp-pungent scents of horse and sweat washed over Janna.

Another girl, slightly older, stood on the far side of Mama. "What time does the ring close?" he asked her.

"Midnight," she replied. Beneath the visor of her black velvet riding helmet, her eyes followed the cantering horse.

Suddenly Janna understood why she and Mama were here. Girls and horses. "Are you thinking what I think you are?"

He nodded. "Grauer's niece is horse-crazy. What better place than this to keep her happily occupied for a few hours?"

"A few hours? We're talking seven or eight on Friday and over twelve on Saturday." Janna shook her head. "That's a long time."

Mama grinned. "Not in horse heaven. You must be one of the few girls born not bitten by the horse bug. When my cousin Genea visited our farm, the first place she always headed was for the horses, and she'd have spent all day every day with them if she'd been allowed to."

It sounded to Janna like an affliction she was fortunate to have missed. "Now we have to establish the girl was here."

He nodded. "Let's start with the riding school office."

It lay off the concourse, a large room but crowded by the four desks in it. At the moment the chairs of three sat empty, leaving only the secretary to answer their questions.

"Do we have a Brin Terrill registered for lessons?" He swiveled to the computer on the ell of his desk, and in a few keystrokes later, replied, "Yes, she's in Tarl Byrne's low intermediate class Wednesday evenings."

Janna frowned. Of course they asked the question, but she never expected that answer. It removed the most logical reason for the girl to alibi Santos . . . as an exchange for something unobtainable any other way.

Mama peered over the secretary's shoulder at the computer monitor. "I remember that a few years back, helping clean stalls Saturday earned a free riding lesson later in the day. Is that still true?"

The jon grinned. "Oh yes. And that bonus class is always filled."

"Is there a record of who rides in it?"

"Not a formal one. Jim Ledders, the head stableman, writes down the names and gives it to whoever happens to be teaching

the class that day, but I've never put the list on the computer.
I don't know if the instructors save the names or not."

"Who taught two Saturdays ago?"

"I don't know. You'll need to ask the instructors." The secretary grinned again. "I think they draw straws for it. Or Ledders
may know."

Mama voted for asking the stableman, and led the way down
a ramp spiraling from a corridor to the side of the riding ring to
the stall rows below. "He should know better than anyone else
who cleaned stalls."

Janna wrinkled her nose as the smells of straw, hay, and
manure enveloped them. "How do you know this place so
well?"

He shrugged. "Some of the other criminal justice students
and I used to come down from the campus every Sunday evening
to watch the P.D. mounted patrol train. The horses are stabled
here. For a while I thought I wanted to be a mounted officer."

She might have known. "Is there anyplace in Kansas City
you *didn't* visit regularly when you were in school here?"

He grinned.

They located the lanky head stableman overseeing the repair
of an automatic water bowl in one of the stalls. "Sure I know
Brin by sight." He moved to one side of the doorway as the
stall's blanketed occupant stretched its head past him to investigate them. "She's one of the regular Saturday gang."

"We need to know whether or not she was here Saturday
before last." Janna reached fingers through the wire netting of
the stall door to touch the horse's velvet-soft muzzle. "Do you
remember?"

Ledders hesitated. "I'm afraid not. You get so used to seeing
some of these kids, you don't notice them beyond writing down
their names as they come in and keeping an eye on them to make
sure they're really working. Sue Rakowski taught the bonus class
that week. Maybe she remembers if Brin was in it."

When they caught the stocky instructor after the finish of a
private lesson, though, she could not remember. She leaned back
against the ring wall shaking her head. "The thing is, that bonus
class is such a mixed bag, everything from green beginners to
upper intermediates, it's impossible to run as a real class. It's
mostly an hour's ride for them—which is all they really want
anyway—so I don't pay much attention to who's there. Unless

one of them does something spectacularly good or bad. Brin's very average.''

"Do you save the lists Ledders gives you?" Mama asked.

She shook her head. "Once the class is over, I throw them away.''

Mama and Janna talked to the two other instructors, and to a number of riders and parents of riders, hoping to find someone who had been at the school that Friday and Saturday. To Janna's surprise, most had. As nearly as she could tell, they came almost every day. None of them, however, remembered whether they had seen Brin Terrill or not.

On the walk back to the hotel for their car, Janna shook her head in disbelief. "In an age when we're colonizing the stars and racing to stake mining claims on the asteroids, I can't believe there are people who do nothing but ride horses.''

"Yes, it is amazing how people's entire lives can be bound up in a hobby . . . or a job," he added with a side glance at her.

"As amazing as a grown man not being able to stand living alone," Janna shot back. Two could play the barb game. Then she returned to their problem. "So . . . we can't prove Santos left the girl at the riding school. Maybe she didn't. If the girl's there so often, why would she be willing to lie for Santos to spend more time there, and why, most of all, would she lie to her uncle for Santos?"

Mama pushed his glasses up his nose. "Let's ask her.''

If talking to them without her uncle present disturbed the girl, she did not show it. She took a chair in the assistant principal's office with the same self-possession she showed earlier. "How can I help you now?"

Sitting down in a chair facing her, Janna said, "We're having trouble finding the gallery café where you and Lessa went." She reached into her trench coat pocket to tap on her microcorder. "What kind of artwork did it display?"

The girl hesitated, forehead puckering. The reaction rang an alert in Janna's head. They had seen this before when they asked where Santos took her . . . a deliberate kind of gesture. Practiced. "Paintings, I think. I don't really remember. We were looking at people." Her voice went carefully casual. "Why do you want to know? Is Lessa in some kind of trouble?"

Sooner or later she was bound to ask that. Janna kept smiling. "We hope not. But . . ." Now for the bluff. ". . . we can't seem to find anyone in Westport who remembers seeing the two of you that week end."

For a split second the girl stared through her, then focused and without a blink said, "I think people forget who they saw when unless they're friends or had a fight with them or something."

A fair observation, Janna agreed. Perhaps a bit mature for a child her age? Also, the average innocent person in this situation reacted with surprise at not being remembered, with disbelief and dismay, even indignation . . . not with excuses for being overlooked. She glanced at Mama. Time for the heavy artillery of bluff number two.

He shifted position on the edge of the desk. "People do remember people they know. Jim Ledders, for example, recalls quite clearly that you cleaned stalls that Saturday, and Sue Rakowski that you rode in the bonus class."

The girl went rigid.

Triumph crackled through Janna. Bullseye! She leaned toward the girl. "Brin, where did Lessa really go?"

The wide eyes stared through her. "I told you . . . we went to Westport. I didn't clean stalls or ride. They're getting confused with another week end."

Janna sighed inwardly. So the girl was going to stick with the story.

"No, Brin." Mama shook his head. "Ms. Rakowski remembers because you fell off at one of the jumps."

The girl stiffened, nostrils flaring. "That's a lie! I stayed on over every single jump, even the In and Out. I haven't fallen off in—" She broke off. Too late. The angry compression of her mouth said she realized that.

Janna let the silence stretch out for a minute, then asked, "Why did you lie for Lessa?"

The girl bit her lip. "Promise me you won't tell my uncle."

"I'm sorry, we can't do that," Mama said.

Her hands clenched. "But he'll be so angry at Lessa!"

To say the least. "Brin." Janna waited for the girl to look at her before continuing. "This is a very serious matter. Your uncle will be much angrier if you don't tell us the truth."

Indecision twisted the girl's face, but finally she said, "Lessa

wanted to record some people in a neighborhood where Uncle
Frank told her never to go alone. She needed those images, she
said, but she didn't want my uncle to know she'd gone there.
So would I help her keep him from finding out by pretending
I'd asked to go along and that we went to Westport together.''
She looked up at them, forehead creased in protest. "It was a
lie, but it didn't hurt anything, just kept my uncle from worrying.
I like Lessa. Why shouldn't I help her?''

   Leaving the school, Mama said, "I'm sorry she'll have to find
out, sooner or later.''

   Fortunately they did not have the dirty job of telling her. "So
much for Santos' alibi. She could have gone to Topeka.''

   Mama nodded. "Now we have to prove she did.''

EIGHTEEN

Proof had to start with means . . . Santos's transportation to Topeka. Logic said it must be the Triton. "The question is where she got it, Mama. Did she buy, borrow, or rent?"

Checking their DMV list of Kansas Triton owners established that Santos had not registered one as Charisma Santos, either.

Their own car bucked in the rising wind. To the west, clouds pushed up over the horizon, heralding another spring storm.

Mama held the wheel steady. "I doubt she borrowed it."

Janna arched her brows at him.

"Whoever she borrowed it from could testify she wasn't in Westport. Let's have Diosdado run her name through DMV in Jefferson City. If that's negative, we'll try local car rental agencies. And self-storage facilities and garage rentals. In her place, I'd want a vehicle set up and ready to go so I wouldn't risk falling behind schedule if I had trouble loading and setting up the desktop."

Janna nodded. No one left a vehicle on the street if it held anything worth stealing.

When they reached Robbery, however, they found Diosdado gone. Janna swore.

An Amerasian she-lion at a nearby desk looked around.

"You're the Topeka detectives, aren't you? Is there anything I can help you with?"

"Thank you, yes." Mama tore a page out of his notebook and handed it to her. "We need to know if there's a car registered to either of these names in Missouri."

"That shouldn't be any problem." She glanced at the page while reaching for her phone. "Oh, before I forget, there's something from Records for you on Diosdado's desk. He asked me to be sure you got it."

Mama headed for Diosdado's desk.

"There's another message, too." The detective rummaged through the papers spread across her desk. "It came in a little after Diosdado left. I don't know now what I did with it. A Lieutanant someone in Topeka who wants you to call as soon —this is Detective Lin in Robbery," she said to the face that appeared on her phone screen. "I have a couple of names to run through DMV."

Lieutenant someone from Topeka had to be Vradel. Janna arched a brow at Mama. "Do you want to call or shall I?"

"Later." Mama passed the information from Records on to Janna.

Glancing through the pages, printouts of the information Santos gave for each ride-along request, Janna saw nothing remarkable, nothing they didn't already know. Less, in fact. The ride-along requests gave her name as Lesandra Santos and listed only a personal address and phone number. If they had had only these to go by, they would never have realized she was also Charisma Santos and worked for Beria.

"I've got your registration query back," Lin called.

Janna copied the information from the detective's phone screen on the back of the Records printout. Negative for Lesandra Santos. She had no vehicle registered in the state of Missouri. Two Charisma Santos's did, but both had Missouri addresses—not near Kansas City—and neither was on a '77 Triton.

That left the rental agencies.

"Thanks," Janna said. "Is there any problem with us using Diosdado's and his partner's phones for some calls?"

"Not with me. But you'd better ask Captain Westfahl."

Diosdado had introduced them to his commanding officer their first trip here, a stocky lion who never quite focused on the person he talked to. As though the conversation was only one of several simultaneous thought trains in his head. They approached him in his office with the request.

He shrugged. "Use them until we need them. Charge any long distance to your own department, though."

They tossed a vending token to divide the calls. Janna won the self-storage facilities and garage rentals. Typing in the category on the alphanumeric keypad of the phone book lying on Diosdado's desk brought her the first of the self-storage listings, the first of many, a quick downscan found.

Before starting on them, then, she called Lieutenant Vradel.

He regarded her deadpan from the screen. "Well, if it isn't one of the gypsies. How nice to hear from you."

The dry tone brought a prickle of heat up her neck, but she kept her face as expressionless as his. "I called as soon as we got your message."

"Thank you. Thank you, too, for the time bomb you left. The detonation is still echoing on the third floor." A corner of his mustache twitched. "You may hear reverberations of it yet when you come home."

No doubt. Janna sighed.

Mama left Diosdado's phone to join her. "Even when we come bearing gifts of corroboration and a possible arrestable suspect?" He outlined what they had learned today.

Vradel listened without reaction or comment until Mama finished. Then he said, "I don't know about the arrestable suspect. Everything sounds circumstantial. Though you're right about Aschke not recruiting Tony Ho. His bank records show several recent trips to Kansas City, but none that include Monday, April eighth."

Mama grinned at Janna.

"According to Weyneth," Vradel continued, "Aschke claims he made the trips to visit Servitron, trying to sell them the design for his guard robot. As long as you're up there, check it out."

"While we're doing that, o great and wise leader, how about trying for a bank warrant on Santos?" Mama asked.

After a few moments of mustache smoothing, the lieutenant nodded. "You just bring home something more concrete on this Santos. Such as the car and a demonstrable interest in criminals using disguise as part of their M.O., and that she had knowledge of Tony Ho."

Checking Servitron was easy enough. Janna called and asked

for the plant manager. Remembering her from their visit the week before, he readily answered her questions.

"Yes, I remember the jon. He's been up here several times. Has some good ideas but needs to work them out a little more."

With a few minutes' thought and checking back through his calendar, the manager worked out the dates of Aschke's visits. None of them fell on or next to Monday the eighth.

That took care of Aschke. Now for the rest of Vradel's request.

Janna sighed, punching off. "With all those evenings riding along and all the questions Santos must have asked, who'll remember her asking about riffers liking disguises? Worse, if she learned about Tony just by keeping her ears open, we'll never —Mama?"

He sat staring at the phone screen.

"What is it?"

A grin spread across the dark face. "Maybe a link, bibi." He headed for Detective Lin's desk. "Would you have time to make another call for us?"

The she-lion looked up. "To DMV?"

"To Records." He sat down in the chair beside her desk. "Last week Diosdado pulled up a file for us. Most of the officer codes on the retrieval log had IVRB and IVFD section designations."

Lin nodded. "Robbery and Fraud."

"One, though, and only one, was a UDMT . . . someone in Metro patrol, Diosdado said." He caught Janna's eye.

A tingle traveled up her spine. Metro patrol. Was he thinking of Grauer?

"Can we find out what officer that code belongs to?"

"I can try." Lin tapped her phone on. "First we need the code. What was the name on the record?" A short time later they had the retrieval log for Tony Ho's file on the screen. Lin jotted down the UDMT code and exited the file, then reached for the keypad again. "You can't learn other lions' codes by asking the computer for them. What I'll have to do is contact a friend of mine in Records."

"Wait," Mama said. "Before you do that, will you request a search for subjects who use disguises as part of their robbery M.O.?"

"What?" Lin frowned at him. "That'll tie up my phone, and me, for God knows how long."

He smiled an apology at her. "I know. I'm sorry. But we can't do it and it's very important to see the retrieval logs on those files."

Her frown deepened. "I'm willing to spend a favor finding out whose access code this is, but I don't have the time for a records search."

Charm poured out of Mama's smile. "Use Diosdado's phone. All we need is your voice reciting your code to get us into the computer, isn't that right? Or does the computer check voices all the time you're logged on?"

The she-lion hesitated, then shook her head. "Not once you're in. All right. I can do that."

Even on a category one search they had to wait almost ten minutes. It seemed like ten hours before the files began appearing on the phone screen. Then Janna quickly forgot the wait. One retrieval log after another listed the UDMT code on Sunday, April seventh. The day before Tony received his letter about the possible job.

Lin called from her desk, "My friend in Records says that access code belongs to a Sergeant Frank Grauer."

"I love you, leo!" Mama blew her a kiss. "Thank you very very much. Where would you like to go for dinner?"

She grinned. "I'd better go home or my husband will be very very pissed."

Janna sucked in her lower lip. Grauer. "Now we need to find out if it was actually Grauer who made the search."

They called him. When he came on the screen, the Metro officer frowned. "You again?"

Mama smiled in apology. "Unfortunately. We have one last question. Sunday, April seventh, did you request a records search for riffers who use disguises in the M.O.?"

Grauer's mouth thinned. "I did not. And Lessa couldn't, either. You know not even a phenomenal mimic can fool a voice recognition program."

"Someone made that search using your code. Has she been present on any occasion when you called into the computer? A microcorder fits in almost any pocket and the best ones have excellent sound reproduction."

His face tightened. With uncertainty? Janna hated what they had to do to him.

Mama sighed. "I'm sorry, Grauer, truly."

"Go to hell."

Watching the stony face fade from the screen, Janna felt anger rise in her. Armenda had been the one killed, but he was just one of the victims in this murder, and the pain of the others had only begun.

She reached for the phone book. "Let's find that damn car."

If and where Santos maintained garage space for the vehicle had to lie within a radius of fifteen klicks, to fit the odometer readings on Grauer's Kobold after Santos used it. That included a large section of the city, granted, but it eliminated storage and garage facilities in outlying areas. Janna also skipped those to the east. Santos needed to go west. It made sense for her to pick a facility in that general direction.

After washing down a sandwich from the building's bank of vending machines with a cup of caff from the squad pot, Janna planted herself at Diosdado's desk and tackled the self-storage listings. Several hours worth of calls, at a rough estimate.

As each storage facility answered, she put on a polite smile and held up her ID to the phone. "This is Sergeant Janna Brill of the Shawnee County Crimes Against Persons squad. Do you, or have you recently had, a unit rented to a Charisma Santos or Lesandra Santos?"

Of course no one at the top of the list had.

"She'll probably turn out to have rented from something called Zeke's Storage."

Mama, calling car rental agencies from the phone on Diosdado's partner's desk, grinned. "Investigation is so action packed."

"Yes," a male face on Janna's phone screen said, "I have a unit rented to a Charisma Santos."

Janna sat bolt upright. Hurriedly, she rechecked the name of the facility. Convenience Storage, Merriam. That would be on the Kansas side. Between here and Topeka. "Do you have an address for her?" Now if only this were not just someone with the same name.

The address was Santos's in Topeka. She had rented the unit number 230 a month and a half ago.

"Mama!"

The whoop turned heads across the squad room. Mama, however, only pointed at the phone book in front of her. "Save the victory celebration until we find the Triton."

An hour later he did. Thrifty Auto Leasing had rented a '77 Triton to Charisma Santos five weeks ago on a month-to-month lease.

They had her! Janna grinned. If Santos were innocent, why would she lease a car and never mention it, just keep on using Grauer's Kobold?

"Does she still have the car?" Mama asked.

On the screen, the dark-haired bibi at Thrifty Auto glanced off to the left of the phone. "No. It was returned Wednesday morning."

Janna sighed. Possession had probably been too much to expect. They still had the vehicle itself, however, and the associative evidence it contained.

"Will you please hold that car until we can examine it?"

Another pause with more attention to the left, then a grimace. "I'm sorry, but it's already gone out again."

Janna swore.

"When it comes back in, hold it. It may contain evidence relating to a murder we're investigating." Disconnecting, he said, "We still have the storage space, bibi. Let's go look at it."

A tall security fence surrounded Convenience Storage. Individual units, white-painted concrete block with brightly colored doors, sat in back-to-back rows, ranging in size from overgrown closets to spaces large enough for the furnishings of an entire house. A group in the mid-range size included number 230, Santos' unit.

Janna leaned against the car watching Mama pace the distance across the blue roll-up door. "It's garage-sized. Santos could have kept the Triton in it."

"And the desktop. She returned the car. What happened to the holo controls, though?" He ran his hand down the door to the lock.

The action sent a warning tingle through Janna. She pushed away from the car. "No, Mama!"

Innocent eyes turned on her. "No, what?"

The wind chased scraps of paper and other small debris down the storage row. Leaden clouds closed overhead. Janna rolled her eyes. "As if you can't guess. No . . . we're not going to break in. There's no point." He knew that. If they found something incriminating, they couldn't touch it. They couldn't even use seeing it as probable cause for obtaining a search warrant. "We're practically on Highway 10 here. That runs to Lawrence, where she could pick up 40 north of Clinton Lake and go straight on into Topeka. It's a perfect route for her purposes, no tolls and not as well patrolled as the Turnpike, so she could make whatever speed necessary for her timetable. We might use that to go after a warrant."

"And while we're building probable cause, what if she moves whatever's left in there?" He tilted his head toward the door.

She shoved her hands in the pockets of her trench coat. "It's a chance we have to take. You know we can't do anything else."

"I can." He swung around and headed up the row in long strides.

Janna scrambled after him. "Mama, what the hell—" She broke off as she realized he was headed for the facility office. "Mama!" Damn the man!

He kept going.

She caught up just as he pushed through the office door. "Damn it, Mama, you   —"

"But I tell you I do smell it."

A jon with the face Janna had seen on the phone looked up from behind the counter. "May I help you?"

Mama pushed his glasses up his nose. "My wife and I have one of your storage spaces, and when we were down there just now, I smelled something terrible. It seemed to be coming from number two-thirty. I thought you ought to know."

So that was the skin. She could short-circuit this. "It's your imagination. *I* didn't smell a thing."

Mama shook his head. "I don't know how you can miss a stench like that, babycheeks. It's like something died. I wonder if a rat got in there."

Babycheeks! He was a dead man. She gave him a sugary smile. "Oh, there's a rat around, but not in there."

The manager frowned. "What unit did you say?"

"Two-thirty."

"He's brainbent," Janna said.

But the manager was already looking down a list behind the counter and picking up a sonic key. He headed out of the office and along the rows to 230. Approaching the unit, he sniffed. "I don't smell anything."

Mama, following him, said, "Is everyone's sense of smell numb? It smells so bad I want to gag."

Frowning and still sniffing, the manager punched a combination on the key, then turned the handle and pushed up the door. Mama peered in over his shoulder.

Since he had the door open, Janna did, too.

The unit was empty. Completely. Not even dust lay on the floor.

"She's right; you're brainbent," the manager said, and hauled the door down in a rattle of vinyl-coated metal. "What's your name and what unit do you have?"

Mama never hesitated. "Keegan, number two-three-five." He headed for the car. "Let's go, my dear."

"So," Janna said a short time later, gunning the car west down Highway 10, "what did that accomplish?"

Mama settled back in his seat with a grin. "We know to bring a vacuum with our search warrant."

"And what if she never brought the desktop and waitron back with her?"

Associative evidence such as fibers from the hotel carpet or Yi's house had to come from the waitron's treads. Santos herself had no personal contact with the crime scenes.

Mama smirked. "If she disposed of them on the way back, we can look all we like without a search warrant."

The car bucked in the wind. Lightning flashed through the purple and black clouds to the west, followed by a booming roll of thunder.

He stared out the window. "In her place, I'd drop them off a bridge, and that helps us, because without a side trip, the only suitable water is the Wakarusa River or Clinton Lake."

"I'll be happy to let you out to look. I'll even tie weights to your ankles to help you dive." Janna bared her teeth at him. "Just say where . . . babycheeks."

Lightning chased through the clouds overhead, followed by more thunder. Farther west, the first rain appeared, scattered large drops splattering heavily on the windshield. The body of the storm hit minutes later. They reached the bridge over the Wakarusa in a deluge.

Mama sighed.

Glimpsing the river below, swift and swollen from the spring rains, Janna did, too. "Let's hope Santos dumped everything in Clinton Lake. With that current, if she chose the river, god knows how far downstream our evidence could be by this time."

"Unless we got lucky and it caught on a snag or washed up on a sandbar." He leaned back in his seat, ticking his tongue.

Some luck like that would be welcome. Janna could not help feeling that without finding the waitron and holo controls somewhere between Topeka and Kansas City, the D. A. would never consider their case against Santos. Bank records might show Santos had purchased a waitron, but building her own was safer. She could shrug off the purchase of a large number of electronic parts, and a trip to Kansas City on the eighth, as part of developing her program. They needed evidence the perpetrator had headed east after the murder, a link to Kansas City . . . to Santos with her false alibi and secretly rented car and storage unit. Better yet: "What we could *really* use is an eye witness placing Santos in Topeka those Friday and Saturday nights."

"If we're wishing, there's nothing better than . . ." His voice trailed off.

Janna glanced sideways. He sat staring ahead through the streaming windshield, lips pursed. She continued driving, letting his wheels grind, but when they reached the edge of Topeka and he had said nothing more, she asked, "Are you going to tell me what's going on in your head?"

He stretched. "Where were you planning to go now?"

"The office, to see if we have a bank warrant on Santos." She yawned. Two nights without much sleep were catching up to her, stimulants or not.

"Let's stop at Beria first."

A jolt of adrenalin short-circuited a second yawn. "To talk to Santos?"

"Don't we usually interview suspects?" He pushed his glasses up his nose. "After all, there's nothing that solves a case better than a confession."

At Beria, they had to wait for their chance at Santos. The storm was playing the usual havoc with electrical systems and she had gone out to check and readjust an alarm.

Shortly after six o'clock, however, their suspect strolled into the employee lounge, pushing escaping wet wisps of her topknot off her face. Janna looked Santos over . . . paying close attention for the first time. The small bibi looked no different. Janna saw the same petite stature, the same narrow face, the same intelligent dark eyes. Nothing about her suggested a killer. Seeing them in two of the chairs there, Santos' brows hopped, but without uneasiness, only surprise.

She smiled in greeting—"A wet evening, isn't it?"—and poured herself a cup of caff. "I suppose I ought to enjoy the rain while I can, though. I won't see any on Mars."

"We heard about your new job," Mama said. "When's your last day here?"

"Day after tomorrow." Santos sipped the steaming caff. "Speaking of jobs, how is your case coming?"

Janna reached into her trench coat pocket and tapped on her microcorder. "We know who killed Armenda."

Santos frowned. "You're not thinking it's Jason Aschke, I hope."

"No."

The relief in Santos's face surprised Janna. Mama, however, nodded, as though the comment was one he expected. "He just distracted us for a while. Which was your intention in mentioning his robots, I suspect. Only, he didn't distract us quite long enough."

Santos stiffened. "I beg your pardon? What are you talking about?"

Mama's smile broadened. "Diversion . . . to keep suspicion away from yourself."

The dark eyes went wary. "I still don't understand."

Janna stood so she looked down at the smaller bibi. "I think you do, Miss Charisma Lesandra Santos."

Mama stood, too. "We know the gunmen were holos, projected by the projector you refused to turn over to Armenda."

Give Santos credit for being prepared, and for acting ability. Her jaw dropped. "Those gunmen were *my* holos?" No attempt to deny who she was. No attempt to deny either the projector or the existence of the holos. "You mean some of the ones I've recorded for—"

"For your alleged shoot/don't shoot program," Janna interrupted. "Yes. But you know that already. Santos, we've talked to Grauer's niece. She told us where she spent the Friday and Saturday evenings of the robberies, when the two of you claimed to be together in Westport."

Santos barely hesitated before replying. "Did she tell you why I asked her to alibi me?"

"She told us the reason you gave her," Mama said. "We don't believe it. You lied to her, just as you lied to Grauer about when you recorded those images you showed him that Friday night. Because we also know about the Triton you leased, and the storage unit in Merriam . . . at Convenience Storage . . . now carefully cleaned out. Too bad when you tossed the holo controls and waitron in the water you didn't stay around to be sure they sank. In spite of the projector holes in it, the waitron must have had some buoyancy. We found it washed up on shore. And despite it being in the water, traces of its builder and handler will still be there . . . a flake of skin here, a hair there. Which DNA fingerprinting will prove are yours."

Now Santos reacted. Fear slashed across her face. Janna had just time to see that and the first motion of the hand holding the cup, then scalding caff sprayed her face and eyes. She doubled, swearing, clutching at her face.

A cup clattered to the floor, followed by the thud of feet in rapid retreat.

Pain vanished beneath a surge of apprehension, triumph, and adrenaline. "Mama!" Janna scrubbed at her eyes with her sleeve. "She's running!"

A blurry Mama with coffee-spattered glasses vanished through the lounge door.

Janna stumbled for the door, too. Should she follow Mama or go out the front and try to head Santos off? Then she remembered that someone would have to let her out the front. She pounded down the hallway after Mama.

A closing door showed them where Santos had left the hallway. That took them through a workshop and down back stairs, through another door into a large garage with a row of parked service vans. Two of the bays stood empty. In the far wall, the door lowered with a soft hiss of rollers down vertical tracks.

Adrenaline jolted Janna again. If it closed, they would have to backtrack to find someone to let them out! She flung herself after Mama . . . between vans and toward the descending door. Less than a meter of clearance remained. Eighty centimers. Sixty. Forty.

They dived for the narrowing slit . . . rolling. The bar on the bottom brushed Janna's shoulder, then she was underneath and in the alley outside . . . clear. And instantly drenched.

She ignored the rain. Nothing mattered right now except the Beria van. Racing for the nearest mouth of the alley, they were in time to see ruby and amber taillights headed west.

They pounded up the block toward Kansas Avenue . . . skidded around the corner . . . flung themselves into their own car. It bucked up off its parking rollers, fans screaming.

"Get us some backup, bibi!"

The car heeled sharply as Mama pulled it in a U turn and around the corner after the van. Ahead, the tail lights canted as the van turned right.

Janna shoved streaming hair off her face to reach her ear, only to remember she was not wearing her radio button. She grabbed the mike of the car radio. "Indian Thirty, Capitol! In pursuit of blue Beria Security service van, bearing plates Adam Adam Union two three three, headed north on Topeka Boulevard from Third and Topeka! Female driver is a possible signal nine." Labeling her a felony suspect would bring everyone in the area running. "Unknown if signal one." Although she assaulted them with only coffee, they could not afford to ignore the chance that she still had the needler used in killing Armenda.

On the radio, Dispatch repeated Janna's information.

They swung onto Topeka, the Meteor heeling sharply. The van raced ahead of them, its taillights reflected in blurred streaks of amber and ruby on the puddled paving.

"Vehicle is approaching the bridge."

The van shot onto the bridge over the Kaw River. Halfway across, however, the taillights flared. Reversing fans kicked up a spray of rainwater from the paving in front of the vehicle. Lights at the far end of the bridge told Janna why. Those chasing bands of red, white, and blue could only be light rails atop watch units from the Soldier Creek Division pulled sideways in a roadblock. More light rails flashing on the Meteor's rear scanner indicated backup coming to close off this end of the bridge, too.

Janna grinned. "Now we've got her."

The van settled to the paving, its side rear door sliding open. Santos jumped out and stood half crouched, twisting to peer one direction, then the other. Distance and the rain blurred her expression but she moved like an animal at bay. For a minute she just stood, then, as the Meteor set down and Janna and Mama slid open their doors, she launched herself across the northbound lanes toward the bridge railing.

Mama bailed out of the car. "Santos! No!"

The small bibi never paused. Reaching the railing, she vaulted over it, to Janna's shocked disbelief, and vanished.

Janna reached the rail seconds behind Mama. Together they peered over. But saw no sign of Santos. Staring down with dismay knotting her gut, Janna found only rain and deepening darkness and the swift, muddy water of the river below.

NINETEEN

In the first stunned moments, thought and emotion churned in Janna's head with the turbulence of the water below. Why had Santos done it? How could she be so desperate? Then footsteps pounded up behind them and lions from the watch cars crowded the rail beside Mama and her.

"Jesus! I can't believe that. She went straight over," a she-lion exclaimed.

"I can't believe it, either," Mama said. "Will someone loan me a flashlight?"

That launched the search. They started with the bridge, peering over both railings, shining flashlights down where the pilings entered the water. An exercise in futility. The rain ate the beams before they covered half the distance. When someone produced a rope, Janna tied it around her waist and went over the rail for a look at the understructure of the bridge. But Santos had not tricked them by somehow scrambling to safety there.

The search spread downstream along both banks, aided by a boat and the arrival of more officers . . . including Cruz and Zavara. The light rails' flashing bands of color lighted up the night, reflecting off wet slickers and helmets and the puddled pavement in an incongruous air of festiveness. It drew the inevitable crowd of onlookers and media videographers, and members of each who slipped past the watchcar barracade and had to be escorted off the bridge.

"Brill, what the hell happened?" Cruz asked.

Zavara grunted. "Looks to me like Santos saved the state the expense of prosecution."

"We talked to her, that's all," Janna said. Holding the lapel of her trench coat out so it sheltered the microcorder, she played back the recording of their interview with Santos.

When it ended, Zavara shook her head. "She panicked at that? But . . . she sounded so controlled."

Mama nodded. "She looked controlled, too." He frowned toward the van. "Too controlled to fall apart that fast."

"We all know people can look that way even when they're pulled so tight they're at the breaking point," Cruz said. "Santos has probably been living on the edge since the murder and this was more stress than she could tolerate."

"A possibility I'm sure Maxwell counted on," Lieutenant Vradel's voice said from behind them.

They spun to see his burly, umbrella-carrying form striding up the bridge.

"Right, Brill?"

With him looking straight at her, she could not sidestep answering. She shoved her hands in the pockets of her trench coat. "We hoped she would make some incriminating statement, yes. We didn't expect . . . this."

"Which explains why you felt it unnecessary to confide your plans to any of your colleagues, despite the fact that this investigation is supposed to be a team effort, and didn't arrange to have anyone covering the entrances while you went in?" Vradel shook his head. "I'm disappointed in you, Brill."

Again. She bit her lip, swearing silently.

"Just a minute, sir." Mama stepped between her and the lieutenant. "All this was my idea, as usual."

"Which your partner freely chose to go along with." The umbrella twirled over Vradel's head. "Didn't you even consider seeing what the bank records showed before confronting Santos?"

Janna swore again. What had they found? Something flatly incriminating, something that would have let them arrest her and avoid this tragedy?

"We thought we knew." Mama pushed rain-streaked glasses

up his nose. "It did show she's bought extensive amounts of electronic parts and was in Kansas City on the eighth, didn't it?"

Zavara said, "It also shows she's been earning extra credit making independent security installations and modifications here and in Kansas City."

Such as adding voiced recognition to housekeepers.

"But the interesting find," Cruz said, "is that she also bought a large number of unset gems."

Janna exchanged glances with Mama. Gems. Tony Ho's pay for his part in the riffs? Once they could show that his carry matched the purchased gems, Santos was tied to Tony as firmly as if a witness had seen them together.

"Yet you didn't bring Santos in for questioning," Mama said.

Cruz shrugged. "We were waiting to hear if you'd found the Triton and tied it to her."

So by not pooling their information, they had arrived . . . here. Janna eyed the bridge railing and swore. She and Mama certainly screwed up this time.

"Sergeant Maxwell." A she-lion approached them, rain streaming from her helmet and slicker. "We can't find any sign of the body and the boat's been downstream as far as Tecumseh."

"Let's call it for tonight, then," Vradel said. He sighed. "We'll alert law enforcement agencies on downstream so they can be watching for the body."

The she-lion saluted. "Yes, sir."

They all glanced east. Zavara pulled her shoulders back in one of her fluid stretch/flexes. "Maybe it's a good thing for us she panicked. If she'd stayed iced when you talked to her, she could have cut cloud after you left and gone mole until time to catch her shuttle flight. We might have lost her."

Vradel's mustache twitched. "No, that, at least, wouldn't work. Once she disappeared, we'd be watching the—"

"Son of a bitch," Mama interrupted. He pounded the heel of his hand against his forehead. "Lieutenant, I'm a world-class lightwit."

"You heard it here first, boys and girls," Cruz murmured.

Vradel frowned at him. "Zip it. Go on, Maxwell."

"If there's one distinguishing feature of Armenda's murder, it's careful planning." Mama headed for the Beria van. "Why wouldn't she plan her escape, too? The computer tech at Beria said Santos first applied for Mars a year ago." He climbed into the van, still standing open, and after switching on the dome light, began peering around the interior.

The rest of them watched from the door. Shelves with pull-out bins lined both sides. On the top shelf facing the door, half a dozen little CCD cameras sat packed in a neat row, three with their lenses peering over the edge, three equipped with cable for a remote camera head.

Mama ran his hand along the top of the cameras. "It stands to reason she'd have contingencies in case we appeared to be closing in on her." His fingers traced from them down the inside of the shelf support. "One way to insure we wouldn't stake out bus and air terminals looking for her is to make us think she's dead."

By going off the bridge? Janna frowned. That was a hell of a risk. Too risky.

Zavara echoed the thought, shaking her head. "No. She'd have to be brainbent to do it this way. I'm a strong swimmer and *I* wouldn't gamble that I could survive the fall and swim to safety."

Cruz nodded in agreement.

"There's no risk if she didn't jump."

"But you saw—" Cruz began.

"Not exactly," Mama said. "We saw this." He pushed something behind the shelf support.

Santos appeared in the doorway. Shock jolted Janna, echoed by indrawn breath from the others. But even as reflex backed her away from the woman jumping out of the van, she understood what Santos had done. Reaching out, Janna passed an arm through the petite figure.

"Son of a bitch," Cruz breathed.

"A holo?" Zavara groped in the space occupied by the image's face. "Jesus!"

A profanity Janna felt like echoing. Even this close, her hand apparently buried in the middle of Santos's chest, the image twisting left and right still looked real. The onlookers at the ends of the bridge certainly thought so. They gasped as the holo raced through the group for the railing. They might have screamed when it vaulted over, except Mama's hand moved again, and the holo winked out of existence short of its leap.

Vradel's brows skipped. "Then with everyone's attention focused on the river, Santos just walked away."

Mama nodded.

Or had even been escorted off the bridge. Janna recalled the civilians and videographers that watchcar officers chased away earlier.

"Then we'd better dismantle this carnival and start looking for her, hadn't we," Vradel said.

Where she hid out, they could not discover, not without revealing they knew Santos was alive, but they did learn from coworkers at Beria that she had booked her flight to the Glenn platform on the shuttle Eclipse. A call to Forbes established that the Eclipse would be lifting from there in three days. So they let the newscanner stations run the bridge story as Santos intended everyone to believe it, and when the passengers for the Eclipse gathered in the shuttle lounge of the terminal, Cruz and Singer watched from the observation window of the terminal supervisor's office, high above the concourse.

Janna and Mama sat in the snack shop, waiting for their Go signal to come over ear buttons set to an operations frequency that let all the team members talk to each other.

"There goes the attendant's pen into his hair," Cruz's voice said in Janna's ear. "Passenger C. L. Santos has checked in."

They stood and sauntered out of the snack bar and across the concourse. The guard admitted them to the shuttle lounge. When they caught the attendant's eye, he nodded toward a figure looking out the windows. Janna gave thanks for the attendant's cooperation. On her own she might have been fooled by what appeared to be an adolescent boy with blue-and-orange hair that matched the colors of his tiger-striped jumpsuit.

They drifted up on either side of her. Outside sat the Eclipse, awesome in size despite its distance from them on the far side of the parking apron, white portions gleaming against the flawless cobalt of the morning sky. A beautiful sky, Janna mused, on a fine May day made perfect by wrapping this case.

"Hello, Santos," Mama said. "Guess what. We found the holo projector in the van."

Blue mirror lenses hid the small bibi's eyes but her body stiffened.

Janna smiled and pulled her wrapstrap out of her thigh boot. "You're under arrest for the murder of Carel Armenda. I don't know how many escape plans you have, but think twice before trying one of them. There are only two ways out of here. Take a look at them."

Santos turned her head the directions of both. Weyneth filled the boarding exit with Showalter tucked in beside him. Zavara and Threefoxes blocked the door back onto the concourse, showing wolfish smiles that invited her to try passing them.

After a long minute, Santos held out her wrists. "I didn't start out to kill him."

Quickly, Janna said, "You have the right to remain silent." If Santos intended to confess, Janna wanted it admissible.

While she recited the Miranda, Janna pulled Santos's hands behind her back and gave the wrapstrap a practiced flip that wrapped it around both wrists before adhering to itself.

"Do you understand your rights?" Mama asked when Janna finished.

Santos nodded. Apparently choosing silence. She said nothing more while they led her out to the car.

There Mama and Janna sat on either side of her in the back seat. Cruz and Singer rode up front. The two Crimes Against Property teams followed in another car.

Cruz guided the car onto the highway and headed north toward downtown. Santos shifted position, grimacing. "Car seats aren't made for sitting with your hands behind you, are they." She shifted again. "Planning the murder was a game."

Janna slipped a hand into her jacket pocket and tapped on her microcorder.

Singer twisted in his seat to look back at them. "Are you giving up your right to remain silent?"

She did not appear to hear him. "He made me so . . ." Her face twisted. "Angry isn't a strong enough word. He . . . infuriated me, filled me with outrage." Her voice rose. "I felt so . . . helpless to stop him from stealing what was *mine*!"

"Helpless?" Cruz gunned the car past a dawdling Bonsai runabout. "You filed suit."

Santos snorted. "That's when I still thought Armenda played by fair rules. I was so proud of myself for not losing my temper, too. I thought, I would handle this by the book and I would win because I was in the right. But you know what he did? He had me come to the manager's office there at Konza and he sneered at me. He said, 'You might as well drop this pitiful suit because you don't have a snowball's chance in hell of winning. No jury's ever going to believe *you* invented this projector. A young woman on her first job out of school, a young *Hispanic* woman, with her E.E. degree from a *Kansas* university, accomplishing *this* by herself?' "

Janna exchanged glances with Mama over Santos's head. She had seen this before . . . suspects pouring out bottled-up feelings, seemingly unable to stop themselves no matter how self-destructive and incriminating the statements.

"He said, 'They'll say it's impossible . . . like expecting an elephant to fly, or a crow to sing. They'll say you must have had help from the men working with you, or at the very least used research done at MIT or some other real engineering school. You'll be laughed out of court.' "

Anger flared in Janna. She could imagine how Santos felt. That insufferable son of a bitch! She would have turned Armenda into a pretzel.

Santos bit her lip. "The longer I thought about what he said, the madder I got. He had all those awards for supposedly being such a wonderful employer and then he did *that* to me? And he treated my heritage as though it gave me tacos for brains? That made me angriest of all. How could he, of all people, do that!"

"You mean," Mama said, "you expected better treatment just because he's Hispanic descent, too?"

"Foolish, wasn't I?" Santos laughed, a short, bitter bark of sound. "After a bit, keeping the projector away from him wasn't enough. I fantasized about killing him. At first it was very direct . . . run him down with a car or shoot him, or maybe go to his office and while pretending to agree to surrender the projector, poison him. Then I started seeing that it was like an engineering problem and I began working out how I might really do it, and get away with it." She paused. "It's amazing how much information you can learn about guests lists and personal records with a modem and a little patience, despite all the entry safeguards on computers."

Disbelief spread through Janna, and more anger, now directed at Santos. She wanted to slap Santos. "You killed him to *see if it could be done*!"

"No!" Santos recoiled as though she had been slapped. "I

just planned it. I never meant to really *do* it. I applied for Mars.
I thought, the acceptance would come and I'd leave and that
would be that. But it didn't come and didn't come and when it
did, I'd already built the waitron and desktop. I'd learned where
the fund-raisers would be and hacked into the hotel and caterer's
files to find who would be serving at them that I could have
someone replace. I had license plates spotted and Tony waiting
for word from me.''

The traffic had thickened as they neared the center of town.
Cruz encroached on the bicycle lane to avoid a Peterbuilt straying
out of the commercial lane. ''What I want to know is how Tony
passed the r-scan at the hotel.''

She shrugged. ''That's easy with access to the security system.
I programmed the computer to ignore the retinal scan for that
Scib card on that particular evening, and afterward, forget it had
ever been given any such instructions.''

Just like that. No black magic. No destruction of the Scib
system integrity. Janna felt everyone's relief.

Anger still washed through her, however. ''You must have
seen you had a wonderful thing in your shoot/don't shoot program. Why didn't you just concentrate on developing that, sell
your projector to some company that could fight Armenda for
the right to it, and forget about the murder?''

Santos slunk down in the seat, biting her lip. ''I thought about
it. I wanted to. But . . . the farther things went, the more they
had a force of their own. It was like being on an icy hill. I
couldn't stop.''

''So you've wasted your creativity and intelligence, and betrayed a lot of people who thought you were their friend,'' Mama
said.

''Yes.'' The word emerged as a whisper. Santos pulled in on
herself. ''Maybe I can finish the program in prison.''

Providing the state did not execute her.

Presently they turned down the ramp into the headquarters
garage, and from there, took Santos up to the holding cells on
the third floor. As the elevator doors opened, however, they
found themselves facing a silver-haired man in a grey paisley
tunic and breeches.

Janna frowned. Why was the most expensive criminal lawyer
in town meeting them?

He nodded at Santos. "Miss Santos, my name is Halian McVey. I'm your attorney."

Santos gaped at him. "I don't understand."

Cruz scowled. "She hasn't called an attorney yet."

McVey smiled. "An interested party contacted me and offered a retainer on her behalf."

"Sydney Armenda?" Mama asked.

McVey nodded. "She will be visiting you shortly, Miss Santos. She asked me to tell you she has a business proposition, one that will be with her, personally, not Armenord. She hopes you will find it much more acceptable than the one proposed by her father."

Santos's mouth still hung open.

Singer smirked. "You'll find this a tough one, McVey. She's already confessed."

The lawyer's smile never wavered. "A challenge, perhaps, but not hopeless. Being careful officers, I'm sure you have the confession recorded, so you will of course see that I'm given a copy of the microcorder chip. And now, Sergeant Cruz, may we proceed with the formalities of booking? I'd like to confer with my client as soon as possible."

He led the way up the corridor toward the cell section, followed by Santos, Cruz, and Singer.

Janna and Mama found themselves left at the elevator. She frowned after the group. "Surely not even McVey can get her off."

"But he'll keep her alive, bibi."

Janna sighed. "So Santos lives and Sydney ends up with the projector, which she'll parlay into control and probably possession of Armenord. Vining can bask in the glory of announcing *case closed* to the media. And we get to file reports."

Mama smiled. "A little more than that." He headed for the stairs. "We solved the case, law enforcement agencies everywhere will soon have a wonderful training aid . . . and you get your fondest wish."

She ran to keep up. "What fondest wish?"

"I'm moving out." He pushed through the stair door and headed down two steps at a time.

"Out?" She followed. "On your own?"

"Not quite." He paused at the landing to look back. "I'm

moving downstairs with Arianna. You don't have to resume paying the entire rent on your apartment, however. Arianna knows a dancer with the Topeka Ballet who's looking for a place to live. Arianna says you'll love her. She treats living quarters like a bivouac, too. Owns one trunk of possessions and a portable barre so she can practice at home. She and Arianna are coming for dinner tonight so you can meet her.''

"That's nice, before you move her in.''

"Arianna and I thought it was only fair.'' He pushed his glasses up his nose. "It's an ideal arrangement. I'll still be close enough to provide you with advice and guidance.''

Janna rolled her eyes. "I knew there'd be a catch.''

He grinned. "It isn't a perfect world, bibi.''

"No,'' she agreed, sobering. Catching Santos preserved the rules, but it did not change back the lives touched and forever altered by the violence between her and Armenda. "It isn't perfect.''

As though reading her mind, Mama smiled up at her. "But it's all we have, Jan, so we just have to keep caring about it and doing what we can to make it better. We've accomplished at least a little of that today, haven't we?''

After a moment she shrugged. Maybe. A little. In any case, it would have to do.

They continued on down the stairs to start their reports.